The Puppeteer

Lynda Kempsey

authorHOUSE

AuthorHouse™ UK Ltd.
500 Avebury Boulevard
Central Milton Keynes, MK9 2BE
www.authorhouse.co.uk
Phone: 08001974150

© 2010 Lynda Kempsey. All rights reserved.

No part of this book may be reproduced, stored in a retrieval system, or transmitted by any means without the written permission of the author.

First published by AuthorHouse 3/19/2010

ISBN: 978-1-4490-5453-3 (sc)

This book is printed on acid-free paper.

Preamble

The view from one of Redgate's many perches has not altered much. It still shows the route from a hidden Drysdale; the narrow road tumbling down to the bridge, which crosses the Wear, which flows by Bradley Hall, which stands facing the field where the archers would practise, just in case.

The landscape has proved more constant than the men who lived in it. Some were puppeteers: deftly giving a wrong name here; a grimace there; a helping hand at just the right time to vibrate the strings with a series of sickening jolts.

And centuries old landscapes may throw up clues, but only reveal half truths. Streets like Meadhope and Angate still follow their medieval curves, causing vehicles that have just descended Redgate's swollen slopes to pause courteously, allowing on comers to pass by. Those descending find it hard to stop, while those ascending find it hard to start and wagons hauling heavy loads climb at a similar rate to when they were horse drawn; only very gradually overtaking those on foot. Those unknowing feet have gradually made dust of the rubble once littering the tortuous climb to Redgate's crest. Now, at one with the layers of leaf mould, lie secrets once fiercely kept, and the fragments of a letter deliberately torn in two by its author in April 1174.

This is the story of how they came to be there.

PART ONE

Chapter One

1148 - A Place To Hide

Once over the threshold, he realised there were very few places he could conceal himself. There wasn't even a shadow. The room was almost empty of furniture but for a wooden chair and a barrel as tall as he was in each corner to either side of the door. The walls were very pale and the floor was bare. No one lived here. Strong sunlight came in through the one window, which faced down the moor at the far end of the building, two steps down from where he stood. Its wooden shutters were unbarred and knocked against each other, so that shadow and light danced together erratically. Quickly, he looked about him as the man and his mother grew closer. Just in time, he wriggled behind the barrel to his right.

His mother was led in and the ill-fitting door secured against the gale outside. The shutters at the window were next, so for a few moments they were left in darkness. Saul's eyes felt large against the gloom until light dropped from the roof above his mother's head. The old smoke hole had been opened.

The man was smiling at his mother and talking in a kindly way. He did not untie her hands but asked if she wanted a drink of water. A pitcher stood on the one chair a few feet in front of Saul's hiding place. He tried to will himself smaller as the man approached to pour water into a cup. Her hands shook when she reached for it, but her face was still and she thanked him with a polite whisper. Saul watched his mother's pale throat as she swallowed. He imagined the water leaving a cool line as it made its way to her stomach.

A sudden pounding at the door sent a shock through his heart. His mother stood very still, as if she was holding her breath.

"Open the door! The King orders it."

The man looked apologetically at his mother. "Have some pity. There should be no rude interruptions at a time like this."

The shouting came again. "You are to free the woman called Mary Gill. King Stephen demands it. He sent us to intervene before it is too late!"

"Then I suggest you leave as quickly as possible and find the lady you are searching for. There is no Mary here."

From his hiding place, Saul looked to the crack of light framing the door, listening for an answer. The people went away. His mother was very still. She looked at the man, then at the floor. Gently, he took her cup from her and placed it on the chair where a coil of rope was draped. It was only then that Saul noticed a thick peg jutting from the roof beam just above the two steps down to the lower half of the building. The man busied himself with the rope. By the time Saul realised what was happening and buried his head in his hands, it was too late. He closed his eyes against the image of his mother's twisted, discoloured face, but it stayed in his head and made him feel like he was unable to breathe too. He could hear her choke, gag and struggle and the horror of it made him desperate to run and help her; to hit the man; to take the chair and try to cut the rope; to be brave. But he could not. His legs shook and it was only the lack of room in his hiding place that kept him on his feet. So he kept his eyes screwed shut and his fists clenched until the only sound was the creak of the rope that prevented her feet from just touching the ground.

When he heard the man eventually leave the stone house for good, he allowed his body to uncrumple itself from the cramped corner, unsure now of his reason for doing so. He moved awkwardly because of the numbness in his feet and the clinging cold of his clothes where he had wet himself. The room was as it had been when they first entered: sun-washed and wind swept, except now his mother had been laid out on the floor at the foot of the two steps. He stepped down towards her carefully. The outer layers of her clothing had been raised to cover her face.

He did not uncover her, but waited with a sickly ache in his stomach. Was that it? Would she never wake?

He would have stayed there, only allowing himself to look at her shoes, but he heard a cart approaching and then men's voices and grew afraid. He could not leave by the door which faced the road. The only way was the window.

He was tall for a five year old; otherwise he might not have been able to climb onto the lower frame. He struggled up. The wind tried to push him back into the room so he felt sure that the men would come in before he had time to get out. He looked back once, knowing he would probably never see her again. The force of the wind wrenched at him while he held onto a shutter and this time he was pulled roughly out. A small bone in his knee knocked against the corner of the wood and he could not help but cry aloud. Screwing his eyes shut, he forced himself to let go and dropped to the silvery grass beneath. He rubbed his leg to dull the sharp pain, then crept to the side of the house where he would be able to see what they would do with his mother.

When the men entered, they saw only the covered body they had been sent to collect and the open window. Saul heard the shutters closing above his head then the men's shuffling footsteps as they left the house, carrying his mother to the cart. They swung her, dropped her roughly into the back and then secured her covering so the wind would not dislodge it as they travelled.

They climbed up and drove away. Saul watched as the cart taking his mother grew smaller and quieter then disappeared over the brow of the hill. His lip trembled.

Chapter Two

Early February, 1158 – Birth and Death

Bran was quietly proud of his paging with the Northern, as was his friend, Marc, who, like himself, had lost both parents early and violently. Unlike Bran, Marc had not been advised to change his name to protect his identity.

In their familiar meeting place by the river, at a midway point between the two households where they paged, the two friends were deep in conversation. That is, for the most part, Bran was trying to keep his patience while Marc shared his angst over the likelihood of discovering how Susan at Redgate felt about him before he embarked on an overseas pilgrimage with his older cousin.

"Why don't you tell her, if you are so worried that someone else will beat you to her?"

The two of them were sitting in a tree by the Wear, wrapped tightly in their warmest cloaks to ward off the last of the winter cold. The February air this late afternoon was still and had swathed the treetops eerily with a long, pale loop of fog. Bran's question turned to mist and hung in the branches they huddled amongst, as if waiting for the answer.

Marc was oblivious to their cold and wet surroundings, his own internal river churned up by what he thought to be an impossible situation.

"I would if I thought she might like me."

"Why wouldn't she like you? You'll be a Knight one day soon. You'll come back from the East with all sorts of stories. I wish I was so lucky. William is trying to avoid service overseas because he had such a bad case of dysentery last time. Ben has been reluctant to leave Margery since she fell pregnant again. The furthest I'm likely to get is......"

"But there could already be someone else. Have you seen her talking to anyone? You know....a man?"

Bran decided to have some fun.

"Well there was one fellow I saw her with at Martinmas."

Marc swung round quickly. "Martinmas! Why didn't you tell me before? That's three months ago."

"Didn't I tell you? Um, must have forgotten about it." Bran looked nonchalantly to the further riverbank.

"What did he look like?"

"What did who look like?"

"The one Susan spoke to."

"Oh, I don't know. I can't really remember. It was a long time ago."

"Come on, Bran, think. Have you seen him at Redgate since? I bet it was that strutting story-teller with the ridiculously short tunic."

Bran creased his brow, "No, I would have remembered that. Besides, I don't think Susan would feel comfortable if confronted with that much leg."

"Well, I may as well forget the whole idea," said Marc dejectedly.

Bran ignored his tone, which craved a contradiction, saying, "Yes, it's probably for the best," and made as if to climb down from the tree. He stopped at the next branch down and looked up at his friend, who was sullenly pulling at the bark.

"Oh for Goodness' sake, Marc. Most men don't even entertain the thought of love when considering marriage."

"Ben and Margery did. That is why she did not marry Edwin."

Bran looked at him through the bare boughs. "How do you know that?"

"My Uncle Robert, told me." He looked down at Bran, worried in case he was getting his Uncle into trouble. "He wasn't being malicious; quite the opposite in fact. Remember, he came from Margery's family home to Ben's smaller household at Redgate by choice. Anyway, what if I tell her and she laughs at me?"

Bran could not help grinning at his friend's self-induced entrapment.

"What do you think I should say?"

"You're asking for so much advice on this, I might as well just tell her myself."

"What?"

"I'll be there in two weeks' time. Margery is due to give birth in the Spring. She has never carried for so long before." Bran looked at the sky, considering. "This must be her ninth pregnancy since they took me in. Will has decided it is as good a time as any to return to Redgate and begin my squiring with Ben."

"Don't tell her. I'll do it."

"When?" Bran did not believe it.

"Soon."

"How soon?"

Marc chewed his lip, thinking. "I'll write it in a letter and you can give it to her. She can read well."

"When I go to Redgate, I shall travel via Crossgate to pick up this letter."

Bran climbed down and allowed himself to drop the last few inches, brushing bark dust from his palms.

Eventually, Marc followed. To Bran's relief, he even dropped the subject while they walked their horses along the lane to where they would have to part ways. The mist was thickening and the damp began to soak into their hair and clothes. The air muffled the usual sounds of evening and the young men remained quiet until they reached the fork in the road. Both glanced up each path they would need to travel. Both quietly thought how ominously still the trees now seemed to each side of the ghostly-looking track.

Bran broke the silence. "Don't forget that letter."

"Oh, I won't." Marc's laugh was cut shorter than usual, the fog snatching the sound as soon as it was uttered.

"See you in a week. Safe journey."

They parted ways; both travelling as fast as they dared in the poor light.

****

Once Redgate's hounds had recognised Bran and ceased their barking, it was quiet, except for the intermittent cries of a baby. Perhaps all was well. He'd heard knights who had returned from the east telling amazing medical stories. Some had witnessed Muslim doctors performing operations that saved both mother and child.

Strange that only last week, Marc and he had been wrapped in extra layers of clothing, poor visibility filling their journeys homeward with menace. Now, it was one of those warm February days, an isolated incident which happens every year and yet still takes everyone by surprise, leaving them hot and flustered in their layers of Winter clothing. The door was open to help cool the main room of the house. Here Janet sat next to her daughter, Susan, who cradled a baby that was wrapped tightly in a length of soft cloth. The baby wriggled and complained to be free and Susan, kind-hearted and broody at thirteen, loosened some of the swaddling.

"It cannot hurt her to feel the air in this weather," she said in reply to her mother's concerned glance.

Bran's shadow falling across them caused mother and daughter to look up at him as he stood in the doorway. He looked to Janet for answers.

She smiled uncertainly. "This is Anna. At least her mother said that if it was a girl that was the name they would give her."

Bran stepped forward for a closer look. Janet smiled at his awkward stance.

"Not even half a day old. Isn't she beautiful?"

His unspoken question hung above them sadistically. Susan moved some of the cloth away from the baby's face in order that Bran might see her more clearly. Two startled eyes looked up at him for a moment, then screwed shut again. He looked at Janet. He did not ask the most obvious question, but instead, "Where is Ben?"

"He's in the room with her. He won't let us in. He sent the doctor away and now he won't speak." She tried to breathe steadily. "I have no idea whether she is dead or alive. Even the priest is met with silence. The doctor said she has lost a lot of blood."

Bran's heart sank. He asked if she would try knocking one more time. It was not long before she returned. "You would think the room was empty. There's not a sound."

"How long since they ate?"

"About a day and a half - since the pains started."

Bran left the women and passed through the shadows. He hesitated at the door, feeling more useless the longer he paused.

"Ben," he called. He did not know whether to say Margery's name too.

There was no sound. He returned to the main room and passed through it, Janet and Susan staring after him. When he did not stop, they rose from the table and followed. Outside, he turned and passed the kitchen, which jutted out from the main house. He stopped and tried to judge where the room holding Ben and Margery would be. The entire house was on a slope, which meant that the small window above the kitchen roof would bring him into their room.

He looked down at the clothes he was wearing: not the best climbing attire. He pulled the deep blue robe and his chemise over his head, as if they were one garment, leaving him in leggings. Without a word, he climbed onto the barrel he himself had positioned to catch rainwater. He balanced carefully so as not to give himself a dunking, placed the palms of his hands on the kitchen roof and raised himself up quite effortlessly.

He looked at the shutters which he judged belonged to Margery's chamber window. Through a slight crack in the wood he could see the birthing table, apparently unused, and the bed, which was empty apart from a few twisted sheets - some with brown stains, which he recognised as dried blood. He leaned back a little to judge the size of the window. It would be big enough to squeeze his shoulders through if he could wriggle sideways. He gave a sharp rap and the shutters swung gently towards him. He grasped the top of the aperture and stepped onto the sill. A small gathering watched as his brown form shifted sideways to allow his shoulders to fit through the opening, then dropped out of sight.

As he had thought, the window which required a climb to reach it from the outside was no more than hip height on the inside. It was relatively dark and he stood a moment while his eyes adjusted. Sunlight cut through the dust-filled air from a window to his left, which looked down the hill, over the tree tops to the small town below. People went about their daily business as usual. The bed faced him and, as he had already seen from outside, it only held the stained linen. The fireplace in the wall to his right was dark. The room was stuffy and had an unpleasant smell. Deciding to open the door to allow in more light and air, he stopped mid-step. His way was barred. He'd thought more bedclothes were piled on a chair, but now he realised his mistake. He'd found Ben and Margery.

The chair faced the largest window and thus the tree tops. Ben stared out with such a stillness that Bran was fearful at first that he was lifeless. A shuddering sigh revealed that this was not so. Ben did not acknowledge Bran but stared sightlessly out of the window. Margery was in his lap with her head against his left shoulder. He'd wrapped the heavier bedclothes around her; Bran guessed to hide her bleeding.

One or two twists of Margery's red hair hung over Ben's shoulder, moving slightly as the older man sighed again. Bran reached up to smooth her hair away from her cold brow. Ben did not protest, but acknowledged him simply, by allowing his cheek to rest where Bran's hand stroked Margery's hair. Just as Ben had done when he had arrived at Redgate ten years before, Bran knelt before him, knowing he would have to be gentle. There was no colour in Margery's face. He took his hand and looked at him until, eventually, Ben met his gaze.

"Will you let me carry her to the bed?"

Ben closed his eyes and nodded.

Bran lifted her and carried her to the pallet, careful to keep the covers about her. Ben rose stiffly, watching Bran. He wanted neither to cross to the bed nor to leave the room. Bran spoke, simply to have the sound of a familiar voice distracting from the sadness of the time. He was old enough now to understand the seemingly callous chatter of the man who had executed his mother. He was simply filling the silences to push away some of the horror.

"Perhaps Thomas's sister can nurse the baby. Janet will want to see her… and the priest."

Bran sat on the bed and looked at what had been Margery. Her hair seemed brighter against the paleness of her skin. He felt Ben sit next to him. When he spoke, his voice was hoarse. "You won't believe what the priest will say."

Bran answered simply, "She would."

The older man nodded resignedly. It had not been a remark about religious beliefs so much as another delaying tactic to push away the moment when he would have to relinquish his wife to others.

"You have a beautiful daughter. Will you call her Anna the way you planned?"

Ben gave a non-committal shrug.

Silence fell over the three of them for a while.

Eventually, Bran spoke again. "When the time comes, many of us will not be with the person we love most." He left it at that.

"What shall I do without her, Bran?"

Bran looked at him. He could think of little else to say to comfort him. "There is no reason for me to return to Bankside. My paging is almost over. It makes sense to stay."

"Yes," he nodded. He looked at Bran, as if just waking up. "Where are your clothes?" he asked.

"I left them outside. I couldn't climb in them?"

"Climb?"

"I came in through the window."

Ben looked confused.

"You didn't hear me calling," explained Bran. The conversation seemed to have taken an incongruous turn. Bran could not help thinking that if Margery had lived, she would have laughed at them both.

"Shall I let them in or would you rather wait?"

Ben shook his head. "Let them in."

Bran leaned over and kissed Margery's brow then crossed the room to speak with the quietly waiting household. At the door he looked back. Ben was still once again, gazing at Margery's face. He guessed, wrongly, that the older man was still blaming himself.

Chapter Three

1163 - The Letter

An early mist still wrapped itself about the trees around Redgate and the sounds of chattering, scolding and hammering floated up the hillside from the fields by the river. Beneath Ben's window, Joss studied the diagram drawn for him in the dry soil, imagining the varied trajectories Bran's vision promised.

Ben gazed out at them: the student teaching the mentor. Bran straightened, his mood change visible when five year old Anna arrived. He lifted her so that her unknowing feet might not distort the drawing that Joss still studied.

"I shall go to the fair tomorrow," she announced, seemingly out of the blue, but it had been all her heart's desire for two weeks now.

Ben stood and crossed to the window and called, "Anna, go and help Janet and Susan."

She sighed, but skipped away.

"Bran, I need to speak with you."

The younger man took his leave and joined his foster father indoors.

The older man had been unusually quiet since Will's visit earlier in the morning. "Just three days until your trip to Spain. Have you chosen a constable to look after your affairs at Drysdale?"

"I had settled on Marc," Bran answered.

"A wise choice," Ben nodded. "Speaking of Marc, Thomas tells me he has shown an interest in his daughter, Susan."

Bran smiled, "Yes. He has been infatuated with her for five years."

Ben stroked his chin. "Marc will make a fine knight one day. It is likely he could choose from several wealthier daughters."

Bran pondered, "Yes, but his heart would still be here."

Ben smiled. "And that would be too much of an imposition on any marriage."

Bran nodded.

"And, of course, you have your friends' interests at heart."

The younger man saw no point in denying it.

Ben considered, "She's a rather outspoken young lady."

Bran, again unable to deny the observation, said, "Yes, but she has intelligence and good morals. I think Marc's idealism and Susan's logic will create a perfect balance."

Ben stood and took the opportunity to stretch, having sat for most of the morning settling the matters of others. Bran studied him, realising that this meeting was not solely for the benefit of Marc and Susan. Ben walked to the window once more and looked out. Joss had crossed the grass to judge the developing horsemanship of the pages.

"Have you considered marriage?"

Ben, still standing at the window, seemed to address someone outside, so it was not until he turned and looked at Bran, eyebrows raised, that the younger man realised the question was addressed to him.

Bran shook his head. The first and last time Bran had wished for a wife, he was seven years old and bidding farewell to Margery before setting off to Bankside to begin his paging years with Will. He had idolised Margery since the day his mother died, and the pangs he felt, he supposed at the time, were the closest to romance he had experienced.

Ben resumed his seat and sighed. "They say Edwin has his eye on you as a prospective husband for Catherine, his step-daughter."

A crease formed between the younger man's brows. "Edwin would not value a marriage between his family and mine."

"Precisely. I think we ought to expect trouble." The older man studied his hands. "Will did bring some good news this morning: the King values what you do at Drysdale."

Bran looked at his foster father blankly. "The King? Henry?"

"Yes, that is he," Ben laughed. "Will came direct from Winchester to let us know. He thinks the King might even call in unexpectedly one day.... I see that disturbs you."

"Should I cancel my visit to Harun in Spain?"

Ben shook his head. "No, the King wants to encourage your studies, not restrict them. It might be wise to have someone make a copy of all your findings. Will knows the King loves innovation and simply described some of your activities up here. Apparently, he was spellbound. It's good news for you and for the Northern. Joss and Will have always been pleased with your progress, but now you have royal support too."

He allowed some time for the compliment to register with his young squire before changing the subject.

"While at the fair tomorrow, I suggest you keep an eye out for Edwin and his hangers on. He has such a large….family…that a man would be hard pressed to recognise whether he was speaking to a friend or an enemy."

"I'll be careful."

"Good. And I would keep out of the contests. It only takes one wrestling bout to dislocate a shoulder: not what you want just before a long voyage."

Bran's mind was still on the King. "Does the King know about my ….religious dilemma?"

"Yes. I think Henry sees it as a guarantee of impartiality. Things haven't been going the way he planned with Beckett." Ben could sense his reticence. "What's on your mind?"

"Of course I am glad..it's just that, now the King is involved, everything I do could be interpreted as me finding ways to ingratiate myself. We already know that Edwin would leap at any excuse to take Drysdale."

"It's a well known maxim that with power comes responsibility," Ben concurred.

"With this amount of power comes vulnerability."

"You have been vulnerable since you were born, Bran. The Order will protect you. You are a young man with an amazing reputation - made all the better because you have never abused your place as a favourite. Besides, you have the backing of both the King and Pudsey, so your land is safe. You deserve power. I'm proud of you."

Bran pondered. He stroked his forefinger across his lips trying to hide his uneasiness with a shrug. "Carp diem?"

Ben smiled and nodded. "Best course of action is to seize the day; especially when you have no choice in the matter."

Bran sighed and then, to show that he had resigned himself to the idea, he asked, "Shall we go and eat?" Ben's look showed him that matters were not yet concluded.

"I feel our good news has blown me from the course of more serious matters closer to home."

Bran had already had warnings from both Joss and Will about staying away from ladies before and during his time in Spain and resigned himself to hearing the same advice from Ben. The only lady he felt merited a warning was Isabel of Stanmere and he was far too wise to allow himself to be trapped by someone of her reputation.

"It is hard to know where to start with this matter. In some ways, it is not important because you will be leaving soon – and be away for months at least. But, if anything occurred at the fair tomorrow, I would feel I ought to have made more of this Edwin business."

He looked at Bran. "You know there is no love lost between Edwin and myself?"

Bran nodded.

"I know you have a vague idea of the reasons for that, although I have never explained it to you directly. Perhaps if I explain the background, it will help you to understand." He drew a hand across his eyes before settling further into his chair and becoming storyteller. "At one time, he would visit Margery's father and he made his intentions known that he would like to marry her. Her father, Martin, had been granted land on the Northern side of Durham by the Prince Bishop for his military services. Margery was his only child of marriageable age so, obviously, she had no shortage of suitors. Her father was careful about making promises, especially as she was still so young. He did not exactly agree to a marriage between she and Edwin, but Edwin thought of himself as the future husband."

"How did you come to know Margery?"

"She was in Durham with a group of other young women. We had just established the Northern Order - as soon as we were knighted - Joss, Will and myself. Big ideas we had. We were only about twenty - your age. November - freezing cold it was." Ben smiled into the fire.

"It was a wicked day. It was so cold we had to break the ice on the troughs when we tethered the horses. Everyone out that day seemed to be in a foul mood, wrapped up in layer upon layer to keep out the cold. When Margery and her friends came into the market place, they were instantly noticeable. Instead of huddling and glaring about them sullenly, they were chattering and laughing at something or other. We were on our way to the cobbler on Soutergate. I needed my shoes adjusting as I had just been given my first decent mail from my father. As soon as the sound of young ladies' laughter cut through the air, our ears pricked up. They were unaccompanied and completely oblivious to us. I'm ashamed to say, we felt a little surprised: we expected to be swatting ladies like flies once we had risen from Squire to Knight. They were all rosy cheeked and animated with the laughter and the cold. All were brightly dressed, except for Margery, but her red hair stood out against her dark cloak." He smiled and glanced across at Bran without really seeing him. "I could not take my eyes off her. I was unaware that Will and Joss were waiting for me. And then, she looked across at me. Right at me. It hit me like a punch. I suppose that's why they describe it as being smitten."

"Of course, Will and Joss had noticed this by now, but a few snide comments and exaggerated throat-clearings were not going to be enough to put me off; especially, when she kept glancing at me to see if I looked at her still. I remember she was blushing as her little group swirled away from me, turning the corner to wander along the street leading up to the Cathedral - the saddler's street. I suddenly decided that my errand with the cobbler was far less important than a visit to the saddler.　Joss commented, "Looks like the cobbler comes last."

How Will groaned at Joss's pun! They both looked at me, with arms crossed and sympathetic expressions, as I watched Margery getting further away."

There was a gentle knock at the door. Ben paused for a moment. Thomas's voice called from beyond it. "Will you eat in the hall, Sir?"

"We'll have trenchers brought in, thank you, Thomas."

They waited until his footsteps had retreated, then Ben continued.

"I almost decided that the best course of action was to forget the incident. If I saw her again with Will and Joss, she might have been intimidated by their fooling. Even if I managed to make an excuse to leave them and catch up with her, I would be intimidated by her friends."

Bran laughed.

"Seriously," Ben gave a quick nod of the head. "Do not underestimate the humiliation that can be inflicted by a woman's closest friends. Margery's father was a pony ride compared to those screeching harbingers."

"You caught up with them then?"

"Oh yes," Ben commented wryly. "Her friends were teasing her almost as much as Will and Joss were teasing me. I was in quite a quandary as you can imagine. Half of me wanted to ignore everyone else and talk to Margery as if she was alone, but the other half could see that she was looking equally uncomfortable and I did not want to make things worse. The only thought I could cling to was that I did not want to return home that day without finding out who she was. I decided to take the plunge and asked the lady closest to me if she would mind doing me the favour of asking Margery for her permission to speak. Of course, her friend hammed this up as much as possible and, quite fortuitously as it turns out; she was so loud and embarrassing with her mock curtsies and flamboyant waving of sleeves, that everyone took pity on Margery and drew away - taking the loud one with them. Well, that left Margery and me staring at each other like idiots again. I was too much of a coward to tell her how I felt, so instead I said, "Could you help me to choose a gift to take back to my younger sister?"

She smiled at me and said she would be glad to. We had quite an audience by then. Some less well-mannered people even followed our progress as we talked and made our way around the stalls. Eventually, we had explored every one. There was no real reason to look at most of the wares: we simply wanted to stretch our time together. Margery had helped me to choose a book for my younger sister, Maud. Not a written book, but a bundle of plain pages bound neatly together. Not a bad find. The stallholder scrawled rather proudly, but untidily, an M on the front cover. Margery said that all young women who knew how to write loved to set down their unspoken thoughts. She said it was like having a trustworthy friend to share your secrets with. When I finally regained my wits, I remembered to ask her name. She told me she was Margery and described her father to me. I had met him in the past. Martin supported our idea for a Northern Order and had heard of Joss, Will and myself through our fathers. The knowledge of her father also brought a memory of Edwin and I felt quite downcast. I was aware of at least ten pairs of ears straining to catch some gossip, but I could not let her go without her knowing how I felt. I told her I would like her to have the book and that it was appropriate that she should as her name began with M. She smiled at me and looked around her, maybe to see if a friend of Edwin might be included in the listeners. She thanked me quietly, but said she would have to decline because she could not deprive my sister of such a pretty gift. I told her that if Maud received such a gift she would probably scribble nonsense and lose it within the week. She said, in that case she had better accept it in order to prevent unscrupulous people discovering Maud's secrets….and when I handed her the book and she blushed because our fingers had brushed, I asked her not to marry Edwin. She explained that nothing had been agreed on that score. I said, "Good" and felt rather pleased with myself at having been so brave, so I threw caution to the wind and told her that she deserved to marry someone who would think nothing of reminding her every day of how special she was. And someone she might trust enough to read her secrets to. Of course, the listeners had to join in with their "oohs" and "ahs" and "Just listen to God's gift." But I didn't care anymore because she seemed pleased to listen. I would have carried on but Will and Joss returned with her friends, reminding me of how early it grew dark in November and that we should really escort the ladies to their homes as we had kept them so late. I can never repay them enough for that suggestion. That day's journey led to a friendship between Margery's father and I and I knew straight away that I would marry her." His voice quietened. "I still have that little book."

The sound of cheers from outside gave him an excuse to walk to the window. Looking out, he spoke again. "I need to tell you more about the rumours I have been hearing. As I said, they involve Edwin and his step-daughter, Catherine. She is Margery's younger and only surviving sibling by her father, Martin."

He paused, gazing down at Anna as she struggled to climb onto the mild-mannered pony he'd asked Thomas and John to train for her. She had been helped to mount the animal and was being led in a wide circle, past the pigs and through the geese. Every now and then, Thomas helped her to regain her balance as she slipped, her small hands trying to find a grip in the dark mane.

As Bran waited, he tried to imagine Edwin as a real man. He had never seen him. Ben finally turned to face him, his face a silhouette against the light from the window.

"What do you know of Edwin?" he asked.

Bran simply continued his line of thought and replied as if answering a question on philosophy. "I know nothing of his appearance, which makes him more dangerous. He is not to be trusted, by enemies or allies. He does not do 'business' face to face, but prefers to manipulate people through threats of violence or promises of wealth so that he can disassociate himself after the event. He has married his way into land - land that was rightfully yours and Margery's. He probably found some method of coercion to bring about his marriage to Margery's mother so soon after her father's death. He has, and will, encourage his children, step children - legitimate or otherwise - to also marry into land. Many of those who began as his allies have been killed; some executed under false pretences or seeming to vanish into thin air. He is probably the man responsible for my mother's death and for 'arranging' my father's accident. If I ever find proof of these, I will endeavour to have him executed for murder."

Ben was looking at him intently. "I had no idea that you had plans for him."

"I treat it as a problem to be solved. It's easier."

Ben clasped his hands and continued carefully. "I've often wondered about his involvement in your father's death. Edwin was down country at the time, but the accident had all the typical features you would expect of a scheme thought up by him. The older Saul, sorry..your father… was a favourite, just as you are. Because of his ingenuity, nothing more, he had almost forty square miles of land. The land was valuable only because of the uses he put it to, and because he educated the villeins so that they were skilled and healthy enough to keep it well. Many freemen headed straight to Drysdale, knowing that if they were honest and able he would ensure the good health and welfare of themselves and their families. Of course, Edwin could have learned from this and increased the productivity of his own land, but instead he was jealous of Saul. Ignorant people never see the value of increasing their knowledge. Their view of the world simply divides it into what they have and what they have not. They can only covet rather than create. In Edwin's hands your land would simply have returned to useless moor and fenland. Still, I do not think that all is lost. I have a great faith in the King's ability to maintain his legal system. Already, people are being tried far more fairly and actually being made to face a trial by jury. Next time Edwin makes a mistake we should be ready for him."

"How was it that you did not gain the land? It would have made life so much simpler if you and I were landholding neighbours."

"Margery's father was a canny man and he knew Edwin's nose would be put out of joint if he accepted my marriage proposal to Margery. He wanted the best for her. He declared publicly that any man who married her would gain only the tenancy of Redgate, here on your land. Saul had given Martin Redgate as a gift, knowing they could work together. When Edwin realised that a marriage to Margery would mean he would only gain a hunting lodge, and that he would be an underling to Saul, he changed his mind about matrimony. I was more than happy. Life as a knight with a small manor to oversee was far more manageable to me. It led to my friendship with your father and mother. I do not know whether Margery's father intended us to eventually inherit the rights to his estate, but shortly after his death, Edwin married Margery's mother; thirteen years her junior. Of course, this is all history now, except I'm wondering whether I have been too complacent."

Bran shifted a little uncomfortably. "If he was so against my father he surely wouldn't wish his daughter to marry me."

Ben nodded. "What you have to remember, Bran, is that Edwin is a logical rather than a sentimental man. He wants Drysdale and you have the tenancy. Now,

I could make the assumption that Henry would skin him alive if he thought you were being threatened by an upstart like him, but there are other ways of getting what you want. A marriage would be a way of him moving closer to achieving his aims. It worries me, because people in the way of Edwin's ambitions tend to die. It would be dangerous for you, for me and for Anna. Edwin will probably see her as one of his major hurdles. That's why I was hesitant about a simple jaunt to the fair."

"I have no intention of marrying just yet. Besides, I leave in three days time. And the Order always makes sure that our households are well-protected. Edwin will know that."

"I know," Ben sighed. He turned to face the window again. "Of course, this lady - Catherine - would not be likely to present herself to a man from the Northern as Edwin's daughter. But, it should be easy for you to recognise her if she does approach you."

He turned back to Bran, who looked up at him expectantly. "They say she looks uncannily like Margery: a seventeen year old Margery, of course."

Bran governed his feelings, simply saying, "Then I'll know her and be forewarned. But isn't it more logical for him to tempt you with a copy of Margery?"

Ben shook his head. "He wants your larger expanse of land; Drysdale. Remember, he turned down the opportunity of winning Redgate and paying dues to your father. This would be no different. Just be careful tomorrow."

"I have no desire to marry just yet."

"Umm, I remember saying the same thing to my father three days before I met Margery."

The door opened and Thomas carried in their meal.

Chapter Four

The Fair

Laughter, shouting, singing, touting, sampling of strangely aromatic wares, flashes of colour and sometimes flames, bartering and dancing assaulted their senses. Marc exchanged a silver penny with a stallholder and brought them all some gingerbread. Susan and Anna compared their gifts. The brightly coloured silks and aromatic spices reminded Bran of his imminent journey. He would ask Janet to cut him mint and nettles in case his stomach needed time to adjust to the movement of the boat.

They squeezed past a man bartering for a hawk and watched a group of musicians trying to teach a new dance from France. Eventually, they were back at the arena where the wrestlers had just begun their bout. Individuals in the crowd cheered for the man on whom they had placed their money. They fought, bare-chested and red-faced, trying to stick to the rules they had agreed before the game. Marc and Bran watched with interest, aware of how much extra weight the men were carrying and how they often relied on each other for balance. It was a cumbersome coupling. There were so many times that each man remained on his feet due to, rather than in spite of, the other's grip that it was quite easy to see that the whole bout was choreographed. Still, they were entertaining enough and when, eventually, the larger man landed on his back with a satisfying thump, wheeze and contortion of the face, one half of the crowd erupted into cheers. Bran and Marc joined with a show of good nature.

"Hope you're not tempted to show them how it's done." Unnoticed, Ben had joined the crowd of spectators. He was accompanied by Thomas and Janet. The latter took the sleeping Anna from Bran.

"I'll take her home. Come on, Susan. There are things to be done before the guests arrive."

Susan did not try to hide her disappointment, but dutifully joined her mother and made her way back through the crowds. Marc's disappointment was equally evident. It was obvious that Susan's father, Thomas, was lingering so he could have a word with him and he wasn't sure whether the outcome would be favourable. He hoped it would go well. He had asked Thomas' permission to accompany Susan to the fair just the night before and he had seemed happy at the prospect. Bran and Ben tactfully moved away.

"Come on then, lad," beckoned Thomas.

Ben glanced over to Will and Joss, who were eyeing up a couple of mares. "Will has asked some of his men from Bankside to help prepare things in case the King pays a surprise visit. He trusts you will take it in good spirit."

"Is it likely?" Bran asked, thinking of the prototypes he had not perfected yet.

Ben made light of it with a shrug and a smile. "Best to be prepared."

Bran nodded. "Any help is welcome. Would you advise me to go to Drysdale tonight?"

"No, no," smiled Ben. "Redgate for the feasting tonight. You and Marc are guests of honour."

Bran looked at him, head to one side.

"Cannot tell you any more than that, but you will be sorry you missed it if you go to Drysdale tonight."

Bran knew better than to press. His guess was that Marc had Thomas's blessing to marry Susan. Bran would be needed to give a formal approval of the match.

Ben looked about him and sighed. "I used to love the clamour and strangeness of these things," he said, casting his eyes about. "Now, all I want is to be away from the crowds and to enjoy the feast at the end of the day. It doesn't seem the same now the king has banned the free-for-all. Must be getting old."

Bran grinned. "It's hardly a sign of old age if it's the free-for-all that you miss."

He waited for a response but there was none. Ben had stopped in his tracks and was staring ahead of him. He followed his gaze to where a man and young woman stood a little away from the busier crowds, apparently listening to the musicians. Bran's eyes were drawn to the girl. She stood a little awkwardly, her arms held self-consciously across her chest. In spite of the sunlight, she seemed cold. Her skin and lips were pale, in contrast to her deep red hair. Bran knew enough of human nature to see that, although looking away, both were aware of their presence. The resemblance between Margery and this younger woman told him that her companion must be Edwin. He could not help but continue to look. Could this man of unremarkable height, with mousy coloured hair and skin to match, be responsible for so much terror?

Ben said quietly, "That is Edwin and Catherine." Unusually for Ben, he did not break his gaze. Stories of Edwin's doings were rife amongst people along the dale and as far as Durham. Those who were local stopped their chattering and watched closely to see what would emerge. Will and Joss noted the change in atmosphere from the tree-lined edge of the river. Twenty pairs of eyes from the Northern joined theirs. Ben noticed that two of their men now accompanied the females back up Redgate's bank and relaxed a little.

Catherine felt a torturous embarrassment. It had seemed so easy this morning as she pondered how to marry her own plans to help her mother with Edwin's plans for Saul. Her mother had said they were good people and not to be afraid, but now it seemed a very different story. In a matter of seconds, they had become the major attraction at the fair. She wondered if Edwin was growing angry with her. How should she behave? They so rarely had company of the respectable sort at Beau Repaire that she was hard-pressed to know the etiquette involved. But she must do something: the idea that she should stand so purposelessly made her pinch her own fingernails into her flesh with embarrassment. She decided to walk forwards as if the falconer's birds had taken her interest. Edwin had always said he would let her have a merlin one day - should they ever have guests with whom she could go a-hawking. She must not let her mother down.

Edwin watched her closely. She wasn't a bad prospect - even on first impressions. Her hair was freshly washed and her skin suitably pale. Her complexion matched well with the green dress her mother had suggested. He considered his position. There was no outward reason why he should not approach Ben and his Squire.

Nonchalantly, he called to his step-daughter, "Don't wander too far, Catherine," then approached Ben and Drysdale. He smiled at the two men, fully aware that Bran could order him off this land having been given jurisdiction by Pudsey, the Prince Bishop, but that he would probably not as it would be ill-mannered to do it publicly. He smiled at the two men. Both knew this was a public display and that if they did not wish to be cast as the villains, they would have to be careful.

"Good day to you both."

Both nodded somewhat curtly. Ben asked, "How is Marion?"

Edwin frowned. "Very ill, I'm afraid..." He would have continued but Ben interrupted.

"Marion? Ill? But she always seemed so healthy."

Edwin ignored the veiled accusation and gave a grave nod of the head. "She has refused to see anyone from the medical profession. She is quite stubborn in her ill-health."

Bran looked at Catherine. He alone noticed that her back had stiffened at talk of her mother. Still looking at Catherine, he asked, "What sort of illness is it? There are those at Drysdale who could help."

Edwin noted with satisfaction that Bran was studying Catherine. She threw a quick, nervous glance over her shoulder at Bran. She looked afraid. If there was any plotting afoot he could not believe that she was a willing part of it.

He looked at Edwin, who immediately averted his gaze before answering the question. "Hard to say what ails her when she will not allow herself to be examined. She is simply wasting away." He gave his step-daughter a concerned, fatherly look and added, "I just hope it is not infectious."

Joss and Will approached the small group. Edwin gave them a disarming smile and held out a beckoning hand. "Catherine. Leave those birds for now. Come and meet the founders of the Northern Order."

Bran could not help thinking that he was using her like a shield. Catherine swallowed and, remembering her mother's words, tried to look amiable. She empathised with the hawks, tied by their jesses to their perches. She just wanted to fly away too - although, thankfully, Drysdale did look rather agreeable. As she approached the men, their unsmiling faces incongruous in such a festive context, she was suddenly pushed off course by three running girls; Isabel of Stanmere amongst them. They ran, shrieking with laughter, pursued by two troubadours, who no longer saw the funny side as they tried to retrieve their hats. Catherine, to her shame, lost her footing and fell upon the grass. Bran would have thought the whole thing an elaborate lure, had it not been for Catherine's obvious humiliation which reddened her pale face. He stooped to her aid. Joss held out one arm across the pathway of the young revellers. They slowed to a walk immediately and apologised as they passed him. He would have insisted that they apologise to Catherine but she was so painfully embarrassed already that he let them go on their way.

Catherine's instinct was to get to her feet, but she had wrenched her ankle quite badly as she fell and knew that it would be too soon to allow the foot to take her weight. Bran helped her. "Did you twist your ankle?"

She nodded, nervous of what Edwin would think. "Just a little. It's nothing really."

He did as he would if he was unsure of one of the page's injuries. He stepped back and watched her feet as she walked. She could not help but limp a little. Edwin was quietly impressed. She was either very good at pretending or genuinely in pain. Joss and Ben were thinking exactly the same. Will, on the other hand, erred on the side of gentlemanly and brought a small empty barrel for her to sit on, removing his own cloak and covering it for her. Bran held her hand as she lowered herself down self-consciously.

"Just for a short while," he reassured her with a smile. He finally allowed himself to look into her face as she thanked him.

Joss felt his heart sink as he watched Bran. He guessed, correctly, that Bran had noticed the large brown eyes, the clear intelligent brow and the slight but shapely hands and body that both Catherine and Margery had inherited from their mother.

Ben intervened. "I have not seen you since you were a baby, Catherine. Have you been well?"

Catherine nodded. "Yes, Sir, I am well, but I do worry about my mother."

As a generous hearted father himself, he could tell this was an unhappy child. Will, sounding as if nothing at all was amiss, entered the conversation.

"Well, Edwin. I think Marion should be seen to, whether she likes it or not. Those nearest and dearest to her are so concerned, it would be a sin not to do something constructive. I would like to make so bold as to suggest that Marion is brought to Drysdale so a treatment can be decided. I would suggest Bankside, but Drysdale is far more salubrious," he grinned, "and the road less pitted."

Ben and Joss turned to look at him, willing him to remember the possibility of a royal visit.

Edwin replied, "I'm afraid she is too ill to ride, Sir."

"That's not important. She could be brought over - as soon as possible as Bran leaves soon. Of course, I realise you may be too busy to make the journey yourself; especially as we do not know how long Marion would need to stay and recuperate. A land holder's responsibilities give him so little free time." Will pretended to ponder, then as if suddenly being struck by some bright idea, he announced, "I have it! I have men who could take a cart for Marion. It is covered so it would not matter if it rained. They could set out for Beau Repaire tomorrow and have her back in Drysdale by the afternoon." He looked at Catherine, who had begun to rotate her foot, and was no longer able to catch everything which Edwin uttered in that quiet way of his. Will continued. "Catherine could accompany her - make sure her journey is as comfortable as possible." He raised his eyebrows, waiting for Edwin's response.

Edwin had not counted on Will's irritating frankness, but he could see some advantages in the plan. He rubbed his chin, pondering. He certainly liked the idea that Catherine should spend some time at Drysdale. But Marion being treated? They would see her wounds. He had intended to send her on her way with a mix of monk's hood and yew berries. It would not take much in her present condition so he certainly did not want her regaining any strength. Suddenly, it fell into place.

"I would hate to burden you, but it is a welcome idea. Anything to help dear Marion." Although quietly spoken, his words rang with hollow insincerity to everyone but Edwin, who had no idea how true sentiment for a wife sounded. "It seems a shame to give Catherine all that extra travelling. Catherine could remain behind today and I could send Marion's lady, Emma, to ride alongside her tomorrow. Perhaps Catherine could help with your festivities tonight. She sings well. I would be happy to help furnish your tables at a future date as a token of thanks."

Edwin was not foolish enough to invite himself into such hostile company. He also knew he would never have to honour his offer of cuisine. No-one would trust him enough to eat food he had provided.

"So you'll see your mother tomorrow, Catherine."

Bran looked down at Catherine. She had blanched again, and no wonder. He was suggesting she be left in the company of strangers. Strangers she had been probably taught to consider as enemies. Edwin now looked at her too.

Ben smiled at her. He really wanted to keep Bran and Catherine separated until his trip, but he could not help pitying her. He could tell she was afraid. As Edwin bade Catherine farewell, Joss glared at Will, who remained undeterred.

"The priority is that we get the girl and Marion out of there to safety. Don't the Northern pride themselves on doing what is right?"

Joss sighed at his friend's over-simplification of what could become very complicated. She was far from being the only daughter that would be used as a pawn to fulfil her family's interests.

"Besides," Will added, "Bran leaves soon. He could meet an array of beauties while he is travelling."

"Um," muttered Ben. "Like Marc could have. Away almost five years and he's all set to marry Susan of Redgate."

"And a fine girl too," grinned Will, completely ignoring the irony.

Edwin had already gone, leaving Catherine to be helped to her feet by Bran. Bran knew he had been forewarned, and he knew what Ben was probably thinking, but he could not leave her to suffer alone while his friends bickered. Besides, Catherine seemed intelligent enough to recognise that she was their topic of conversation. He held out his hand and smiled. "Shall we see how your ankle feels now?"

Her hand seemed small and pale when she took his. She stood and rocked her weight a little from one foot to the other, just as the music began again.

"No need to dance for me, Catherine," he grinned. "A couple of steps will do."

She couldn't help but smile. "It's better now," she decided.

"Good," he grinned. She had a nice smile. "I think you should ride up to Redgate: it's taxing at the best of times."

Bran led Catherine to the higher path and helped her to mount his courser. She gave him a nervous smile.

He tried to reassure her. "It's just a short distance. You mustn't worry about coming to Redgate. They always give a warm welcome to visitors." He gave her another grin. "And if you have heard any stories about me, you mustn't worry about that either. I'll be too busy sacrificing small children and counting money to have time to sell you into slavery."

She coloured and gave a nervous laugh at his awareness of the rumours that were spread about him. "If you have a list of intended victims, might I suggest you add my step-brothers?" Bran laughed. She was beginning to feel more comfortable, but her head still spun at the task that lay ahead. She wondered if he ate what everyone else did. He certainly did not look like a man who would worship the devil and blight crops.

The three older men watched the two as they talked and gave each other dismayed glances. "Some good could come of this," Will insisted quietly. "And there has never been a time when I have not been able to talk us out of a complicated situation."

Neither of his friends reminded him of the obvious fact that he was usually the one that had talked them into the complicated situation in the first place. As they mounted their horses, Joss muttered, "This isn't a poem based in some fantasy world of chivalric ideals, Will. We cannot step outside when we have had enough."

"Exactly. Neither can Marion and Catherine. Why purport to have ideals at all if we do not live up to them simply because it does not feel convenient? If anything ever happens to me and my sons, leaving Leona and my daughters in the King's gift, I just pray there will be an interfering busy-body like me to keep a close eye on them."

Ben knew better than to add his own opinion. His friends needed to let their feathers settle first. A draught of Redgate ale after the steep ride would do the trick.

As they crested the hill and dropped a little to the manor house, the sound of music, chattering and laughing became more audible, given a theatrical echo by the surrounding hillside and stonework. Sheep chewed nonchalantly in the surrounding fields. Catherine looked about her: so many smiling people; so many greeting each other. They had a different look to those of Beau Repaire. And not just those of rank. The mood was the obvious difference, but perhaps that was brought about by the fair. No. It wasn't just the smiles. Their eyes were brighter; their clothes were cleaner; their skin seemed to glow. The men of rank were obviously athletes: even those her step-father's age. The house stood in fetlocks of hartstongue, mint, sorrel and vervain; grass between worn footways was sprinkled with colour from heartsease, columbine, ox-eye daisies and camomile; while the further slopes fell away from the stonework in mists of garlic and yarrow. Catherine knew already that she would find it difficult to leave here.

Bran watched her reaction as he helped her dismount. If she liked Redgate, he wondered what she would make of Drysdale. The king's potential visit crossed his mind. Somehow it did not seem to matter so much anymore. Will got them into this: he could decide how it should be played.

Edwin met his small band of men on the Durham road and set off for Beau Repaire in haste. As yet, he was still unsure of how Marion would die before morning. He did not like to be rushed into decisions, but he was determined that she would not survive the night.

At Redgate, Bran introduced Catherine to Janet and Susan so she would have some female company. Janet seemed stunned at first, then gave her a hug.

"I'm sorry for staring," she apologised. "Your sister and I were good friends. You look so alike. It quite startled me." She took her hand. "Come and see your niece." She led Catherine over to a happily eating Anna, whose blank look showed she was quite unaware of this lady's resemblance to her mother.

Catherine was not allowed to do any work. Instead she was given a trencher piled with game and frumenty and a mug of ale and made to sit in the window, where she could watch the goings on. "Just a word of caution," said Janet. "Redgate ale is very strong. We have good water here so there is no need to brew mild ale as a cleaner substitute. Sir Drysdale has a plentiful supply of water which he pipes over here."

Catherine did not understand. "Pipes?"

"He's a very clever man." nodded Janet. "Knows a lot about the old Roman ways. Anyway, the reason I tell you is that over there.." she pointed with her cloth to two barrels in a corner, "is water for drinking. I will give you a spare pot so that now and then you can drink from there and water down the ale. Otherwise your head will be splitting in the morning."

Janet was whisked away and Catherine was left to watch the company. On finishing her plate, she sniffed at the ale. It certainly smelt quite strong. She took a sip. She felt nothing at first and, it being a hot day, she took a few more gulps. It was rather nice at Redgate. She could not remember a time she had felt so at ease. She watched the happy company, even joining in one or two of the dances as time passed. She tried to protest and said that she did not know the steps, but her cries fell on deaf ears and she was marched and twirled around the room, out of the door to where a different tune was being played, and back again. She could feel a smile on her face and wondered how it had got there. She decided it might be a good time to water down her ale as Janet had advised and then withdrew to her window-seat, where Janet found her and invited her to join the company outside.

Catherine was pleased to see that Bran was a member of their group. After the ale and the dancing, Joss did not seem so menacing to her. Anna sat on her father's lap, holding a little woollen doll. Another party of guests arrived and a delighted Will stood up to greet the company. Catherine wondered who the two young knights, the lady and four flaxen haired girls, perhaps between the ages of seven and twelve, could be. The girls were helped from their mounts by the young men, who she could now tell must be their brothers. As soon as they reached solid ground, they ran towards Will giggling. He opened his arms theatrically and bellowed, "Ah! What is this brilliance of angels!"

He embraced them all simultaneously, then stood on noticing one of his sons about to help his wife to dismount. "Ah, ah," he smiled. "My duty, I think."

Catherine watched and smiled. He helped her down, whispering something tender judging by the way she looked at him. He didn't put her down until she had reached their group. Only then could Catherine tell that the lady was expecting a child. Anna had wriggled from her father's knee and was pulling at Will's sleeve.

"Am I an angel?"

He laughed and scooped her up high into the air. "Of course you are, Sweetheart. Look at you up there in Heaven!" He twirled her down to the floor again and all five girls ran into the house calling for Susan. How different this was from her family.

Bran was looking at her.

"Are all the families you know so close?"

He smiled. "Will makes more of a show of it than most."

Catherine was introduced time upon time as new company arrived. All of them remarked on her resemblance to Margery. None of them remarked on her kinship to Edwin, although the first faltering moments of each introduction reminded her of the strangeness of her being a guest here. Eventually, as the evening drew on and she had drunk another pot of ale, she became more relaxed: even contemplative. She cooled herself by leaning against the stonework of the house and simply allowed the story-telling to wash over her. Bran was much in demand, especially in the hour following Marc and Susan's announcement that they were to be married. Bran fulfilled his duty of formalising the agreement by giving his permission for his vassal to marry. Others came to him with strange looking gadgets or drew shapes in the dust of the pathway, perplexed looks on their faces. He seemed to enjoy solving their problems. As far as she could see, his humour was not brought about by the ale. He had only water all evening. Just as the sun dropped below the roof, Ben hammered on the table top with the hilt of Joss's sword. Immediately, the music stopped and a crowd gathered about them.

"A very, very important announcement is to be made," he declared sombrely, "so listen carefully."

A hush fell on the gathered company.

"Today, the Prince Bishop gave his official approval of this very, very important event." He looked about him at the faces in the crowd. "I say 'very, very' because it involves two young men, rather than one." He held out his hands, beckoning. "Bran, Marc - stand up please and follow me."

The two friends looked at each other and did as they were bid. Joss and Will joined Ben and led them to a place beneath the trees. The on-lookers began to smile at their confusion. Ben laughed and shook his head. "You must be the only two people here who do not realise what is about to happen." He leaned towards them, playfully, and gave a theatrical whisper. "You need to appear pleased."

The company laughed.

Ben continued. "In two days time, these deserving young men will need to prepare themselves with a day of cleansing and meditation. Then they will be in a state of readiness to be knighted."

Both young men looked at each other and smiled.

"But, we need to know one thing - if offered a place with the Northern Order, would you accept it and agree to live by the rules and ideals they cherish?"

After some nodding of heads, the crowd gave a cheer and they were allowed to hide their embarrassment by rejoining the company again.

Ben announced, "As Bran is leaving us soon, you are all ordered to enjoy yourselves as much as possible now rather than waiting until after the ceremony."

A cheer went up again. Congratulations poured over the two but, eventually, the company receded a little, eager to do just as Ben had said. Susan stood in the doorway, shyly, wondering whether to join Marc. He looked for her and went to her, finally daring to kiss her in public, much to the delight of the younger members of the company. From his kitchen window, Robert smiled at his nephew's good fortune. Their family were not doing too badly, in spite of their humble beginnings.

Catherine decided to draw away a little, feeling that it was not really her place to intrude amongst the well-wishers. She felt a little down-hearted that Bran was to go away, but she blamed this mood on the ale. She hardly knew him. Still, she could not help wondering where he was going and for how long. She knew she would not dare to ask him in case he thought it was something Edwin had asked her to find out. As people around their original table became sparse, she noticed Bran looking at her. She smiled a congratulatory smile and he came over to join her.

"May I sit with you?"

She was taken aback by his manners.

There was still a lot of noise from the house, so he led her to the bank side opposite, laying down his cloak so they could sit more comfortably on the grass.

Ben watched from the house. He considered whether to watch them for a while, but decided against it. Bran knew they needed more information if they were to help the girl and her mother without mishap, so he would trust him to do it his way.

"This is a happy place," smiled Catherine, hugging her knees.

Bran nodded. "Ben takes his duty of care very seriously."

Catherine considered. "As does Edwin, but the results are very different for the people of Beau Repaire."

He looked at her to gauge her mood.

"How long have you known Ben?" she asked.

"Since I was five years old. He took me in when my...." he faltered, realising Edwin's implication in his mother's murder, but decided it was best not to be guarded in his own speech if he wanted her to be open. "When my mother was killed."

"And your father?"

"He died two months before that."

They looked at each other, seeing that they shared some common ground. She took a deep breath and said, "I believe Edwin killed my father."

In the face of her candour, he remained silent. Her tone had a dreamlike, otherworldly quality which seemed incongruous with her blunt home-truths.

"I know I was very young, but I hear people's stories and, besides..." she looked at Bran, "I am old enough to judge his character now and..." she faltered again, realising how abrupt this must sound, but needing to let him know so something could be done. "And I feel that if no one intervenes, he will kill my mother very soon." She spoke quietly, her eyes almost misted with the thoughtfulness required to say exactly what she meant – as one recently awoken from a dream, needing to explain it before the memory of it eluded her.

He felt quite hypnotised by her. "What makes you think it, Catherine? Does he beat her?"

She shook her head. "No. I did see him knock her to the ground once - a few years ago now. No, not that. It's the way he has isolated her. He fabricates her moods. He says she is stubborn and will not see any one, but he has a guard at the door, preventing anyone from entering." She looked about warily. "He may have spies who will report back. It will make things worse for my mother."

Bran took her hand. "All Northern households are constantly watched over. Any hidden observer would have been discovered by now."

She looked across the pine topped banks, as if to verify what he had said.

Bran gave a gentle push. "Who is Emma? Can she offer some protection?"

Catherine shook her head. "Emma left Beau Repaire months ago: before Christmas. Edwin said she had gained her freedom and gone to marry a man in Lincoln, but I'm not so...." She stopped, noticing Bran's face.

"Is there another Emma? Someone he would send to ride with your mother to Drysdale?"

There was no need to ponder. There were no other females at Beau Repaire, save those fly by nights that visited from God knows where. She shook her head. Bran looked at the sky. There was little light left. "Catherine, will you come with me? This is serious news."

She was confused. What had she said to change his mood? He helped her to her feet and led her into the house. He scanned the room for his mentors, but they were already aware of him.

He whispered to Ben. "We need to talk privately without delay."

This was just what Ben had feared: trouble dispelling the good cheer.

Ben led the party into the smaller room at the back of the house and closed the door on the revellers outside. The window facing down the bank was open. The carefree company seemed a long way off now. The four men turned to face Catherine and she suddenly felt alarmed and took a step back towards the door like a cornered hind. Was this a trick? Did they mean to ill-use her to teach Edwin a lesson?

Bran spoke, eager to put them all at ease as quickly as possible. "Catherine does not know why I brought her here, but she just told me something of great import. You remember the arrangements Edwin said he would make for Marion being accompanied to Drysdale in the morning," he addressed this to the men, who nodded, then he turned back to Catherine.

"Catherine. Don't be afraid. We want only to protect you. Remember you are Margery's sister."

She nodded, but watchful eyes showed she was still fearful.

"Please tell the gentlemen here what you just said about Emma."

It did not seem the most important part of what she had told him. She gave a slight shake of the head. "Simply that Emma has not lived at Beau Repaire since before Christmas last."

The other three looked at each other. Ben spoke. "Does she live close by then?"

Catherine shook her head again. "No. It is said she is gone to marry in Lincoln."

The men looked at each other. Ben asked her. "Have you seen your mother lately?"

"I saw her this morning and yesterday evening." She looked at Bran nervously. "I wish to be truthful with you. To be completely honest, I saw her yesterday afternoon after being denied access to her for weeks. I climbed through her chamber window. Please do not tell Edwin."

The older men again wondered if she was a good liar or sincere in her fear of her step-father.

Ben continued. "How was she? Did you recognise any of her symptoms?"

"She was far worse in the afternoon, when I saw her alone, than later in the evening, when Edwin insisted on accompanying me. On my first visit, there had been no fire lit. She was bed-ridden. Her skin was grey, her lips cracked and she could barely speak or raise her hand." Catherine stopped. Her own hand was raised as if miming her mother's condition. Even in the shadows of the dusky chamber they could see the moistness in the girls' eyes. "I know it is Summer and the lack of a fire seems of no importance, but this is a shaded room. It gets the sun for only one hour a day. And the fire was not lit. Not until the meeting Edwin arranged for me later in the day. And the chamber window had been left open wide. That was what finally prompted me to climb up to it by the apple tree."

The men stayed quiet. They realised Marion could be dead already. They conferred quietly. Bran tried to give Catherine a reassuring smile. The others turned again. Ben spoke once more. "We are very concerned for your mother's safety, Catherine, and for yours. Before we take action, we need you to tell us if you have any knowledge of plans afoot that might be harmful to anyone linked to the Northern."

Catherine gave a hopeless shrug. "Edwin is always plotting but I know nothing of the details." She looked across at Bran again.

"If there is something we should know, tell us now, Catherine, no matter how difficult it might seem."

Even before the fair, she had spent some time considering how she would word things when revealing Edwin's plans, but it still was not easy. She took a deep breath. "Edwin has painted a black picture of the Northern since I was a little girl. Suddenly, yesterday, he asked me to be brave and to ...." she burned with embarrassment and looked at the floor, "to make myself attractive to you." It was nothing they had not already guessed. Bran tried to fill the silence.

"Thank you, Catherine. I know this is hard, but is there anything else he has told you? Are Will's sons likely to ride into a trap tomorrow when they go to fetch your mother?"

She tried to think. "I want to help but I don't know. He never speaks in straight forward truths. Like saying my mother is stubborn and refuses help. If you'd seen the look in her eyes. She's desperate. She wants to live." She wrung her hands. "I really do want to help."

Joss approached her. His deep voice was surprisingly gentle. "Catherine. I think you have been honest with us and we now need to be honest with you. You need to understand our reasons for being wary. Apart from the twisted truths about Ben's engagement to Margery which you have probably already heard, we also believe that Edwin was responsible for the murders of Bran's father and mother. Two people who did nothing but good for the community they led. Nothing ever happened to bring Edwin to task, partly because he threatened those who were chosen to speak for his character. You need to answer this carefully, Catherine. Only tell us what you think you can do, not what you wish you could. If we find a reason to bring Edwin to trial, will you testify that you think him murderous or deceitful? Only telling what you know to be true, of course."

Catherine nodded. She cleared her throat nervously. "Would I be able to stay somewhere safe? Just in case?"

Ben intervened. "Of course. That would be a priority."

Joss continued. "We feel that your mother needs us tonight. It's more urgent than we thought."

Catherine's heart began to pound.

"Edwin said that Emma would accompany your mother tomorrow."

He gave time for the information and its implications to sink in.

Will elaborated. "It's a weakness of the liar to feel there ought to be 'realistic' details woven amongst the main thread of his lie. It's usually the thing that finds him out. I was going to send my two boys over there tomorrow with an extra few men to guard their backs, but I do not want to endanger them. There may be no ambush. It may be that Edwin intends them to go tomorrow and discover that your mother has already passed away. He could continue with his plans for you and Bran regardless."

The longer Catherine thought about it, the heavier her heart weighed. "He could be about it now." Her hand came to her mouth. "Even now. Or have already done it. While I have been safe - drinking ale and dancing." Suddenly, it felt like they could not get there soon enough.

Joss spoke again. "We will leave immediately. I want you to stay here where it is safe, Catherine. Do you give us your word that you will help us against Edwin?"

She thought of how her step-father had touched her the night before; how he breathed over her when he thought she was sleeping. How he probably killed her father, altering the course of her life. She met Joss's steady gaze, "Yes."

"We will say nothing of what you have told us. He must think that you are still a willing participant in his plans. We will tell him that we would like you to stay at Drysdale for a while. That Bran has become close. In that time, Edwin may meet with you. Tell you things, or, better still, write things that will incriminate himself. Do you see how this is unfolding, Catherine?"

She knew it was unlikely he would write. Like many knights, he had not learned. Besides, he would not leave anything that could be used as evidence. Still, she nodded, simply eager to have them make their way to her mother as soon as possible.

Joss gave a rare smile. This could be all they needed to finally be rid of Edwin. The king himself might even preside over the hearings if all went according to tonight's plan. If Marion was still alive, they would have two who would speak against him. From the doorway, Ben waved Janet over. "Show Catherine where she can sleep. Leave the torches lit on the outer gates - it is likely to be dark when we get back."

Bran turned to Catherine. "This must all seem strange to you, but try to get some rest." And with that he left her.

Horses and arms were brought. She saw Ben shaking his head at Bran. She strained to hear them speak. "You are his main game, Saul. We cannot risk it."

Bran said something in reply which she could not catch, but it made Will shake his head.

"He's right," added Joss. "Stay here with Marc and organise the men in case he has already prepared a counter attack. This way, he still needs Catherine."

They rode away, leaving Bran looking dejected on the bank side. It was a while until he noticed Catherine still standing there in the half light. Janet held back tactfully. He bent down to retrieve something from the grass then came towards her. The company had all melted away into the twilight. She wondered if he would be angry with her for spoiling his evening and flinched away from him as he raised his hands. He stepped back. He was holding his cloak. "You look cold," he explained. "Here," he raised his hands again, "use this to keep warm. It'll cool down through the night." He draped it over her shoulders and led her to Janet, who took her through the house to where Susan, her sisters and Anna shared a room.

Bran pondered as he went to find Marc. Catherine probably wouldn't sleep. They all had a long night ahead of them. But he was getting closer to solving his problem.

Chapter Five

A Long Night

Catherine watched the road east from the chamber window. She tried to focus through the darkness to the point where she knew the men would have to pass, once they had descended the bank and swerved along the dale towards Beau Repaire. Twilight had arrived, making stark silhouettes of branches against the mid blue sky. She wondered how they would handle it once they arrived. If they were to catch Edwin out, they would have to play it carefully. Quite soon, she spotted the five torches of the group as they moved between the trees. Once swallowed by the forest, her eyes could make nothing of the inky black so she looked down into the courtyard instead.

Bran was there. At intervals of about twenty yards, wending through the nearest woodland, she could see more torches. She felt a pang of guilt that it was her visit that aroused so much suspicion. What would Will's pregnant wife think of her? Three of the party of five were from her family. And Susan? Her engagement celebrations had been cut short. Bran wore his hauberk now: hardly a way to prepare spiritually for his oncoming knighthood.

She looked down at his dark head. He was absorbed in his watch, unaware of her gaze. Presently, Marc joined him, spoke briefly then made his way into the trees. Susan came into the room shortly after, smiling in spite of the threat of trouble. Catherine returned the smile as Susan took to her bed, then resumed her watch from the window. She tried not to worry about her mother. Realistically, she could have been dead for a while now. Thinking of it only shot frantic darts of worry through her chest. Her mother had faith in the Northern. So would she.

After a while, she realised that there was a pattern of movement to the torches. A very definite signalling occurred at regular intervals, travelling down the line. The watch was constant and the men along the watch-line continually informed of the level of safety.

She turned away. There was no point torturing herself. It would be another three hours at least before Joss came back from Beau Repaire, and they could only be that quick if her mother was not with them. She slipped onto the pallet next to Anna, who slept soundly with Woolly in her hand. Catherine lay staring at the purpling sky, unable to sleep or even to know what to pray for.

****

Rising up from the dale to the scrubland around Beau Repaire gave the small party from the Northern an extra hour of twilight. Taking care not to climb high enough to be seen on the skyline, they gathered for talks.

"I could go in first," suggested Will. "He knows I offered to help Marion. It would not seem so provocative."

Joss shook his head. "If it is advantageous to Edwin to see this visit as an attack, he will interpret it as such."

Ben nodded his agreement. "We are not dealing with a man of honour or moral standing. I suggest we go in unannounced, assess Marion's condition and make sure we leave with her - if she is still alive."

Joss turned to Will's sons, Raymond and Leonard, "Stay here. We will leave our torches, but keep them burning where they can be seen from the bank top. It will give the appearance of numbers."

The three older men turned and began the further winding ascent to Edwin's home.

****

Edwin was very irritated: especially at Will with his generous offers. He hated to be rushed. He stared at his wife who, although displaying the signs of blood poisoning, was an annoyingly long way from death.

Marion watched her husband warily from her bed.

"Where is Catherine?" she asked, her voice fighting against a swollen dryness in her throat.

Edwin decided there could be some advantage in a bedside chat and seated himself with a smile.

"It seems Drysdale was quite taken with our Catherine. She was invited to join the festivities at Redgate."

Marion smiled. She would be safe there.

"You sound thirsty. I had some juice prepared for you. The berries are unusually ripe for August - in places which catch the most sun." He reached for a cup at her bedside. "Here, drink."

He put one hand behind her head and held the cup to her lips. She knew better than to drink, although she could not help some of the liquid going into her mouth. He put the cup to one side.

"There. Close your eyes and see if you can get some sleep."

She did not want to, but if she feigned sleep, perhaps he would leave her alone for now. Long enough for the Northern to find out about her illness. She closed her eyes as she was told but listened for his movements. Eventually, she felt the motion of the pallet as he stood. He moved away from her. She thought he was going to the doorway, but at the hearth he stopped and she heard more logs being lifted and dropped onto the fire. From there, his footsteps crossed the room and she heard the chest being opened. He came back to the bed and she sensed him leaning over her. She wished he would hurry up and go so that she could spit out the juice she still held in her mouth.

He was silent for such a long time that she was tempted to open her eyes again, but she did not. She heard him take a deep breath and wished him gone so that she could too. A heavy force suddenly pressed upon her face. So heavy that she could not sink any further back into the pallet in order to twist her head and free her airways. She tried to push him away but he lay across her, pinning her down under his body weight. She felt the blood begin to pound in her head and panic shot through her. She tried to call out, but her cries were muted under the bruising pressure. Finally, as the sound of her pulsing blood became more of a scraping, she tried to claw at the hands which suffocated her, but Edwin's need was too great to allow a few scratches to deter him.

Long after her struggling had stopped, he still lay across her, the bundle of cloth pressed hard to her face and mouth - just to make sure. When he finally peeled it away, he studied her face in the poor light. He contemplated the open mouth and eyes. She looked far too stricken. He tried to close them and turned her head a little to one side. Better. An alien footstep on the stairs made him act quickly. He rolled the cloth and put it behind her head then sat at the bedside once more. The door opened.

As soon as Ben saw Marion and Edwin framed by the open doorway, he knew it was too late. He waited for no invitation and crossed the room to the bedside. Joss and Will stood so that Edwin could not run, even though they knew this wasn't his style. Ben studied Marion's face.

"How long has she been dead?" he asked.

Edwin, who had positioned himself with elbows on knees and head in hands, turned around blearily, as if waking up. "Dead? You mean she has gone?"

Ben felt his anger rising but did not let it control his actions. What happened next was very important. He reached across the bed and felt the bedclothes just beneath her neck.

"Still warm," he murmured to Will and Joss.

Ben looked to the window: it was closed. Then to the fire: flames leapt upwards. He made pretence of straightening her covers. Behind her head lay a folded nightgown. Edwin shifted a little and held out a hand, "She won't need that now."

Now that Edwin wanted it, Ben saw the garment in a far more significant light. Gently, he pulled the cloth from behind her head. As it unfolded, several russet stains became apparent. Ben studied them. The stains were of varying intensity, but all of a similar shape, as if something damp had marked the cloth in one place and seeped through the folded layers. Slowly and deliberately, Ben folded the chemise then held it in his palm with the darkest stains facing upwards. He positioned his hand so that it hovered an inch over Marion's face. Joss and Will watched closely, as did Edwin.

"She was coughing up blood today," sighed Edwin, but Ben was not listening. He knew the stain was not blood and looked to the bedside. The cup of juice caught his eye. He held it to his nose and sniffed, then turned to Edwin and raised an inquiring eyebrow.

"Blackberry juice," said Edwin. "I thought it would help give her some nourishment. She would not eat, you see."

Ben, already convinced that this was a lie, dipped the tip of a finger into the liquid. "Young at heart as I am, Edwin," he murmured, watching his finger just break the surface, "I still enjoy blackberrying every year. The only embarrassing drawback is being discovered by one's unexpected guests." Here he nodded towards Will and Joss. "You see, the main pitfall of blackberrying is that the juice stains the fingers quite unmistakably. It gives you away. The juice's stains always remind me of the purple-red of birth marks."

At this point, he held up his fingertip, which was now an unequivocal orange-brown. Ben studied it and said nothing. He rubbed his fingers together and the juice became invisible to the eye. "Takes a lot of scrubbing to rid yourself of tell-tale blackberry stains," he added.

Will took out his water bag, took a long drink, crossed to the window, opened it and emptied the remainder. He then crossed the room to Ben, who poured the contents of the cup inside. Edwin was no fool. He knew their intentions, but he also knew that to protest so early would smack of guilt. He reached for his wife's hand and squeezed it, his eyes closed. He tried to think fast. Ben's calm voice wended its way between his racing thoughts.

"Did you pick the blackberries yourself, Edwin?" he asked.

Good. He could answer no, then it would not matter that the berries were not the type he had said. "No, I sent the Cook's boy."

"Oh, I thought perhaps you had picked them."

"No." Edwin shook his head. He looked up at Ben, now confident enough in his advantage to look him in the face. Ben was not returning his gaze, but looking pointedly to where Edwin covered Marion's hand in his. Stung, Edwin immediately saw his mistake and instinctively withdrew his hand. But it was too late.

"If you had picked the berries yourself, it may have explained the scratches on the back of your hands and your wrists."

Edwin's heartbeat quickened. "I don't like your implication, Sir." He would take offence to buy more time. Ben ignored him and held Marion's hand so he could inspect her fingernails more closely. Joss brought two candles to the bedside.

Edwin snorted derisively. "Who gave you permission to come here? Who on Earth do you think you are, interrupting at a time like this? Has a husband no right to be alone with his wife? Has he no time to pray for her departing soul without the gloating eyes of his old enemies pressing upon him?"

Until now, Ben had ignored him completely, turning Marion's fingers this way and that in the candle light.

"Oh!" he said in feigned surprise. "Are we enemies, Edwin? Why would that be?"

Edwin blustered further. "You know full well."

Ben turned from him to his companions. "Marion's nails on both hands are broken. She has been scratching at something quite frantically. With all the strength she had left, I would say."

Will and Joss remained silent, but stared pointedly at Edwin.

"I will not put up with this in my own home."

"Put up with what?" asked Ben.

"I know the source of this. It all stems from Margery."

Ben, Will and Joss looked at each other then at Edwin, blankly. Even Edwin felt the ludicrousness of his own statement. Here he sat with one dead wife while lamenting the loss of another.

There was a silence. "You need to elaborate for us, I'm afraid." proffered Will.

"Jealousy!" Edwin was quickly realising that feigned anger was not going to work. He chose to keep a stubborn silence instead.

Ben knelt by the bedside as if saying a prayer. While on his knees, he swept a hand under the bed. His fingertips brushed against several light and fragile objects. Leaves? He scooped them up as he got to his feet. He bent to kiss Marion's brow, noticing as he did so, the same russet stains at her lips.

The three men walked to the door. Ben turned. "I take it from your displeasure that you will be insisting on Catherine being returned home as soon as possible."

Things were not going the way Edwin had planned. With a force of will, he turned to them, shaking his head apologetically.

"Forgive my curt words. Grieving men often speak out of turn. If Catherine has been troublesome, I can have her collected, however, I would humbly ask a favour." He waited for a signal to continue, but receiving none, he pressed on uninvited. "Until we know what killed Marion, perhaps it would be safer for Catherine to stay at Redgate."

The irony was not lost on any of them.

"She will certainly be safer at Redgate," agreed Ben. He glanced at the bed. "Marion should lie next to Margery. We shall arrange it so."

All three left the room. They made their way through the dark house to their waiting mounts, checking for tampering before climbing into their saddles. They were aware of Edwin watching them as they left. Edwin knew he was not out of the woods. He also knew there was no point trying to waylay the men in order to take the evidence which would prove his guilt. He had no men who could match the combat skills of the Northern. To hold a failed ambush would be to simply implicate himself further. He would use his time to gather character witnesses instead. The people of Beau Repaire were all aware of his capabilities. It would not take much persuasion for them to lie.

None of the trio spoke until reaching the circle of torchlight where Leonard and Raymond were waiting. Even then, it was only Will who spoke to his sons, saying simply, "Too late." In silence, they took their torches and began the dark journey back to Redgate. With Edwin behind them, a grim mood had descended. All three of the older men were thinking of the last time they had been together at Beau Repaire. Marion had been alive and well and still married to Martin. The men had hidden their feelings in front of their enemy, but now a sadness tinged with guilt coloured their thoughts, making them oblivious to the cloudless-night chill.

Returning to familiar territory made their journey homeward seem shorter. At Redgate, Will bade his sons good evening and the young men retired to the largest room in the house to find a place to make a bed for what was left of the night. Marc and Bran crossed the grass to join their mentors, helping the older men to dismount. Ben waved them back. "You're not squires anymore, remember."

Leona looked down from her window, relieved that all of her family were back under the same roof. Joss turned and gave a hand signal into the trees to indicate that only the standard number for a watch was necessary now. The five men moved silently through the main house, along the passage and into the smaller chamber for talks.

Not having slept, Catherine knew that in the time they had been away, her mother could not have returned with the men. She would have slowed their journey. She heard Susan sit up and leave her bed. The room darkened slightly as she moved to the window. Catherine rose too, wanting to know the news. Below them, the subdued voices of the men came through the floorboards, but their words were unclear. The young women looked at each other, unable to hide their anxiety. The tone was serious. Catherine, knowing the news could not be good, felt something give way inside her. She could not prevent her mouth from giving an involuntary twist. Susan put a comforting hand on her shoulder, "Perhaps it's not all bad news."

Catherine tried to smile. Both sat quietly in the window, watching the torches' intermittent movements in the trees.

Downstairs, Joss leaned against a wall, seemingly lost in thought. Eventually, he looked at Will. "You were right."

"About what?"

"Trying to bring Marion back here. I was wrong to doubt your instincts - simply because they were instincts."

Marc and Bran had been told the night's events. They stood awkwardly, wondering at which point they ought to tell Joss what had happened soon after they had left Redgate. They were surprised he had not noticed himself. He must have been affected deeply by what happened tonight. In front of them were the leaves Ben had retrieved from beneath Marion's bed and Will's water bag.

Ben brought a cup from the shelf. "It is best to transfer it and keep it out of harm's way."

Bran watched as he poured the honey coloured liquid into the cup.

Will sighed and passed a hand across his brow. "When we arrived, it seemed like only yesterday that we accompanied Margery and her friends home from market. Do you remember? A bitterly cold day. It's eighteen years, you know?"

Ben and Joss nodded, sharing the memory.

"And then, expecting to see Marion as she had been...." His words petered away. It was clear to all that Edwin had murdered his wife and probably Martin too. Should Catherine be deemed a burden, unable to marry as he wished, then she would probably meet a similar fate.

Will stood up and sought some comfort in the remaining embers. "Did anyone else wonder how, in that eighteen years, we came so far and seemed to achieve so much and yet allowed this to pass us by?"

The room fell silent. Marc and Bran looked at each other, unused to seeing them in such a low mood.

Joss broke the silence at last. "If we are to ensure Edwin faces punishment this time, we need to act quickly. The king's visit would be perfectly timed. We would not need to travel to Durham for the services of the shire reeve - or even the Prince Bishop with such an important case. Henry often acts as judiciary on his travels. We have the evidence. We simply need twelve people to speak truthfully of Edwin's character."

Ben intervened. "But he will have the right to choose his own character witnesses."

"Yes, but we have the evidence. When witnesses see that they may feel more reassured about telling the truth without fear of repercussions." He glanced across at the cup and the leaves. "Failing that, we could suggest publicly that he chooses trial by combat if he is so certain that God will prove he is telling the truth."

"I thought we weren't doing that anymore in order to champion Henry's new legal system."

Joss nodded. "But Edwin doesn't know that. A rumour to the contrary may make him keep his head low. However, our priority is to substantiate the evidence - make sure he cannot make a plea of ignorance. We need witnesses to see his hands in case they have time to heal before Henry arrives. Marion's fingernails will still be broken. There may be even more evidence of ill treatment under her nightgown. We should question whoever prepares her body for the funeral."

Will and Ben began to stir themselves, realising Joss was right. Joss glanced across at Marc. "Is Susan abed?"

Marc blushed at the unintended implication but answered evenly, "I believe so, Sir."

The older man looked to the window. The air was beginning to lighten. "Do you think she would mind being woken?"

Marc shook his head. "She will want to help."

Ben murmured to himself, "We need to break the news to Catherine."

Bran stepped forward. "I can do that."

The other three looked at him. Joss nodded. The two younger men left the room, their unspoken orders understood.

Will sighed. "How do we feel about Bran becoming....attached to Catherine?"

Ben simply said, "If it happens, it happens."

Joss looked at Will, understanding his concern. "We want to protect Catherine, but she could lead him into trouble, even though she promised to be our ally. Trouble for Bran is trouble for the rest of us."

Ben shook his head, as if he had already given the matter a lot of thought. "He won't pursue her unless his feelings are reciprocated. He may be nostalgic because of her likeness to Margery, but he is not a sentimental fool. Besides, if we are shortly to be rid of Edwin, the source of any potential trouble is nipped in the bud."

Will nodded. "I believed her earlier when she said she was willing to help us against Edwin." He walked to the window. Looking down, he beckoned the others to join him. "Here's our chance to judge whether her grief for her mother is stronger than her fear of Edwin." His brow creased, as a thought struck him. "It would look odd on Edwin's part if he tried to reject his stepdaughter as a character witness, wouldn't it?"

Below them, Catherine was seated, back straight, as if already braced to take the bad news. The two had found a place away from the company sleeping in their tents, and sheltered from the wind. Bran knelt on the grass in front of her. He spoke and she nodded - almost politely at first, then brought her hands up quickly to her face to hide the tears. He put his arms around her and continued to talk. She nodded intermittently and wiped her eyes as he spoke. The men could tell that, even now, she was apologising. Bran continued to talk, shaking his head gently and stroking her hair.

Ben spoke quietly. "Where on Earth did he learn such empathy?"

His two friends looked at each other then back at Bran.

"From you," said Joss.

A knock at the door brought them from the window. Marc and Susan entered.

Ben pulled up a stool for her. "We are in need of your expertise, Susan. Your mother has always said you are good with your herbs. We believe Edwin has committed a murder, but we need to make sure we can prove it."

Susan sat and waited politely. Will picked up the cup. "We believe he helped her on her way with this juice. Is there anything from your study of simples which can help us?"

Susan took the juice and looked into the cup. She held it to her nose and inhaled. She dipped her finger into the liquid and examined the colour in the candlelight.

"It could be yew berries."

Joss intervened. "Yew? Poisonous then?"

Susan chewed her bottom lip then looked at him. "The seeds of the yew are very poisonous - but the flesh around the seed is not so." She stood to make the most of the dwindling light from the window. "If he had ground the seeds and added them, the juice would not be so clear - not so translucent." She swirled the cup, looking into it. "I see no residue."

Will thought. "Edwin told us this was blackberry juice, which is an obvious lie. Why would a man give his wife yew berries and lie about it?"

Susan thought again. "The flesh of the berry, in the right amounts, can have a very strong hallucinogenic effect - well..." she rethought her phrasing, "almost the opposite of hallucinogenic.." She looked around her as if trying to find a clearer explanation. "Have you ever been woken from a very deep sleep, held a conversation then fallen back into sleep, only to have no recollection of it when you are reminded of it the next day?"

The men nodded.

"That's the effect this juice could have on you. Perhaps he chose to administer it to discover whether she was keeping things from him."

"This is interesting. A truth drug," pondered Will. "And she would not remember?"

Susan shook her head.

"Could you make people act in a particular way, as well as speak?" Joss asked.

"I have not heard of it," she shrugged apologetically, "but that does not mean it is not possible." She pondered. "Are you thinking he could have made someone else commit the murder, which they would not recollect?"

Joss nodded.

"Might I add that many people think that yew berries are poisonous - and indeed, if they still contain the seed, they are deadly - but not many know of the effects of the berry's flesh alone. If I was ignorant of all the properties of yew and I wished to poison someone, I might, in ignorance, remove the seeds in case the liquid seemed less palatable and they did not drink a sufficient amount."

Joss smiled at her intuition. "And this could help our case because?" he pushed her gently.

"It is a man's intention to kill which makes him worthy of punishment, not whether he succeeds in the attempt. Edwin's basic knowledge of herbs let him down, but that does not let him off the hook. Ignorance does not equal innocence."

They all smiled. Marc gazed at her proudly. Ben moved quickly and brought the leaves into the light. She took them and laid the spear shapes flat on her palm. Some were branched while others lay separate. They were rather dry now, but still identifiable.

"These are leaves from monk's hood."

They all recognised the name of the poisonous plant.

"Are you sure?" asked Ben. "It's not just wishful thinking? It couldn't be something innocent - sage perhaps."

Susan shook her head. "Even without the blue flowers, I would recognise this. From being very young, we were taught to know it by our mother. She would not have it by the houses in case we came to harm, but she realised we might come across it in the meadows and so made sure we would know it. It could easily be used to kill someone. Even in small amounts, the only good use I have seen it put to is to numb a patient. To anaesthetise. It would only be used in extreme conditions - if a patient was to undergo an operation - even then, it is risky as it affects the heartbeat."

Will put a hand inside his surcoat and pulled out some cloth. "So, with the monk's hood and the yew berry juice, this might help to seal Edwin's fate." He gave the cloth a shake. "The stained chemise Ben examined in Marion's chamber."

Joss shook his head and smiled, "Unbelievable."

"Hadn't you noticed?" grinned Will. "I expected Edwin to miss it, with all that eye rubbing, but not you." He laid it on the bench.

"Once Leonard and Raymond have caught up on sleep, I'll send them to fetch Marion's body."

It seemed to all of them that Edwin's time had finally come.

The sound of a throat being ostentatiously cleared in the corner of the room made them turn quickly, swords drawn. A red haired, roughly dressed man of about thirty years sat on a stool in the corner, mug of Redgate ale in hand. He looked at them, head to one side. He smiled and in French said, "Good morning, Sirs."

Recognition dawned and the surrounding company bowed low to their King.

"The young man you call Bran was quite perturbed when I asked him not to make my arrival known to you, but did as he was asked." He drained his mug. "He is obviously a man who possesses a trustworthy character as well as an innovative mind. Now," he placed his empty cup on the floor, "where will we find this Edwin?"

Chapter Six

Thinking Time

At intervals, clouds of smoke billowed back into the room. Oblivious, Edwin sat at Marion's bedside, his thoughts racing in time to the rush of wind at the chimney. He already had people in mind who would be too afraid or too greedy not to speak for him when questioned about his character. He paced from the bed to the fireplace, from the fireplace to the window, from the window back to the bed. The sky was lightening to a pale morning blue. Any clouds were sent skimming westwards. What were the main obstacles? He rubbed his chin in irritation.

Ben, Will and Joss would speak out against him; tell what they had seen. They would also suggest Catherine be involved. Could he trust her? He cursed himself for not having spent more time shaping her attitude throughout her girlhood. People at Beau Repaire would say what he told them to or be left homeless, but would anyone believe them in the face of the Northern's reputation for truth?

In the centre of the room, a pang of panic stopped him in his tracks. He had not even considered the most obvious piece of evidence against him: the body. The shire reeve would wish to see it. And the Northern had taken the juice. He stooped quickly and pulled at the crumpled bedclothes, inwardly cursing the tightening legal system that made his life so difficult these days. Where was the stained nightgown? He looked on the floor around the bed, heart racing. It was nowhere to be seen. He fell onto the bed, breathing hard, fists clenched. Damn them. They must have taken it. He stood again, ready to pace, then stopped. He looked at Marion, remembering all Ben had said. In a rage, he picked up the now empty cup, which still stood at her bedside and hurled it at the fire.

What was he to do? This was all Will's fault. Meddling bastard. Forcing him to rush his plans. As he stood, fuming at the predicament the Northern had put him in, the logs on the fire shifted and the cup he had thrown rolled, half charred, onto the hearth. He glared and kicked it savagely to the back of the fireplace. The force was such that it simply bounced back defiantly into the room, bringing a smouldering splinter of wood with it. He took two quick steps, his instincts telling him to stamp it out to stop the rug from catching fire. But even as he raised his foot, he stopped and smiled. Of course, an accidental fire. He quickly looked about him for materials to encourage a blaze. Marion's cloak lay on a stool at the foot of the bed. It had been there for weeks. He teased the fabric a little so that one sleeve fell on the hearthrug and the other on the bed. He watched the smouldering wood carefully. As it lay on the matting, its glow grew in intensity until a flame began to nibble at the wool. He continued to observe, thankful for the wind which continued to blow smoke back from the chimney. As the draught breathed over the contents of the room, the flame's appetite increased. Once satisfied that it would take hold, he gingerly moved a burning stick from the grate and dropped it between the covers nearest Marion. He stood back quickly as the fire spread, then hurriedly left the room, locking it behind him.

At the bottom of the stairs, he picked his way between the quietly sleeping residents. Midway, he covered the mouth of Alric, his son, and tugged at his hair to wake him. The twelve year old awoke, wide-eyed, and flailed a little until he recognised his tormentor. Edwin hauled him to his feet. Once outside, he glanced around him, suspiciously.

"Now, Alric," he began. "Are you awake enough to let my words soak in?"

The boy looked bewildered and dishevelled, but the breeze was helping to bring him to his senses. He nodded, blearily.

"On Wednesday, I want you to ride to the forest between Beau Repaire and Drysdale. Remember the place we killed the deer? We had to keep it a secret. Do you remember?"

Alric nodded again.

"I want you to take the hounds – all three. Tell no one. Go when everyone else is still asleep." Alric looked towards the kennels. Edwin shook the boy by the collar. "Are you listening, Alric?"

"Yes, Sir. Take the three hounds to the forest."

"Leave them tied there. Tie them so they cannot fight. Then go to Drysdale. If Catherine is there, stay hidden and when you think she is alone, take her back to the forest. Tell her you need help. Tell her your favourite hound is caught in a trap and you need her to help because you do not like to hurt him. If she says she will fetch help from Drysdale tell her no. Tell her that poaching is severely punished by the Prince Bishop and you are afraid of being found out."

"What if she is not at Drysdale, Sir."

"It's unlikely, but, if not, ride quickly to Redgate. Fetch her from there. It is the same distance into the forest. I will be waiting in that place, where we killed the deer, from early Wednesday evening onwards. Do not tell her that I will be there. Tell her nothing but what I have told you to. That is very important. Do you understand?"

"Yes, Sir." He would not go against his father. He had seen the beatings he could inflict on the other boys.

"There is one more thing, which is even more important. From now, do not feed the hounds. Forbid others from doing so. It is better for the hunting. That is why I asked you to tie them separately, in case they fight."

"Why are we asking Catherine to meet us in the forest? Why not just bring her home?"

"Because Catherine does not know the danger she is in. I am concerned that if I show my face at Drysdale, it might start a skirmish. This is easier. It is for this reason that you must persuade her to leave without telling anyone. If they know she is trying to leave, they might hurt her."

Alric nodded earnestly, remembering everything his father had ever told him about Drysdale. Perhaps he wanted the dogs hungry so they would be better protection against enemies.

"I am leaving now. You won't see me until Wednesday. I cannot tell you where I am going in case someone from the Northern tries to question you. Now, quickly! Go saddle the courser."

Alric scurried off to do as he was told. This intrigue was quite exciting. Nothing like this ever happened at their house. Perhaps he would get to see some people killed in a fight.

Edwin glanced at the house. He could smell the smoke now. He crossed to the well and dropped the key into it. It was some seconds before it hit the surface of the water. Presently, Alric returned with Edwin's mount. He climbed into the saddle.

"Do not let me down, Alric."

"No, Sir."

"Good." He leaned forward in the saddle. "If you do, that hound of yours will take the brunt of my disappointment in you. Do you understand? Catherine needs us."

Alric's dog was his only companion. His two older brothers left him out of their doings. "I shall do everything as you said, Sir. I shall tell no one."

Edwin smiled, patted the boy's shoulder then turned his mount and galloped away. He avoided the roads leading from Redgate and Drysdale. His route led to Durham and the Cathedral and sanctuary. Thinking time.

****

As the party of five from the Northern set off once more for Beau Repaire with their royal guest, the remainder of the entourage accompanied Anna, Susan, Catherine, Leona and her daughters from Redgate to Drysdale. Raymond and Leonard kept a watchful eye at the rear. Joss discreetly passed a handful of heath peas to his small group. "The King has the energy of a maniac. I want us to be as alert and focused as possible. This will keep any hunger pangs at bay and keep your mind on the task ahead."

The return journey took on a different hue, daylight now revealing the outline of the tree covered hills which ensconced the winding route to Beau Repaire. Joss did not like the idea of following such a vulnerable road without forerunners, but the fact that they travelled with the King allayed some of his insecurity.

As the day brightened and they gained the summit of the hill bordering Edwin's land, they were greeted by the urgent cries of men and women, the barking of dogs and the throat stinging smell of thick smoke. They squinted as they approached the frantic activity of those who tried to quell the flames with pitifully small vessels of water carried over an excruciatingly long distance. The wind hampered them as they blindly tried to gain access to the house again and again. The visitors shielded their faces, peering upwards. From what they could see, the origin of the flames stemmed from one room on the upper storey. Those attempting to fight the fire were made to climb all the way to the roof with their water in order to try to gain enough height to drop the water onto the flames, there being no access to the room from the doorway. There were not enough people to form an effective chain and save time. They were fighting a losing battle. Shortly there would be no part of the roof left safe for them to get a foothold. From below, the party ascertained that instead of trying to deal with the larger fire, there would be more use in preventing its spread to other parts of the building. Water was thrown onto the neighbouring roofs and, intermittently, people emerged from the lower chamber doorways, carrying furniture to safety.

The King turned to the others, visibly bristling at this obstacle to the legal process. "I take it that that is the dead lady's chamber?S"

They nodded grimly.

Joss rode forward, looking amongst the people, searching for Edwin. The rest of the group took four other routes, like spokes travelling outwards from a wheel's hub. They scanned the activities and beyond in case their quarry was in the process of making his escape, but it was obvious to them all that Edwin would be long gone.

Eventually, they reconvened. Joss spoke, "I imagine he left shortly after we did. I was naïve not to leave a watch."

He approached the weary people once more, eager to salvage what he could of the situation. A young woman sat on the grass, wiping her brow with the back of a hand.

She looked up as Joss's mount stopped in front of her feet. "Are any of Edwin's children about?"

She looked up at him alarmed then scanned the bustling community. She pointed to a boy, conspicuous through his relative lack of movement. "The boy in the blue hood," she replied.

Joss trotted over. "Are you Edwin's son?"

The boy pulled his hood away from his brow in an effort to see the speaker better. Joss's appearance was so imposing that he felt it was necessary to stand before replying. "Yes Sir."

"Where is your father?"

The boy looked at him steadily. "I do not know, Sir."

Joss watched him carefully. "Has he gone to the Cathedral?"

The boy took off his hood and looked down, twisting the fabric as he spoke. "I do not know Sir. I have not seen him since yesterday."

Joss could tell he was lying. He returned to the King and addressed him in French. "I suggest we go forward to the Cathedral. Edwin knows he has the option of forty days of sanctuary in Durham."

The king nodded, obviously irritated by this man Edwin he had never even met. "The church had better not interfere against the Crown," he muttered. Joss spoke quickly to the rest knowing Henry would be keen to continue without further delay. "Better return to Drysdale. Make sure the guests are safe. Organise a watch for Redgate." Then, in a spiral of hooves, they were gone.

"Are they safe enough travelling alone?" asked Bran.

Ben nodded. "Joss will ride ahead so that the King follows him on the safest paths. Even Edwin would not be so foolish to harm the King or try to take on Joss man to man. Shame really. It would be the quickest way to be rid of him."

Will moved away from the others then called back. "Ben. I think you and I should see to retrieving Marion's body."

He turned to Bran and Marc. "The two of you ride ahead to Drysdale. It is closer. Prepare a private place where what is left of the body can be laid out. Poor lady."

And as the activity of the fire fighters became less frantic and the smoke coming from the chamber window less dark and dense, Ben and Will covered their faces once more and approached the building while the two younger men turned about and made their way to Drysdale.

Chapter Seven

A Lesson In Control

Joss calmly recounted how Henry had ranted and raved outside the Cathedral, yelling that it must surely be sacrilege to provide a safe-haven for a man who had broken one of the most important commandments and to aid a murderous outlaw who had sound evidence stacked against him. The church was a sore point with Henry. His meeting with Beckett in July at Woodstock had not gone in his favour.

Playing the waiting game was torturous. Catherine found some solace in her new found friendship with Susan and managed to focus on more positive things by helping her with the wedding plans. Marc had no land to call his own as yet, so Drysdale was to be the venue. Bran had more than enough to keep his mind occupied. The King was stunned by the innovative use of water power at Drysdale. He immediately noticed the superior health of the people. They were clean, as were their houses, which had stone floors that could be washed as well as swept. In the main house, the fire was not in the centre of the room, but somehow built into the wall, as it had been at Redgate. Henry was dubious about this, remembering the fire at Beau

Repaire – yet another that had been engineered by Bran's late father.

Lead was mined at the edges of his land from a series of bell pits so Drysdale had financial bargaining power. They had linen clothes and sheets that could be laundered and dried quickly in the right weather. Their beds were not made of straw, this was left to the animals, which were housed separately, the hearths in the walls meaning the extra warmth from the beasts was not necessary. The King quickly recognized that, not only had Bran's people been allowed to share in the comforts provided by his ideas, but they now had some knowledge which could be passed onto others. Bran demonstrated how water power ran the machines that separated lead from the waste sediment and made and dyed the linen. Henry lingered over each so that he had not even seen the siege engines yet, nor followed the water ducts to Redgate where the community was assured of clean drinking water. He had sat staring into the fireplace, as if wary that the chimney wall would catch fire, being used to the fire burning in the centre of the room and the smoke escaping through a gap in the roof. The king felt like he was in the company of a magician. "Dream driven!" he pronounced one evening during a debate in which he tried to sum up Bran's sheer industry.

"I thought he was Jewish," he said to Joss.

"His father was and his mother Christian. If you remember, this was part of his Grandfather's land on his mother's side."

Henry looked about him and shook his head. "I have never known a man take his duty of care so seriously. I wish the whole kingdom could follow this young man's example."

He made Bran's building of a Christian place of worship, in spite of his own background, a topic for one of his philosophical debates.

The King kept Bran busy and made it difficult for him to see to Catherine's welfare and make preparations for Marion's funeral, let alone prepare for his and Marc's knighting ceremony and his friend's marriage to Susan. The trip overseas seemed to be pushed further and further to the bottom of his list of priorities. In fact, he was not even sure that he wanted to go now. Not right now, anyway, with Edwin's trial coming up. It was a situation he would like to see resolved before he left.

It was Wednesday morning, the day before Marion's funeral, at the time between explaining to Henry how the water levels in the man-made reservoirs could be controlled and arranging to have yet more food transported from Durham to feed the hungry royal entourage without putting too much strain on Redgate's resources that Bran received a message from Ben requesting that he see him that day. His heart sank a little. If his journey to Outremer was to go ahead, his only remaining planning time was that afternoon. Perhaps, if the meeting was short, he could ride back the same day. He swallowed his annoyance, realising that this must be a bad time for Ben. He had to prepare the tomb to accommodate Margery and her mother, as well as being reminded of his own mortality as he would obviously want to leave enough space to be laid to rest next to his wife in the future. Having arranged that both Susan and Marc would escort Catherine to her mother's funeral the following day should he not return in time, he set off cross country for Redgate.

In contrast to Bran's internal turmoil of rushing to catch up with all that needed to be done, Ben seemed thoughtful and reticent. When he was welcomed into the same room where they had met just three days before, Bran realised that there had been little point in Ben's chat at that time. It was as if fate had decided to toy with them regardless of their prior knowledge.

"This Edwin business has come at a very unfortunate time." Ben began. Bran remained quiet. He felt he knew what was coming already.

"I felt that, with your own personal grievances against the man, you might want to delay your trip."

Strangely, now that the news had been broken, instead of feeling disappointment, Bran felt the burden lightening.

"I had thought it might be too much too soon," he concurred.

Ben came closer to the hearth, and seated himself for the more important part of his discussion. "The King has talked of you with me, you still being my Squire for the next few days."

Bran listened attentively.

"He wants you to delay your journey even longer in order to travel to Winchester and spread what you have been teaching up here."

Now Bran's heart did sink and he spoke before his manners had time to reword his thoughts. "It would be so much easier to use Drysdale as a teaching base. Why start from scratch elsewhere?" Aware of the petulance in his voice, he took a deep breath and focused on the practical. "Do you remember Harun? He visited Drysdale with Joss two years ago." Ben nodded.

"During a tour of Drysdale, while we followed the aqueduct towards Redgate, I explained that I wasn't entirely happy with the system because it would be easy to sabotage the water supply. Harun said that people who lived in hot countries learned to look for waterways in places other than the surface of the land. That got me thinking. With a party of squires, I have been searching underground. Harun was absolutely right."

Ben raised his eyebrows, sensing the younger man's enthusiasm returning.

"The land is hiding many waterways. We spent months building an aqueduct on the surface when there was already a subterranean fresh water channel covering half the distance to Redgate. There must be ways we can harness underwater currents too. The reason the king is impressed is because of the way ideas benefit the community, so there seems no sense in taking the ideas out of context. And necessity is the mother of invention. Besides," his brow creased and he shook his head, "why should all of the North's best ideas end up in the South." He stopped suddenly, realising his self-pity had returned. He would have no choice in the matter anyway. Part of him even wondered whether Henry could have sneaked into the room to hear his reaction before he arrived.

Ben smiled. "Roughly what I said. We shall speak again and I shall see whether I can make him see the benefits of sending his people to us up here." He shook his head in wonder at his foster son.

Bran had resigned himself to the fact that his journey would no longer go ahead as planned. "How long does he have in mind?" he asked, guardedly.

"I believe he envisages years rather than months."

Bran sighed. He realised it would be difficult to argue a case which would disappoint his King, especially when the essence of it was to benefit the King's people. He stroked his forefinger across his lips then looked at Ben, saying resignedly, "I suppose the voyage being delayed has several advantages. The timescale for getting things done seems far less urgent. Less urgency means more scope for rational thought: isn't that what Joss would say? We do not want Edwin slipping through the net. He's the main problem to be solved. That would improve things well into the future. Besides," he offered hopefully, "maybe the delay need not be too many years hence. I can teach others who can then teach without me. Perhaps that will give me some freedom to leave the country for a while."

Ben smiled and patted the younger man's shoulder, aware that the sacrifice was far greater than he was putting into words. "It also means that you and Marc can leave a more diplomatic space of time between Marion's funeral and receiving your knightly status. A much better way of achieving the quiet meditation intended to leave you in a state of readiness. And then, of course, the wedding! By then, you'll be feeling it's high time we all had something happy to celebrate."

"Yes."

"The King would like to be present at the dubbing. To preside over things actually."

Bran looked up quickly. "I was hoping it would be you."

Ben was pleased and did not try to hide it. "You will still be accepted into the Northern. I must confess, I had always imagined that I would lead the events. You know I have come to think of you as I would a son. But, this is quite an honour– for you and the Northern. The only differences it really makes are positive ones. The King's presence makes you and Drysdale, and therefore Redgate, more secure; people are less likely to question his authority; more security for Drysdale means that there is less chance of your claims to the land ever being used as a weakness in the Northern's armour. And, after all, if it pleases Henry, perhaps we should give him his way. He works very hard to keep his kingdom prosperous. Soon, with the disappearance of Edwin's sons, those sons we know of, he will have to decide what happens to Beau Repaire. We champion his ideals- this Winchester idea is his way of showing he champions ours – even if he unwittingly kicks the North in the teeth in doing so. We would all agree that learning is important." He looked at Bran with a mischievous grin. "You are his mascot."

Bran gave a wry smile and rubbed his brow as if clearing away thoughts of the future so he could concentrate on the here and now.

"Would it be ill-mannered of me to return to Drysdale straight away? I would like to accompany Catherine here in the morning. It'll be a sad journey."

"Of course not." Ben looked at him closely, gaining a questioning glance in return. Bran felt a perverse need to grin, but kept his face under control. Ben pushed a little further.

"I don't like to pry, but I'm going to anyway," he smiled. "How do you feel about Catherine? And," he held up a hand "I don't mean pity at her poor mother's death. I mean feelings of the love and marriage variety."

Bran was taken aback at Ben's candour. He shook his head slowly, unable to meet Ben's eye, especially as he was sitting in the same room where, just three days before, he had denied any interest in romance. "I don't know how to answer. I hadn't considered it."

Ben walked back to the window to hide his smile at Bran's expense. "She's very pretty," he said to the sky. "Although, of course, I am biased. She has a look of Margery."

Bran said nothing.

Ben helped him. "I think she has escaped Edwin's influence, miraculous though it seems. She seems an intelligent and trustworthy young lady." Bran was aware that Ben was fishing for clues, but he enjoyed hearing Catherine being praised and remained silent. "Susan likes her and she is a shrewd judge of character."

Bran allowed himself a nod.

Ben turned to him so he could study his face. "It came as no surprise to find that she is betrothed already, in spite of us being considered so remote."

Bran's face fell. "She is?"

Ben grinned, "No: just helping to sort out your feelings."

Bran gave an embarrassed sigh of relief. "Yes, it would have disappointed me, but I truly haven't had time to think it through. I have no idea how she feels about me either." He grinned up at Ben. "Isn't trying to find that out the hardest part?" he asked, recalling Ben's description of his first meeting with Margery.

"If it helps, I'll support your decision no matter what you decide. The poor girl is going to need a new home soon so she will be hoping to marry well. There is a chance that it could be to someone she has never met if she wants to keep her home at Beau Repaire. Of course, the King may be so pleased with you that he may decide to reward you with your old adversary's land. Then Catherine's difficulties would be over-marriage or not, you would not see her homeless. You could even have Marc take the tenancy so that he has a place to oversee with his new family and you have a reliable man in charge."

Bran got to his feet and with a shuffle and a "We'll see" he bid Ben farewell and made his way back to Drysdale while there was still time.

Late afternoon was turning to early evening by the time he arrived. There was still a heat to the day and he discarded his top layers of clothing in order to wash in the courtyard before entering. He was pleased to see through the open door that the tables were being prepared: somewhere along the line, he had missed a meal. Catherine looked down from the chamber window where she was chatting with Susan. As she watched Bran scoop water over his face, neck and shoulders, she felt herself blush and moved further into the room. Susan was sewing.

"Is that the veil for your wedding?" she asked, admiringly.

Susan nodded and smiled. Her eyes were beginning to tire so she laid the fine cloth to one side and asked, "Shall we go and eat?"

Catherine nodded and the two young ladies linked. A long moaning sigh from the room above them made Catherine stop in her tracks. She listened, looking upwards. "What is that?"

Susan looked at her, a little embarrassed. "It sounds like Leona."

"Is she all right? Should we go and see?"

Susan looked at Catherine, wondering how to word her next sentence. "I think it's a sound of pleasure not pain."

Catherine's brow creased in confusion, then the truth dawned and she blushed. "You mean she and Will?"

Susan laughed, relieved not to have to elaborate any further. "Well, it will not be anyone else."

"Oh," she bit her bottom lip, unsure of how to react.

"Um," Susan nodded.

"Does it happen a lot?" She realised how silly the question sounded. "What I mean is…is…you don't seem surprised."

Susan shrugged, trying to be nonchalant, "All the Northern are," she cast around for a polite phrase, "good to their wives." She looked around conspiratorially and whispered, "They are taught.

They believe that strong marriages make strong families – no sudden embarrassing claims to land through illegitimate children – that sort of thing. And I believe there is a Muslim belief that …happier marriages create stronger children."

Catherine now realised what her mother had meant when she told her that wives of the Northern have broader smiles. She thought about it. "Is it safe when she's having a baby?"

Susan smiled. "It didn't hurt any of the others. Besides, I'm sure he's very gentle. Anyway, there's more than one way of – well, you know – of giving pleasure."

Catherine looked at her blankly then a completely separate thought struck her and her eyes widened and shone at her new friend. "Oh, Susan. That means Marc and you…."

Now that the conversation had come closer to home, Susan felt rather more self-conscious. She pushed her smile aside with a shrug and changed the topic back to appetites of another sort. "Come on, let's eat. Robert has been yelling at the boys all afternoon so we should be in for a treat."

They descended via the gloomy stone stairs and emerged into the brightly lit courtyard, choosing to cross here to go to the Hall, rather than taking the more labyrinthine internal route. Marc was checking his courser's shoes. He stood and smiled a greeting as they passed. Bran, his skin having dried in the sunlight, was dressing again. The girls looked at each other, then scurried, laughing, into the hall. Bran and

Marc glanced at each other, eyebrows raised, and shrugged.

Robert had certainly done them proud, eventually. He thought it would never come together on time. It was less than hour ago that he had been yelling, "Don't be afraid of it, Lad! It's only an egg for God's Sake!" to one of the pages drafted into the kitchen to help out making the sweet courses. The tables, already groaning with mouth-watering dishes were still being rearranged to make room for more. Flushed boys carried platter after platter – some needing two to carry the weight between them. The aroma itself was enough to satisfy the hungriest stomach. The girls stood back to allow the procession past, craning their necks to better identify the dishes going by. A glossy display of roasted lamb with richly coloured spiced wine was the first platter to set their mouths watering: then neat rows of pheasant and quail; clouds of rice with almonds floated by; pots of dark golden honey were placed between every two diners; then beautifully decorated pies, six inches high, illustrated with symbols giving clues as to their fillings, bobbed between the eagerly turning heads of the company. At one point, Robert entered the room and cast a critical eye over the table tops. He was greeted with shouts of approval, but ignored this. He had not sent out the sweet puddings yet and there was little room to spare. He spurred the pages into action. The boys ran quickly, moving a platter here, a pot there, more afraid of Robert than the royal company. Then four pages entered, carrying the dish which would set apart the royal table from the rest. They held a corner each and carefully, hardly daring to breathe, hoisted the platter above their heads. A hush fell over the guests as a stuffed peacock, looking for all the world like it still lived and sat with tail feathers resplendent, was carried on high and laid at the centre of the top table. The King gazed at it appreciatively and nodded across to Bran, who had just entered and stood behind Catherine and Susan. Bran quickly shook his head and held up a hand towards Robert to indicate that one man alone deserved all the glory. Henry turned to Joss next to him to be sure of his English. He then turned back to the company, grinned, stood, took a bow in Robert's direction and announced, "This man surely deserves a knighthood."

The company laughed appreciatively, apart from Robert, who simply looked awkward, took a very hasty bow and retreated to the safety of his kitchen. Even now, as the girls made their way to seats near the back of the room, dishes were being brought forth. Catherine wondered how there had been room for it all. Every table was delivered of a marzipan castle with turrets and little figures on the battlements and the base. The King noticed there was even a perfect siege engine on the royal version. Trays of pine candy were offered to the children so they could take them and eat them at leisure afterwards, while sugar cones and rose pudding were squeezed into the only available spaces left. After a quick scan to see that everyone was happy, he realised that Susan and Catherine were picking their way to the bottom of the Hall with the lower ranks. He caught up with them as they cast about for empty spaces on the benches. He caught their eye and beckoned, then escorted them to seats running at right angles just below the table he would share with the King on the dais. As they seated themselves, they glanced at him self-consciously, feeling like upstarts amongst the guest knights from the Northern. But no one seemed perturbed. The main focus of attention was the feast and soon they were chatting as comfortably as the rest. Redgate ale meant that the hall soon rang to the rafters with laughter. Even before the tables were cleared away, music began in the gallery and, in spite of full bellies, dancing commenced.

Catherine stayed in her seat and chose water over ale, wanting to stay clear headed for the funeral the next day. She knew she would grow maudlin if she took a stronger drink. She noticed that the children ate together, giggling as they compared their figures of marzipan, and that Will and Leona were still absent. It must be love if Will would miss a banquet of this quality. As the dancers swirled, side-stepped and clapped, she noticed how Marc and Susan kept glancing at each other. After weighing up the morals, she concluded that noisy afternoon lovemaking between man and wife was far preferable to Edwin's private adulterous affairs and horrible, crablike wandering hands.

Bran, seeing that she was alone and quite unaware that Henry was gazing across at her in the hope of catching her eye, decided to go to her to spare her the embarrassment of having to refuse royal advances.

"Would you like to walk in the fresh air for a while? The heat won't be so oppressive now." He took her hand and led her out of harm's way into the rosy evening framed by the open door, stooping on the way to pick up his cloak. Alric, watching from his hiding place in the trees, gave a sigh of relief, having finally located his sister.

****

Edwin had wanted to bide his time. He did not have a plan for leaving the Cathedral unseen as such, rather he thought that if he watched and waited long enough, the perfect opportunity would present itself. It usually worked that way. But, after several hours, he realised he was going to need to give opportunity a helping hand. He guessed they would have lookouts stationed at strategic points between here and the coast, but no one would actually be expecting him to move closer to them and the King. They would probably also expect him to use the full forty days' sanctuary. He had no delusions about Pudsey being more loyal to himself rather than the King, so he would keep his departure a secret. He had no intention of missing his meeting with Catherine.

He knew that by evening prayers, he would have to reconvene with the other 'guests' at the rear of the Cathedral. He also knew that there was a cell where monks unfortunate enough to fall asleep during prayers were taken as punishment. From its position in the outer wall and the amount of hours a monk would be incarcerated, he guessed there would be a garderobe. Not the best escape route he had ever used, but an escape route nonetheless. But first, he would need to find a way of having himself imprisoned there, rather than being kept in the more public place within the main body of the church.

From the window in the passage where he stood, he could observe the novices moving about their daily business: gardening, going to prayers, leaving prayers, returning to their dormitory. It was those who ran messages and left the Palace Green who interested him most. He leaned against the wall nonchalantly, as an anxious looking novice scuttled towards him. As the boy drew level, he stepped forward and gave a polite, "Excuse me."

The boy looked at him warily.

"Won't keep you long," he smiled. "I wonder if you could answer a question."

The boy said nothing, in accordance with his vow of silence, but waited patiently.

"I have a female friend. Very friendly as it turns out. I was wondering if you have a key to that door. She is waiting for me on the other side, you see."

The boy took a step back and shook his head then turned and scuttled back the way he had come.

Edwin called after him. "Then do you know which monks would allow me to play with them? Just a little fondling would do?"

His voice rang out, amplified by the stonework. He leaned back and waited. Presently, the boy returned with three older men. He pointed to Edwin then held back while they approached.

"This is very accommodating. I would have been satisfied with one." He smiled, pulling his cloak to one side as if about to untie his breeches.

The three monks picked up the pace, two of them taking an arm each and frog marching him after the third who led the way to the cell, unlocked the door, told the young monk already within to get to prayers and then locked the door again, this time with Edwin on the inside. Once within he seated himself, calling, "What have I done? I demand an explanation."

He listened for some time, until he could deduce that prayers must be well underway. Then he got the first, and foulest, part of his plan underway, knowing there was little time to lose.

As he suspected, there was a garderobe. He looked down the narrow gap, wrinkling his nose. He looked at the aperture this way and that, hoping he was not to be beaten before he began. Eventually, he stood with a foot to either side of the drop, stooped to rest a hand next to each foot, then took his bodyweight on his hands and tentatively allowed his feet to snake below and through the passage. He wriggled his way through the first tight squeeze, then felt his feet find freedom. If his hips did not become stuck, he could do this. Knowing there was no guarantee that the fall would not knock him unconscious or worse, he took a deep breath, raised his hands above his head, gave another wriggle on realising he was wedged, then slipped, knocking knees and elbows in the darkness, until he landed in a heap of filfth a couple of yards from the river. Grimacing and holding his arms away from his body, he looked down at the smears of excrement covering his clothes. He needed to borrow new ones before caught something deadly. He stood up, resting his weight warily on the foot that had taken a blow to the ankle. It did not seem to be broken. He looked about him, noting with satisfaction that he was now without the Cathedral walls.

Again, he waited. At long last prayers were over, and novices carried on with their busy itinerary. He tried to discern where they exited the Cathedral. They did not use the same entrance as the lay worshippers and pilgrims. Eventually, just as he thought it would, the opportunity presented itself in the guise of a querulous-looking young novice with quite a pronounced limp. Once he was quite certain that it was the right leg that was the weakest and that the young man was not being met at the doorway, he made his way into the shadows. The novice was obviously in quite a hurry, judging by his hasty if scuffling step and his heavy breathing. As he rounded the corner and passed Edwin, the older man stepped out, placed both hands firmly round the young man's neck and squeezed tightly on the pressure points which he knew would prevent breathing and calling out. In slow moving silence, the boy's knees crumpled and Edwin allowed him to gradually collapse to the flagstones. He quickly relieved him of his robe. He had observed well. They were of similar height.

With the same hurrying gait, Edwin limped to the street, where he pulled up his hood, then made his way with a sense of purpose past the buildings on the perimeter of the green. He passed straight by to Saddlergate, then on past Soutergate, then twisted under the arches of the ever busy Elvet Bridge, silently thanking Pudsey for having it built three years previously. He entered its shadows as monk, discarded the habit and emerged into the sunlight as lay citizen, hoping his lower layers of clothing were not so soiled that they would attract attention. He then made his way back to the level of the town and, having discreetly relieved a very drunken gentleman of his mount and his cloak at the back of the market tavern, he made his way to the forest to see if Alric had managed to follow his instructions.

Bran led Catherine through the courtyard, away from the clamour of the building, through the tents pitched to house the Northern's guests, then twisted along the willow-draped paths to a cooler place behind the mews. He found them a grassy seat by one of the reservoirs and spread his cloak so she was protected by the dampness in the ground. She smiled her thanks, wondering why he had brought her to such a private place.

Bran seemed a little awkward now. Not the landholder at all. He picked up a few nearby twigs and threw them into the water's edge. He turned to her to find she was looking at him expectantly. She looked back to the water to seem less rude.

He spoke. "Tomorrow, for the funeral, I would like to escort you to Redgate."

"Thank you." She seemed to speak to the dragonfly bouncing at the water's surface. "I am grateful for everything you are doing – especially at such a busy time. I would have been lost without your help."

He loved the trance-like way that she spoke – such a contrast to the purposeful logic and planning he had been used to. He brushed the dust from his hands. "Ben has organised much of it. He wanted to. I think there's a rightness for him – to have Margery and Marion together again, I mean."

There was a stillness in the air around them accentuated by the muted music from the house.

She nodded, then said quietly. "It doesn't seem final." She hugged her knees, looking at him over her shoulder. "I don't seem to be feeling anything real." She felt foolish being unable to express her thoughts clearly. "I should feel bereft. My mother, my home – all changed forever. I cannot explain."

He placed his hand on her wrist. "I understand, believe me. It's like watching a drama, rather than being part of it. It almost has to end before you can pick out its meanings. It needs to be rounded off somehow, before the examination can begin. I suppose that's why the living need rituals. They give a framework to pick at." He creased his brow. "Still, with something like this, figuring out the whys and wherefores is difficult."

She thought about it and nodded. He had been through much the same as her and this made her respect his opinions more. "It's hard to accept that there aren't any good reasons. When there's no logic to it – or maybe too much." She shrugged. "It just shouldn't be. Such precious people being wrenched from us."

He squeezed her hand gently. "It'll be a hard day tomorrow."

Catherine smiled. Her existence had been quite solitary at Beau Repaire. It was good to have friends.

"You have a pretty smile."

She blushed.

"Sorry. You're so much like your sister that I feel like I've known you for much longer."

Catherine turned to the water again and hugged her knees awkwardly before taking a deep breath and saying, "Susan seems to think you were in love with Margery."

Bran laughed self-consciously and allowed himself to lie back on the grass to hide his embarrassment. He put his hands behind his head, declaring, "Susan says exactly what she thinks." He closed his eyes against the low sun, pleased to have a reason to draw a curtain over his feelings.

She twisted towards him, leaning on one hand so she could look down at him. "I suppose an answer like that means that it's true."

He grinned and opened one eye to deliver his answer. "I was very young." He closed his eyes again and thought. "Actually, it wasn't so much being in love …urm.. how can I put it?"

He opened his eyes again to look at her. She waited, feeling flattered that this important man was confiding in her. "It sounds pompous," he warned, self-consciously.

"Tell me."

He paused. "She was my saviour. She was the one who helped me to feel safe again, even before the worst day of my life was over."

She gazed down at him, wanting to tell him that was exactly how she felt about him. They looked at each other a little while and, quite suddenly, a wave of the elusive sadness finally swept through her. She tried to look away again before it reached her eyes, but he'd already seen it. "We'll look after you, Catherine. You won't be left alone in the world."

She nodded, but said nothing, knowing her voice would only betray her weakness.

Alric watched from his hiding place, concerned at the way the Jew was touching his sister. Was he trying to seduce her? He could see her face now. It looked like she was trying not to cry. Should he go to her rescue? But no. Catherine turned to face Drysdale, her hand, now claw-like, half covering her face. She sat up, gave a crooked smile and tried to dry her face with the back of her hands. Bran leaned up on one elbow and helped her to wipe her tears away. "I promise it will get better, Catherine."

She smiled again, a little more convincingly this time. He stroked one or two damp strands of hair from her face, noticing how pale and smooth her skin was. She thanked him in a whisper, not able to trust her voice yet. Her lashes were damp. He could not help but gaze at her. He had an urge to say, "Marry me. I'll keep you safe. I'll solve all of your problems." But he knew it was not a good time. Not a memory that could be looked back upon fondly. She looked up at him. His shadow prevented the low sun from being a nuisance. His skin was honey brown in the evening light. She reached up and stroked the hair away from his eyes and he bent close and kissed her brow. Then closer still and kissed her mouth.

He leaned up again, his heart pounding. He should lead her back to the house, but there were so many people in there. He didn't feel ready to face them – to assume that other role and discard this one so quickly. He lay on his back by her side. "May we stay here for a while? Just the two of us?"

She turned her head to look at him and squeezed his hand. He turned to face her and they gazed at one another again. "Does being together feel as good to you as it does to me?" he asked.

She smiled. A breeze, a little cooler now, blew over them. He sat up. He could hear voices, mainly drunken voices, growing louder as the revellers spilled out of the house into the evening air. He stood up and held out a hand. "Come with me," he said. "If we want peace and quiet, we need to find a better hiding place."

They walked down the grassy slope that dropped to the trace room. He led her through the doorway and shut out the night air. The western window cast a red glow into the room as the sun sank a little further. He wrapped his cloak around her shoulders, intending to then find her a seat, but on looking at her, he suddenly found himself unable to move. She was beautiful and somehow vulnerable, swathed in his over sized clothing. In spite of this vulnerability, he was struck by her hair, now a fiery red; and her eyes, the deepest, softest brown he had ever looked into. He stood transfixed while she reached up to his face, raised herself on tiptoe and slowly and gently kissed his mouth. His heart leapt and he pulled her closer, needing to more readily feel her warmth, her skin, to tangle his fingers in her hair, to make any contact that would continue these shocks of pleasure running through him. He forced himself to pull away from her, leaving them both gasping and gazing and beautifully surprised at how each could make the other feel.

She pulled the gown more tightly around her shoulders. "I'm sorry. I should go."

His instinct told him to say, "No you should not." But he said nothing, and they remained looking at each other a little self-consciously. Laughter from outside brought him back to his senses. "I suppose a goodnight kiss wouldn't hurt?" he suggested.

She shook her head, smiling and blushing under his gaze. "I suppose not."

He cupped her face in his hands and kissed her mouth then held her close. She lay her head against his shoulder and he rested his chin on her hair. Their hearts were pounding. He hoped she couldn't feel how aroused he was through their clothing. The sounds from outside seemed far away. Strange that he had organized the whole affair, but now it all seemed so alien. He spoke as he held her, finding it easier to say what was on his mind while his face was hidden, "Perhaps, after the funeral, when you feel ready, when you know how you truly feel, we could speak alone again."

Sensing his awkwardness, she looked up at him.

He took a deep breath, "We could see then how you would feel about...well, about me. About..."

She smiled, "About being yours?"

He liked the way it sounded. He nodded. "Yes. Being mine. Being my wife."

"Wife?"

He shrugged, suffering under her question. "No need to answer now. Take time to think."

She smiled and rested her cheek at his shoulder again, then suddenly perplexed, she straightened.

"Will a marriage between us make Edwin more dangerous to you?"

He stroked her hair. "That problem will be solved soon."

"Perhaps I could speak with him, try to make him see that an alliance with a community like yours could only be a benefit."

Bran kissed her hand. "First things first. For now, I just want to keep you safe and that means keeping you as far away from Edwin as possible." He could see that she was undecided. "I know it's a little early for promises and commitments, but I would feel easier in my mind if you could promise that you won't try to speak with him just yet."

She nodded resignedly. He kissed her brow, eager to change the subject. He did not want Edwin stealing away his euphoria. "We'll sort out Edwin when the time is right, then I can concentrate on making your world happier too." Suddenly a thought struck him. He took her hand and led her out of the trace room.

Alric bit his lip. He was running out of time. One building then another. What were they doing? The daylight could only last so long, even in late August. He shuddered to think what might happen if he let Edwin down. And what if someone came across the hounds and took them? Even the dancers had gone back indoors now to escape the evening chill. Eventually, much to his relief, he heard the stable door open and could make out Catherine and Drysdale's figures. He glanced outside, then bent to kiss her. He said something that made Catherine smile, then she unwrapped herself from his cloak, passing it back to him and made her way towards the main building.

Alric panicked. He would have to work fast. First, he checked that Drysdale was still busy in the stables, then he slithered from his perch and scampered along the edge of the tree line so he could reach the house corner before she did. She approached with a dreamy look on her face.

"Catherine," he hissed.

She jumped and looked about her.

"Over here."

She peered around the stonework at him. "Alric! What on earth are you doing here?"

He beat the palms of his hands downwards, whispering urgently, "Shush. I'm not supposed to be here." He beckoned her to come closer to him so he could speak quietly. "I need your help. Gripper has his foot caught in a trap. He's in pain."

She looked at him, her brow creased. "I'll fetch help."

He shook his head. "I was poaching. I've been living in the forest. The Prince Bishop would be angry. They'll punish me."

"No they won't. They're fair people."

"No, please, Catherine," he pleaded. "Please just come and help. I'm afraid for Gripper and he's been suffering for a long time already."

She bit her lip. This is not the way she had wanted the night to end. She had wanted to go back to the upstairs chamber and lie with her eyes closed, pretending to sleep but really recounting all that Bran had said and done earlier. Trust her younger brother to turn up and spoil it all. "What on earth are you doing this far from home?"

Alric thought on his feet. "It seemed like a good time to explore with father gone and unable to forbid it."

She felt sorry for him now. The past few days could not have been easy. She wondered whether Alric would want to attend the funeral. It seemed unlikely, given that Edwin had estranged his sons from their own mother.

She sighed a big sister sigh. "Where is Gripper? Let's get this over and done."

Alric pointed roughly in the direction of Beau Repaire. "It's about a mile into the forest."

Catherine's eyes widened, "A mile?"

"Please! It won't take long. I have a horse tethered nearby."

"Oh, Alric!" she glanced back at the stable, wondering whether to confide in Bran, but she had given him so much to contend with lately, she decided against it. She felt embarrassed that her infuriating younger brother would add to his burdens. She would tell him in the morning after the problem had been solved. "Come on. Show me. And you had better give me a ride back afterwards. I have no intention of sleeping in the forest until dawn."

Alric trotted into the undergrowth and Catherine, a little wary of the uneven pathway in the dimming light, followed after as quickly as she could. As he had said, a horse stood tethered. It snorted and its ears twitched nervously as they approached. Alric mounted and walked his mount to where the ground sloped so that she might climb aboard more easily.

"Keep your head low," he warned and set off at a tooth-jarring trot through the trees.

After a while, they reached a clearing, much to Catherine's relief. The denser trees en route had stolen away the remaining daylight and made her wonder at the wisdom of taking up Alric's quest. They dismounted. She looked about her trying to pierce the dark grey shadows that were speckled with pale dots from straining her eyes. She could not hear a hound, but as her eyes adjusted to the light, she could make out not one but three animals. She moved a little closer, thinking her eyes must be deceiving her. There were indeed three and their mouths were muzzled. There was no sign of Gripper being caught in a trap. Perplexed she looked to Alric, then froze, an icy fear stabbing her chest. Standing next to Alric was Edwin.

He smiled at her. "Catherine. I have taken it upon myself to check up on your welfare. I hope you didn't think I would abandon you, just because I have had troubles of my own."

She said nothing. He looked at her a while, then turned away to speak quietly with Alric.

"Go and stand over there, but don't get too close to the hounds. Watch carefully. You are about to learn a lesson in control. The objective is to make someone do exactly as you wish without them realising it."

Alric did as his father said and watched carefully, although truthfully, he had had enough of watching Catherine for one night.

While Edwin murmured to Alric, Catherine looked about her wondering whether to make an escape or to pretend that she was still going along with his plans. She knew that her mother's death would probably make him assume that she was now against him. Being wary made her watchful, even calculating, and somehow the cloaking darkness gave her an extra layer of bravery. She felt almost confident that she would outwit Edwin if she thought logically about her situation. She noticed how Edwin led Alric's horse aside but did not tether it. She knew she was fit and strong enough to mount the animal from a run if she waited until an opportune time. On her way here, she had been shrewd enough to memorise the pattern of branches through which they had emerged, so that she had a marker for getting back to the path that would lead to Drysdale. It would be easier to join the broader, adjacent path first, should she be at a gallop, but it forked to the correct path after several yards. If she kept her cool and things went wrong, she still had a good chance of escape. Still, she might be able to talk Edwin out of insisting that she leave with him. The dogs were tied and muzzled so they presented no danger. Her main worry was no longer whether Edwin would know that she was lying. She had learned so much about him in the past few days that she felt it her duty to outmatch his dishonesty if it would help her get back to Drysdale where she would prefer to live out her life. He deserved no more loyalty.

Edwin turned to her, smiling. She felt so strangely brave that, before he could speak, she asked, "How are you? I've been worried about you?"

A slight flicker of surprise crossed his eyes, then disappeared. "Likewise. I felt guilty about leaving you in the wolf's lair for so long."

"They said you were under the protection of the monks. An outlaw."

"Well," he held out his arms, turning his palms upwards, "they were lying." He came closer making her take a step back. As soon as she had done so, she realised her mistake. He now knew she did not trust him.

She was still conscious of her possible escape route in her peripheral vision but forced her eyes to stay on Edwin so as not to give away her intentions. An owl screeched overhead and she jumped. She covered her nervousness by laughing at herself and clapping her hands to her heart. "I was trying to be brave for Alric's sake, but I'm really quite afraid of the dark. I'm glad that you are here. Is Gripper all right now?"

Edwin ignored the reference to the dog and moved towards her again. Alric side stepped a little to the right. If he was to watch and learn from his father, his father ought to stop getting in the way. Even though Edwin's back was to him, he could tell by the way he inclined his head and held out his hands and took hers that he was smiling. Catherine held his gaze.

"How are you getting on with Drysdale, Catherine?" Edwin was too close for comfort. She needed a reason to free her hands.

"I believe he likes me," she said. "Is it still what you want?"

He ignored the question and narrowed his eyes at her. "How can you tell he likes you?"

She shrugged, elaborating on her words with her hands so she could be free of his grip. "He told me so. This evening. He even seated me next to the king's table."

Edwin's mouth became a thin line and he raised his eyebrows. "I'm impressed." He rubbed his chin. "But I think you need a little fatherly advice, Catherine. I am a man so I know how men think. A lot of times, men say and do things to please women, just to see how…. compliant they are. To judge whether there's a chance of lying with you."

Catherine shook her head, taking another step back. Too late, she felt a tree root behind her heel and after three quick backward stumbling steps, she felt a trunk against her back and leaned against it awkwardly. Rather than help her upright, Edwin moved forward, placing a palm at either side of her ribs, caging her in. He brought his face closer. She tried to think quickly.

"He has mentioned marriage. He says we should discuss it after mother's funeral."

"Oh, Catherine. He seems so eager after three days." He leaned his weight on one arm, freeing the other. "Of course he's mentioned marriage. Your stepfather unable to protect you and, well, look at you." He put a hand on her breast. "I bet he's awake all night wondering what it would be like to touch you." He stroked his thumb firmly across the fabric so that it began to pull to one side. He pinned her more firmly against the tree with his hips and pushed his hand inside her dress, stroking her skin and cupping her breast in his hand. He could feel how rapidly her heart was beating and smiled, aroused by her fear of him. Desperate to get away, but afraid that he would use more strength to trap her if he sensed it, she whispered quickly, "He said I could take my time to think about it." She felt his hand squeeze again and he began to lift the folds of her dress. He pushed his hips against her and she could feel his hardness as her hem was raised. "I thought it would please you." Her feet were beginning to slip where they struggled for a firm hold on the uneven network of roots. He enjoyed the desperation in her face and voice. Another time he could have teased her like this for hours. On feeling her slipping, he removed his hand from her dress, stood back a little and allowed her to fall to the base of the tree in an awkward little heap.

Alric watched from the shadows. Part of him watched in heart pounding sympathy for his half sister. He was beginning to realise he had judged events quite wrongly. But, another part of his nearly thirteen year old brain – the part that was becoming obsessed by the female form, compelled him to watch as his father's hands continued to push and grab at her body: even as he swept up the hem of her dress and attempted to open her legs with his knee. The roots made his balance unsteady. Alric watched wide-eyed as Edwin's fingers tried to probe further up her tightly closed thighs.

"Has he been at you already?" His voice was steady and calm, as if he was concerned for her welfare.

"No!" She wasn't answering his question so much as telling him to stop. She used both hands to catch at his fingers as he sought to find out the answer for himself, digging her heels into the dirt and trying desperately to shuffle backwards in spite of the tree roots pushing harshly into her back. Face straight, he caught at her ankles as she struggled, then pulled her roughly along the ground towards him, moving back himself to allow more leeway. He lay over her, pinning her to the ground with his hips. The humiliation at her powerlessness was finally too much. She felt her face crumple and began to cry.

"Just you keep it that way, Catherine. Be warned." He pushed hard against her pelvis with his, giving her a sharp pain, even through the folds of her dress. Although she looked past him at the pattern of dark branches against the sky, she nodded quickly, unwilling to give him a reason to push so hard again.

Then, without warning, he stood up and brushed himself down, as if he had simply stumbled. He looked down at her, a look of disgust on his face.

"Get up, girl. Tidy your hair. Put your dress straight." He walked back towards Alric and the hounds, untying the two older dogs, who began to strain at their leashes. Catherine struggled shakily to her feet, face burning. It was now or never. She just wanted to get back to safety. She ran for the horse, not so certain of her abilities now. Although she felt unsteady, adrenalin gave her a welcome extra measure of strength and she leapt onto the horse's back without a struggle. She bent her head low, too terrified to look back. She was afraid of what Edwin might do should she fall. She forced the horse to an immediate gallop onto the wider path, which would take her onto the one that she had taken from Drysdale.

As she rode into the trees, she heard sharp barking from the hounds. They were unmuzzled. She kicked harder, hearing herself whimper in desperation. She urged the horse forward through the branches and urged herself to keep her focus on safety. She could still do this. Drysdale was only a mile hence. Even less.

But something was wrong. As if in a nightmare, her mount would not do as she commanded. Instead, it reared up, whinnied in pain, spiralled, landed heavily on all four hooves, gave an almost human scream far worse than before and reared again. As Catherine fell, she tried to push herself away from the animal so as to stop herself being crushed under its weight when it was so agitated, but the branches ensnared her, robbing her of space. She felt her head make contact with one of the limbs, then rider and horse were crashing heavily to the forest floor. It was so dark that for a split second, she wondered whether she had lost consciousness, but before the thought had time to register properly, a pain in her ribs and chest and the snarling of the fast approaching hounds, told her that she was still awake. In spite of the pain, she struggled to free herself from the weight of the horse, but the dogs moved too quickly. She could feel the ground vibrate as they barged through the undergrowth nearby.

Edwin stood next to Alric, muzzles still hanging from one hand, gazing along the path where smaller branches were now snapped. "You see, Alric. Put all parts of the equation in place beforehand: an attractive escape route scattered with caltrops, hungry and bad-tempered hounds, a reason for a woman to feel she has to get away quickly; and people become nothing more than puppets. They do exactly as you wish. No need for foul play. No links to the death."

Although Alric could not see the figures clearly, he heard Catherine's one sharp scream, suddenly cut short, her throat being vulnerable and the strength in her arms too outweighed by fear to have any effect against the frantic energy of the dogs tearing at her. The hounds did not stop, but fought over the prey; even after the horse, glossy with sweat and blood and shivering from the shock, had limped away into the trees without a fight. Edwin left them to it for a while. He had no intention of risking being bitten while he tried to muzzle them again.

Alric's knees shook and his scalp crawled with icy gooseflesh. His legs buckled and he dropped into the long dewy grass, shivering in the darkness.

Chapter Eight

The Tallow Man

Not knowing that Bran had elected to sit by himself for a while, thinking over his evening's conversation with Catherine, Thomas came into the stables to have some things prepared in readiness for the next morning. Bran had a polite but brief conversation relating to the marriage of Marc and Susan, then made his excuses and found a quiet place to sit between the trace room and the main house. He looked at the chamber window above the main doorway, a little to the right of centre. A light still burned. He wondered what Catherine was doing now. Would she keep their conversation a secret or had she confided in her new friend already? He found he really didn't mind either way.

He also found himself sighing a lot – happily for the most part. He was contented yet dissatisfied, rested yet restless, confident that she felt the same as he did, but wary of being confident lest she should change her mind. He found himself basking in occasional waves of pleasure, when, on the third or fourth time of recalling something she had said or done, he remembered an extra piece of information that had previously slipped away: perhaps a nuance to her voice or a smile at just the right time. Something that showed she really must like him. Mustn't she?

Above the inky silhouette of the tree-line, the sky was a bloodshot purple, spreading to mid blue overhead. It was not long to nightfall. From dusky shadows around the grounds, tents emitted snores or final shuffles as people bedded down. Insects twitched the grass blades irregularly around his feet. One or two voices in the Hall still lingered on, more hushed now that people were settling for the night. From the open kitchen window, he could hear the fire being raked over. He imagined Robert making himself comfortable in the comparative luxury of his more private sleeping space.

The grey definitions of trebuchets, willows and tents began to melt as the sky darkened. Bran stood, feeling it would be better to pick his way through the sleepy household now, rather than wait and risk creating a disturbance when all the candles were out. Once on his feet, he stretched, more aware of his body than usual. He glanced towards the upper casement again, then stepped down towards the main house.

A sharp two raps from one of the watchers by the lakes caused him to quickly stoop into the shadows and creep to a place where he could safely assess how best to arm himself. Heads emerged from tents at the call to arms, although most were only half-dressed. Squires rushed from the main building, bearing torches to cast light on the turn of events.

Ray and Will stepped into the courtyard. Bran joined them. He glanced up at the window again.

Susan was straining to see. Leonard ran down from his watch.

"I sounded the alarm. A rider is coming this way."

All was quiet. No-one needed to be told to listen. And now the sound of hooves could be discerned. A gallop. As the seconds passed, the urgency of the rider became more apparent from the agitated snorts of the approaching mount, which slew to a halt in the courtyard. Joss and the King had joined the company now.

"Friend," called Joss, recognising Wilfred, the young knight he had left posted at the Cathedral in case of mishap.

Wilfred slid from the saddle, out of breath. "The Prince Bishop has reported Edwin missing from the Cathedral. After Compline, a novice was found half naked and unconscious just off the North aisle. Pudsey immediately informed me and ordered a search. We cannot find Edwin anywhere inside the building. Those posted on coastal routes know to be vigilant, but I thought I should come this way to warn Drysdale and Redgate."

Joss rubbed his chin then spoke. "Raymond, Leonard, stay wary and make your way to Redgate – ensure it is safe…"

His orders were interrupted by a call from the trees.

"Better to wait," he added.

The King watched with interest. He did not need a good command of English to be impressed by the combined effort of these men in their common cause.

Joss took Leonard's torch and he, Bran and Will moved towards the voice.

"By the lakeshore," it called again.

A large shadow stumbled by the water, righted itself just in time and stood again. Joss passed his torch to Bran and approached the animal that swayed and shuddered there. It seemed to have been making attempts to drink, but was unable to lower its head without losing its balance and its legs buckling. Eventually, it simply stood, coat quivering.

Bran and Will held their torches aloft to enable Joss to see, but stayed at a distance that would not threaten the animal. Joss moved slowly. If anyone could gain the animal's trust it was he.

From the Hall doorway, Susan watched and looked about for Marc. He went to her and she whispered urgently. Marc listened then left her and approached the lakeside. Joss was shaking his head.

"This animal has been attacked. Perhaps by wolves – maybe dogs, although I cannot imagine why." He squatted and pointed to the horse's belly. "See?" Flesh hung where teeth had ripped at the tender underside.

Bran and Will peered more closely. "Not a bear or boar?" Will asked.

Joss shook his head. "This is no courser or destrier….good enough for a page perhaps. A mount like this may have been able to put up a desperate fight to fend off wolves or dogs, but I cannot see him surviving anything larger. Still, it makes little difference now. Poor creature is so shocked it is no longer quite conscious of the pain." The horse indeed seemed confused at its inability to perform the most instinctive of actions: lowering its head to water. Joss sighed and stood again. "It'll have to be destroyed."

Bran turned away, intending to find Thomas so that he could deal with the unpalatable task of destroying the horse and disposing of its body. Marc intercepted him en route.

"Have you seen Catherine?" he asked.

Bran nodded. "I said goodnight to her about an hour..no... maybe two hours ago now. She went to join Anna and Susan in their chamber."

Marc shook his head. "Susan has just told me that she has not seen Catherine since we ate this evening."

Bran looked at his friend, perplexed. "But I said goodbye to her from the stables."

It dawned on him that he had not watched her enter the house. Suddenly things seemed more urgent. He turned back to Will and Joss. "We need to mount a search. Catherine is missing."

Marc explained, "We thought she had retired to the solar with Susan and Anna, but she hasn't been seen for two hours now."

Joss and Will glanced at each other, then the latter spoke to Raymond. "Go wake your mother. Help her to take the girls to the solar. They are less vulnerable if they sleep in one place tonight."

As Ray set off on his task, Will added, "Assure her nothing is wrong. It's just to be safe. And don't let her carry the girls. Make more than one journey if they're fast asleep."

"Who is the last person to have seen Catherine?" asked Joss.

"Me," said Bran. "I spoke to her in the stables about the arrangements for travelling to the funeral at Redgate tomorrow."

"And this was two hours ago?"

"A little less."

"Did you see her go back to the house?"

Bran shook his head, unsure of how to answer. "I said goodbye to her at the stable entrance. I watched her walk towards the Hall doorway. All I can think is that she did not make it indoors. She can only have been several footsteps away when whatever it was that diverted her caught her attention."

Will sensed his awkwardness. "Did you watch her from the door for the sake of discretion?"

Bran nodded. "I swear I have treated her honorably – but," his voice petered away as he realised his ineptitude in discussing his private feelings. He took a breath and ploughed on. "I wanted to allow her the time to think about a match between us. If people saw me accompanying her, they may have pre-empted things. Made her feel she had to go along with it."

Joss came to his rescue. "So we need to ascertain what took her in another direction and which direction that was. Also, whether there is anyone else missing from the house; someone that would be a likely rider for this horse. If not, they may have come here from elsewhere. Perhaps that will help us provide a clue as to Catherine's whereabouts." He turned to Leonard. "Did you notice anyone acting in an unusual way – any strangers? Someone not linked to royal or Northern guests?" He realised this was a tall order.

Leonard shook his head. "There is no-one I have not come to recognise amongst the Knights and Squires, although I must confess, it is harder to place the pages."

Joss summoned a handful of men. Each was given an area to search from the house itself, the outbuildings, the lakes and surrounding undergrowth. He then prepared to set out with Will, Bran, Marc, Wilfred and Leonard into the forest. They armed themselves first. The forest at night time was not a place for the faint-hearted. Still, Edwin could be relying on that. Thomas, having let Joss know that all in the stables was as it should be, quietly led the injured horse away.

Raymond came back out to the courtyard. "All are accounted for indoors. Apart from Catherine, there is no one missing."

Joss mounted. As he pulled on his gloves, he asked of Bran, "What was Catherine's mood tonight? Did she seem agitated at all?"

Bran guessed that he was trying to see whether Catherine had planned to go all along. "I think she had every intention of going back to the house. All things considered, she seemed the happiest she had been in days. I don't think she ever wanted to go back to Beau Repaire or see Edwin again."

Joss nodded. "This is a serious situation until we prove otherwise. Treat any movement in the forest with suspicion. This threat is too close for comfort."

Each man took a torch, and moved to a position about three yards from the next man. It soon became apparent that the forest was so dark that to search properly they would need to dismount. Perhaps no bad thing as their mounts would give an extra wall of protection against attack. Apart from the screech of owls and the sudden flutterings of birds as they were disturbed by this twilit intrusion, the forest offered them no sounds. The men formed a broad arrowhead formation with Joss at the front. The boughs were so thick in places that it was hard to cast light into potential hiding places without risking setting fire to the undergrowth. As they searched silently, rumblings began overhead. Thunder. Bran's heart sank. Heavy rain would not help them. Joss seemed unperturbed. About half a mile into the forest, it began. Drops sounded on the canopy above them. Not the pattering drops of a welcome rainfall, but large, bruising, penetrating drops, which battered at the upper leaves, punching them downwards then splashing again onto the underlying foliage. The drops gradually increased and the thunder grew louder. Soon it seemed the forest was alive with unseen creatures shaking the undergrowth as the rain pummelled and tore at the ferns and lower branches. The torch flames spat and shuddered and the wetness soon found its chilly way into their clothing. Joss held his shield so that there was no danger of his flame going out and the others followed suit. Soon, they stepped, slowly and methodically into a clearing. They ignored the atrocious weather, keeping up their methodical search. Then, two raps of a sword's butt against a shield put them all on alert.

It was Marc. "Over here!"

Bran, Will, Joss and Henry hurried to join him, while Wilfred kept a watchful eye on the dark trees.

Marc beckoned, his shield held aloft above the spot he had found. The other four men created a roof with their shields to protect Marc's find. Bran peered at the ground. It was hard to see: to know what he was looking for. Marc squatted and pointed with his torch. The ground was wet, but not like the rest of the rain-sodden floor. Here the wetness darkened the soil as expected, but that darkness spread itself over grass and ferns. And there were what seemed to be bundles of rags.

"Bran, Marc. Can you please stand over us with your shields and torches held just so?" suggested Will.

They did so. He had hoped to make Bran stand back before he recognised what he was looking at. But too late. The lightning cracked over their heads and now that they were in the clearing, the scene was illuminated, perhaps to an even greater extent than in daylight.

Henry stooped. There was something dark in this area of flattened grass. He loved hunting enough to recognise a kill, but he was finding it difficult to see what had been the prey. He looked up at Joss and Will, eyebrows raised.

Will picked something up and asked gently of Bran, "What was Catherine wearing tonight?"

Bran took the bloodstained fragment of sage green cloth from the older man. "A green dress."

Henry began to recognise what they had found. Quietly he stooped down next to Joss, who scraped his wet hair from his brow in order to see more clearly. While he picked carefully at the grass he said, "Create a roof of shields over this clearing. Two volunteers to stay on watch, the rest to split between Drysdale and Redgate."

Marc looked at Bran then said, "We'll stay."

Joss shook his head. "No. You have a funeral to escort." He stood and took a bag from his saddle. Carefully he put something inside then placed the bag inside his cloak to try to protect it from the relentless rain.

Henry and Joss stood. They conferred quietly. "I haven't seen anything this bad on the battlefield. I'll have documents drawn up. All citizens have the power to arrest this man wherever he is found. I'll publicise the danger he poses so that if he is found anywhere in the kingdom, including France, he will be brought back here for trial in Durham. As soon as we are back at Drysdale, I will send men to bring the Prince Bishop back to this site in the morning. He needs to see it with his own eyes so that the sentence matches the severity of the crime. In the few days since I arrived he has killed two women and attacked a monk in the very church that was giving him sanctuary."

Wilfred and Leonard took up watch; Joss, Will and Marc approached their mounts, but Bran lingered behind. His eyes were adjusting now that the underbelly of the roof of shields danced with light from several torches. The rain set up a clamour over his head as he stooped to make a closer inspection. Scattered clues identified what he looked at as Catherine: matted red hair; green cloth stained red; the occasional startlingly white flash of skin where part of her lay relatively untouched. Will put a hand on his shoulder, "Come on, Bran. The land is quite high here. No danger of flooding………….. should you need to come back. It is unfortunate, but it is best to leave her like this until Pudsey has visited the scene. He needs to see what an animal Edwin is."

Wet through from the rain, Bran mounted his courser. They rode in silence.

Back at Drysdale, Bran sat alone. Joss went to him, made him take off his cloak and wet outer garments and steered him in front of the fire. He then did the same for himself, placing the bag carefully to one side. Bran looked at it.

Joss explained. "Perhaps this poor daughter needs to be with her mother again. To share the same ritual so they can move on together."

"Such a small bag," observed Bran.

Joss nodded, "We only ever really deal with a token of the physical once we have passed on." He shifted a little, wondering whether to continue.

Bran looked at him. "And Catherine's token is?"

Joss gave him a level look. "Her heart was whole."

"Is there any way it might not have been her? The owner of that injured horse perhaps."

"I cannot say what you want me to Bran; her hair, dress, shoes."

Bran closed his eyes momentarily, then shook his head. He gave Joss a look so strange that at first the older man thought he was going to refute what he had said. Bran shook his head again and brought up his right hand between them in front of the fire. His forefinger and thumb were held so that they almost touched. He looked at Joss and made sure he saw his hand. "This close. You see?"

Joss looked, not comprehending. "Tell me."

Bran shook his head again. "Always this close." His hand began to quiver and he gave it a deliberate shake as if to banish his trembling. Slowly and deliberately, he brought his hand up again, watched as his forefinger almost met his thumb, then, as if it was the most important thing in the world to make his mentor understand, he threw another glance at Joss. "You see. You see how close it always is?" The hand shook again, so he brought it down sharply on his knee then held it shoulder height again. "I was this close to my mother when she choked to death." Joss realised something was descending on Bran that was more far reaching than the night's events.

Bran gave his knee another blow and resumed his former position. "Her feet were this close to the ground when he pulled her up on the rope. She tried, but she was just out of reach. She couldn't breathe. This close." His brow was a confusion of furrows as he shook his head. "If Anna had been born just two years later, I could have saved Margery. I'm sure I could. And Marion. Ben said the body was still warm when you got to her. And tonight. Tonight. If I'd watched her into the house, if she had only come and told me what was happening. I asked her to keep herself safe, to allow me the time to solve her problems." He looked at Joss again, mouth trying to form the words, but no sound coming out.

Joss took Bran by the shoulders. A tremor ran right through him and, still shaking his head, he looked into the air around him as if searching for the words that would sum up his anger, his helplessness, his disbelief at how quickly these precious people could suddenly be no more than memories.

Joss took his shoulders, forcing him to focus on his eyes. "Bran. Look at me." He waited until Bran focused. "None of this is your fault. None of it. There is only one man to blame and soon everyone in the country will know what he has done."

Bran stood up. He shook his head. "The things going through my head right now make me unfit to breathe the same air as the rest of this company. If he was here now, I'd flay him, chop him into messes..." He stopped, swallowed, shook his head, put his fingertips to his brow. "In here, right now, I'm no better than he is. I need to go. I need to be on my own to think."

Joss stood too. "This is your house, Bran, and you are entitled to do as you wish, but I suggest that you should not be alone. Let Marc come with you."

Bran shrugged and left the room. Marc looked to Joss, who nodded, then followed his friend to his chamber. Joss wondered whether Bran would search for Edwin himself. He wasn't in a state of mind that would help him to achieve anything useful. Perhaps having Marc around would allow him to reflect more safely on what had been happening.

Bran lay on the pallet silently. Marc allowed him the luxury of ignoring him and looked from the window to where he could see the light from the chamber where Susan lay. He could not help being glad she was safe; glad that Catherine had not confided in her new friend. He knew Susan. She would have wanted to help; she would have considered herself capable of keeping them both out of trouble in the forest. If things had been just a little different, there could have been two deaths tonight.

Bran did not sleep. He tried not to think of Catherine's final moments. Still, he ached with guilt that she had been so brutally alone in that vicious dark.

The next day, the funeral went by with Bran taking very little in. Later, he realised that parts of the day were a blank to him. He could not remember crossing the river on the journey to Redgate, nor what people said to him. The King, realising Bran's state of mind, conferred with Ben instead and it was agreed that Bran would use Drysdale as a teaching base for two years, then as long as Bran saw fit. Joss met with Puiset, the Prince Bishop, and clearly stated the evidence against Edwin. All they had to do was find him. It was decided that, officially, Beau Repaire would revert to the Prince Bishop in the hope that it would lure him back, but that, in the mean time, it would be managed by the Northern: Ben and Marc shared the responsibility, feeling Bran had enough to do. Joss took it upon himself to search for Edwin, but to no avail. He had sunk without trace.

Marc and Bran were knighted one week after the funeral, shortly before the King left for further negotiations with Beckett. Susan and Marc decided that they would like a longer delay before the wedding. Catherine's death was too shocking for them to contemplate such a happy occasion. Besides it would not have been fair to Bran when he had so many other things on his mind. Instead they merged Christmas and matrimony in a ceremony beautifully fringed by red and white berries and evergreens, by which time, Bran seemed to be more like his old purposeful self, although his old humour did not return. He worked intensely: building, experimenting, teaching non-stop.

When Henry sent for a report, it was written the same day and dispatched, based on the copious notes he had already made and had copied. When Joss requested help in a case requiring diplomacy from an outsider, he set out immediately, dealt with it and returned. When everyone else lay in bed, Bran's light still burned in the trace room. While Marc and Susan created their first child, Richard, Bran created diagrams, prototypes and reports. When Ben made special journeys from Redgate and entreated his foster son to rest, he did so for an afternoon perhaps, but fidgeted and seemed distracted and eager to return to his designs or his lead pits.

With Edwin's whereabouts still unknown, Bran felt that he was always there, at his shoulder. Part of him worked hard so that there was no room for the lurking fury he felt at the deaths of those who didn't deserve it, and another part was preparing, just incase he was the next to go. If Bran was to suddenly disappear, someone else would be able to take over. There was nothing that wasn't documented. It was as if he was tallow: a man turned candle, just biding time until he was burned out. His loss was a gain for those he taught and for the silversmiths of Durham. Henry, a tireless man himself, was greatly impressed.

Ben wished he could stop the suffering which was making Bran feel he should work so hard. In Bran he saw reflections of Joss- another who chose to do everything himself rather than allow himself the time to reflect on the killings of his wife and children when he had been away from them, proving his loyalty elsewhere through battle. Thomas, on the other hand, thought Bran needed a woman who would treat him to "a good, hard shag," and although Janet scolded him for being so forthright about the young overlord, she couldn't help but agree with him.

It took two years of furious industry before sleep finally overtook him during daylight hours. One sunny afternoon, when Ben returned from the annual fair, he found his former squire head down and sound asleep across the desk in the trace room. Anna was with him and before Ben had time to warn her not to wake him, she had giggled and pulled at his sleeve.

"Wake up, Bran. You'll get ink on your face!"

"Shush, Anna," but too late.

Bran sat up blearily, looking about him to get his bearings.

"Sorry, Bran. I tried to stop her. We are just returned from the fair."

Bran came to his senses slowly. "Was Edwin there?" he asked.

Ben shook his head.

Bran rested his elbows on the desk top and sighed, pushing back his hair from his eyes with both hands. He thought deeply, then looked at Ben. "I need to go now. I've done all I can here."

Ben said nothing, thinking he simply meant to return to the main house. Anna looked up at her father then at Bran. "Where will you go?"

"Overseas. Spain maybe. Arrange to meet Harun. I'm not sure. I need to learn something different for a while." He shrugged. "I have neglected medicine for too long."

Ben wasn't sure that was what Bran needed at all.

Anna put her arms around Bran's waist and lay her head against his ribs. "Do not go, Bran. You are sad, that is all."

Bran gave her a hug. "I am not sad, I am just tired." And then, bringing up a forefinger and stroking it absently against his lips, without a sound, he began to cry.

Ben stepped forward and held his poor, broken boy.

PART TWO

Chapter Nine

1173 - The Homecoming

Bran deliberately rode ahead of the party in order to travel down to Redgate alone. He wanted to absorb every part of the homecoming and knew that this would be impossible with a party of pilgrims at his heels. He had invited them to stay at Drysdale so they could make a further shorter journey to Saint Cuthbert's shrine at the Cathedral in Durham over the next few days, but he would send his Squire with them to Drysdale, rather than go himself. For now, after eight years, all Bran wanted was to see Ben and Anna and the household at Redgate: to feel their familiarity; their easy acceptance of him: to be shocked by the contrast of Springtime moorland and forest compared to the recent memories of red earth and palm.

High up, at the edge of the moor, where heather gave way to grassy pasture, Bran stopped to listen. Layers of birdsong sounded about him and buzzing insects twitched the grass by his feet. This fallow land was easier underfoot. He looked about him before he dismounted, taking in the shape of the hills, their surfaces creased in places with narrow crevices and littered with rocks. He walked his mount down the path worn by sheep and wound his way down to the more verdant meadowland. From here he could see only the tops of the pine trees, the older branches turning finger-like fronds upwards as if offering him a hand down. The day was still and the sun warm. A bee flew at man and horse before spiralling up and past them to the sweeter lure of the heather.

He remembered how he had run along here as a boy and thanked the land for making the path obvious. He hadn't known it until he was older, but he had already run a few miles more than necessary and, for a tired child, the easiest way was between this series of descending banks. The community was not visible, but by following this narrow ribbon of relatively flatter land, you were led straight to it.

Bran walked slowly, savouring the familiar territory and the better memories it roused in him. He decided he would wake early tomorrow so he could go out alone to bank's edge simply to listen to the sound of at least a hundred doves in the surrounding lime and chestnut trees. To stand and look was good enough, but then to stand and look again and let the life amongst the branches gradually dawn upon the eye: becoming aware of what had been invisible -

scores of birds - fluttering, preening, and moving from branch to branch; like an illusionist's living work of art - that was special.

He gave a deep, satisfied sigh. As he had hoped, time had weakened the worst of his memories leaving him with the euphoria of a man returning to the people and places he loved.

As he walked, his thoughts turned to the practical. He wondered whether he should build a channel at Drysdale which replicated this path. A flash flood would be easily diverted past the house and buildings to the fenland below, rather than spreading itself across his precious fields, returning them to marsh. He had reached one of the steepest parts of the path, where it seemed it would fall almost vertically. Here the pine was joined by chestnut trees. He peered between two large, moss-spattered boulders at the steepest and narrowest part of the path, making sure his courser would be able to cope. He was reassured and led Seer carefully between the rocks. There was another flatter glade, followed by a final steep and leafy descent, then he would be able to see the rooftops of Redgate. He let go of the reins, confident that the animal, after a couple of initial snorts and exaggerated nods, would follow carefully and obediently. He stepped across the grass and allowed himself to slide down the earthy bank to the large chestnut overlooking the dale.

He lingered for a while, enjoying both the closeness to and the distance from the community he considered to be home. Eight years had seemed so long until now. He breathed deeply, as if he could literally internalise his familiar surroundings. For a short while, he would be a voyeur of the place he had not seen since he was twenty two years old. He would wait until he had familiarised himself again with every stone and branch, then he would make himself known.

His plans were interrupted, not unpleasantly, by voices: several happy voices. They brought him back to reality and he grew curious as to who the speakers could be. In a community of this size, he was bound to know them. Two or three young children shrieked in delighted terror at whoever was chasing them and making inhuman monster type sounds. A voice he recognised instantly as Susan's was giving the man a good-natured scolding for scaring the little ones.

A movement of orange cloth between the branches revealed that a further person, probably a young woman, was making her way to the bank where he stood. He stayed where he was, there being no reason to hide - this was his land after all. As the lady stooped to pass under the lower branches to a grassy ledge, which he knew from personal experience made a comfortable seat, she became visible piece by piece. The first part he saw was her gown below the knees. Her shoes slipped a little on the grass so she put her hands out in front of her to make the ascent easier. In one hand, she carried an open book. Even from here, he could see the pages were crammed with tiny writing, as if she valued the space. He noticed the pages were paper not vellum and guessed she was writing on paper made at Drysdale. Her free hand lifted her hemline a little to prevent tripping. She ducked under another branch, bringing her a little closer and a little higher. He now had a view of the top of her bowed head, which was uncovered, revealing very light brown hair, fair in places from previous years' sunlight. She made a final step up to the flatter grass, only an arm's length below him, and stood up straight, her fingers taking a few wayward strands of hair away from her face.

She did not see him at first. Her cheeks were flushed from the climb and, as she was without headwear, her hair shone in the light which fell through the leafy canopy. She was beautiful. He felt his heart beat faster and wondered what he could say to her in order that she would stay rather than retreat hastily through the trees to her companions. He wondered what was written in the book that she held. Perhaps he could ask her about it. Realising it would be rude to stare without making his presence known, especially as she looked like she had come here for privacy, he cleared his throat. Two startled brown eyes looked into his. If being shot in the chest by an arrow could bring pleasure instead of pain, that would be exactly what Bran felt now. He tried to appear nonchalant, hoping his face was not letting him down.

He smiled, "Good day. I did not mean to shock you."

To him, his voice sounded unnatural, but she must have been reassured because the brown eyes had now lost their look of fear and were joining the rest of her face in smiling up at him. She even held out an arm to him so she could join him on his level. He reached out and gently took her wrist, pulling her easily towards him. He could only stare at her foolishly, not yet trusting himself to form a coherent sentence.

She smiled up at him, catching her breath, then spoke. "Bran! Is it really you? Away such a long time and then you just...appear!" She hugged him, her head resting momentarily against his chest, then she stood back to look up at him again. "Does father know you're back?"

Bran gazed down at her, unable to make a family link, but grateful for the intimacy she was showing him. He heard himself saying, "I wanted to surprise everyone."

She looked pleased. "So I'm the first!"

Footsteps sounded from the foliage nearby. A familiar but wary voice called up the bank. "Anna, who are you talking to?" Marc emerged from the undergrowth.

"It's Bran! Come and see!"

Bran looked at her. At Anna. Then he looked beyond her to his best friend, who had stopped in his tracks, amazed. "Bran?" He began to laugh.

Reluctantly, Bran stepped back, letting his arms drop from Anna's shoulders, and going to his friend. "We didn't know you were on your way. People are going to be so pleased to know you're home - especially the King." He glanced around him and whispered, "Family problems." He then resumed his former tone, "We were just talking about you."

Anna laughed, "We are always talking about you: we have all missed you so much. It's not the same just hearing about you from the people you send."

She took his hand to encourage the party to begin the short journey back to the house. In spite of the hot day and the climb, her skin was cool. He grinned at her and bent to kiss her hand. Having regained his composure, he stepped back in order to drink her in. "My God, Anna. I didn't recognise you at first." He took both of her hands in his and smiled down at her. "Although, I should have guessed when I saw you carrying a book." He studied her face, glad of an excuse to do so. "I can see your mother in you."

"Really? Most people think I look more like my father."

He nodded, not sure whether he should feel guilty about the way he felt about her. She led him back to the path where Marc had joined Susan, picked up two of his three children and was now waiting for Bran to reach them. "This is Bobby," he said, raising his right arm, "and this is Agnes," he raised his left. He placed both back at his feet.

"Hello! Oh, there's another one." A third child, a little girl, hid behind Susan's skirts.

"This is Janey. She is the oldest of the three, but the shyest." Bran smiled at her and gave Susan a hug. "Three more children!"

"No, no," laughed Mark, beckoning Bran to follow them down to the house. "We left the youngest at home with Janet. She was fast asleep anyway. Besides, it's a hot day for carrying babies. Then there's Richard of course. The plan is to send him to Will's soon as a page."

"Old enough to page already? Have you asked Will yet? You know Richard is welcome at Drysdale if you'd prefer. It's time for me to concentrate on home for a while."

"I was hoping you would say that," his friend replied. "You know what a stay-at-home Will can be, especially now he's past fifty. He tends to stay at Redgate more than Bankside these days."

Bran laughed, thinking of Will's love of home comforts, "How is he?"

"Oh, the same as ever - never quite as ill as he says he feels."

Bran stopped, realising his horse was still standing obediently on the level where he had first spoken to Anna. "I'll follow you down. I had better fetch Seer - make sure he avoids the shale."

Marc nodded and continued down with his family. Anna stayed further up the incline preferring to wait for Bran. From below, Susan watched him as he returned. She noticed the way he lingered over letting go of Anna's hand and smiled as he reached her on his way back down. Susan nodded and looked at Marc. She stood on tiptoe in order to whisper to him without the children hearing, "Bran's in love."

Marc looked from his wife to Bran and back to his wife again.

"Don't look! He'll know we're talking about him!" she whispered urgently, linking his arm and turning him to face downhill.

"How do you know? Who with?"

Susan laughed and shook her head. "I'll tell you later." She turned again and walked down the slope, trailing her children behind her. Marc, looking somewhat perplexed, turned to look back up the hill at his friends. As Bran walked behind Anna, his look was clearly focused on her as she chatted, probably about what she had read lately. It dawned on Marc that his wife was right - as usual. He turned and called after her, "I'm with you now!" He ran to catch up with her. "Is it allowed?" he asked.

"What?"

Marc waited until the children had trotted out of earshot. "Godfathers and God-daughters - marriage between undecided Jew and Christian; urm, let's see - a relationship between foster brother and foster sister?"

"Oh, they're just little things." His wife seemed resolute. "His father married a Christian." Susan pondered further. "And lots of men have married their wards. Besides, he was allowed to be her sponsor wasn't he? If anything had happened to Ben, he would have been entrusted to raise her."

"You've got this all worked out, haven't you?" said Marc smiling.

She shrugged and grinned. "She deserves the best and the best is following at her heels like a puppy."

"The best?" He raised his eyebrows at his wife.

"Well, the best apart from you then and you're already taken. And he would have turned thirty in January this year - 1173 - it's time he thought about having children."

"For all we know, he may have married while he was away. I heard him tell Anna he wanted to surprise everyone."

Susan looked back at Bran and studied. "No," she was certain. "We'd have heard. Besides, you heard him say she looked like her mother."

Marc shrugged. "Which means?"

"Which means I'm right. When we were children, Bran always adored Margery. He worshipped her. Remember Catherine? All those girls trying to catch his attention, but Catherine was the only one who turned his head. A slight realignment of the heart and there it is. Bran is in love with Anna." While his wife continued to walk to the house, completely convinced she was right, Marc glanced up again. Anna was smiling and nodding at something Bran had said. Marc wondered how Anna felt about him. She knew men were taking an interest in her now that she was fifteen, but Susan had told him that it annoyed Anna, as if it was something that interrupted her daily routine. He knew Ben hoped she would marry a man from the Northern, but many were intimidated by her in spite of their learning - not all of them read as widely as she and even if they did, Galen was not who they had come to talk about. Perhaps, if Susan was right, Bran was the perfect solution.

From within the house, Ben was quite surprised to see the little band returning so quickly. He hastily began rolling the sketches he had been studying and adding to with Will and Joss.

"Come on, help me! We cannot let her see. Marc said he would try to keep her away for at least two hours!" He was a little annoyed at his old friends for leaving him to struggle alone and he only just managed to tuck it behind a chair before Marc opened the door.

Will and Joss moved their heads away from the window where they had peered, checking whether it was really Bran they saw accompanying the little tribe that had left the house only one hour before. As Marc stepped into the room, a taller and darker shadow followed.

Ben had only just righted himself and stood staring at Bran in disbelief. "Bran! My God! Bran!" There wasn't a day that went by without him wishing that his foster son was there to help with the secret plans for Anna's library, so at first he wondered whether this silhouette in the doorway was a product of his own wishful thinking. It was only when the shadow stepped across the room and hugged him that the company came out of their trance. Bran was generally buffeted and slapped, before being seated at a trestle table with Will, Joss, Ben and Marc.

Susan took the children through to Janet before rejoining the company. At the table, questions were thrown while each talked over the answers. Marc watched his friend's mild manner come to the fore as he tried to attend to all of their demands simultaneously. He was doing a good job of it.

"Have you performed any operations?" asked Will, with a tone of macabre curiosity.

"Oh, of course he has." Ben answered for him. "What about bones? Osteo - whatsit. Will's a slave to his knees these days."

Bran grinned at their enthusiasm and self-deprecation. It was obvious they were still much fitter than many men half their age. "I've learned a little about a lot. I could look at your knees some time, if you really wish."

"What is it they were saying about building a tower at Pisa?" asked Joss. "Have you had a look at the plans? They seem to think it'll be impressive."

Bran shifted uncomfortably, not wanting to seem immodest. "Um." he nodded. "I did take a look."

The others looked at him expectantly. He gave a tight smile and a slight shrug. "I wasn't really convinced it would work. Still," he added, as if to compensate, "if mortar was as strong as their enthusiasm, it would never topple."

A door opened behind them and a much greyer haired Robert entered from the kitchen carrying three cups and a jug of ale. On noticing Bran, he stopped for only a couple of seconds, gave an impatient sigh, placed the ale on the table and returned to the kitchen.

"Excuse me," said Bran and went to his bag, which he had left just inside the doorway. He picked out a smaller bundle and placed it on the table. "A present for Robert - spices."

Attercop the cat, named by Anna ten years before, approached the bag, gave a tentative sniff and withdrew hastily.

"Still with us," Bran observed. "Is every man and beast in Drysdale so healthy?"

They all nodded apart from Will. Ben nudged him. "He said Drysdale."

Speaking of health stirred something in Marc's memory. "Oh, there was some bad news a couple of years after your departure - although not unexpected. I'm afraid Godric passed away."

"They say he was a hundred and five years old," mused Will.

"Not bad for a man who lived with snakes," added Marc.

"I hope they don't begin prescribing it as an elixir." Will wrinkled his nose.

Ben looked about him furtively to make sure Anna was out of the room. Noting her absence, he leant towards Bran conspiratorially. "Never mind medicine for now, Bran. We need your brain to help with some architectural details. But Anna must not know. We are building her a library."

Bran smiled at the affection in Ben's face. "That's a wonderful idea. She was speaking of a library earlier though. Perhaps it's not the secret you imagine."

Will looked perplexed, but Ben put him at ease, unharried by the news. "At present, she has a small collection of books and rolls of letters at one end of her private chamber. She often refers to this jumble as her library, but really she needs a much better place to house it. I'm quite proud of her."

"She could put the area back on the map - like Bede hundreds of years ago," nodded Will. His grey hair stood at angles from his head, like a cornfield after heavy rain. Bran recognised this as a sign that Will had been thinking hard about things that bored him.

Joss joined in. "But Ben is useless when it comes to designing buildings."

"Thank you, Joss." Ben rolled his eyes as he looked at Bran, but admitted wryly, "Of course, I cannot take offence because it's absolutely true."

Will nodded. "Every day we say 'If only Bran were here. He'd come up with something special.'"

"Umm," Joss concurred. "The plans we have made so far make a stable look imaginative."

"Shall we look now?" Bran's curiosity had got the better of him. Robert returned with more ale and pottage for Bran. The fact that it was rather a generous helping was the only clue which revealed he was pleased to see him. Wordlessly, Bran handed the bag of spices to him. Robert nodded cordially and with a brief but polite "Thank you, Sir," he took his leave of them.

"Eat first," said Ben, remembering his manners. "In the mean time we'll find an excuse to keep Anna away from here for a while longer."

"I don't mind eating and working," said Bran. "I often do."

"What a mind," said Will, admiringly.

Ben turned to Susan. "Do you think you could find an excuse to keep Anna away for an hour?"

"I can think of five good excuses," Susan grinned and rose from the table, "although she'll be eager to see Bran I imagine. I'll think of something."

Bran was glad the Eastern sun had darkened his skin. He could feel himself colouring at the thought of Anna being eager to see him.

As Susan left, Ben reached into the hiding place and unrolled the plans so that Bran could see them properly. Bran leaned back and stretched as if his brain needed to limber up before the hard work began. Joss stood and opened the door to its furthest point to allow more daylight to fall across the table.

Will carefully raised cups and bowls so that the plans lay flat and secure. They stared down at Ben's crude drawings in charcoal.

In a flat voice, Joss remarked, "Good, isn't it?"

Marc watched Bran's face. He had transformed, now seeming completely absorbed in his task. One elbow rested on the table, fingers holding the stick of charcoal almost to his lips. The other arm rested comfortably across the plans, keeping them flat. He spoke.

"This isn't bad at all," he said.

"That's the diplomat in him," Will remarked to the others and they all laughed.

Bran looked up at Ben. "Where do you see this being built?"

"Midway between the house and the stables, where it's flat, but it will still catch a lot of light. It's better for her eyes."

"And is there a time you would like it to be built by?"

"Let's see. It's March now...eleven months until her sixteenth birthday. Of course, we cannot hide the building from her until then but we can pretend it is for a different purpose. Tell her to keep away while dangerous work is underway."

He looked at his foster son as he pondered the plans. Again, he reminded him of the older Saul. "I know it's the books that are the most important element, but I want the building to be worthy of housing them...and big enough to allow the collection to grow."

Bran sat up a little and said without looking away from his task, "Do you mind if I start again on the back? I always find it easier to begin from scratch."

"No, no. Go on," urged Ben.

Cups and bowl were repositioned. Bran stared down for a few moments, as if the design was already there, lurking under the texture of the paper. He brought the charcoal down from his lips and let it hover close to the surface. As he worked, he spoke.

"Right. If it is to be in a central position, where it will catch the light all day but from different angles, let's give it more than four sides." He thought of the domed roofs in Jerusalem. "Perhaps make it octagonal. I won't worry too much about scale for these initial plans." He lightly traced an eight sided shape in the middle of the paper. On each straight side he pressed a shorter darker line of grey. "In each wall we have a window." The three older men watched the brown hand making deft strokes as he talked them through the idea. Marc stood and positioned himself so he could see over his friend's shoulder without blocking any light from the doorway. "We could have shelves built from floor to ceiling. As well as being placed against the walls, between the windows, we could have a double sided case of shelves coming from the wall towards the centre of the room." He drew an aerial view of these, producing something that looked not unlike spokes of a wheel without a hub. "Here," he drew a circle in the centre of the octagon, "we have a table. A round table, so she can make the most of the light. She can move as the sun moves."

"Ah, yes," the company nodded.

"At the end of each bookcase, we could have more shelves, or drawers, for more books, or to store paper or whatever. I could change that for her, if she states a preference once she has worked in there for a while." He brought his free hand to his mouth and absentmindedly stroked a finger across his lips. "Against one of the eight walls, we'll have a fireplace, so Anna can be warm in the winter. Each of the eight sections will be large enough for a chair and another smaller desk. Perhaps there will be monks willing to scribe in return for...oh, whatever, I'll think of something. Blanchland should be able to offer a few educated hands. A new monastic order will be eager to associate itself with the neighbouring communities. We could exchange a few ideas." His brow creased a little as his thoughts unravelled.

"If she doesn't insist on doing it all herself. She's far too headstrong." Ben shook his head, although his expression did not look as sorry as his words implied.

"Once she sees all the empty shelves, she might accept help in filling them," offered Will helpfully.

Bran smiled at his optimism. "Yes. And if we are doing this because we have faith in her ability to produce something impressive, we need to allow a lot of space so it can grow." He paused, looking at the paper again. "We'll have a high ceiling." He slid what he had drawn thus far to one side so that he now looked down on another blank area. "There will be galleries - broad ones - so that books can also stand on a second floor...which will also have windows. We will build in stairs so she can easily access the whole collection." Bran stopped. He quickly scribbled a question in the top right hand corner of the paper: "Ways of lifting texts? Pulleys? A wheel between floors?" He then allowed himself to come back to the main drawing. "We'll have another fireplace above the one on the ground floor. This building will fight off even the coldest winter weather."

His hands moved quickly now and the enthusiasm in his voice was growing. The men could tell that Bran could now actually see, and move about in, the idea he was creating. Marc smiled as he watched this labour of love.

"Sometimes, she'll simply want to enjoy this place, with no thought of working. To read for pleasure rather than for learning. Up here, we can have an area near the fire. We can extend the gallery at this point so that it fits a more comfortable seat. The platform will be high enough for her to see from a large window here" - he drew a dotted line diagonally opposite the fireplace to the outer wall and shaded the area the window would occupy - "She should be able to see right down into the valley from here, but no one will be able to see her. She'll enjoy perfect privacy." Bran straightened to rid himself of the ache in his back and looked at his work. The pottage remained half eaten. "Now for the aesthetics." He pointed to the large window in the diagram. He said nothing. It was almost as if the action of pointing would suggest the idea. He gave his mind time to imagine, scribbling a few simple tree shapes in the area outside the window. He thought aloud. "Because we have brought out the gallery floor to here, to make it a larger space, a larger space will also be created beneath - by the pillars supporting the floor above. She can feel more enclosed there. We could even create walls of books to make it the warmest area in the winter. It would still be large enough to entertain friends - to talk about what has been read or written, or even just sit for an idle chat.... or not so idle, knowing Anna." Marc did not have to see his friend's face to know that he was smiling. "The six windows will be enough to send light to the centre of the room, but, when she is lost in her writing, she won't stop work once the light grows dim or the sun moves to a less convenient position..." he paused. "Ha!"

The others jumped.

"What?" asked Will rather perturbed.

"A glass ceiling: it will allow light to fall straight down."

"You can do that?" asked Joss, amazed.

"Yes, with a little thought. It could work on the same principle as a portcullis - they are only wood in an iron wrapping after all. Either that or stone tracework. It's the other windows that may be more difficult to design without Anna knowing about the project. I was thinking that we could design the windows in such a way that some of her favourite things were captured in the trace work - you know, something like a book, or a scene from the Arthurian tales, but..." he looked at Ben. "It makes me realise how long it is since I was here. I'm not really sure what her favourite things are anymore." He looked at Marc. "Maybe Susan could help with that."

Marc nodded. "She would be happy to help, although you might do better."

Bran threw him a questioning glance.

"We are all so happy to see you back and Anna has kept notes of things she would like to discuss with you. You asked her to keep a book of thoughts, so she has produced several. There is bound to be something in there that shows you the secret Anna."

Bran looked at Ben, who was nodding. "He is right. She won't divulge anything to anyone else. It's for your eyes only. I have a horrible feeling that we are all in there - warts and all." Ben suddenly brightened. "I have an idea! Tomorrow we could go hunting. If we can gain permission from our overlord of course."

Bran grinned, "Granted."

"After a rousing morning, we can feast in the safer part of the forest. She will expect us to do something a little different to celebrate your return, so she should not grow suspicious. Robert always organises these feasts so well. We'll ask Anna, Susan, Robert and the servants to meet for the feast at a particular time. It'll be the perfect time for conviviality and talk."

The idea met with approval.

"We'll make sure you have some time to speak a little way from us," said Joss, "to allow her to confide in you." Like Susan, he had noticed Bran's demeanour when he spoke of Anna.

Ben added a cautionary note, "I feel your only problem will be transforming her favourite things into some sort of solid or symbolic form: most of her favourite things are ideas - or views perhaps."

Marc watched Bran's face looking for clues as to how he felt about the idea of being allowed time to speak with Anna alone, but his friend was inscrutable. Robert returned with more ale and rush dips to light the table. Ben loved these ideas, but was beginning to feel a little uncomfortable at the cost implications. Bran routinely designed for very wealthy men in the East. If this building was to live up to the idea, it was going to need the best quality craftsmen and materials. It would stretch his purse to the limits.

Bran sat back, his head to one side. For now he was satisfied with the way things were taking shape. He stood up and moved to the doorway to view the proposed site. He stepped out into the evening. It was far lighter outdoors than in, even though the sky was turning from its earlier pale blue to pink. The birds still sang clearly above the stream that ran noisily past the house on his left. For once, there was no breeze. He loved it here. He turned to the others, smiling. "I can see it already," he said.

Joss was studying the octagon. "These shelves," he said, tapping a finger at the sheet where the shelves ran like spokes from the outer rim towards the centre of the room. "How will you ensure their stability? It would be a shame to spread papers and rolls inconveniently just to balance the weight."

Bran re-entered. "I intend to put something at their top shelf near the centre: something that will enable them to pivot. He became animated again " - through three hundred and sixty degrees if she wishes it. At intervals, she can stop the motion so she can create different shaped rooms within the larger space. Look! If all of these shelves have the ability to pivot....." he drew pale lines with arrows, "look how many variations she could have. She could even have several scribes, with a private work area for each and still more than enough room for herself. I'll give it more thought - I'm sure I can think of something that will suit the purpose more closely."

"Now that," said Ben, "would suit Anna beautifully. She is so restless - always complaining that women have to put up with the same old walls. I know it's not quite what she meant, but at least it is some variation."

There was a gentle knock at the inner door. Silence fell over the men. Marc stood to answer it. His son, Richard, was on the other side, looking a little anxious. "Anna's on her way," he whispered.

The drawing was rolled up and hidden once more and the men picked up their ales and stools and carried them out into the rosy-but-darkening evening air. Bran, manners impeccable as always, held back to allow the older men through first. Marc stood next to him as the others bickered and shoved their way through the doorway.

The two younger men smiled at each other. "They taught us everything we know!" Marc whispered, donning a worried expression.

"When did they grow so wonderfully cantankerous with each other?" Bran asked.

"Oh, it was a gradual process, "Marc surmised. "It will be more obvious to you because you haven't seen them for a while. It's hard to imagine that Will can still break a man's neck more quickly than he can down a small cup of mead."

He looked a little more closely at Bran as his friend glanced at the inner door then away, having heard Anna's footsteps. "Will you tell her?" he asked.

"No, of course not," replied Bran. "It would spoil the surprise."

"I'm not talking about the library."

Bran looked back at him, head on one side.

"Oh, all right. Don't tell me," laughed Marc. "Just don't throw me that 'I'm not with you' look." And he went outside to join the rest.

Bran looked after him. Was it that obvious? He followed after, trying to focus on the solution to telling Ben that he would pay for the building costs in a way that would not offend him.

Chapter Ten

Darkening Skies

Good conversation and too much Redgate ale made the small company forgetful of the darkness and its accompanying chill, so that they sat in the dusk for quite some time, with only the light from the fire indoors and a few rush dips, which Robert had brought out unnoticed, dimly illuminating their faces. Bran's return could not have been better timed. Not only had so many old friends decided to descend on Redgate all at once, but news of a threat from William in Scotland had made Joss wary and he felt that now he had one of his strongest men back in England, he could relax a little. He knew Henry took it for granted that the Northern would be loyal -but loyalty was only useful if the men behind it were strong.

Light thrown from the doorway made a shadow play of the company. The older friends grinned as Will stroked his full stomach. "I love the time leading up to Lent," he exhaled dreamily. "I must say, it's rather good of you to time your return so well, Bran."

The others nodded their agreement.

"It must be three months since I visited Ben here and Joss at the same time..." he turned to look at his old friend, who had stood to allow Susan to pass back into the house with a tired little boy in her arms. "How long is it since we were all together properly? For entertainment, I mean, not business."

Joss resumed his seat and smiled at Bran. "Over a year," he answered.

"Umm," Ben nodded, taking another sip of ale. "For the wedding."

"The wedding?" Bran questioned. He could not guess whose.

"Oh, of course!" Will exclaimed. "You will not have been told, because Lord Discretion would not want it passing from country to country that he had remarried." Will grinned as he cut himself a generous helping of game, deliberately trying to keep Bran in the dark.

"Oh, come on Will, tell me who married."

Will was quite prepared to spin it out in order to see what guesses Bran would make, but his fun was curtailed by a rebuke from Joss. "Oh for goodness sake, man!" snapped Joss. "It was me, Bran."

Bran looked across at his mentor's face, hardly able to make out his features in the shadows. "Congratulations!" he said, rather falteringly.

Everyone laughed. Even Joss. "Is it that much of a surprise that a woman would agree to marry me?"

"No, of course not. I just imagined ...well... I don't really know why I am shocked. In fact, the more I think of it, the more I see you are the obvious choice. Yes," he added weakly, "Lord Discretion: I ought to have guessed." He glanced around him. "Where is your wife?"

"She'll be here tonight. She should have finally rid herself of kin who only intended to stay until twelfth night, but who decided that the North offered far more than they'd realised."

"Do I know her?"

"You may have heard of her. She's an excellent horsewoman. It's how we met. She accused me of trying to cheat her out of an excellent mare for a derisory price, which I was of course."

They grinned.

"You still ended up with far more than you bargained for," smiled Will.

Joss smiled. "She'll join us for the hunt tomorrow, I'm sure. Although I hope she isn't travelling in the dark...I'd prefer that she was late rather than putting herself..." as if thinking of her had summoned her, the sound of hooves broke into his sentence. The men faced the small but noisy band of travellers who approached the house and stood as one to welcome them. It was obvious from their laughter and breathless calls to their horses that they had been racing each other. A dark haired, olive-skinned lady, veil now hanging limply over her shoulders and riding astride her horse, began to climb down even before her mount had stopped. It was hard to determine her age. Bran was useless at that sort of thing anyway. He felt she could have been anything between twenty-five and forty. Even in the dim light, her black courser's coat shone. Joss crossed the grass to meet her and she allowed herself to be lifted down, even though it was obvious that she needed no help in reaching the ground.

"At last!" she laughed, looking up into his face, "I thought they would never go home. We have not stopped during the whole journey just so we could be here tonight rather than arrive in the morning." Joss held her closely; twenty years younger in an instant. He introduced his wife's brothers and father. Their colouring and accents suggested that they were of French descent. He and his wife then turned to the politely waiting company. "You have met everyone here before, except for Bran."

Bran stepped forward and bowed his head politely. "This is a pleasant surprise." He became aware of the fact that he did not know her name and tried to cover this by adding. "I apologise that my congratulations are late. I can see you are very happy."

She smiled her thanks. "I am so pleased to meet you at last. There isn't a day that passes without your name being mentioned in our home."

Thomas came out of the house. "The tables are set, Sir."

"Ah, excellent timing!" announced Will, obviously feeling that his stomach was now ready to take more food.

They filed into the house, all in good spirits, while Thomas' son, John, saw to the newcomers' four horses.

Bran held back to allow Anna to enter just ahead of him. Quietly, he whispered, "Anna."

She stopped and looked up at him.

"Can you help me? I have no idea what Joss's wife is called."

She smiled and stood on tip toe to be able to speak in his ear.

"Adela," she said and stepped back to see his reaction. "She doesn't look like an Adela does she?"

He grinned and whispered back, "More of a Diana."

The room seemed to have shrunk with so many people in it. The tables groaned under the weight of so much food and Will's ecstatic voice was heard to proclaim yet again how much he loved the time leading up to Lent. The feasting and laughing filled the room, while outside the horses crunched on their oats, twitching their ears at the occasional guffaw from Ben, who was truly happy to be in such good company. They spoke of hunting, pilgrims, voyages, where the energetic King Henry could be now, his planned pilgrimage and penance at Canterbury, illnesses, the strength of the ale at Redgate, weddings, until, eventually, the company began to disperse to various parts of the house. Will would share Ben's chamber, although Ben warned that he'd better not keep up that damned snoring like the previous night. Marc, Susan and the children had already found space in the downstairs room along the passage - the room where Anna had been born. Ben had told Bran that he was welcome to make up a bed in front of the fire downstairs - the warmest room in the house - if he did not mind waiting for Anna to stop reading by the light of the fire before he got any sleep. Bran realised how much Ben trusted him with his daughter. He wondered if that was because the older man did not consider it feasible that there could ever be more than a platonic relationship between the two of them. Adela's male relatives had come equipped with tents and drunkenly insisted on using them. Luckily, their less drunken Squires had erected them while there was still some light to see by. Joss and Adela had volunteered to sleep in the upper storey of the barn, which had surprised Bran as Joss was the biggest land holder in the company, but no-one protested and the couple seemed strangely happy with the arrangement.

Before each dispersed, Joss asked that they would stay a little while longer - he wished to speak more seriously of plans he wished to make to safeguard the north from William in Scotland while Henry sorted out the rebellion in France. The women were not excluded from the planning: after all, what affected the men would eventually affect the women and children, but the men drew their stools together in a tighter circle so that they could speak more quietly.

Joss, aware of his wife's gaze, began. "The King's family are rebelling yet again. Eleanor and her sons' disloyalty is nothing new, but this time the threat is greater. Henry realises this." Joss looked at Bran. "The younger Henry has gone to France to negotiate with Louis. Eleanor had intended to follow, but the king has detained her, having no intention of being ousted by her former husband. William of Scotland and Henry's eldest have also been colluding. On top of this, our forces need to be split. While the Princes are planning to visit Paris, there are those in England who are behaving as if Henry is already beaten. Only this morning I heard that Norfolk, Leicester and Derby have declared for the younger Henry."

Bran's brow creased and he shook his head. He wondered what could be in it for the rebels. Each would be expecting a share of land; how much could they expect when it involved so many?

"And what is more," Joss looked to Bran again, "Edwin's youngest, Alric, has suddenly raised his head again."

Bran hid his feelings and simply asked, "Are we ready for a fight?"

Joss gave a quick nod. "I dare say we will be fitter than they - although I would like to see us at our peak. It may put them off trying again later. I've been rallying the Knights, from within and without the Order and we should easily outnumber their forces, in spite of Pudsey remaining neutral and a few barons showing allegiance to the Princes. Obviously, we'll be better skilled - whether looking at combat man to man or strategic thinking." Joss said this with no air of arrogance. The Northern prided themselves in always going a few steps beyond what was needed.

Joss continued, "I know you train on a daily basis, but I want us to restart the more arduous preparations that make us fighting fit."

Quietly, Will's heart sank.

Joss was the wonder of the Order. At fifty, he still seemed to be at the peak of fitness. Rumours amongst the superstitious spoke of his invulnerability, even immortality, because God secretly sided with his mother after her rape. She had been declared guilty of seduction by the Church and given the choice of execution or banishment. To her, one seemed as bad as the other. The story went that she prepared herself a potion and took her own life, but not before learning the secrets of reincarnation. What these secrets were and who taught them remained vague, but there were those who were convinced that she had learned how to step out of purgatory and into another life, so by association, her son was allowed the same legendary status. Many, superstitious or not, assumed he was ageless. "This may all blow over," he said, with a casual wave of his hand, "but there is no harm in being prepared."

"There are already prototype siege engines at Drysdale," offered Bran. "I can restart tests and build the best here too - although I'd prefer it if the trouble did not come so close."

Bran thought further. "Do we know Alric's position on this rebellion or whether Edwin is likely to become involved? He knows the King has no trust in him."

Joss answered. "I am waiting for him to make the first move. If he is still alive, I am quite sure that he will side with whoever seems to be the stronger - even if that means changing loyalties midway. I imagine that at first, he will say he sides with the King and, therefore, the Northern. He will probably approach us as allies. However, if William and the Younger Henry seem strong - or worse - if it seems they only need one more ally to win, I feel Edwin will change his mind, and a defeat would leave us landless after the troubles."

"And worse," brooded Ben. "The Princes seem as selfish as he. I imagine there would be little sympathy for those who did not join the rebellion in the event of our defeat. Our unlikely defeat," he added, smiling at Anna.

"How strong is he?" asked Marc.

"Impossible to say as yet. Certainly, the men old enough to remember how bad things were under Stephen would be reluctant to fight against Henry. They would see the benefits in maintaining the status quo. What about Drysdale? Would your people be willing to block a possible advance?"

Bran considered. "We are healthy and strong enough." Bran's predicament was unique. He was not a Lord who could insist that those dwelling on his land did as he said. He had always fulfilled lordly duties to protect them, but his father had built up the community from an uninhabited, marshy wasteland, so none of the people now living there were tied to the land. They had come of their own free will and were free to leave whenever they wanted. "I'll speak to them. Remind them that their lifestyles would deteriorate rapidly should the Northern or the King be defeated."

Will nodded, more focused now that his mind was on battle rather than food.

"This has its advantages all round I'd say. We show our loyalty to the King - he will be grateful for our support - lighten some of the load - he's still reeling from Beckett. And should Edwin appear, we can start where we left off eight years ago. Then of course, should Edwin try anything underhand, we finally have an excuse to be rid of him once and for all. If he goes against us, he goes against the King."

Again, the company nodded. Bran thought how his years of absence had done nothing to rid him of his old troubles. He spoke. "I suggest that at any hint of trouble the Redgate community should come to Drysdale. You are not well protected here." He looked at Anna, who looked at her father for a response. She loved Drysdale.

"I think you are right." Ben nodded.

Bran continued, "At the next opportunity, I'll request permission from the King to fortify Redgate. It may be the ideal time."

Ben knew it made sense. He also realised that his suggested deadline for the completion of the library was very probably too optimistic.

Joss clapped his hands, breaking the grim mood. "For tonight, let's think no further than tomorrow and the hunt." He drained the last of his ale. "No need to mar a welcome home party completely. Besides, hunting is a good way of sharpening skills needed in battle." The rest of the company raised their cups to Bran and finished their drinks too.

Susan and Mark left the company first, on hearing a baby cry. Next was Will, who said he still needed the sleep of a man less than half his age, as if this was a quality that proved his youthfulness. Joss and Adela left with her brothers, suddenly leaving the room much emptier. Anna read by the fire.

A number of Squires were hidden in the trees around the perimeter of the house, just in case. Thomas had seen to Seer and the hounds and was making his final preparations for the hunt before allowing himself to go to his rest.

Ben stretched and yawned. "Will the hearth suffice, Bran?"

"Of course." Bran stood to wish him goodnight. "I'm not tired yet. I think my mind is confused after the long journey. It seems like a week since I arrived in port this morning." He looked down at Anna, who now sat curled on her bench near the glowing ashes. "Are you away to your bed, or shall I have company if I stay awake a while longer?"

"I can stay," she smiled.

"Oh yes, she can stay," agreed Ben, wandering to the narrow stairs. "She often pretends to retire to her chamber to sleep, but eavesdroppers hear the turning of pages well past the middle of the night."

Anna grinned and stood to hug her father, "Goodnight."

"Goodnight to you both." At the door he turned and looked at them both fondly. "It is so good to have you back, Bran. If there is anything you need, remember Janet or Thomas will be more than happy to see to it. They know what a long journey you have had."

"I'm content," Bran smiled. The older man left the room.

Bran moved his stool so that he sat opposite Anna and looked into the embers. He bent forward and lifted one or two lighter sticks from the hearth to liven the fire a little. When he sat up, Anna was looking at him.

"It's hard to believe you're really here. You've been a memory for so long and then you just appear."

"A good memory I hope."

They smiled at each other. Half of her face was lit by the low fire, her hair turned to red by its glow. Her eyes were large and dark in the dim light.

"When I'm away, I miss Redgate more than Drysdale. Drysdale takes up my business thoughts, but it's Redgate I think of as home," he said. "I'm hoping it'll be a long time before I'm required to leave England again."

"You miss Redgate more? Even though you've made Drysdale such a wonderland of ...invention? Don't we seem boring to you after your travels?"

"Boring?" he laughed. "No. People are more important than places. Inventions only come about because of people's needs and desires. Besides, boring is good. It can only exist when we feel safe."

Thomas knocked and entered. "Forgive me, Sir. I took the liberty of unsaddling your horse and thought you might like your bags."

Bran took them from him. "Thank you. I had forgotten them." He placed the bag at his feet and Thomas left for his bed.

"Where is your favourite place?" Anna asked him.

"Favourite place in the whole world?" he queried.

She nodded.

He considered. Various images and memories crossed his mind. "There are several." He then stood, crossed the room and opened the door. A cool draught met him. He beckoned that she should stand by him in the doorway. She did so and he pointed into the darkness. He bent his head deliciously close to hers so that she could follow his line of vision. "It can't be seen right now, but that is my favourite place. The grassy ledge at the top of a steep climb. It makes a comfortable resting place when you want to hide from the world awhile."

She looked up at him, disbelievingly. "Are you teasing me?"

He shook his head.

"Where I met you today?"

"Umm, truly," he nodded. "From there I can see moorland, forest, river, sky and the rooftops. And I hear all the sounds that they bring: like an amphitheatre. It's a strange paradox - to be so close to people and yet part of something so much bigger. And yet it feels safe up there. Insular. Thomas carried me from there when I first came to Redgate as a young boy."

"You mean out of all the places you have seen in the world, your favourite place is within a stone's throw of our house?"

He nodded again. "I'm not teasing you," he smiled down at her. "Although I do have more than one favourite place. Like the trace room at Drysdale. Just before I left, I had the water diverted to keep the reservoir filled. Now, the water casts dancing lights onto the walls and roof. When I was away, I often pictured myself sitting there. You should come to visit me there one day."

Anna pictured it and smiled. "I would like that."

"What about you? What are your favourite places?"

Anna thought. She shrugged slightly and shook her head. "I really don't know. I like lots of places and I love Drysdale."

Bran felt something very pleasant move in his chest. He wondered if she realised that Drysdale could be taken to refer to the man as well as the land. "What do you love about Drysdale?"

"The way it looks and feels like a dreamworld... an enchanted place. So many beautiful trees and falls - and they are repeated over in the reflections from the lakes. And then, there are the enormous engines - so incongruous that they give the place a feeling of the fantastical." She grinned at him. "There is no definitive line between what is real and what is not. It's a place where the imagination can slip anchor. And everyone at Drysdale seems so happy of course. There's an atmosphere that is so cheering."

"You know, that's what the King noticed on his first visit. He said he ought to move in. Fortunately, it was just one of his little jokes."

Anna giggled at Bran's discomfort at the memory. "I heard he likes these little jokes. Is it true that he used to ride his horse up to Beckett's dining table and vault onto his seat waiting to be fed?"

Bran nodded. "He did that at Drysdale too. Just the once. I don't think he saw the irony of holding a discussion about healthy diet while his horse kept slobbering over the diners' bowls."

"What did you do?" Anna's eyes were sparkling at the picture Bran was creating.

"Ignored it politely of course. He is King after all. But, we were talking about you, not Henry. Your favourite places."

"Yes, we were," she concurred. "Well, apart from Drysdale, I feel I am happy anywhere. My favourite places are where I happen to be at the time, I suppose. Like now."

Bran looked at her admiringly as she turned to go back to the warmth of the fire. He followed her. "Now that is true contentment. Being happy in your own skin."

"Um," she nodded, pleased with the conclusion. "Although I used to be quite dissatisfied. I was always comparing what I was permitted to do or be with what a man was allowed to achieve. A recipe for disappointment."

"What changed your mood?"

She looked to the fire. "I realised that I was never going to wake up one morning and find I had transformed into a man, so I would have to make the best of it." She looked up at him. "To be honest, the main reason is that Susan told me to stop moaning - to compare myself with other women - then I would see how fortunate I was. And she was right." She closed her book in her lap and rested her hands upon it. "I think I would make a rather mediocre man, at best," she grinned, "but as a woman I've come to realise that I'm rather ..." She shrugged slightly and looked about her as if searching for the right word.

Bran gazed at her. "Special?" he offered.

She looked at him aghast, some colour coming to her face. "No, no," she protested. "I was trying to find a word closer to spoilt. I know my father allows me to do as I wish, as long as household duties are not neglected. And," she smiled across at him, "having a Godfather who encourages me and sends me teachings that very few men have access to." She petered out, feeling that she was talking too much.

"You're very special to the two of us. And from what your father tells me, you are certainly more than a match for any man I know - mediocre or otherwise."

She blushed again and looked down at her hands.

Bran thought it best to change the subject. A wave of paranoia made him wonder if Ben was listening to the conversation through the floorboards. Bran sat down and reached into the bag at his feet. He felt about inside then pulled something out, holding it towards her. "Guess who!" he grinned.

She leaned forward for a closer look, then laughed. "Woolly! You still have him after all this time?"

"Of course. I don't part with gifts given so generously." He pointed to Woolly's head. "See. He has the same amount of eyes he left with. Although I have to say, it's becoming a little embarrassing at tournaments. Thank goodness Henry has banned jousts in this country - I don't think I could live it down if I had to sport him over here."

She smiled. "Is there a lady who could offer you her sleeve as a replacement to Woolly?"

He shook his head. "No." He smiled, trying to discern how interested she was in his relationships with women, but she was either completely innocent or completely inscrutable.

"Father wondered whether you would be married by now."

"He did?"

She nodded. "Um. I think he worries about you."

He smiled. "And marriage would make him worry less?"

"Yes. He thinks you need an heir."

"He has no need to worry. I would like to marry."

"You know someone?" Anna was curious.

"Oh yes. She is as close to me as it is possible to be."

Anna put her head to one side, not wanting to seem overly curious about Bran's private life. "Has she come with you?"

Bran grinned. "I suppose you could say she is always with me, seeing as though she is a figment of my imagination."

"Oh." Anna seemed disappointed. "You are teasing me now. Is there no lady?"

"Who can say? Maybe she does exist. Maybe I'll never find out."

"Well, maybe I could help." Anna was warming to the banter. "What is this imaginary lady like? I may know of a real lady who would be willing to take her place - although she may prefer you to carry her in your heart rather than your mind."

"I would hope she would like to be carried in heart and mind - if she is the woman I have created."

Anna was curious to know more, but a strange noise made her pause. They both looked a little startled. It came again. She gave a relieved sigh. "It's Will snoring."

Bran laughed. "I'd forgotten the sound. It's always louder when he has a full stomach. Which is nearly always."

She smiled. "Poor father. How is he so fit and slender?"

"Goodness knows. Janet always said he must have worms."

They laughed.

The opportunity for talking of his ideal woman slipped away.

"Are you looking forward to the hunt tomorrow?"

"Oh yes," she replied. "Robert always provides such a wonderful feast."

"Will you ride with us?"

"Father doesn't like me too. He says there is only one of me so I ought to be careful."

"Quite right."

"Although I would quite like to bring my hawk."

"Perhaps you could bring your journal. Ben says you have something for me."

She blushed again. "I wish I hadn't been so outspoken about it now. Now that you are here, I feel quite silly. It's nothing special. Just thoughts."

He smiled. "Thoughts are special. Show me when you feel comfortable. Or leave them with me and I'll read them when I'm alone. However you like." He gave a gesture with both palms upturned. "I'll be here or at Drysdale for some time now."

She smiled at him warmly, "I'm glad you're back. I've missed you."

"And I you."

She stood up to take her leave of him, forgetting about her book, which fell to the floor. They both stooped to pick it up. Her hair brushed against his face and he felt a wave of pleasure tingle through him.

She took the book from him and placed it on the trestle table. It was so hard to judge how she felt about him, even without worrying how he ought to feel about her. "Do you have everything you need? Is there anything I can do to make you more comfortable?"

He shook his head. "I'm perfectly happy." And he was.

She looked up at him and smiled. "I'm so glad you're back with us." She looked so happy that he instinctively gave her a hug, feeling almost fatherly towards her. She spoke while her head rested against his chest. "I promise I won't speak so much tomorrow."

"I hope it's a promise you don't keep. I like talking with you."

She stepped back from him and smiled.

"Goodnight, Bran."

He put his hands on her shoulders and kissed her brow. "Goodnight, Anna. Sweet dreams." And she left him standing there, wondering how he was going to deal with his feelings for her. And what Ben would think.

As he made up a bed on the longer bench near the fire, he almost tripped over his bag. He realised he had forgotten to give her the length of coloured silk he had carried all the way back from Spain for her. Still, maybe it was for the best. He would have a good excuse to ask her if he could take a piece so he could be seen wearing his lady's colours -or something. He shook his head a few times to clear his mind and focus on preparing for sleep. The room was warm. He pulled his gown and his chemise over his head but decided to leave the leggings. He put out the remaining candles and settled down in the firelight, still feeling the motion of the boat beneath his back. As he turned to make himself comfortable for the night, his eyes rested on the book that she had left lying on the table. He wondered if she had meant to. Was it her journal? Or was it simply some other writing that interested her? He wondered whether he should get up and take a look. Perhaps this was her way of letting him read her thoughts without it being too obvious, making it less of a risk to her pride. He decided he would take a glance.

Upstairs, Anna fumbled her way to her bedside in the dark. Her fire had been lit, but the red glow was very weak by now. She had not thought to bring up a candle. It was not until she was seated and was in the process of removing her shoes that she realised she had left her book behind. She wondered whether she should retrieve it. She did not want to disturb Bran after his hard journey. Then again, it was only a short while since she had left the room. He would hardly have had time to make up a bed, let alone fall into a sleep. She bit her bottom lip. Should she or shouldn't she? It was not important that she have it tonight. She was tired and wanted to sleep. And the book was not one she had promised to show him - just an old favourite that she had often read as a little girl -Arthurian tales. But she would be embarrassed if he looked at the leaves in the back of the book. When younger, she had drawn a heart around his name. Later, she had wondered whether to smudge it away with water and her thumb, but the ink was made from an oak gall of good biting quality and the design would be still quite discernible to anyone who cared to look.

The more she thought about it, the more of an issue it seemed. She decided she would go and fetch it. She did not want him to see it. He might laugh at her - he was renowned for his manners, but even he might find it amusing that one of his vassals had doted on him in such a childish way.

She made her tentative way back down the stairs. She would knock quietly so that if he was sleeping she would not disturb him, but if he was still awake, she would be able to complete her task.

Just as Bran reached the table and picked up the book, Anna knocked gently. He gave a guilty start and set the book down again. "Come in."

Anna entered. She was taken aback to see him standing half naked in the middle of the room and muttered a hasty apology.

"I didn't want to disturb you. I came back for my book."

Bran became aware of the cause for her embarrassment and stood a little awkwardly. He picked up the book again, as if seeing it for the first time and walked across to her. Noticing her discomfort, he gave her a disarming smile as he handed it to her.

They both began to talk simultaneously and then laughed, awkwardly. She turned to go and stopped at the door to say goodnight. He was still smiling at her, his head to one side. She felt reassured enough to joke with him. " Isabelle of Stanmere would give her right arm to swap places with me."

He gave a wry smile. "I would rather you took mine."

She smiled and he was not sure whether she had taken his hint. "Goodnight again."

"Goodnight, Anna. Sleep well."

She left him again. It wasn't long after she reached her bed that she fell into a deep sleep. She dreamt of Bran fighting half naked against the Picts. Bran, however, did not fall asleep for some time. He could not take his mind off her. He wondered whether she could love him and, even if she could, whether religion would be an issue. Or her safety. His mother, Margery, Catherine - all the women he had loved were wrenched away from him. What if he brought the same bad luck to Anna? And she was so young. He was prepared to wait, but what if others approached her in the mean time?

After a while he stopped torturing himself and tried to imagine what it would be like if there were no problems in the way. He could not sleep for thinking of her. He had set out on his journey from port over a day ago, but still he could not sleep. He wondered about the hunt and whether she would want to speak to him about her favourite things as her father and Marc had suggested. He thought he would eventually drift off to sleep, but his mind and, admittedly, his libido would not let him go. It did not help that he could hear Marc and Susan making love now that Will's snoring had ceased. He sat up and glanced around the room for a distraction. His mug of ale lay unfinished on the hearth. He did not usually drink more than one cup of Redgate ale as it was so strong, but tonight he would make an exception. He reached for the cup and downed it quickly then lay back. After a short time, he heard hooves outside. He would have been alarmed but he heard Joss urging on the mount that he and Adela shared. He guessed they would be going for a midnight ride so they could be out of earshot. He wished Marc and Susan could quieten it down a little. Good God. He sometimes felt like he was the only man in the world who wasn't lying with a woman. He turned over, trying to dispel his bad humour by lying with his hands over his ears.

Upstairs, Anna slept soundly, her dreams influenced by the sounds of the house. Now she rode behind Bran as he fought. Danger was all around, but she felt safe, enjoying the feel of his bare skin.

Bran resorted to thinking of a way to create a device that would serve the purpose of allowing the shelves for the new library to pivot while being strong enough to support their weight when fully laden with books. This seemed to do the trick. He became aware of the rocking motion in his blood again and his eyes became heavier as he finally fell into a slumber.

Chapter Eleven

The Hunt

Spring had painted a contrasting picture to the landscapes Bran had become accustomed to over recent years. Twenty shades of green surrounded the hunting party; wild garlic, sorrel and bluebells patched the forest floor; hooves otherwise cushioned by a thick, straw-coloured layer of Winter pine needles. Above them, the canopy emitted a green light, most of the leaves having stretched their way out of their budlike clumps to spread in the sun. The laughter and calls from Adela's brothers ricocheted from floor to canopy and back again, mingling with the birdsong from blackbirds and robins. Bran breathed in deeply. He absorbed every sound: the creak of leather as horsemen bent low to avoid branches; the dull thumps from hooves on the soft ground; the sound of his own breathing. There was something satisfyingly simple in the way the men had been temporarily stripped of their rank, and therefore responsibilities, by their earthy coloured hunting garb. Contentment flowed through his veins. He was glad he had returned. Perhaps he could have come home sooner after all. But he had found an acceptance of Judaism in Outremer that had lifted some of the guilt he had always felt when he thought of his father.

He took a deep breath, eager to savour his surroundings before the rest of the huntsmen arrived and the yelping of the hounds held sway. It was a bright and perfect morning for spending in cheerful company.

Adela had joined the men, while Anna and Susan, on seeing how fair the weather was, had decided to walk the mile from the house to the sheltered place Robert had chosen to stage his movable feast. Every time there was a hunt, some optimist told him there would be no need to provide a main meat dish because the hunt would yield all they needed. And every time the huntsmen returned to the feast: tired, hungry and in need of immediate gratification, they were pleased that he had ignored their instructions rather than beginning the cooking on their arrival. Susan put aside a spray of herbs she had collected en route and remarked, "It's good to know Bran is back safe and sound isn't it?"

Anna nodded and smiled.

Susan considered. "You probably remember him as all work no play." She spread a cover on the ground to protect them from the damp.

"Wasn't he considering marrying my aunt?" Anna asked.

Susan nodded. "Even though he hardly knew her. But, perhaps Bran knows exactly what he wants in a wife." She looked at Anna to see if she could read a reaction.

Anna thought back to the previous evening's conversation and Bran's imaginary lady.

Susan continued. "Anyway, it was doomed from the start. Poor lady met a horrible end."

"Did you know her?"

"Only for a short time."

"I asked father about it once. He seemed reluctant to talk. All that he would tell me was that she was murdered by her stepfather and that I wasn't to ask Bran about it."

Susan looked at her as they seated themselves. "He's right. I think he was protecting you. To know it would only have given you nightmares. Especially as her stepfather has never been caught and tried."

"Why is that?"

"He has never been found."

Anna had been planning to empty her bag of reading materials to pass her time, but she put these to one side as she pondered. "Men my father's age look back and say that the laws have improved people's lives in comparison to when they were young. They say that in Stephen and Matilda's time it would have been impossible to ride from one side of the country to the other without fear of being attacked as you can now. Yet this murderer is still roaming free."

"Edwin is a different kettle of fish. He calculates. He plans things well in advance so that he can influence events without seeming to have any involvement in them. It is thought he was responsible for the murders of Bran's parents too."

Anna thought more deeply now and her sympathies were more readily evoked. She could not really identify with the loss of one to whom she was betrothed, but losing her father would be unthinkable.

Still, she could not help some logical thought shaping her words: she was a daughter of the Northern after all.

"So really, Edwin and Bran have a lot in common."

Susan felt a pang of shock at the statement. "What a thing to say."

"What I mean is they both plan. They both calculate in order to solve a problem. They both see ideas through in logical ways. The thing that sets them apart is their morals. Bran's humanity and Edwin's lack of it. Bran's logic benefits everyone. I assume Edwin's only benefits himself." Her brow creased as she rationalised. "What exactly did Edwin hope to gain?"

Susan thought. "There is no easy answer anymore. At first, I suppose it was land and rents. Then, once he had started to commit crimes, he needed to continue in order to cover his tracks. I think he killed Catherine, and your grandmother, because they knew enough to incriminate him."

"If he was found now, would there be enough evidence to condemn him?"

"Oh yes. It's all documented. Even the items used or found by the bodies have been retained. They are in Durham under the Prince Bishop's protection. Henry would not allow anyone of lower rank to oversee the case to decrease the risk of bribery."

Anna hugged her knees. "Would it follow that anyone involved as a witness on those occasions is still likely to be in danger as Edwin has never been apprehended?"

Susan felt cold gooseflesh spread across her skin. This was not what she had intended. She tried to switch the course of the conversation. "If he is still alive, of course. It seems odd that he could have disappeared without a trace, especially with Joss on his heels. Bran once told Marc that he thought of himself as the common denominator in all the misfortunes that had happened to those around him. I suppose that is his logical way of calling himself a jinx."

"I wonder if now he's back, he'll be able to see things in a different light."

"You never know. Perhaps he will find someone who will make him glad he decided to come back."

Anna smiled. "Last night he told me he had an imaginary lady in his head." She raised a conspiratorial eyebrow. "He's looking for her."

Susan's mouth became an O of surprise. "He must feel close to you to confide about his feelings in such a way."

Anna frowned self-consciously. "You don't think he meant me to keep it a secret do you?"

Susan considered. "How much did he tell?"

Anna thought back, "Not much. Will began to snore and we lost track of the conversation."

Susan shook her head. "No harm then. Although, I imagine if he returned and knew we had been discussing it, he might be a little embarrassed. Men don't often share their feelings – well," she reconsidered, "their good feelings. It would seem the two of you have a special relationship all of your own."

Anna looked at her. "What do you mean?"

"Well, you have set down your thoughts for him as he asked. Only he is allowed to see them. And when you were born, he promised to keep you safe. That's special, wouldn't you say?"

Anna pondered. "He was so considerate when he realised I was embarrassed about what I have written for him."

Susan decided to play Devil's advocate. "Why? Are your papers so shocking?" she grinned.

"No. But even I read them and cringe at how serious I was about silly things when I was younger. I don't think I could possibly let him read them now without spending at least an afternoon explaining myself."

"Well, today is your chance. Bran has always preferred good talk to good ale, so I expect he'll be eager to chat with you in some quiet corner."

Susan had wished to judge Anna's reaction to this, but several people; her own brother, mother and father included; suddenly appeared, pink, panting and laden, from the undergrowth. After a little initial bickering, trestles were dressed with linen, dishes, pewter ware – in fact anything usually associated with grand dining indoors. John surveyed the area and began a fire in what he considered to be the safest place. Before long, a train of pages arrived with foodstuffs to be prepared. A sense of duty stirred the two young women, who struggled to their feet to help. Within a couple of hours the aroma of Robert's beautifully prepared food spread through the forest.

Susan took a deep breath, her stomach rumbling appreciatively. "If this doesn't bring them back well before nightfall, I'll start to worry."

"Will won't allow it any other way."

Susan seated herself with baby Maud and was immediately climbed upon by three of her other offspring. Anna smiled and commented, "Sometimes it seems as if children are simply roosting on you."

Come mid-afternoon, as predicted, the party returned, jubilantly as it turned out. Suddenly, the peaceful clearing was alive with bodies: human, equine and canine. The boar they had run to ground was an absolute monster. They had decided not to portion it until they reached the feast so that it could be done in a more ceremonious manner. Several hares were also dumped, rather less ceremoniously, at a spare table top.

Marc and Bran rode in together and sought Susan and Anna, who having saved themselves for the feast, escorted them as quickly and courteously as possible to the trestles so they could pick from their favourite dishes.

Soon the forest rang with talking, laughter and tall tales once more. As time passed and stomachs filled, the company moved to more comfortable seats of their own choosing around the forest floor. Joss and Adela joined Ben and Will, invited to share their jug of ale. Marc and Susan found a reason to join Susan's family.

Anna studied Bran as he reclined against a large chestnut trunk. His face was still slightly flushed from the morning's exertion. He looked at her and smiled a dreamily tired smile.

"You look very contented," she observed.

He nodded. "I am." He felt like he was swaddled in something warm and pleasant and, although physically tired through the hunt and a full belly, his mind felt alert and ready for good conversation. "Have you been here long?"

"Since the latter part of the morning. Susan and I decided to walk"

"Will you ride back with me?"

She was pleased he had offered. "Thank you."

"I need to talk to you." She looked a little perturbed, making him smile. "Nothing serious. It's just that out of all the people I said goodbye to eight years ago, you're the one who is likely to have changed the most. I have a lot of catching up to do. Since our conversation last night, I realise I can't continue to talk to you as if you are seven years old anymore."

She relaxed a little and made herself more comfortable by leaning against the same trunk. It provided ample space for both of them and they could share the same view of the company. "There's little to tell really. I'm much the same."

He smiled as he looked into the trees. "It's harder to see it for yourself."

She twisted a little to her side so she could study him more closely. "You can see a change?"

He looked at her, head to one side, smiling. "Well, yes, of course. On my way to Redgate yesterday, I imagined greeting my old friends, and tried to envisage our first words. I have to say that, quite foolishly, I imagined you would be a taller version of the same little girl. Perhaps you would pull on my sleeve, enquire after Woolly, and ask me if I would mind scolding Attercop the Cat for chasing squirrels."

Anna laughed, remembering how worried she had been.

"And then, when I did see you I didn't recognise you."

"You didn't?"

"No. Not until Marc said your name."

"Am I that changed?"

He grinned and nodded, "Oh yes."

He noticed Ben glancing across at them and decided to change the topic. Perhaps it was a good time to find out about her likes and dislikes as planned.

"Has your taste in books changed? You used to love the Arthurian Tales."

She shook her head. "Still do. Although the stories that are my favourites now are not necessarily the ones I favoured as a child. Perhaps you feel differently about characters as you learn more about the world. I also read more of medicine and philosophy now. It used to irritate me when I was younger – knowing there was something important in there but being put off the reading as soon as I came across a word I didn't understand."

"One day, I'd like to be able to treat people at Drysdale. Now I'm back, I suppose I can start to plan it more seriously."

"Could you really do that?"

Bran shrugged. "We have the know-how, although it may be safer to wait until the King's troubles are sorted out successfully. Then again," he said, remembering the difficulties Henry was having with his sons were nothing new, "we could carry on saying that forever. I met people overseas who said they would gladly stay for a while – so we have the benefit of experienced doctors. The only problem I can foresee is the attitude of some towards foreigners. People can be superstitious about medicine anyway, throw a different religion or two into the equation and people will assume the worst."

Anna considered. "Did your find your parents' influence a help when you were away? I mean, did it break down barriers or give rise to more?"

He sighed. The East had given him a greater freedom and it was hard to fence his ideas inside the old attitudes once again. "I know my parents were probably doing their free-thinking best. They had a complete acceptance of each other and so could not deny one part or the other in me. They probably meant well when they decided to let me choose one path or the other, but that's a lot of responsibility. They left me to deny one of them."

There was a pause as the enormity hit him now that he had spoken it aloud. He glanced at Anna. "Sorry. It isn't really the sort of conversation expected on a day like this. Do you mind?"

"Talking about problems can help to tame them. At least, I always find talking to Susan a help."

He smiled his agreement.

"It is a difficult problem to solve. Perhaps," she offered tentatively, not wishing to be presumptuous regarding her Landlord's parents, "just for the sake of exploring the argument and cutting it down to size, they were expecting you to treat religion like philosophy – study then choose – even come up with a hybrid and call it your own."

Bran latched onto her words. "Yes, exactly. But religion isn't a philosophy. It involves faith, belief, commitment and, hence, guilt. It makes us what we are." He considered then asked her, "Does belief in two Gods make me doubly committed or does one counteract the other leaving me with no commitment at all?" He became more animated as he thought. "Does seeing what they both have in common make me doubly certain of their underlying truths – as if they are different interpretations of the same God, or does it make me completely uncertain? Should I feel guilty for being singularly Godless or twice as pious for claiming more than one?"

She shook her head and smiled. "Ah, there you are again. Never pious. You punish yourself too much."

He shook his head and grinned. "I'm a poor Godfather. I should be mentoring *you*. Are there any worries or qualms I could help you to banish?"

She realised he was joking, but perhaps there was something. Her problem was so embarrassing; she hadn't even mentioned it to Susan. He guessed from her look that he had hit on something. He waited.

"Father is the only person who knows about this. Well, the only one amongst the present company. He said he would be discreet so the decision could be my own."

At certain times in his life, Bran had felt like he could read minds. One such time was when he was very young. His mother had asked him to stop his errands outside and to come into the house. She had asked him to sit down. She said she had something very important to say. Somehow, before she even began, Bran knew she was going to tell him that his father had died. Now he felt that same dread creeping into his chest.

Before speaking, Anna looked around self-consciously, to make sure they weren't overheard. "Someone has made a marriage proposal."

Bran covered his disappointment. "I thought you were going to say that."

"How could you?"

He tried to make light of it. "You look so disappointed."

She gave an uncomfortable smile.

"It's a little embarrassing."

"Why?" he grinned. "Is he ugly?"

She tried not to laugh. "I don't know." She shrugged. "I don't really have any interest in marriage. I know it's selfish, but I cannot really see how my life would take a turn for anything but the worse."

He smiled. "That would depend on the husband." He was beginning to feel more at ease. "It sounds to me like you already know the answer. You're embarrassed to talk about him and you think he would make you unhappy."

Anna nodded, still looking perplexed.

Bran continued. "When it's the right time you'll talk about him happily with others. In fact, you'll probably talk about him too much." He noticed she still seemed unsure. "What's troubling you, Anna? I cannot imagine that Ben would make you feel obliged to agree to a match that you did not want. I know a lot of fathers use their daughters' marriages to improve their families' status, but there's no need for that with the Northern."

She shook her head. "He mentioned it because he did not want to keep it from me, but has left the decision about meeting him to me." She sighed. "It's just that with this latest threat against Henry, especially with it being closer to home this time with Scotland being involved, if anything happened…well…you know." She was reluctant to plainly state her fears that Bran and her father's lives were at risk.

"You're worried you could be in the King's gift. Furthermore, you cannot be sure who the King would be if Henry was beaten. Either way, you could be married off to someone you loathe."

She gave a crooked smile and nodded. Bran sighed. "So at least considering this other fellow, you feel like you would be spreading your chances of …well, not happiness… escape? Not a good reason to marry."

He wondered whether to tell her how he felt, but dismissed this as a bad idea almost as soon as it came into his head. His instincts told her she was too young. In fact, it galled him that someone else should go blundering ahead when she was only fifteen. Besides, what if he told her how he felt and she rejected him? Would he ever enjoy this sort of intimacy with her again?

"Remember, you could end up in the King's gift even if you married the man of your dreams – except, if he was the sort of man your father and I would like you to marry, he would care enough about you to prepare for such an eventuality. I wouldn't be surprised if Ben had done that already. If anything happened to Ben and I, Joss, Will and Marc would see to your welfare, I'm sure."

Anna didn't like to say that if the rebellion was successful, it was likely that no-one in the Northern would be trusted enough to be allowed to hold onto their land. Obviously, this was not something Bran considered feasible.

He wanted to know more. "He cannot be a man from the Northern."

She shook her head. "How did you know?"

"Because he would not make a proposal without meeting you. His proposal would be based on knowing you and loving you. Who is it? Do you know anything of him?"

"I've not met him. His name is Walter. From Yorkshire. Helmislay. You know of the Abbey near there? Rievieulx?"

Bran scanned his memory. I know of a Walter Espec of Helmislay, but…" he faltered.

"Please- do say – I really need information on which to base my refusal."

Bran, heartened by this, found himself smiling. "Well, the Walter I am thinking of – and I've never met him you understand – has a reputation for fairness and generosity. I think he also has military honours, but…" he petered off again.

Anna looked at him expectantly.

"Well, he's older than your father. I know that's not unusual in other marriages, but…"

Anna's mouth had become a thin line. She shook her head slightly. "I don't think it can be the same

Walter. Father said there was a ten year difference in our ages."

Bran felt his spirits tumble again. There was less of an age difference than that between him and Anna. "I can find out for you. It doesn't do to ruminate too much. Before you know it you have moulded the man to fill in the gaps you don't know about – the imagination can be cruelly misleading in the long run."

She glanced at him. "You sound like you're speaking from experience."

He gave her a conspiratorial look. "Very nearly. I almost convinced myself I was in love while I was away. So much so, that I did not dare open my mouth to the lady. I think she thought me very aloof. Then, one day, I had my eyes horribly opened."

Anna was intrigued. "What happened?"

"I saw her kissing the master mason, who was married."

"How disappointing. Especially for the master mason's wife."

"Umm. Not particularly," said Bran. "She was the master mason's wife."

Anna threw him a quizzical look.

"I'd often seen them in each other's company and I knew he was married, but I had convinced myself that she was his daughter. It was what I wanted to believe."

"Were you greatly disappointed?"

"Funnily enough, no. All she had really been was a figment of my imagination dressed up in the real lady's body. When I realised my error, she had no place there anymore."

"So, is the lady in your head you mentioned last night a reflection of the lady overseas?"

"Oh no," he smiled. "Still, this doesn't solve your problem. I could make a few discreet enquiries at Drysdale. We have visitors from all over the country."

Anna considered. "Do you think I should simply say no?"

"Only you can answer that, Anna."

"Oh, please Bran. You've known me since I was born. I can trust you. If you were me, what would you say?"

"Very well. Say no. If it embarrasses you to discuss him, he's not the right man. You have no need to marry for security, financial or otherwise."

"Right," she seemed decided, then immediately frowned. "But what if I waste what might be my only decent proposal?"

Bran laughed and looked at her. He quickly straightened his face when he realised she was serious. "I shall make enquiries to help you make a decision, but, really, you should rest assured that this will not be your only proposal."

She shook her head. "But we don't know that."

"I'm certain," he said. "I reckon there'll be a few men in the Northern who are just waiting until you are old enough to have decided what you want in a husband. And you can rely on men from the order."

"How do you know?"

Bran knew he was not permitted to tell too much, besides, the whole truth could only be off-putting for a young woman who, as yet, took a pessimistic view of relationships. She would only consider it presumptuous that men thought they could reach a greater understanding of women simply through studying it like an exact science. He played it safe. "Consider all the people you know who are married, then divide them into those who are part of the Northern and those who are not. Which families are the happiest and how do you know?"

Anna thought, unconsciously letting her eyes skim over Marc, Will and Joss. "I think I see."

"It wouldn't hurt to wait awhile, Anna." Mid-conversation, Bran suddenly sat up a little straighter, a thought having struck him. He pulled at his collar, delved inside his clothing and pulled out the silk he had forgotten to give her the night before. He had rolled it to prevent it creasing during the hunt. "I should have given you this last night," he apologised, "but I was sidetracked by Woolly." He handed her the rich green and amber cloth.

She passed her palm over its glossy smoothness. It was warm from his body heat. "You brought this for me?"

He nodded, making the most of gazing at her while she pored over the pattern of the fabric.

"It's beautiful." She smiled and looked up at him. "Were you thinking of me as a seven year old when you chose such a beautiful gift?"

He smiled back at her. "I used a little guesswork." He allowed himself to look into her eyes, trying to gauge her feelings. "Wait a little longer, Anna. There's no need to hurry into marriage." Was it her pleasure in receiving the silk or was there really a special look that passed between them? "I care about you. Take your time. Someone special like you can afford to wait."

Unnoticed by them, the company had begun to stir. The hounds and most of the food had already been taken away. A shadow fell over them. It was Joss.

"Anna, your father will take you back to Redgate. Will, Marc, Susan and Adela will go as well. Leona will be waiting there for us.

Joss continued, "Before we go our separate ways, Bran, could I speak with you regarding the King? We need to firm up plans for protecting the Dale and the Borders."

Bran nodded, "Of course."

He stood up and helped Anna to her feet, feeling slightly deflated that their conversation had been cut short. Perhaps that was why Joss had intervened. He watched her place the silk carefully in her bag before being helped onto her mount. As she and Ben rode away, Joss outlined his thoughts on the threat facing the King. Soon, practicalities and firm decision making subdued his earlier glow, and by the time tactics had been outlined – all the quicker because the Northern were always prepared – the gloom in the forest covered all clues that Spring had been there. Joss would go to Durham tonight to meet with Pudsey and ascertain just how neutral he intended to remain. Even neutral was very annoying and did nothing to show allegiance to Henry.

Bran mounted Seer. He was reluctant to go straight back to Drysdale. If he made haste, perhaps he could call at Redgate and invite them to join him the day after tomorrow, before travelling onto Drysdale where the pilgrims expected to see him before nightfall.

Chapter Twelve

Left in the Dark

A merrily chattering Will rode just behind Ben and Anna, which gave her an excuse to remain quiet and think about what had just happened in the forest. Had Bran been a more ordinary man, someone of her own rank, she might have thought that he liked her in a way other than that expected of a Godfather. Although it would have been pleasant to bask in the glow such a thought gave her, she knew entertaining it might only delude and then disappoint her. He had said he cared for her, but of course he would. He cared for her in the same way as her father did or an older protective brother. And he was renowned for his manners and considerate nature. It would be very easy to confuse kindness with love. Besides, she had no idea whether God daughters were allowed to fall in love with their Godfathers, especially when the God issue was so problematical. But then her father must not have deemed it a problem when he chose Bran as Godfather in the first place. As the journey ended and she poured scorn on her thoughts, she caught Will looking at her. Had she missed something he said? She tried to give a neutral smile, at which he turned back to Ben and continued to wax lyrical about whether the chase really was better than the catch.

The small party did not take long to cover the short distance to the house. Once she had dismounted, she thanked her father and made an excuse to be on her own for a while. She had good reason. The damp from the forest floor had seeped into her dress and left her feeling quite chilly so she would need to change, or at least fetch her cloak. Once she had gained her room, she undressed and sat on the edge of the bed in the half light. She opened her bag and pulled out the silk, holding it towards the window. Daylight was in its golden stage. Only half of the enormous sun was visible over the black forest. She unfolded the silk to see how much there was. Should she make a complete garment or trim existing ones? Once unfolded, there was enough to fall lightly across her lap and drape in generous ripples all the way to the end of the bed. It was such fine stuff that its size had been quite deceiving when rolled up. She stood and held it high above her head and still there was enough to lie in folds around her feet. She found that she could make the fabric billow simply by giving a foppish wave from the wrist with each hand. The golden light from the window turned her skin tawny and burnished the amber pattern in the cloth. She smiled and wafted the material again, this time turning on the spot so the silk draped across and around her. She looked down enjoying the touch of it on her bare skin. She now wore a haphazard sari, rather too revealing in places, and she could not help thinking that if she were to be a bride, such a delicate garment would make rather a nice surprise for her new husband – whoever he might happen to be.

A knock at the door brought her out of her reverie. Susan called from the other side.

"Anna. Leona is here. Shall we join the company?"

Anna hastily unwrapped herself and looked about for a more suitable dress. "Yes. I'll meet you down there."

"Better be quick. Adela's brothers have a hearty thirst."

Anna gave a last look at the forest tops then left the chamber to join in the fun.

It wasn't really until Seer reared for a second time that Bran realised something was terribly wrong. He was an intelligent mount and could sense danger well before his rider. Bran guessed something was amiss at approximately the same time as he felt a sharp blow to his temple. In spite of his vision being clouded by dancing spots of light from whatever had hit him, he was immediately on guard. There were still people from Redgate in the forest, mainly pages who had been helping Robert. Stephen, Will's nine year old son, and Richard were among them. They would be well versed in what to do in the event of an attack and would run and tell their fathers if need be. No need to panic just yet. He reached for his sword to strike the two warning raps, but before he could grasp the hilt, Seer reared again. He figured there must be caltrops in the grass as the animal had been trained to stay calm in the presence of danger. He slipped from the saddle to give himself more cover, but instead of making contact with the forest floor, he found himself falling extra feet down a ravine. He had thought he knew this part of the forest well. Another dizzying blow to the head sent him closer to losing consciousness. As he went under he felt further blows to his arms, legs, stomach.

Strangely, he found himself thinking positively. Blacking out made the pain more bearable. At least, his throat had not been struck. One of his worst fears was of choking to death. As he went under, he thought of his mother.

The forest was so thickly black it was hard for him to recognise when he finally came to. First, he thought he could hear voices and hooves. Then he felt a blend of extreme cold and pain.

Everywhere.

Scalp, face, arms, ribs. Even his feet hurt. He felt like he was lying down but could not recognise what position he lay in. He heard a distant voice call his name. Was it Ben? In spite of the cold, his ears burned and seemed swollen, impairing his hearing. He tried to call out but, like a child trying to summon his parents after a nightmare, his voice wouldn't do his bidding. It was only then that he realised how thirsty he was. How long had he been here? Lights flashed in time with his laboured pulse. As his eyes gradually became accustomed to the dark, he realised his vision was obscured on the right. He either lay in a place which blocked out the light on that side or his right eye was truly less efficient. He stirred to touch his brow with his finger and thought at first that he could not raise his arm. It was only when he felt something brushing his head that he found his arm was doing as he wanted, but it was so numb he had not been aware of it. Was it that cold?

The voice called again. Called his name. Was it Marc? Was it really fainter now or was he losing consciousness? Where was Seer? This time, when he succumbed he was uneasy. His clothes were cold and wet. He knew he stood a greater chance of surviving until he was found if he could remove them but he knew it would be impossible in his present state. Maybe this would be the last time he heard a familiar voice. The pain in his head throbbed slow and deep. Perhaps this was for the best. But no. With a start, he cart-wheeled back into consciousness. What had happened? He still had the pain but his position was now more recognisable. It had been eight years since he had last lain here, but he could feel it was his own bed in his chamber at Drysdale. Had it all been a nightmare?

It was lighter now, although the shutters were closed over the window at the foot of the bed. The fire was lit and the flames sent an embracing warmth into the room. He heard a stirring to his left. In an attempt to see who shared the room with him, a sharp pain shot through his neck and behind his eyes. The window on his right was uncovered. He allowed his eyes to rest on the familiar scene. There was the brow of the hill where forest ended and moor land began. Had he been able to raise his head, he would have been able to see the valley floor and deduce the point in the trees, halfway up the opposite slope, where a tiny Redgate was hidden. Lazily, he let his eyes scan the hilltop horizon. There wasn't one shape or shadow he could not account for. Just as he had every time he stayed at Drysdale as a child, he recited in his head the well known lumps and bumps on the skyline so he would know if enemies were approaching well in advance: from left to right, three crooked trees all bent eastwards; an even rectangular block then a gap where the wall was down; one tree; one pole where people were hanged in Stephen's time (push image of mother from mind); nineteen trees, all obligingly separate and distinct, up to the westward point where the hill was creased. At the seventeenth tree, he fell asleep again.

The softest voice whispered, "It's all right, Bran. You must be careful. Lie still. Save your energy for the healing."

Had he been dreaming? He tried to focus on the real world. Was it real? All but the fire was simply shadows. A hand took his and the whisper came again.

"It's good to see you awake. If you can drink, I can do more to stop the pain."

He gradually had a cleaner vision.

"Anna?" He began to cough.

"Yes, but shush. Try not to talk just yet. You have had nothing to eat or drink since the forest feast four days ago."

Four days? How could that be?

Anna continued softly speaking. "I'll let father know you have woken up. Everyone has been praying for you. Lie still. Don't struggle anymore. I'll return soon and after you've tried to eat and I've bandaged your hurts again, I'll tell you the little we know of what happened."

She left him for the briefest of times, but in spite of her haste and the familiarity and womb-like warmth of the room, he began to panic. He still found it difficult to move. How had he ended up like this? Was he destined to consider home unsafe? Unable to look at or move his hands over his body, he tried to simply sense his position. As far as he could tell, he was only lightly covered with a sheet. A sheet woven at Drysdale. He decided to rely on his other senses as his sight was not giving him any answers. Through waves of nausea and pains in his head, he could hear birdsong. The smell of hyssop and cowslip based ointment was in the air. The windows had now been draped across. He was pleased. The direct light would probably be too much for his head to bear. He found he could move his fingers so he brushed them against his ribs. He felt bandage rather than skin. Bracing himself, he took a deep breath to ascertain how badly broken his ribs might be. Sharp pains cut him short but at least both of his lungs seemed to be fully functioning. His medical knowledge provided him with little comfort now that he was patient rather than doctor.

How could he lose four days without knowing? Having arrived back so recently and seen so many changing landscapes on his travels, the line between dream and reality was blurred. Had he really fallen in love with Anna? Designed a building around her? Given her silk? Or was it some weird effect of the blows to the head?

Out of range of his vision, the door opened. Ben came and sat at his bedside and smiled down at him.

Bran tried to speak but Ben put up a hand, gesturing that he should not try. "Give yourself some time, Bran. Anna will feed you. It may take some time, being so thirsty and tired."

Anna stood behind her father, stirring something in a bowl. Still beautiful. Real rather than a dream.

Ben rose. "I'll leave you to it." He stood awkwardly. "Please don't let this take you away again. We have the culprits. Anna will tell the details while she tends to you."

He walked to the door. "I'll let Joss and Will know that you're back with us. They have gone to fetch Alric in case there is a link with the attack and his return. Marc said he would give you time to eat then he would come to see you. The food may make you drowsy so allow yourself to sleep if it comes over you."

He left the room and Anna rested the bowl on a shelf near the bed.

In spite of Ben's warning, he tried to speak. His voice came out as a hoarse whisper. "Are you going to feed me that or rub it on my wounds?"

She smiled. "It's pottage. I can rub it on if you wish."

His face felt strangely encumbered when he tried to return her smile. "What happened?"

Anna continued to see to his needs while she spoke. "Just let me raise your head a little." She put a cushion of fabric behind his neck. "It'll help you to swallow. There." She smiled at him again. He watched her. She had tied her hair back. She brought a spoon towards him. "Don't worry if this irritates your throat at first: I'm prepared for anything." She grinned and held up a cloth. "I've learned a lot from watching Susan weaning her children."

His stomach complained of hunger as he took a mouthful. It was delicious. "Is Robert here?" he asked.

"You can tell Robert cooked this from one mouthful?"

He smiled, having quickly realised that nodding was too taxing. "What happened?" he asked again.

Anna held up another spoonful. "Well, we were told that you were mistakenly set upon by the Prince Bishop's men who thought you were poaching. Of course, we don't believe that, especially as Joss had just said his farewells, judging by where you were found. Also, it all seemed very well planned. A ditch had been dug and there were three men all waiting to waylay you. There were caltrops scattered in the grass too. Besides, Joss rode to the Prince Bishop. Pudsey told him they were not his orders and anyway, everyone knew you had been granted freedom to hunt because you do so much to improve the Dale; nor could he think of anyone in his employ that would go to such extremes. It is their job to apprehend, not deal out the punishment. Joss has gone to fetch Alric. He says it smacks of Edwin so he will start by questioning his son."

Bran felt a strange mix of emotions. His head throbbed at the mention of Edwin and the thought that he might see him get his comeuppance at last, but he also felt a deep disappointment. "Back home only a few hours and someone wants me dead already."

Anna looked at him and rested the spoon in its bowl. "Perhaps not." She could sense his hurt. "You were the last of us out of the forest, apart from Robert's little group of pages. It is only chance that made you decide to ride by the ditch and over the caltrops. And the downturn in the weather, of course. It's unusual to have frost this far into Spring. Joss thinks an attack was planned, but feels it was aimed at the Northern generally rather than you alone. It would be unlikely that they knew of your return. The culprits have been caught. They were paid for their work, they say. We are holding them for you. It seemed right that you should be the one to decide the punishment."

"They confess to doing it?"

"Yes, but we cannot get to the bottom of why they did it or for whom. They are being questioned further. It's just as well they were so unreliable. They seem to have spent their pay on drink first. Heaven knows what might have happened had they been sober. You are covered head to toe in bruises but have only a few broken bones."

"Is that all?" He felt ashamed at having been beaten by such an amateurish mob.

"Your ribs and head took the worst of it. I'll give you something for the pain shortly."

Bran's mind wandered as she tended to him. She stole glances at him now and then. Beneath the bruises, his expression was grim. He obviously had a lot on his mind. Bran felt his wounds pulse more heavily. Damn Edwin. How was it he could travel so extensively, meet all sorts of people, solve all sorts of problems and then the merest thought that Edwin might be involved in his life again wiped his mind of all logical thoughts. His fears were stuck deep in Edwin. It annoyed and shamed him. Perhaps it stemmed from when he was a little boy. He had been powerless to do anything about him then and it seemed he was no further forward. Also, at the back of his mind there was the thought that if he showed Anna any affection, she might suffer a similar fate to Catherine. He couldn't let that happen. Before he could tell Anna and Ben how he felt, he would have to deal with Edwin first. In his heart of hearts he knew that no matter how fondly Ben thought of him, he would not want to risk Anna's safety for the sake of a marriage to a man of rank. Besides, with this latest threat from France, Scotland and Henry's sons, none of the Northern was guaranteed to hold their strong position if the King was defeated.

Anna began clearing away the bowls and ointments she had been using, bringing Bran back to the present. "How old is Alric now?"

Anna's mouth became a thin line as she thought. "About twenty, I would say. Joss will bring him here for questioning. Do you mind?"

He had thought she was asking about Alric and said no, then realised she was asking for permission to pull down the covers so she could check his ribs. She sat on the edge of the bed, taking some of his weight while he leaned forward. He felt as helpless and imbalanced as a baby. She reached around his waist and unwound the cloth while talking. "Father thought it best if we came to Drysdale as it's better fortified here. With the likely rebellion and now this, he thought it best if we take precautions."

Bran looked at himself while she tended to him. Most of his skin was either badly bruised or scribbled with abrasions.

Anna noticed him looking. "You must be very sore." She helped him to lie back.

A thought struck Bran. "Are the pilgrims still here?"

Anna shook her head. "They've gone to Durham to pay a visit to Cuthbert's bones. We have a lot to thank them for."

"Really?" Bran asked, raising a cynical eyebrow. This particular party had been unusually haughty and sanctimonious so he found it difficult to imagine how they had made themselves useful.

She nodded. "If it wasn't for the short man named Rupert taking it upon himself to come to us at Redgate in order to complain that you had not met them as you said you would, we would not have known you were in trouble. Although Seer arriving here without you had already alerted us. He is fine by the way."

Bran couldn't help smiling. "How did you find Rupert?"

She grinned. "You worried in case people saw you as pious. I didn't really know how pious conducted itself until Rupert descended on us in the middle of supper."

Bran laughed, then immediately winced as a pain stabbed at his head. "That was God's way of telling me to show more gratitude. Even to men who shout when they can talk and wear enormous hats to make up what they lack in height."

She reached for the pestle and mortar and used her fingers to scoop up some paste from inside. She focused on Bran's brow. "This will sting a little." She moved closer to him and he felt a gentle dabbing. The ointment was cold and he felt a tide of gooseflesh spread across his chest. She must have noticed because she pulled the covers up towards his shoulders, warming him immediately. He felt drowsy. He watched her as she leant near. Her eyes were dark in the candlelight. Occasionally, his own eyes closed. He felt like he was in a dream. She would come near and touch his brow, his eyes would close for what only seemed a few seconds, then he would open them to find her by the fire, adding more wood, then again, only seconds later, he would open them again and she was sitting on a stool by the window tearing cloth into strips. A little while later, he opened his eyes and Susan and Marc were just leaving the room. His manners tried to make him call out and ask them to wait, but his voice could not do his bidding against the wave of weariness washing over him. He drifted in and out of consciousness for hours, until he woke and it was daylight again. Anna was still there, sitting by his bedside, reading.

She didn't notice he had woken at first. He gazed at her. He wondered if she had stayed all night rather than allowing someone to help her watch over him. It was a nice thought. Although he guessed she would not want to burden Susan when she already had her hands full with her children. Anna's wrists were pale and delicate, just visible at the cuffs of her orange dress. Her hair was coming loose from the binding she had used to tie it. The book she held was angled towards the window to make the most of the light. She looked up, saw him awake and smiled. "Good morning."

"What are you reading?"

"A rather long-winded poem."

"Is it a good one?"

"That would depend on what you like in a ballad."

"Is there a hero?"

"Yes."

"A beautiful lady?"

"Several."

"Is the hero worthy of several beautiful ladies?"

"I think he only loves one."

"Good."

"You approve?"

"Yes. A hero who loves several beautiful ladies quickly becomes a villain. Does she know?"

"Who?"

"The beautiful lady. That he loves her."

"As far as I can tell," said Anna, "it's unrequited at present."

"As far as you can tell?"

She shrugged. "I imagine she refuses him, not because she does not find him appealing, but because she has an evil fiancé or admirer who has threatened terrible things if she tries to take another."

"You can tell all that?"

She smiled. "It would be a boring poem if she simply didn't like him because of the colour of his hair."

Bran smiled, "His hair?"

Anna blushed, "Or whatever else it is that makes men seem less attractive to women."

"You make it sound like you have no idea what makes men attractive."

Susan's voice came from the open doorway. "That's because you have been surrounded by good looking men all your life." She threw a glance back at Marc who followed her. "Spoilt rotten."

Marc glanced at Bran grinning, then turned to Susan shaking his head, "He's not so good looking now though."

Susan assumed a sympathetic expression. "No. Poor soul. Still, it's only a matter of time. The bruises will heal and the swelling will go down."

Bran felt uncomfortable and wondered how long his friends had been eavesdropping. He also felt strangely embarrassed at being reminded of his injuries. He tried to compensate by continuing his conversation with Anna.

"You said it was all unrequited at present. Do you think she'll come round in the end?"

"Oh yes, they always see it in the end." Bran wanted to ask what it was they saw, but Anna became preoccupied. She dipped a cloth in the bowl, squeezed out the excess water then gently washed his face. It was beautifully warm.

Susan and Marc sat at the foot of the bed. "I rather like all this pampering," Bran mused. "Is that selfish of me?"

Anna dabbed gently at the cut on his temple. "I don't think so. You paid a high price for it."

Marc nodded and added dryly. "Anyone forced to spend three months in Rupert's company deserves far more than a little pampering."

Although the window was closed, the sound of hooves in the bailey was clearly audible. Marc crossed the room to look. "It's Joss with Alric. I don't think it'll be long before we get to the bottom of this."

Bran felt his head begin to hurt and his pulse quicken again. It wasn't long before Joss joined them in the chamber.

"Are you well enough to join us while we question Alric?"

Bran nodded.

Joss turned to Anna. "Is he well enough to join us while we question Alric?"

Anna glanced at Bran apologetically. "Nowhere near. Unless you don't mind being carried into the Hall."

"We'll delay until tomorrow. That gives you a chance to think through any questions you would like us to ask. It's more important that you build up your strength. There are far more enemies than Alric creeping out of the woodwork."

"Where are you holding him?" asked Bran.

"We thought you could suggest the best place."

"The trace room is probably the easiest place to secure."

Joss nodded as he walked to the window then called instructions to the men below. He came back to the bedside. "There may be plans already – he did not put up a fight when I told him of our intentions. In fact, he seemed quite resigned to it. Even fatalistic. He either wants to get it over with, as he said, or he has an ulterior motive for coming to Drysdale." Joss rubbed his chin for the briefest of moments then turned to Anna and Susan. "You know the safe places should Drysdale come under attack?"

They nodded.

"It's unlikely, but best to be prepared," he said and strode from the room.

Chapter Thirteen

Alric

Alric was woken after only a couple of hours sleep by a sharp shaft of sunlight lying across his face. He lay on the floor fully clothed, wrapped closely in his cloak. He could not decide whether it was the cold or the anticipation of what lay ahead which troubled him the most, but he had been kept awake until well into the wee hours. As soon as he resigned himself to the fact that he was awake again, he opened his eyes and immediately felt more alert. He wondered whether Isabel would really have met him in the town like she said, or whether she was just a flirt. She was several years older than him, but it's not as if he wanted anything long lasting with her. She seemed no stranger to men – of any age. He allowed himself to ponder on just how experienced she might have been. Too late to find out now. Besides, Roger would only have taken an interest and had his way with her, flirt or not. He freed a hand from its warm cover and shielded his eyes in order to assess his whereabouts. The simple square window framed a chalky blue sky, interrupted with what seemed to be part of an enormous siege engine. He had noticed on his arrival that they were well prepared for an attack.

He shifted uncomfortably on the hard floor, wondering whether he was being watched from a hiding place. He certainly would have spied on his captives. Shame he could not be sure of his privacy. Thinking of the voluptuous Isabel had a warming effect. He turned his mind to the forthcoming interrogation. What he would be asked, where he would be asked it, who would be his questioner. Joss? The Jew? How should he address Joss? He had so much land that he would be hard-pressed to know which title to use. What would happen if there was an answer he could not give? Worse still, what would happen if he gave an answer they did not like? Or if they forced him to say something they wanted to hear through torture?

He heard the community coming slowly to life: footsteps then the stable doors swinging open; the heavy, ponderous early morning stamp of hooves; the cry of a baby; the complaint of a cat shooed away from the mews; an impatient voice barking orders in the kitchen; the scrape of wood on stone as trestles were laid out. He had been away from his birthplace for so many years that he thought being brought here, only fifteen miles from Beau Repaire, would have given him a sense of coming home, but it felt alien to him. Probably just as well. What would people have thought if he had felt at home on land held by a Jew? Alric felt that he belonged nowhere. It was a long time since he had first realised it and it no longer gave him the pang it used to when he was younger. Besides, some people thrived on it. A lot of men of rank had more than one home; constantly on the move from one castle to the other; a crusade here, a pilgrimage there. Not for Alric though. He was tired of it.

The latch lifted with a clatter and he sat up. A trencher of frumenty, honey and water was brought to him. He took it greedily. His nerves had made him thirsty.

"You'll be taken to the main house shortly." Then the door was closed on him again.

Alric wished that his bladder was not so full. He wondered if and when he would have the opportunity to relieve himself. He had neither seen nor smelt a midden when he was brought in through the outer village. By the time he had eaten his fill, the sun had moved to a higher window and the latch sounded again.

"It's time to go." He was led from the trace room to the main house. There was a frost and it was a beautifully clean morning. People stood and stared after him. Before he entered the main building, he heard voices echoing. These stopped as soon as he crossed the threshold. Someone showed him through a door on his left.

"You have nearly an hour to prepare. Make the most of it." Then the door was closed, leaving him standing in a small shadowy chamber. There was a bowl and a jug of water on the cup board. In the corner furthest from the door was a curtain. He looked behind it and gave a grateful sigh. The garderobe. He hastily relieved himself then made another closer inspection of the room. He had been told to prepare. Prepare for what? He tested the water in the bowl. It was warm. He washed his face and hands and dried them with the smaller of two cloths that had been laid ready. He looked about him again. A bath had been prepared and stood steaming in the cold air. He regarded it suspiciously. Why would his questioners be so hospitable? Was it really filled with warm water? What if they had added something? Some drug or poison. He looked into the wooden vessel. A cloth had been laid inside to protect his skin from splinters. Alric did not think he needed a bath. It was only three weeks since his last one, but it did look inviting. He watched the steam curling upwards as he pondered. Rolling up his sleeve, he waggled his fingers at the water's surface. It was a good temperature. He looked to the door, almost expecting it to open now that he had decided he might like a bath after all. If he was going to do this, he ought to do it quickly. He pulled off his clothes and stepped over the edge. He quickly lifted his foot back out of the water as sharp needles of pain stabbed through his cold feet. Another dip made it slightly better as his foot warmed to the temperature of the water. Tentatively, he introduced the other foot. He sank into the warmth and watched his breath join forces with the steam. He could not help but muse on the strangeness of it all. Did they treat all of their suspects like this? The more he thought about it, the less he was able to enjoy it. Perhaps they were going to execute him regardless of anything he said today and believed a body had to be clean before the sentence was passed. There had to be some trickery involved. He climbed out, cursing himself for leaving the dry cloth at the end of a long cold walk at the other side of the room. Gooseflesh rendered his skin and he dried himself as vigorously as possible to keep the chills at bay.

After dressing, he sat on a stool awaiting his captors. After a while, he went to the window. He could see very little from there. He went back to the stool and waited again. The bath water had stopped its steaming. Sitting quietly made him chilly so he stood up and invented excuses to move. He counted out how many paces there were to the room's length and breadth. This done, he carried on pacing. He could not prevent his mind from anticipating what might happen today. How much would he need to tell? It was a difficult line to tread: enough to keep them happy without making Roger angry. Was it wise to favour the devil you knew? Maybe not in Roger's case.

Why were they taking so long? He paced out the length of the room backwards. Then sideways. He sat down again. They were taking a very long time. Or were they? He had no way of knowing. Prepare for what? His mind started to play tricks on him. Had they said to wait or had they told him to knock when he was ready? His memory was foggy. He really wasn't sure. Should he knock anyway? Could they have forgotten him? Perhaps they had no intention of coming back. Perhaps he would never be released. He had heard of such things.

The scraping of trestles being cleared away gave him more patience. He heard voices again, and laughter, then, finally, footsteps. The latch lifted. Joss stepped over the threshold. He said nothing as he looked at Alric. His eyes were expressionless. For no particular reason, Alric felt like apologising. He shifted uncomfortably and stood up from his stool, gave a little bob of the head and a mumbled, "Morning Sir."

Joss was amused but didn't let it show. Keeping prisoners waiting always did the trick. "Come with me."

He strode into the main hall and Alric followed like an obedient puppy. The room was big. It had two fires, both of which were lit. Three tall windows on the courtyard side allowed Alric to see his surroundings quite clearly. On the dais were three chairs, two of which were already filled. He assumed these were Ben and Will from descriptions he had been given. Joss walked to the third chair and took his seat. There was no sign of the Jew. Tapestries hung on the walls, adding colour and warmth to the stonework.

Alric stood before them. No seat had been provided for him. The tall fair man in the centre spoke. "Confirm your name for us."

"Alric."

"Once you lived at Beau Repaire?"

"Yes."

"Your father is Edwin?"

"Yes."

"You had a sister, Catherine?"

"A half-sister, yes."

"What happened to Catherine?"

"She was killed in the forest."

"How do you know?"

Alric swallowed. Now or never. "I was there, Sir."

"You killed her?"

Alric paused. "No Sir."

Will leaned across to Joss then Ben, whispering. They both glanced at each other and nodded. Will continued. "Tell us everything you know about Catherine's death."

Alric swallowed. He did not know where to begin.

Ben asked. "Was Catherine's death murder?"

Alric remembered the way Edwin had coldly set out his trap for Catherine to walk into. "I believe it was, Sir."

"You sound unsure. Explain."

"Catherine was killed by the hounds from Beau Repaire, but it was planned."

Will took over. "By you?"

Alric looked shocked. "No, Sir."

"Who took the hounds to the forest?"

Alric began to panic and stuttered, "I..I..did Sir, but I was told to."

Will's accusatory tone had worked. Alric did not want to shoulder the blame for Catherine's death.

"My father…"

"Edwin?" Joss snapped.

"Yes. It was him. He said to starve the hounds and take them to the forest." Alric began to recount the night's events. As he spoke all three Knights watched him carefully. He made little eye contact. He stuttered and stumbled as he tried to recall the exact way that things had happened. His hands shook and as he told of the dogs' savagery, his voice trembled and broke.

When he had finished, the three conferred.

"Most annoying," said Will. "His behaviour could indicate he is lying or that he is telling the truth and merely upset."

Ben murmured, "I hope Bran is not regretting his decision to listen in."

They resumed their seats and Joss took over the questioning. "I am the person with the power to release you, imprison you, have character witnesses brought before you and to decide whether you need to be sentenced to death. So far you have told us that you were an accomplice in the murder of your sister."

Panic made Alric brave. He interrupted, "But I did not know his intentions. He told me that Catherine needed to be rescued from the Jew. He said we would need to do it quietly to avoid a battle."

Joss stared at him and said nothing. Alric wrung his hands. "I cannot be held responsible for Catherine's death."

Joss kept staring.

"I am not lying."

Joss finally spoke. "Did you tell anyone of what had happened? Did you report this appalling murder to the appropriate authorities?"

Alric looked at his feet and shook his head.

"Why not?"

"I was afraid he would kill me too."

"Where is Edwin now?"

"He is dead, Sir?"

The three old friends resisted the urge to look at each other to assess whether Alric had just said what they thought. In the doorway hidden by a tapestry, Bran and Anna held their breath.

"How long has he been dead?"

"Since one week after Catherine's death."

"You seem very sure."

Alric swallowed. "I know because I killed him, Sir."

Joss narrowed his eyes. "Tell me exactly what you mean."

Alric took a deep breath. "I was twelve years old. When I saw Catherine killed, I felt sick. It didn't seem to bother my father. In fact he seemed pleased with himself because he had planned it so that she was killed without there being any clues that would link him to the murder. I could not get the sounds out of my head. The horse's screaming. Hers. And the silence was even worse. He wanted us to leave immediately. He told me to stop being so cowardly, to pull myself together. I honestly cannot recall how far we travelled that night. I felt cold through to the bones. I realised that if I became troublesome to him, he would do the same to me. And no one would ever know about it. We travelled through the forest most of the time and I got it into my head that he planned to do away with me before we came to the more open roads. He said nothing to reassure me otherwise. In fact, he said little at all. I could not sleep, feeling that he might attack at any time. If he gave me an errand, I treated it with suspicion, recalling how he laid traps rather than being more direct. Eventually, after five nights without sleep, constantly wondering when my death would come, I decided that the best form of defence was attack. I was young and weak compared to him so it would have to be underhand. I couldn't poison him, because our food was so basic that anything added would have been noted. If he caught me he would kill me. Besides, I am not very clever with things like that.

On the morning of the day I killed him, he told me to tighten his saddle strap. When I tried to do so, I found that it had stretched and that it would not fasten any tighter without stabbing the leather. I remember the next part quite clearly."

All three men watched him carefully. He certainly seemed to be reliving the event.

"I said to him, 'I need to cut the leather, it has stretched.' He glanced at me and took his knife from his belt. As he handed it to me, he hesitated and stared into my eyes. I felt a cold feeling come over me. In that one moment, I knew he had lost trust in me. That was all it had taken for him to decide to kill Catherine. I remember reaching for the knife as if cutting the leather was the only thing on my mind. I fumbled at the job due to lack of sleep and my state of mind. When I finished, I had intended to return the knife and to bide my time - perhaps to try to make my escape under cover of darkness – but when I looked up from my task, I could not see him. My heart began to pound. I thought he would be at me any moment. I looked around wildly. He cleared his throat behind me and asked, "Is something troubling you, Alric?" Convinced that I was in danger, I span round wildly. He swore at me. I had slashed his arm. He would never have forgiven me for that. He knew for sure there was no trust between us now. He swung with his good arm, but I ducked and jabbed him in the ribs. He swore again. I was surprised when he fell. There was blood. He was so angry. Although he was the one who was injured, I was scared. He tried to get to his feet and I stabbed again. Even as I did it, I felt cruel. I had to put a stop to it. The only way to do that was to keep on stabbing. To stop him from living." Alric looked at Joss. "I know it sounds like madness, but I had to kill him." Joss could understand it, but said nothing. "I kept on stabbing him. Even when his clothes were shining red because there was so much blood.

Eventually, I ran into the trees. I hid myself in the undergrowth, half thinking that if he survived he would be after me with a vengeance yet shaking with the horror of what I had done. My mind raced and then, strangely, I fell asleep. For the first time in a week. When I awoke, it was starting to get dark again and I was cold. That was my first thought. Then I began to remember what I had done. I hoped that I had only dreamt it, but my clothes and skin were spattered with his blood. I roused myself and forced myself to go back and find his body. It took a while to find it as I had run so wildly to be away from him, but eventually I came to the place. The knife was next to him. His face was pale and stone cold to the touch; the eyes open. His clothes were stained beyond recognition. I felt a heavy guilt. It was me that took the life from him. And yet I knew that if he was alive, my old fears would have still been with me and I would have been prepared to kill him still to protect myself.

I warmed myself by digging his grave with my bare hands. I made it deep. It grew dark, but I did not stop. When it was almost as deep as he was tall, I rolled him into it. He was cold, stiff and heavy and not at all easy to budge, but I managed it. I removed my clothes and dropped them in with him, then scraped the leaves and soil on top of him and packed it down hard. Even now, I worried that he might have still been breathing and that he would be after me. I stamped the soil down as hard as I could, so that if he was still alive, he would suffocate. Then I waited for daylight, washed in the stream, took my cloak from the back of my mount and left him. It was the first time I had been warm in days."

Joss interrupted. "Where did you go?"

"I continued through the forest until I came upon a village. I kept outside, realising that village folk would be suspicious of anyone coming out of the forest. I knew there was quite a broad road on the outskirts so I followed this. The further I rode, the more travellers there seemed to be. Upon enquiry, I was told that I was coming into York. This suited me. A town gave me anonymity and I had enough money from Edwin's pouch to earn me respect in spite of my age. I concocted a story that my father had told me to find work in the town and to find a master who would teach me a respectable trade. Most people sent me on my way with a warning to be careful who I confided in. Another robbed me, and another tried but found I had nothing left to take but my cloak, which was too small for him. Finding the town people too threatening now, I lived in that flat unsheltered land outside of the walls, trying to escape the night breezes by lying against balks dividing the land.

Eventually, starved and desperate, I decided to take my chances in the town once more. If not I would surely die. On my walk back, I had little hope. Hunger made my stomach growl and my vision blurred and as I entered the town once more, I fell in the streets. When I awoke, I was in a tavern. A lady gave me water and bread, but made no pretence of any further hospitality. A man seated nearby asked if I would like to help him. He said he was a tailor and needed an apprentice with better eyes than he. I was eager to have a roof over my head and said yes." Alric looked at the men in front of him. "That's how it happened."

Joss asked, "What brought you back from York?"

"The tailor died, Sir. He left little money and his family did not want me claiming anything of his. I decided I ought to return to Durham, perhaps take up the work I had learned from him. I can also make shoes and I had a childhood memory of Soutergate in Durham. Perhaps I could set myself up as a shoemaker there. For no stronger reason than this, I decided it was time to come home."

Joss looked at him levelly. The final part of the story seemed to ring the least true.

"So you are confessing to the murder of Edwin, your father?"

Alric grimaced and nodded. "Yes Sir."

"Yet you were eager not to be named as an accomplice in Catherine's murder."

"I had no idea what Edwin had planned for Catherine. I do not want to be accused of something I have not done. On the other hand, I can take the blame for the murder I did commit."

"You realise that killing your father is a capital offence under the law of the land – Edwin being our enemy does not excuse you from that."

Alric swallowed and looked at his feet. He had thought they would give a more favourable reaction.

Will took over. "What do you know of an attack in the forest three nights ago?"

Alric looked at them. "I know nothing of it, Sir."

Will crossed to a door on his left and called through. There were shuffling footsteps and the men who had been caught in the forest were walked into the room.

Alric looked at them. Will addressed the men. "Do you know this man?"

They looked at him closely. Two said no and one said yes. Joss grimaced and gave an impatient sigh. "Make your mind up!" he snapped, making the men jump.

"I do, Sir. I saw him in town last week. He was drunk and calling out rude remarks to a group of women."

Joss sighed again. "Was this you?"

Alric reddened. "I believe so, Sir. It is hard to recall."

"It would seem that thrift is not one of your strong points." said Ben. "You need to earn a living but spend money on drink."

"Yes, Sir."

"With whom do you keep company?" Ben probed.

"With anyone I meet at the time." said Alric. "I have no permanent companions."

Joss did not believe him. "Have those you have met been loyal to Henry, the present King, or his son?"

Alric looked at his feet again. Roger had told him to plead ignorance on this one. "I know nothing of politics, Sir. It is not my lot to choose kings but simply to live by their command, whoever they happen to be."

"To live by their command," repeated Joss. Alric looked up at him and nodded. Joss continued, "The king creates a judicial system to protect his citizens from crime and you live by his command by murdering your father and causing public disturbances."

Alric reddened again and said nothing under Joss's crushing logic.

"I think you live according to your own rules, Alric, and damn everyone else. Could you lead us to the place where your father is buried?"

Alric shrugged. "I could try, Sir, but it was eight years ago and the path we took had no landmarks. All I recall is that it was a few miles outside of York."

Joss interrupted him. "No matter. You have confessed to your father's murder, which is a capital offence. If for some reason you are lying and Edwin is still alive, you have perjured yourself, and if your reasons are treasonous that is basis enough for us to keep you imprisoned until we find out more. Are there any character witnesses you would like to speak for you?"

Alric sighed heavily. The only one he knew was Roger and he had said to keep him out of it. "No, Sir."

"Are you sure?" asked Ben.

Alric nodded.

"You'll be given three days to decide whether you would like to rescind on your confession. If not, you give us no alternative but to sentence you to death by hanging. Should you change your mind about the murder and feel you would like to tell us of Edwin's whereabouts, we may view your plight with a more sympathetic eye. Take him away."

Marc led Alric to a colder place one floor down. It was dark with very little light coming in at the small window. Alric curled into a ball and tucked his cloak tightly about him, ready to sit out the long wait.

All three older men shook their heads. "Give him a week instead," said Joss. "Let him hear the gallows being erected. If he is lying, he will soon change his mind."

"And if he isn't lying?" asked Ben.

"Then he is truly guilty of murder and deserves to face his punishment under law."

Will nodded. "In the meantime, we need to send men to Durham. Let them mingle with the sort of company Alric would keep. See if they can glean any knowledge of a plan. Perhaps Alric is sufficiently foolish to think he is important enough to be saved at the last minute by rebels who wish to take Drysdale and aid the Scots in an attack."

Ben walked to the tapestry and pulled it back. "What did you make of it all?" he asked Bran.

Bran looked uncomfortable. A sheen on his skin gave away his fever. "If I had not had dealings with the family, I would say he sounded convincing. But…" he shook his head, "I just don't feel like Edwin is dead."

"Well, we should find out soon," said Will. "I just hope for all of our sakes that Alric is telling the truth. If not we may end up killing an innocent young man. I do hope he is not trusting that his own father will rush to protect him if he is alive."

While men were dispatched to Durham to mingle with undesirables, Alric, below stairs, tried to keep his mind blank. If one wants to wipe the mind clean it becomes virtually impossible. Alric's mind raced far more than it would have on a usual day. He had no idea of an attack in the forest. Was Roger doing things without his knowledge? If so, why? Would it make things more dangerous for him? His teeth chattered with the cold and he looked about for a source of heat, but there was none. The small window built high into the stonework threw a weak grey light onto the floor a few yards away. He shuffled towards it as if the light would warm him. He pulled the collar of his cloak over his mouth that his breath might warm the inner folds. He clamped his hands between his knees. Damn Roger. It as easy enough to say sit and wait, but this was purgatory. He thought back to the warming bath he had had earlier. It would be so easy to tell them. What had they meant by "sympathetic"? Pardon him? Protect him? One without the other would still be a death sentence. His shoulders were stiff and ached in their fight against the cold air. He had to stay resolute. The Northern would be nothing soon anyway and any protection they might offer him now would be worthless in the long run.

Above stairs, Joss was making plans for Bran. "We need men to stay behind to protect Drysdale and

Redgate. It will be weeks before you are fighting fit again."

"I can be useful in other ways," Bran insisted. "I'll be more of a hindrance than a help if I stay here."

Joss shook his head, "The journey will be too uncomfortable for you. Your bones need to mend."

Bran glanced at Anna. "Anna can provide us with medicine. Once we are based in Scotland I can take the necessary bed rest while helping with tactics and engineering."

Joss looked at Bran then Anna. He considered. "We won't be leaving until we find out more about the younger Henry's plans – and whether Alric is involved. I imagine the King will want a part in this. He has a personal interest in Drysdale's affairs. Perhaps three weeks or more before we need to leave," he muttered. He made a decision. "If you can sit astride a horse at a gallop in three weeks' time, I will consider taking you along, but I have the final decision. I have allies in Scotland who can help us. We will leave others here to defend Drysdale and Redgate."

"Thank you," said Bran.

Chapter Fourteen

A Time of Opposites

Anna weighed up the pros and cons as she pushed down hard just above her knees to help her up the steep incline to where the feverfew flocked thickly. It was a time of opposites: loyalty in the face of treachery; wondering whether to embrace marriage in the face of a strong urge to escape it. She turned a few ideas over in her head, her mission for herbs providing the perfect excuse for solitary musings. The flower heads bobbed, lighter than the insect strewn air around them. She was determined to collect enough in one trip, rather than take the easy way now and regret it later.

On the good side, she had had Bran just about all to herself over the past few weeks. Alric spent extra time in captivity in the hope it would loosen his tongue. The King had involved himself for a while, but the Northern could regain control now that Henry had made his way down the country to face would-be rebels and do penance for Beckett's murder at Canterbury. She wondered if he would really go through with it. A King putting himself forward for a public flogging seemed topsy turvey. Anna pondered. This time next year would she be on Scottish land or English, without even moving a footstep?

Joss's deadline had been exceeded by at least six weeks and to no avail. Alric did not change his story, no traces of rebellion were found in Durham, with or without Edwin, but, she smiled, there was some pleasure in this limbo time.

Bran had gained a more sensible time for healing and was looking much more his usual self. He had read her diaries now and had not laughed at her or scorned her ideas. Instead he had picked out issues they could discuss and had recommended further reading where her views danced in time with philosophies he had read elsewhere. They'd even mingled talking with Bran's therapy, meandering around the lakes and banks and finding a good place to sit and put the world to rights. Even though she knew he would be mad with boredom otherwise, she could not help feeling flattered. And she felt like she was growing somehow. Bettering herself. She had to think more carefully before she spoke in discussion with another, unlike personal writing where anything went. Her father had come to see them one time when they were in mid discussion and scolded Anna for not letting Bran rest, but Bran had said he would be tormented more if he was forced to lie quietly, day after day, and asked Ben to leave her be.

So here she was, the morning of the execution, trying to keep her mind from death and the fact that once Alric was gone, the need to deal with the rebellion would magnify and Bran, her father and the rest of the Northern would need to leave. She didn't like to dwell on this at all. Half of her was glad that she was not a man who would be expected to fight and risk her life, and the other half wished she could go with them, rather than being left at home, thinking the worst.

The morning was warm, which had pleased her at first, but the spring in her step began to elude her as she climbed Drysdale's steep banks, gleaning the best of the herbs. The bag tied at her waste was bulging. She wanted to be prepared if Bran suddenly had to leave and take medicines with him. Finally, she reached the grassy plateau amongst the pine. She stepped into the shadow-striped clearing and breathed in deeply. As her heart quieted and her breathing evened itself, she looked down, through the treetops to the bailey and the land outside the walls. Willow half hid the enormous wooden prototypes that Bran had still been working on, from his bed at first. She reflected on how just a few weeks could bring such a change to her surroundings, not just because of the wooden structures planted on the landscape. It seemed like no time since the boughs were damply brown-black and the brand new buds alarmingly green. Now, the foliage was heavy on every bough and the thick grass shone brightly where the sun caught the remaining dew. Breathing the air seemed to nourish the body. She watched the people of Drysdale, dwarfed by her vantage point, going about their daily business, only the occasional huddle for a chat revealing that anything unusual was going to happen that day. She bent down to pick the feverfew she had climbed so high to reach.

Before she returned, and she knew she must soon, she would go to the stream's edge and watch how it tumbled and weaved its way down the bank side to the river below. As she approached, its babble grew louder. She leaned against an overhanging branch and watched for some time, loving to hear the hundreds of notes rushing over each other.

Eventually, she gave the branch a push in order to lever herself back up the incline and away from the water. Her heart lurched and she heard herself give a startled gasp as the branch broke and she was unable to stop herself from falling head first. The shock of cold water as she fell face downwards made her gasp again and she coughed and pushed down with her hands to keep her head above the fast moving surface. She began to panic even more when she realised that, even though this was only a stream no more than ten feet wide, she was in no position to fight the current and regain her balance.

She felt the water move her rapidly downstream. Her palms and elbows scraped and buffeted against the stony riverbed as she tumbled with the water, headfirst. She tried to grip the rocks, but they were slippery with weed and before she had time to recognise the full extent of her foolishness in having stood so close to the edge, the water had her completely and dragged her roughly downhill, while she tried to find her feet and lift her face out of the torrent.

Water bubbled at her ears and she heard echoes of her own cries amplified then muffled in turn as the water washed over her head. She knew she had to get up or at least turn over so she had a chance to wedge herself or grab at something on the bank. Her forehead hit against something sharply and she clenched her mouth tightly against the instinct to cry out. She turned her face to the side, trying to use the water's momentum to help her to roll onto her back so that she could at least breathe again, and perhaps get her bearings in order to put up a better fight.

Her mouth could not find the air which showed itself to be tantalisingly near as a multitude of swirling sunlit bubbles. So close, but not close enough. It would not be long before the route took her over a series of falls and she would have no chance of slowing her progress then. She still had not managed to catch her breath and, her logic having proved fruitless so far, she began to flail wildly. Her head pounded and she coughed and swallowed water as she was buffeted, lifted and dropped by the current. Just as a strange sense of resignation was taking over, she felt the strap of the herb bag catch on something above her. If it held her for long enough she might just be able to right herself. Ignoring the sharp pains in her wrists, she tried to push down again with her palms. Suddenly she felt herself lifted backwards out of the water.

A world bright with sunlight suddenly embraced her and she felt grass behind her back. Convulsive coughing and gasping shook her from head to toe and she followed the instinct to turn her head to the side. Her stomach lurched and she threw up stream water. She was unable to fight the heaviness in her body and simply lay, foetus-like, waiting for her panic to subside. She felt herself being rolled onto her back once more. The world rotated and she was left staring at the bright blue sky. She searched its blankness for clues. Was it a miracle? Her view was suddenly obstructed by a face: a young man's face; blue eyes, dark hair. Unusual, she thought. And a beard. She wasn't used to beards. He looked concerned. He was talking to her but it was difficult to make out the words with water still in her ears.

She shook her head and squinted, as if focusing would improve her hearing. He spoke again. "Can you speak to me?"

More water caught at her throat and brought on a fit of coughing. He lifted her to a sitting position and rubbed her back. It was some minutes before she felt able to trust her voice again. Her skin was pale and covered in gooseflesh.

"You're cold," he said, and she felt warmth surround her as he put his cloak over her shoulders. He undid the strap of the bag, which now contained only a few bedraggled stems and asked, "Do you think you could get to your feet with a little help?"

"I'll try."

When he took her arm, she was unable to stop herself wincing. He noticed, saying, "I think some bones may be broken." He moved to her other side and helped her up to her feet. She could only put weight on her right leg. "Um." He looked her up and down. "We need to get you home and dried. Do you live down there?" he indicated with his eyes.

She nodded.

"Would you mind if I carried you?" He gave her a bright smile. "You have little choice, of course."

She wondered who he was, how long he had been watching and what the others would say. It was a silly time to happen, what with the hanging and the chance of a visitor from Helmislay any day.

Oh.

He picked her up and carried her quite easily, even though he was only a couple of inches taller than she was. She looked at his face and he grinned at her. "Comfortable?"

She blushed having been caught studying his face, "You're very kind."

"I could hardly leave you up there, could I? It's fortunate that I dropped in when I did – pardon the expression."

She looked at him again. He had a nice face. "Are you Walter?" He stopped in his tracks and looked at her. He seemed to hesitate, then nodded.

"Then I ought to introduce myself and perhaps apologise again," she said. "I am Anna."

He gave another broad smile. "I would shake your hand, but I think it would smart a little. Besides, I think we're past that point." This was fortuitous. He didn't have to make excuses for his unannounced arrival. He would surely be forgiven after pulling this lady from the water.

Susan was the first to notice them. Then Bran, who hobbled over.

Anna tried, as politely as the situation allowed, to introduce everyone. "This is Walter from Helmislay. And this is Sir Drysdale."

Bran led them to his own bed and Walter laid her down. Susan shooed them out, sending Janey to fetch dry clothes, leaving both Bran and Walter standing outside her doorway, Walter holding the herb bag at a loss as to what to do with it. Bran held out his hand, took the bag and laid it to one side in a corner behind him. "Have you come far today?"

Walter shook his head. "I called at Redgate first and then here. I'm just glad the weather was good today, and that I forgot my manners and decided to arrive unannounced, otherwise I may have put off my visit and Anna could have drowned."

Bran indicated a place for them to sit and threw a glance at Robert for food to be brought. He did not like to say that Anna's death was highly unlikely as the hidden watch had already informed him of events.

"What happened exactly?"

Walter recounted all he had seen. He confessed to having watched for some time before the accident happened. He had held back from making his presence known incase he frightened her. He had intended to simply come to the house and be introduced later, although at this point he had no idea that this lady was Anna. He noted Drysdale's manners, which although very much to the fore, did not fully disguise his concern for Anna and the mental fencing he was erecting around her.

"You seem very protective of her," Walter said.

Bran put his head to one side, considering Walter's candour, then smiled. "I am Anna's sponsor. I hate to think of the danger she was in, that's all."

Walter nodded, "Of course."

Bran wanted nothing more than to tell Walter to go home again, but he had no right when he was unsure of how Anna would feel. Someone must have told Ben the news and he came to them and shook Walter's hand vigorously. "She might have drowned if you hadn't chosen to come now."

Walter shrugged modestly and Bran felt his hopes sinking. So far there was nothing to dislike about this man, and rescuing Anna was likely to give him a head start in Anna's affections. And maybe even Ben's. While Walter and Ben talked and Ben explained that it was not usual, but today there was to be a hanging, Bran returned to Anna's bedside to assess her injuries. He noticed Walter looking at him as he closed the door.

Susan was drying her hair and scolding her for being so careless. When she saw Bran enter the room, she made her excuses to leave the two together. "And perhaps you can talk some sense into her." As she passed Bran, she raised an eyebrow, "Silly to rush into things without thinking," she murmured, and left the room, closing the door behind her.

Bran smiled at Anna and sat down at the bedside. "Tell me where it hurts," he said.

She lifted an arm obediently. "This wrist." There was a large swelling on the back of her hand.

Bran looked. He gently took her hand. She winced. "Sorry."

"It's fine," she lied.

He smiled at her. "Anywhere else?"

"My ankle – this one." She pointed to her right leg.

He looked closely. The ankle was bruised and swollen. "Can you move it at all?"

She tried and winced again.

"So far, two breaks. I think you have found a valid excuse for not attending the hanging this afternoon."

She bit her lip. "Sorry for being a nuisance."

He shook his head. "My turn to be doctor for a change." He looked at her skin. Her brow was bruised and on pulling up her sleeves he found there were some ugly cuts and bruises there too.

"I'll prepare some more of the ointment you used on me. It'll help the swelling go down and take some of the pain from those cuts." He had such a strong desire to ask how she felt about Walter that he found he could not broach the subject. While he had been recuperating and they had spent so much time alone together, he had wondered whether to simply grasp the nettle and let her know how he felt. Before then, he had been too reticent, being obsessed with the idea that he would bring bad luck to her. Since the attack in the woods, he had been hoping she would forget about the proposal. But now, this Walter made him rethink. If he was a suitable match, shouldn't Bran stand back and allow the marriage. There was no reason why she should not be keen. Walter was far too good looking for his own good, yet he seemed modest enough. He reached for the bandages and unwound some of the cloth, looking at her as he did so. Still beautiful. He would always think that. It wasn't going to fade. She smiled at him. "What are you thinking?" she asked.

He looked down at his hands again, head to one side, and continued with his task. "I was wondering what you think of Walter." The bandage shrunk in length as he worked.

"Will you be gentle with me?" she grinned.

"Always," he smiled.

"What do you think of him?"

He said nothing until he had finished then gave a sigh and said. "It's not important what I think of Walter. What do you think?"

She gave a little shrug. "I'm glad he was there when I needed him." She looked at Bran, "But apart from that, I don't know. I was hoping you could give me some guidance."

Bran gave a self-deprecating laugh. "I'm hardly an expert on marriage."

Anna felt his reticence but thought the trace of scorn in his tone was surely just her imagination. Perhaps he had been reminded of Catherine. "Do you think he's unsuitable?"

Bran shook his head. "I didn't say that. Spend some time with him. See how you get on. It'll give us time to check out his loyalty to Henry." He hated himself for encouraging the relationship.

There was a dull pragmatism in his voice. Anna felt that Bran was being very logical seeing as though they were discussing what should be an emotional issue. "I am sorry I was so stupid to have fallen in the stream."

"As long as you are here safe and sound: that is all that matters. As for Walter, it's a big decision." He moved further down the bed so he could see to her damaged ankle.

After a closer inspection, he looked at her shaking his head, realising what a close call she must have had. The door opened behind them and Ben and Walter walked in. Bran stood up.

"Breaks to the wrist and ankle," he said to Ben. "You'll have to excuse me, I have some things to see to before this afternoon," and he left. Anna felt a little empty when he had gone. She had hoped he would stay so they could talk about Walter on their own later.

Ben apologised on Bran's behalf, "Sir Drysdale prefers to teach and invent in order to improve life rather than provide a venue for ending it."

"Why the change?" Walter asked.

Ben, although pleased with this young man for saving his daughter, knew it would be terribly naïve to confide in him so soon. "A long story," he said, and he turned his attentions to Anna.

While Ben chastised his daughter for worrying him, Walter studied her. In spite of the bruising and wet hair, she looked rather pretty. He liked the shape of her mouth. The wet dress and having to carry her had already given him a good opinion of her body. He looked away as Ben turned to him and held out an arm to guide him back out of the doorway. "You'll have to forgive me for this Walter, but we need to assess how you feel about the troubles between the King and his sons." He was very careful not to give away his own loyalties.

"Of course," said Walter. "I hear the country is divided."

Ben raised an eyebrow. "Seemingly." They entered another room and Walter was seated at a stool. Bran, Marc, Joss, Will and Ben sat before him. In spite of his heroics with Anna, he saw that he was not accepted yet as Joss and Will did not introduce themselves. Not that it mattered to Walter. He knew who they were anyway. Their reputation made it common knowledge. Ben was the first to speak.

"While I am grateful for your timely arrival, I must remind you that any further talks about marriage will rely on two very important things. Firstly, where your loyalties lie in the pending rebellion and secondly, whether Anna wishes to proceed."

He looked at Walter expectantly. At first, he seemed to ponder in a serious manner, then his face broke into a smile, he shook his head and turned his palms upwards.

"I was going to tell you what distinguished company I was in and that I was flattered to even be considered as a husband for your beautiful daughter, which I am, but I feel that flattery has no value to you. So – the rebellion. I remember my father talking to me about the difference between now and when Stephen and Matilda were fighting over the throne. He told me it was very easy for those who had only known of the good times to lack appreciation of what a good king could do. Especially the young, who feel they can teach their elders and betters a thing or two. I remember him talking of how his castle was besieged a number of times, simply because there was no decisive force preventing it from happening. I was a child when he told me. I remember feeling a sense of outrage that strange men could threaten my father and my home in that way. When I hear of the King's troubles with young Henry, Scotland and France, I feel that same sense of outrage.

I am not a knight of distinction, although I am eager to prove myself loyal to the King. That will not change, even if it means I must give up my suit for Anna and perhaps spend some time in captivity if your loyalties differ from mine. I have few men, my father wishes to protect his home again, but he offers you the services of his son," here he bowed his head, "and fifteen men if you are to fight for the king."

Joss considered him and began a two hour line of questioning involving those he had discovered to have signed over to the rebels' cause.

Below them, Alric was saying his prayers with a brother from the monastery in Durham. He was cold. He wondered if he would feel cold from dread even if he were outside in the sunshine. How would this unravel? He was entrusting his life to others. The monk left. He lay huddled in his cloak, not knowing whether he wished time to stand still or move quickly. Whenever he thought ahead, an icy ache of anxiety made him feel sick.

Above him, Walter was being discussed. "If he knows as much as we do, he could be lying." Joss observed. Walter's answers had all been perfect. "The offer of fifteen men sounds good," he continued, "unless you consider it simply as a way to infiltrate our ranks and turn traitor when we least expect it."

"Wouldn't he have simply left Anna to drown?" asked Will.

Marc's arms were folded across his chest. "I don't trust him."

The others looked at him. In truth, he was simply defending Bran's position as a potential husband for Anna, knowing he would not do it himself. He thought quickly, "Why arrive unannounced? I would never have done that to Susan's father."

Ben rubbed his chin. "To be fair, I heard of Walter's interest a while ago. I let Anna know, but she seemed to show no interest." He smiled. "Better things to do, I think she said. And these days, it seems best to act spontaneously, rather than give enemies time to sabotage your plans." He considered.

Will glanced at Joss then asked, "What do you think, Bran?"

"Play along with his idea. If he is a rebel we might as well have fifteen men preoccupied here, but be ready for any foul play. Perhaps you could warn Anna not to get too close until we are sure. Until the rebellion is crushed. That would give time for Walter to prove which side he is really on. And to see how he treats Anna. It won't be too difficult to keep an eye on them."

"If Anna is still dismissive of the idea of marriage, I'll send him on his way, rebel or not. I won't have her feeling uncomfortable."

Will rubbed his chin. "I know we have never said that daughters of the Northern should marry our knights – after all it could become rather incestuous, but…" he gave Bran a steady look, "shouldn't we make it known that marriage is on the cards for her now. She's rather special and I cannot help thinking that it would take a knight from the Northern to see it."

Ben nodded seemingly unaware of the implications for Bran. "I'll let her know there is no reason for her to agree to a first proposal."

Bran looked away from the company. He felt painfully self-conscious, especially as Ben seemed to have no inkling of what had become more apparent to everyone else.

They turned back to Walter. "You're welcome to stay here," said Bran, "but we will save any decisions about marriage until we're free of present troubles." There was a knock on the door. "Speaking of which," he said, "it would be cruel to keep Alric waiting any longer."

All stood and left the room to be present at Alric's hanging. Joss looked to Marc knowingly and the younger man knew he was to keep an eye on Walter incase there were any plans afoot to sabotage the execution.

There was quite a crowd on the bank top where the gallows had been constructed. Bran had not allowed it in the bailey as he would think of it whenever he passed the place. Unlike executions in Durham, there was neither jeering nor cheering as Alric was helped up the steps. The children had been kept indoors. Men from the Northern meandered amongst the people, taking positions which gave them a good vantage point, not of the criminal to be hanged, but more vulnerable areas on the periphery of the spectators. Marc stayed near the steps to the Hall, having a good view of both Walter's and Alric's faces from there.

Joss, having seniority of rank, reminded Alric of the crime that had led him here and asked if there was anything he would like to say in his defence before it was too late. Alric looked straight ahead, recognising Isabel in the crowd, and gave a brief, "No, Sir."

The hangman stepped forward to put the hood over Alric's head. Alric leaned back a little. "No hood."

"The hood is for the benefit of the people watching, not you," said the executioner.

Alric shook his head again.

The hangman looked to Joss who nodded then watched Alric's eyes carefully. Marc now turned his full attention to Walter. He was watching like a curious child, seeming to examine the structure, the rope, Alric's face. Then looking to see how people around him were reacting.

The rope was placed round Alric's neck. Alric shifted uncomfortably. He glanced about nervously as if he were about to be struck from behind. He looked into the crowd. Isabel had noticed Walter and now looked back to Alric, her mouth a circle of surprise. The hangman tightened the noose. Alric looked about him more wildly as he was led to the edge of the platform, in front of which a deep ditch had been dug to allow a longer fall and hence a more humane neck breaking death.

The hangman took no pleasure in watching people die and did not allow a cruel pause before pushing Alric over the edge. Alric was startled. This was it.

When Alric's body had stopped its twitchings and the crowd began to disperse, Marc continued to watch Walter. To Marc, there seemed nothing underhand in Walter's behaviour – except – perhaps he was wrong, but for a fleeting moment he thought Walter was grinning to himself. Marc doubted his own judgement, thinking he was over compensating to be rid of this rival of Bran's. Just as he relaxed, Walter turned and looked directly at him and tilted his chin sharply upwards as if enquiring, "What do you make of me then?"

Marc held his gaze. Walter did not look away. Marc wasn't one for making lasting judgements based on first impressions, but he was certain he had an enemy. Susan took his hand and he smiled at her then looked back to Walter who was now speaking with Ben. It was a pity no one chose to watch Isabel.

Marc apologised to Susan and took his leave of her in order to find Bran. It took some time. His friend obviously wanted some privacy, but Marc could not let things lie. He went to the trace room and knocked tentatively, knowing this was a place Bran went if he wanted some time to himself.

Bran gave a weary "Come in, Marc," before his friend had time to knock more than once.

Marc entered and gave Bran a grin. "I know I'm disturbing you but I don't care."

Bran leaned his elbows on his desktop and gave Marc a wry look of thanks.

"When are you going to tell her?" asked Marc.

Bran raised his eyebrows at his friend's direct manner. "I am not."

Marc frowned, "Why not?"

"Because if she was interested, she would have let me know by now."

"Maybe she has and you just have not seen it."

Bran shook his head.

"She enjoys your company. She won't let anyone else tend to you. Besides, why should she be the brave one?"

Bran gave him an enquiring look.

"You are too cowardly to tell her you love her... yes see?" he added as Bran winced at the mention of love, "but you would have her reveal all to you. Is that really fair?"

"Ben will tell Anna to consider casting a wider net. If it turns out she is not fond of Walter, I'll tell her then."

Marc shook his head. "I can't believe you would lose her so easily. Perhaps she is better off without you. God knows it would be hard work for her having to squeeze out any sign of affection."

Bran took a deep breath to quell his anger. Part of him knew that his friend was merely playing Devil's advocate.

"If this Walter is good enough for her, and she can love him, she is better off marrying safely. There would be no rest with me. There is always someone trying to claim that Drysdale is not held legally. To get to me it would be very easy to target Anna."

He turned back to his papers. "That is an end to it."

Marc stared at his friend in disbelief. "Is this what travelling taught you? It may have broadened your mind, but your heart is sadly lacking. I know what Will was getting at in there. He wants you to speak up. Tell Ben."

Bran laid down his papers again and, tried to keep his voice even, "Has it ever occurred to you that the last thing Ben wants is for Anna to marry a Jew? That he is hoping this marriage will keep her safe?"

Marc was speechless. He shook his head. "Ben loves you like a son. He chose to bring you up: no one forced him into it. He would be happy to agree a match between you."

"Would he?" There was a sarcastic tone in Bran's voice that Marc had not heard before. Marc made as if to answer, but Bran held up his hand. "Be honest Marc. Imagine Anna and I had children and one of yours fell in love with one of ours. Would you encourage it? Or would your misgivings guide her elsewhere?"

Marc frowned at him. "I would be delighted – unless, of course, your children inherit this self-pitying streak." He changed tack. "All right, let's forget about you, shall we? Obviously, your feelings for her aren't strong enough to make a good marriage anyway. She deserves better." He ignored the angry glare from his friend and continued, "I still say we need to be rid of him. There is something not right. I cannot put my finger on it, but I'm sure."

Bran let his anger subside, knowing his friend's instincts were reliable.

"What is it?"

"I know you want logic and this is not logical," said Marc, taking a deep breath. "When we were out there, I felt sure he was challenging me. He gave me a look as if to say –come on then, find me out." Marc acted out what had happened for his friend. "He lingered behind and grinned, then turned and looked straight at me. It was definitely a challenge. I didn't look away and neither did he. In fact, if Susan hadn't distracted me, we would probably be out there glaring at each other still."

Bran considered. "Maybe he thought of you as a rival for Anna, but then saw you with Susan. He seemed to wonder at my concern when he carried her down – perhaps he's just prone to jealousy, in which case Anna will reject him – she knows how counterproductive jealousy is."

Marc said nothing more. Bran offered, "Tell Joss how you feel. At least the rebellion gives us time to see whether Walter will prove himself worthy."

Marc nodded and turned to go, "Sorry for shouting," he muttered. They grinned at each other foolishly, at which Marc perked up, knowing the argument was forgotten, "It's just that the best thing I ever did was let Susan know how I felt. It was you who advised me to tell her, if you remember. Stop making excuses – just do it." Then he left hastily before Bran could talk himself out of it again.

Left on his own, Bran considered it all more carefully and honestly. The remark about being unworthy of Anna had gone deeper than Marc knew. Cowardice played a large part. If Anna rejected him, he would feel he ought not to spend time alone with her anymore and he loved these times. Ben trusted him, so did Anna for that matter. He looked blindly at the papers in front of him. Perhaps Marc was right. If he let Anna know now and all went well, it might not seem so awkward with Walter having only been here a short while – but the longer he waited the harder it would be. Yes. He would try to tell her as soon as possible. And even if she did turn him down, he would be travelling up country with Joss soon. Distance could do much to dilute the embarrassment.

As soon as he had accepted that this is what he would do, he found himself daydreaming about her, trying to picture the scenario. It was a pleasant way to spend an hour or two, merely dabbling with the paperwork now.

Eventually, the light at the window having submerged the room in honey, he stood up, stretched, picked up his cloak and made his way to the main house. He would tell her before the week was out.

Anna herself had been doing some thinking. Susan had given her food for thought. She told Anna to think of herself as someone precious. It was a fault in girls to be so self-deprecating that they accepted the first offer of marriage that came their way. Some girls had no choice but to let their fathers do the picking, so it would be a shame not to make the most of her freedom.

"I thought Marc was your first proposal," said Anna.

"Oh no." Susan shook her head. "There were others, but I'd always liked Marc and persuaded my father he would prove himself in time." She looked at Anna, then sat by her on the bed. "That's what I am trying to tell you. If I had only considered those of my own rank, I would have married while Marc was overseas." Susan straightened the bed covers. "You could wait it out for someone the likes of Bran to propose. It would not be unrealistic."

"Bran's my brother – well sort of."

Susan looked at her. "As far as I can see, the two of you are most suitably matched: you spend hours together quite happily."

Anna grinned at the ceiling. "Are you telling me I ought to start flirting with my overlord?"

"No," Susan said, her head to one side. "I'm just saying that men don't spend hours alone with women unless they are quite taken with them. Come to think of it," she added, "there aren't many men who would be allowed that freedom. Your father obviously trusts him."

"Oh, stop it. You'll make me feel awkward the next time I see him."

Susan stood to go. "He's the sort of man who would wait until you start showing an interest in marriage." She stooped and pushed the hair away from Anna's brow to make sure the bleeding had stopped. "I am just allowing you to see that your choices may not be as limited as you think." She left Anna to ponder on her own.

And ponder she did. She knew she ought to get some rest yet had never felt so restless. She closed her eyes but her mind raced. Usually, her days were a series of purposes: simples, studying, writing and, lately, seeing to Bran's needs. Quite suddenly, the tide had turned. Bran was out of the sick-bed and she had taken his place. The luxury of the extra time it gave her made her feel like an idle fraud. Still, even if she struggled out of bed, there was little she could do with a broken wrist and ankle.

She knew she ought to be making decisions, but it wasn't easy. Perhaps that was the way it should be. Marriage would change her life after all. Although, according to the stories, her own father had known instantly that he would marry her mother. Had her mother known it too? Never having known her meant that she had little to miss, but today, for the first time, she regretted not being able to turn to her for advice. Perhaps she would say wait – if you are not sure, retain the status quo. Say no. She wondered if she ought to ask Susan. Not only was she happily married, but she was the closest thing to a mother Anna had. But sometimes Susan could be very confusing. What was all that talk about men like Bran. Had she said that because she disliked Walter? Did she simply like the idea of her two closest friends being married? This morning, when Walter had fished her from the stream, the decision had seemed easy – even made for her by a higher force. She had been awash with relief at being helped to safety and Walter had seemed a rather attractive proposition. But now, as she began to take her safety for granted once more, marriage still seemed like an enormous gap to bridge. She knew it was because she had been so fortunate in her life so far. There seemed no incentive to make changes.

She pondered on Susan's earlier words. It sounded so odd to hear her talking about Bran in that way. Anna remembered that Susan had seemed to do that same thing just before the forest feast. If she knew something why did she not just come out with it? Perhaps Marc and Susan wanted a reason to keep Bran at home for longer and had decided between them that Anna was it. Were they speaking to Bran in the same way? She burned with embarrassment at the mere thought, especially when they had spent so much time alone together and him naked under the covers. If they had, had Bran laughed at the implication? Did familiarity really breed contempt? Then again, she reassured herself, he had told her father he enjoyed her company. She pondered herself back into doubting: was that really such a compliment when he had said the alternative was to go mad with boredom? Her head spun and the bruise at her hairline began to throb painfully. This Bran conundrum would have been hard enough even without this morning's fiasco at the stream.

With sleep refusing to come to the rescue, she wished there was some diversion to distract her. Thankfully, her thoughts were interrupted by a knock at the door.

Bran entered. She felt a stab of surprise on looking at him so soon after her musings and hoped the dimming light hid her reddening face. She grasped around for something to say that would sound normal – but it did not help that the day had been so unusual.

"Is Alric executed?"

He nodded and came and sat at her bedside, thinking her discomfort was due to her injuries and the nature of Alric's death. He held up a length of wood which had been fashioned into a crutch. "I found this for you," he said, stroking the wood in a final check for splinters. "I know you will be using it under your left arm, but take it steady at first. If you stumble your reflex may be to save yourself with your injured hand."

She smiled her thanks.

"I couldn't imagine you staying put for long."

"I feel rather ill-mannered taking your bed. You can sleep here tonight?" She could have kicked herself as soon as the words were out.

He grinned and gave a quick raise of the eyebrows, "It's very accommodating of you, Anna, but I won't risk annoying your father by taking advantage of the offer."

Although he had taken the awkwardness from the situation, she found that, even after having spent weeks speaking freely with him, she could not think of anything to say. She wished Susan had kept her opinions to herself. He seemed less talkative than usual too. Or perhaps she was just imagining it – letting her own misgivings magnify every pause. He made another assessment of her injuries and moved about the room, mixing lotions and potions, washing his hands, closing the window. Eventually, he came and sat by her again. He still seemed a little awkward.

"We need to check out Walter's background. I'm sure everything will be fine. His father has sent fifteen men to help put down the rebellion. Once we are sure, it leaves you free to make your choice."

Her mouth became a thin line and she nodded. She wondered if he wanted to know how she felt. She plucked up the courage to look at him. He looked back. She shrugged a little. "Big decision," she proffered.

He nodded. "Remember, no one will force you to rush into things."

She took a sip from the cup of water he held for her. He still looked at her as he took the cup away and placed it back on the shelf. "Perhaps we could try out that crutch tomorrow," he said. "Practise getting you mobile before I have to leave."

She felt a pang. "Will it be soon?"

"Sooner rather than later. There are terrible things happening all over the North. We really should have left before now. Nipped things in the bud. The sooner we move, the further away from our homes the danger is when we meet the Scottish forces."

"Shall I still write for you?" she asked, nonchalantly studying the bandage at her wrist.

He smiled, but his tone belied his true feelings, "If you're not too busy making decisions about marriage proposals."

She looked at him then away again quickly, trying to hide her disappointment in his tone. Contrition made him wish he had kept his mouth shut. Perhaps Marc was right. He did not deserve her. He stroked her cheek and she looked back at him.

"I would love you to write for me, it's just…well," he stumbled a little. "I guess if I was Walter, I would not want my intended setting down her thoughts for another man. It's something you may need to consider."

Anna obviously had not. "Oh. In that case I have no intention of marrying him."

Bran grinned. "For now, let's just say that you will continue your writing. We haven't even checked his background yet. And perhaps there's no harm in writing to a man because he has to be away from home."

She smiled up at him again. With his spirits lifting, he quickly looked away from her eyes, knowing he would give too much away. He made pretence of concentrating on the cut to her head. Maybe, if he was to tell her, it should be now. Quite suddenly, he said, "I'll miss you."

She gazed at him. He escaped her scrutiny by standing up and leaning the crutch in the corner of the room. This done, he turned back to her, but kept the distance he had gained. He put his head to one side then paid rather a lot of attention to the ointment at his fingers, casting about for a cloth to wipe his hands clean. As he did so, he said quietly, "I'll miss you a lot."

She smiled at his endearing awkwardness and opened her mouth to speak, but a knock at the door snatched away the opportunity. Susan, in between feeding her own children, listening to her husband's woes and tending to Anna, came bustling speedily into the room, determined to keep up her usual level of efficiency in spite of the business of the day. On seeing Bran, she stopped dead in her tracks, then completely unfazed she set the bowl of leek soup she was carrying on the shelf by Anna's bedside. She was going to turn on her heels and leave the two alone together, but Bran nodded courteously, saying, "Time I went." Normally, he would have kissed her brow on leaving the room, but this time he did not. At the door, he hesitated, turned and said, "I'll see you tomorrow, Anna," and was gone.

Susan looked from the now closed door to her young friend. "Have I interrupted something?"

"None of your business," Anna replied, hiding her smile by struggling to sit upright using one good hand. In spite of the pain, she felt wonderful.

Walter mused over the situation. A lot of things seemed to hang in the balance. He needed to talk to Anna. If he could not be alone with her, there was no point hanging round. He realised it would be hard to get any privacy. He was well aware of the men keeping a watch within and without Drysdale's walls. His only chance of being alone with her was to be in the sickroom and there were people forever going in and out. If there was to be a lull in visitors, it would be Anna who would need to suggest it. Marc was a pain in the behind. He would have to watch that one. And Drysdale was hard to fathom. What was he to Anna apart from overlord? He knew Ben had brought them both up, but did they think of each other as brother and sister? It was a shame that knights with broken bones were not destroyed like their horses. And he could not help thinking that someone like Anna would have plenty of admirers already. If not, why not? As he approached the bedroom doorway it opened and Susan walked out.

Susan having just gleaned from an unusually cryptic Anna that she would need to have some time alone with Walter to let him down gently, bobbed her head at him courteously and said, "I'll let Anna know you are here and see to it that you have some privacy."

He couldn't believe his luck. Susan left the door open for him and hurried off to tell Marc the good news. Anna was going to reject Walter. Something must have happened with Bran.

Walter stepped over the threshold and closed the door behind him. He noticed her lips were a darker red than before, probably because she had eaten now.

"I'm glad to see some of your colour has returned."

Anna thanked him and he took her smile as an invitation to sit by her on the bed. She felt a little annoyed at his forward manner, but being annoyed at him only made letting him down that much easier.

"I thought we should have some time alone together," Walter began.

Anna thought it best to cut to the main issue quickly to save Walter any embarrassment.

"I'm glad you came," she nodded. "There is something I have to say. It's rather awkward really. You see, I do not really feel like I am ready for marriage."

Walter did not like her tone, but said evenly, "Let me be so impolite as to have my say first. I think from your tone that you feel decided, but please let me speak, then make your final decision."

Anna looked away. She felt tense enough without this. She had felt herself quite brave and assertive dealing with the refusal so quickly. Now her stomach churned and the delay sent painful spasms through her wrist and ankle. She lay stiffly, hoping he would not be too wordy, before she simply had to repeat her rejection. She tried to concentrate half her attention on the familiar sounds of the house in order to lift some of her unease: the trestles being cleared away;

Robert scolding a page's clumsiness; Susan and Marc's children shrieking with glee in some game or other.

Before Walter began, he stroked his thumb and forefinger down his beard, as if thinking carefully. "Most women have little choice in who they marry. You know, I had a cousin who was betrothed before she was even born. The man she married was twenty five years old even then. I used to think that was so old," he smiled. He held his hands palms upwards and shrugged. "And yet, here I am now, that same age, not so old at all, harbouring a heartfelt wish that your father was the type who would make this decision for you. I know that when he checks out the family and their loyalties, he will be happy; but I also know that that does not mean the issue of us is anywhere near finalised. He will leave that to you. Soon, The Northern will make their way towards Scotland. Some will remain behind and I will ask if I may help to protect this area with my own men. I ask this because it will give me time to prove myself to you. I am not pretending to be the best knight and husband the world has ever known, but I will always strive to be so."

Anna's nerves were such that she would have squeezed her hands together if it would not cause so much pain. Why did he have to make it so difficult? She spoke quietly as if it would reduce his embarrassment. "I am touched by your words, Walter, and feel you mean what you say, but I am afraid my mind is made up. It would be unfair to say otherwise."

Something hardened in Walter's face and he folded his arms. "You may live to regret that decision, Anna."

She looked at him, surprised by his arrogance and no longer feeling a need to be polite.

"We have nothing left to say to each other, Walter."

He nodded and said quietly, "Yes. Words lose their strength after a certain point. Actions tend to speak louder." His brow creased as if he was annoyed and, when he sat a little straighter, Anna thought he was getting up to go, but instead he leaned forward and kissed her hard on her mouth. She was so shocked it took a few seconds for the added pain in her wrist to register as she tried to push him away. His mouth was wet and bruising and, for the second time that day, she found it difficult to breathe. She was not strong enough to pull away and felt her heart pounding and a heavy chill in her stomach that something so outrageous could be happening here and now in Bran's bed. Trying to detach herself from the humiliation of it all, she told herself he would have to stop eventually and then she could call out. Her sense of alarm grew when she felt his body weight move further over her. The heel of one of his boots swept against her broken inner ankle making her leg give a rigid judder of pain. This was no enforced kiss simply to teach her a lesson and save him some face. He was not going to stop. He lay over her, holding both of her arms over her head with one of his. The other hand became a gag as soon as he freed his mouth to speak. He could feel the adrenalin of attempted but impossible escape trembling through her.

Glancing at the place above her head where his one hand tightly grasped both of hers, he noticed how pale and lifeless her puppet-like fingers seemed. He looked at her and smiled that disarming smile. "I imagine that really hurts."

Anna, trying hard to breathe, made no response. He grinned and forced her to nod with the hand that muzzled her. "Um. I thought so. Still, there's a good antidote for pain. When I was younger, I complained to my father of a headache. Do you know what he did? He punched me in the stomach to take my mind off it." He lifted his hips and dragged the covers down. Anna struggled, the pain in her wrist now paling into insignificance. She attempted to call out in spite of her mouth being covered. As she tried to move away, he grimaced and his grip tightened. He said calmly, "Someone should explain to women that struggling only makes it all the more enjoyable." He could see there were tears in her eyes. "Just as well. Your eyes aren't so attractive now."

Anna hit out at him as he freed her hands to fumble at his own clothing. Her arms trembled so much she felt as feeble as a kitten as she pulled at his chemise to lift him away from her. She felt him pushing hard against her, trying to find her as she struggled. Momentarily, he stopped, pressing his hand harder against her mouth. No smile now: more a focused anger. She felt his free hand move behind her back to hold her still against him. As soon as he found her, he lunged hard. She felt the pressure hard against her and for a moment thought nothing would give. Perhaps he would stop trying. But no.

Sharp tearing pain and a humiliating misery let her know she had failed to keep him from her. As he carried on, he breathed his stinking breath in her face and the knife-like pain did not stop. She closed her eyes trying to imagine she was suffering something else – another prolonged fall. She felt her stomach lurching and tried to stop herself from retching while he covered her mouth. God let it be over soon. He shifted his weight a little, arching his back, and moved slower but harder with a stifled groan. Keeping his hand over her mouth, he lifted himself from her.

He tried to steady his breathing. "I saw how you looked at me when I carried you down this morning. Act like a whore and you will be treated like one." He paused, looking about the room, listening. "I am going to take my hand from your mouth. You may choose to take the opportunity to call out. If you do you will be sorry. I recognise your sense of right and wrong may be such that you don't care if I carry on hurting you, if it means I'm found out. However, I'm sure you wouldn't want anything to happen to Richard, Bobby, Agnes or Janey. She's a pretty little girl."

He held his head at an angle and said, "Listen."

It was hard to concentrate on anything but she could make out the laughter and squeals of the children. "My men have arrived. I have been surprised at some of the atrocities they will commit just because I pay them to. They make my life so much easier. One word from the window and I'm sure the laughter would stop. Abruptly. It's your choice."

He lifted his hand slowly. Anna's mind raced. It seemed far fetched that he would go through with his threat. On the other hand, she would not have thought him capable of rape. She just wanted him gone. She said nothing. He lifted himself from her. In spite of the awful wetness he had left her with, the pain now burned. She turned her head away, furiously humiliated. How could she have let this happen? How dare he? With her father only yards away?

He carried on talking as he straightened his robes. "Marriage or not, Anna, we are stuck together. I cannot imagine the Northern will want to taint their glowing reputation with a marriage to a lady who has been used, who perhaps even carries another man's child. Take what you can get and be grateful. If you are lucky, I may marry you anyway."

Although she had her back to him, she heard him come back to the bed. She curled up into a tighter ball. He pulled at the bedding so he could inspect the cloth where she had lain. "I thought so," he smiled. "They say you never forget your first time."

He bent over her and spoke quietly in her ear. "Remember, there are fifteen men here. I know they aren't a match for the Northern, but that makes little difference. Even if they lose, there will be deaths. Who would it be I wonder? I imagine they would leave you until last. Or maybe Susan. Not bad after five children." He walked to the door as if leaving, but on glancing at the bed he came back. Her bandages were awry. She flinched when he sat on the bed again. She wanted to cry with the pain, but was afraid to make a noise. She clenched her teeth, breathing through the spasms and wishing he was gone. Half of her felt like a terrified child in the middle of a nightmare: the other half outraged by what had happened yet knowing her urge to strike him would be useless. He undid the dressings and tried to make them neater. She found it impossible to keep the twice injured limbs from twitching. Then he straightened the bedding under her and over her. For a second time at the door, he looked again. With nothing seemingly untoward, he left the room.

Anna stared into space consumed by shame, anger and loneliness in turn. Twice she struggled to the garderobe and vomited. The third time she decided it was pointless to return to the bed and stayed shivering in the corner until her stomach calmed itself. After dark, she felt her way back to the bed. Her head throbbed. She lay in the darkness turning over what had happened. When Susan came in to check on her in the half light cast by her candle, hoping to glean some gossip, Anna lay so still with her back to the door that she thought she was sleeping and left her in peace. When Susan had gone, Anna suddenly needed to know that the door was locked incase Walter decided to come back in the night. She limped to the doorway and secured it.

In spite of the burning humiliation, she shivered. When she limped back to the bed she felt something trickle at her thighs. Holding back angry tears, she swilled a cloth around the bowl of now cold water and attempted to clean herself. She washed again and again, until the bowl was empty and the wet stone floor reflected the pale grey light from the window. Then she lay on the bed again: Bran's bed, her skin prickling with gooseflesh. The anger surged once more. How dare he do this in Drysdale? Her mind raced and her head throbbed so that when a messenger come in the night to warn Joss that Scotland was on the move she heard nothing. Walter was right. It would be so easy to go to her father and tell him, but not now, when they needed to focus on the King's troubles. She had heard terrible stories of families being slaughtered, even babies being killed in the womb. People needed her father and Bran more than she did. If they became the weaker force, they would all be in dire trouble. She had no intention of letting the Northern down.

But if he thought she had given in, he was wrong. She would let him think he was winning to buy time until she could think more clearly. In spite of her outrage at what had happened, she must remember everyone else.

But what if he had left her pregnant? Well maybe that was his plan. If a child was part of the plan then surely she would be safe for a while. Like it or not, she would need to get over this. This wasn't about her. She was sure Walter had bigger plans afoot.

And what of Bran? She thought back to how he had been today. She wanted to smile but could only cry. She deliberately flexed her broken wrist to pull herself out of it. Stop it, Anna. You are a thinker. You will find a way to be rid of Walter without jeopardizing the bigger campaign. Maybe he was arrogant enough to think her capable of falling in love with him, even after … perhaps that was her way forward. Again, she wished she could tell her father, but a skirmish here and now could ruin everything. And then she would be stuck with Walter indefinitely. Besides, Joss would not leave the community unprotected. Perhaps she would be able to avoid Walter for the most part.

As it grew light, she realised she must open the door to prevent suspicion. She did so, then waited for Susan to come.

When her friend arrived, she noticed the older woman had been crying.

"What's wrong?"

Susan shook it off. "They leave today. I know it's the way of things but it doesn't get any easier. Ben will come soon, and Bran." She looked at her friend to gauge her reaction and noticed how pale and ill she looked.

"I'm sorry Anna. I knew I should have woken you to give you more medicine, but you were sleeping so soundly. You look like death."

She busied herself , finally asking, "Have you given Walter your refusal?"

Anna looked away from her friend. "I'd rather not talk about it," she said.

"Well. I suppose it wouldn't be seemly to gloat."

Anna said nothing.

"Does your head ache?"

Anna nodded.

Susan felt her brow. "Feverfew for you."

Susan's comings and goings passed in a blur for Anna. Her older friend paused at the door before she left, brow furrowed. She would keep a closer eye on Anna. The incident at the stream must have been worse than they thought. She might have to reset that wrist. Not something she looked forward to.

A little later, her father arrived, concerned at her sickly look. Anna smiled. "I am fine. I just didn't sleep well that's all. Susan will look after me."

"You know we have to leave today?"

Anna nodded.

"Joss is choosing a guard now to protect the families here."

He stroked her hair. "You don't look well at all, Sweetheart."

"A few days and I'll be fine."

Ben looked about the room. "Ah, there it is. Bran said he had found an old crutch for you. A lot of the pages end up with a broken bone or two." He looked at his nails and said nonchalantly, "He seems in better spirits of late."

She tried to smile, not wanting to divert him from the seriousness of what lay ahead.

He took her hand. "No matter what happens, Anna, there are men who will keep you safe, even if they have to serve under a different king."

Anna looked at him. Was he telling her there was a chance they might lose?

She squeezed his hand. "You will win. I feel it. There is no one stronger."

Ben sighed. "Unfortunately, we don't all fight by the same rules." He noticed her crestfallen look and changed his tone. "Of course, we will win. We just have to be careful: it's not just a case of fending off Scotland. Everyone wants to appear loyal to a potential winner – and gain a reward of land of course."

Anna sighed. "If it is to be shared so many times over, there seems little point fighting for it?"

Ben nodded. "Just what Bran said."

There was a knock at the door. Ben stood and leaned forward to kiss her. "That will be him now. I will leave the two of you to say goodbye. Get better soon, Sweetheart. It won't be long."

He left as Bran came in.

Anna was taken aback at the strength of her feelings on seeing him. Was this God's little joke? Once the man becomes unattainable, make him more attractive. Bran sat at her bedside. Like her previous visitors, he was immediately struck by how ill she looked.

"Have you eaten yet?"

"Susan has gone to fetch something from the kitchen."

He stroked her brow. "You're cold." He said and stood and brought more covers from a chest beneath the window. He tucked them around her.

"I wish we did not have to leave so soon. I feel I ought to be here with you."

Anna shook her head. "It's bad enough that I've taken your bed. Really, I am not so unwell."

He held her hand. Immediately, he noticed a difference in the dressings and began to unwind the cloth, while thinking how to broach the real reason he had come to see her. He had thought about how to say this all night, but it was no easier now that he was here. "I had been hoping to help you walk a little today."

She knew what she had to say, but this was so hard.

He continued, "I'd been hoping we could spend more time together. There's something I need to ask you." He looked from her hands to her face.

She looked away. God, this was unbearable.

"You see," he paused, "I don't want to leave without letting you know how I feel about you."

She looked back at him, reached out and placed her fingers gently against his lips, stopping him before he said anymore.

He took her hand and gently kissed her palm. Then let it go as she shook her head. He looked at her, head to one side, and asked quietly, "No?"

She shook her head again, felt her hand come to her face. It was quiet for such a long time. He reached to stroke her hair away from her forehead. She put her arms around his neck, hid her face in his warmth and cried, whispering, "I'm sorry." She felt him sigh. She wanted him to know. To realise. To be able to see and hear that she was lying. To have grown so close to her that he could tell she was in trouble. He sat back and gently took her hands from his shoulders. "Thank you for being so honest." He kissed her forehead and stood up. "Bye Anna." And quietly, "Still write." Then he was gone.

Anna stared at the closed door, the force of holding back tears making her breath come in deep juddering sighs. It was a time of opposites.

Chapter Fifteen

Apart

Bran stood stony and grim while the pages, Richard and Stephen, busied about him with hauberk and greaves, assuming equally grave expressions on their young faces, thinking this was the way knights looked as they prepared for a campaign. For once, he could not blame Edwin. He blanked out as much of his surroundings as possible, trying to rid himself of the gut churning humiliation of being turned down. He had been arrogant enough to hope that Anna's rejection of Walter meant that he would be accepted as a consequence. And now he was left wondering whether they would ever share the same closeness again – even as brother and sister.

The time for him to join the other men came painfully soon. Marc would expect him to speak of it. He did not allow himself to ponder, but strode out to the group mounted on their destriers. Adela and Leona were there, saying their farewells before making their way to Bankside. His paranoia increased as he approached them. He avoided looking at Marc but as he swung into the saddle, he was aware of his friend turning his mount in order to speak with him. The predictability of it annoyed him.

"How did it go?" The happy note in Marc's voice irked him further.

He looked at him and shook his head, then away to Joss as if awaiting orders. Marc did not let it lie.

"What? She said no? But that cannot be right, she told Susan…"

Bran glared at Marc's irritating insistence. "That's an end to it," he growled and sat proud and upright, wishing Joss would get on with it so he could escape his friend's pity.

Joss was choosing those he wished to stay behind to protect the families. Marc was fearful for his own, especially now when it looked like Walter would be staying at Drysdale. He approached Joss and spoke. Joss shook his head. Marc, who would never do such a thing normally, raised his voice and Bran caught him trying to argue with their commander. Joss and Marc glared at each other.

"I have chosen the men who will remain behind as a safeguard. Wilf will see to it that they treat the families here with the same care as they would their own. He has no family so he will stay focused."

Marc made a final attempt, even though he knew he was pushing it, "Something is not right. Leaving them like this feels…"

Joss interrupted, his face now closed and inscrutable. "I know exactly how it feels to leave a family behind. The men I have chosen will carry out their duties objectively."

Marc fell back, now as uncomfortable as Bran. He did his best to hide it when Susan approached to say her goodbyes. Bran felt his annoyance grow once more as he predicted that Susan would poke her nose into his private affairs, but then Marc caught his eye and nodded towards his chamber window. He glanced up. Anna was there looking down at him. He nodded in acknowledgement and her hand rose in return. Strange that all it takes to restore hope is the tiniest of gestures. She rested her brow against the glass and watched them leaving. As they left, he found that he was able to salvage some of his self respect. At least it looked like they could still be civil to one another. Besides, unrequited love was the fashion now. Perhaps knowing how he felt and this enforced separation would allow her heart to grow fonder.

Anna had never felt so alone. She comforted herself a little by cooling her throbbing forehead against the cold pane. She knew it was feasible that she would see neither her father nor Bran again. But still, she knew Bran had liked her. Maybe his feelings would survive, in spite of the rejection, and when this was all over she could apologise. But what if he stayed away because of her, or worse, returned with a wife? Perhaps a lady who matched the imaginary one he said he carried in his head. She pushed this out of her mind. If she started to believe she had done the wrong thing now it would be unbearable.

Presently, the chamber door opened and Susan, a little out of breath from her quick ascent, bustled in.

"You should be lying down."

Anna turned to face her. In the light from the window, Susan could see her better. "My God. You look awful." She took her arm to help her back into the bed.

Anna resisted. "You know, I feel quite lonely in here. There is nothing to take my mind off things. Now that Marc has gone, would you mind if I stay with you and the children?"

"Anna, the children would hardly let you have a wink of sleep."

Anna pulled her arm away. "Please, Susan, I…" She brought her hand up to her face as her mouth contorted and she tried not to cry.

Susan studied her. "If it means so much to you of course you can come down stairs. I was only thinking of you." The older woman now felt quite selfish. Of course, Anna was upset. She was worried for her father and Bran. It would be good for her to have a friend to talk to, and once the children's chores were done, they could busy themselves out of doors now that the weather was fine. "It is a good idea. It will save me having to come up and down the stairs. Of course, you can come down with us, just rest here a little while longer and I'll make it ready."

Anna smiled her thanks, feeling foolish. She had thought she had spent all of her tears through the night. She now allowed Susan to help her to the bed far happier in the knowledge that it would be harder for Walter to catch her alone. Perhaps, when she was more mobile, she could explain to Wilf that Walter's attentions were not wanted. All she had to do was bide her time until these latest troubles were quelled. She felt a little safer for the present. She could hear the muffled voices of Walter and some other men in the Hall below.

Susan left and set her children the task of tidying and making room for Anna. They immediately grew excitable, loving their older friend. As Susan came back along the passage which would take her through the Hall, she heard the men laughing. She hoped they would have the manners to subdue their voices once it grew dark and the children needed to sleep. She was surprised they were in such good spirits anyway, when they were supposed to be focused on protecting the land and its people. She stopped in her tracks as Walter's voice cut through the laughter once more. It was only now that she realised what he was talking about. "I soon taught her what she really wanted. I thought the sheets would make a fetching wall hanging for the Jew. Anna of Redgate's maidenhead." Susan's stomach turned icy. She peered around the wall, looking to see what Wilf would have to say to this boasting. Obviously, Walter was telling tall tales after his rejection to protect his pride. Wilf stood up and the laughter subsided. By contrast, he spoke very quietly. "That kind of talk is not acceptable here, Walter."

Walter looked at him. He was slumped on the best chair, grinning like an idiot. "Strange," he mused. "Acceptance is the very subject on which I was speaking. Very willing, gasping, heaving acceptance."

A couple of the Walter's men gave a snort. Wilf quieted them with a glare. He turned back to Walter. "We don't do things that way here."

Walter sat up and rested his palms on the arms of the chair. "Oh, believe me Wilf, I know you don't do things that way."

Wilf held his gaze. "We need to talk privately."

Walter gave a short laugh. The other knights watched with interest, the Northern men being busy at their watch made them confident of their strength. Walter had no intention of leaving the room like a child to be chastised. "Leave us alone." The men were reluctant to leave, but no one wanted to be the one to voice his displeasure.

Susan, confident that Wilf would nip this in the bud, made haste to Anna's room, choosing to avoid the route through the Hall. The sooner she had her close by, the better she would feel. It would also give her a chance to warn her off Walter. He may have been rejected but he was deluding himself, and worse, deluding everyone else about it. Reputations were fragile things. And how dare he talk about Bran like that: as if he owned the place.

By the time she had reached Anna, she had made a firm decision not to repeat what Walter had said. If it had sickened Susan, what would it do to Anna? She smiled brightly as she walked back into the room. "Let's get you down there." She flung back the covers breezily and helped Anna back to her feet, then stopped. The sheets were marked: dry and chalky now, but marked all the same. Anna froze. Susan said nothing, but led Anna out and down the stairs, awkwardly trying to shoulder most of her weight to protect her ankle. When they reached the downstairs chamber, the children had already vacated, being under strict orders to allow Anna some peace. Susan led her to the pallet between the window and the wall, helped her into bed and examined her dressings before speaking.

Finally, she looked at her younger friend. "What happened since I saw you last night, Anna?"

Anna's mouth became a thin line. Then she looked about her to be sure they could not be overheard, took a deep breath, shook away the urge to cry and told her friend everything.

In the Hall, Wilf was glaring at Walter. "You had better be lying."

Walter smiled. "What's the matter? Jealous?"

Wilf did not grace the comment with an answer.

Walter played a little longer. "There is more than one way to skin a cat. If it transpires that the rebel forces are not strong enough, there is still the opportunity to get a foothold here through a blood link."

Wilf shook his head. "There is no reason for anyone in this community to come to harm. If I had known you would do this forcibly, I would never have agreed to make sure I was left behind."

Walter laughed. "Forcibly? The Northern have obviously spoilt their women for too long. Don't pretend you had no inkling of what would happen here."

"Leave Anna alone. It is not necessary."

"Are you going to stop me?"

"If need be."

"My men would not bother themselves with fair play if you turned against me."

Wilf gave a short soundless laugh. "You know as well as I do that as soon as your money runs out so will their loyalty."

Walter stood up and crossed the room to join him. "But that is not going to happen is it?"

He undid the fastening of his cloak at the throat, reached for Wilf's hands and arranged his fingers around his bare neck. "If you are tired of me, take advantage of our privacy. Go on. You could probably kill me with one hand, but I allow you two."

Wilf stared at him, taking in the flecked blue eyes, the smooth brow, saying nothing. "I thought so. You cannot kill me can you Wilf? In too deep."

Wilf freed his hands. He spoke almost in a whisper. "Don't goad me, Walter. Don't presume to test me. I have not been here before. I could not predict the outcome myself."

He stepped away. Susan's children ran through the Hall, Janey following with the baby, Maud, whose wet swaddling had prompted their hasty return. Wilf walked away.

"Don't spoil it for yourself. You are in a good position at the moment. When the tide turns and reveals more land, it'll be worth your while."

Wilf stopped at the doorway. He didn't bother to look back. "If you think I joined you because of the promise of land, you don't know me at all. And if you think a rebellion will yield every tenth rebel any more than a mouse's share, you know nothing about this fight."

Walter sat back in his chair, hands in his lap. If he left Anna alone, she was no use to him. If she was no use to him, she might as well be dead, except as a bargaining tool. Would Susan or any one of the children be just as useful there? Drysdale had seemed interested in Anna for himself and he owed her father. Even if it was only brotherly love, he did not seem the type to turn his back on the troubled. Wilf's morals were annoying. He gave an irritated sigh. He would leave Anna until she had healed. That would give him time to see whether she seemed healthy enough to carry a child. According to his father, the mother had had problems.

He stood up and fastened his cloak once more. If he was to leave Anna alone, he would have to find his fun elsewhere, and there was no chance of that with Wilf for the time being. Outside, there was no sign of anyone from the Northern, but Walter knew they would be keeping watch. His men idled in the bailey, wondering when they would have the chance to sample the Redgate ale they had head so much about. Walter called for his horse to be saddled. He cast about for Wilf. There was no sign. Would he have had a change of heart so soon? No. There he was. It was not a good sign that the men were bored. They would create trouble with nothing to occupy them.

"Make yourselves familiar with the land," he called. "Your services could be called upon at any time."

He made a show of designating different tasks to various men, before mounting and setting off for Durham. He did not say where he was going or when he would be back, knowing it would goad Wilf.

Wilf focused on his duties, wishing he knew why it felt impossible to walk away.

Chapter Sixteen

A Long Way From Jerusalem

In spite of the blazing heat and glimmering skies on his arrival, the roads of Durham, ankle deep in mud and worse, told tales on the recent heavy downpour. Normally he would have dismounted but he wanted to save his boots. As horse and rider climbed the bank which ran from Framwellgate Bridge and along Silver Street, he kept his eyes to the right, looking for breaks in the buildings where alleys provided shortcuts to other parts of the town. The whole place was built on a peninsular with the river meandering moat-like at its feet so these alleyways could spare a traveller time and distance, as long as he did not take a wrong turn along the way and end up where he first entered.

A quick succession of bright droplets fell from the eaves; steam rose eerily where the sun warmed the mud and the rooftops; horses and pedestrians plished their way to their various destinations. He glanced to the right again, at last recognising the shape of the alley he preferred. It snaked upwards then turned abruptly to the left. It had yielded women before, and if not this time, he could carry on towards the keep and call for a drink, although with the wetness on the roads he had wanted to avoid Fleshergate, knowing the butchers there took little care to prevent the leftover mess from the slaughtered beasts interrupting the progress of passers by.

He gazed up the alleyway, eyeing the rivulets rippling past him to join the main street below. The way was too narrow to cope with a rider and he wondered whether to dismount. He hesitated. It would make more sense to pay someone at Saddlergate to look after his courser and then explore what the town had to offer. He made his decision, but as he urged his mount to continue up the slippery bank, a red dress caught his eye. He turned just in time to see Isabel disappear down a descending route to the left. It was a broader and steeper alley than those to the right, with buildings to either side. How fortuitous. He could mix business with pleasure. He spurred his horse to catch up with her.

Knowing she could not outrun him, she waited in the shadows. Here the walls were out of reach of the sun making their fabric seem sodden and insubstantial. He looked down at her with a smile.

"Are you following me, Isabel?"

She looked him up and down with a derisory expression, trying to hold her hem away from the mud. His head and shoulders were backed by a now bright blue sky with the narrow space between the high walls framing his shoulders. "Why would I follow you?"

"I came to town looking for entertainment. Could you be it, I wonder?"

She dismissed him with a shake of her head, one fistful of skirt resting on an out-thrust hip. "Some people have work to do."

He dismounted as she turned to go, cornering her against a cold wall. He took her hand and forced it inside his cloak. Her fingers closed on a pouch full of coins. "I intend to pay you for your work. In fact, you might find it is that rare sort of afternoon where you earn enough to be able to take the rest of the week off."

She glanced at the people passing on the main street above them to see if they were watched, then sighed as if she was doing him a favour. He relinquished her hand, knowing she had given in. She led him down a further serpentine alleyway which led to a crooked looking house with wooden outbuildings leaning precariously nearby. The river ran alongside, confusing him for a moment until he remembered that the Wear surrounded the town almost fully. Insects buzzed in thick angry masses near the water's edge. In contrast to the shaded alley, the sun was uncomfortably hot here. The black and rotting vegetation showed that the area was prone to year round flooding.

"Careful where you walk," she said. "The butchers' boys often bring their rubbish down here and dump it in the river."

So that was the stench. Rotten flesh. He noticed the movement of rats amongst the damp undergrowth and the nagging clatter of crows that clamoured for the spoils. She led him to a doorway and stopped.

"You'll have to find a place to leave the horse." She barred the way as if she thought he would actually attempt to bring the mare indoors. He looked about him. To the side of the building the land rose a little.

Here the ground was drier and cleaner. He did as he was bid and then followed Isabel inside.

Beyond the doorway it was dark. Very dark and very quiet. At best, it smelled damp. There was no furniture at all. His footsteps were muted and he felt his feet slip as she led him through the room to a broad ladder. From the state of the floor and walls, it was obvious that the house was prone to flooding too. His horse would have been hard pressed to spoil anything in here. He followed her up the ladder, warily now, unwilling to allow his head above the floorboards without having checked the place out first. The upper room was smaller but drier and the smell less strong. A broad band of sunlight fell across the floor through the one high window which faced the rooftops at the bend of the main street. Two or three of the small panes were either broken or missing completely. He could hear a cart bumping its hard-going way through the deep clarts towards the bridge, the driver's urgings only just out-doing the horse's complaints.

Having quickly scanned the room, he leant against a wooden post which supposedly helped to prop up the rather shapely roof.

"Business slow, Isabel?" he grinned.

She ignored his sarcasm. "I save my money for more important things than the roof over my head."

"Very sensible," he said, mocking her with a serious look, then taking in the one bench and the roughly made pallet on the floor, he added, "With luck you will save enough to be out before Winter sets in."

"I need to see your money properly," she said, protecting her hands with a cloth while she removed her muddy boots.

He put his head to one side. "Don't you trust me?"

"Did Alric?" she asked.

He sighed, bringing a hand to his brow, but he watched her face carefully. "There was nothing I could do for Alric. He committed a murder and paid the price. The past would have caught up with him in the end."

"I would have thought watching your younger half brother dying would have moved you more."

"I have a great many half-brothers, older and younger. Sisters too for that matter. My father was not very good at keeping his hands to himself. My mother raised me to be hard with those she considered to be getting a better deal than we were." He paused. "Anyway, I did not come here to talk. Are we here for business or not? You hardly knew Alric."

"More than most." She crossed, barefoot, to a nook in the wall and lifted down a jug and two goblets. "If you want a seat, you will have to use the bed." She threw a glance in the direction of the pallet and poured out two cups of ale. "But take off your boots before you cross the room."

"I am overwhelmed by your bedside manner," he grinned, giving a deferential bow of his head. He took the pouch from his cloak and placed it on the bench next to the jug, noticing with satisfaction that she could not help but glance at it from the corner of her eye. Knowing women like Isabel were a mine of information, he continued to converse a while.

"You said you had better things to spend your money on."

She handed him a cup and took hers to the bed, seating herself with her back against the wall. "Escape, is what I want."

"Escape from what?" he asked, trying to kick off his boots without using his hands.

"People who know me."

He laughed. "Outremer is a long way."

Her face remained straight and he realised he had stumbled upon her true intentions. He continued to undress. "So you think a journey to Jerusalem will cleanse you of your sins, Isabel?"

Her brow creased, her temper rising that he should mock her personal longings. "Apparently, it's all that is needed to be absolved of murdering bishops in their Cathedrals," she snapped.

He took a drink. "Ah, but women are the gateway to Hell."

She ignored him.

"I thought Drysdale would be a place where you could live safely."

She glared at him. "I could exist there, but I want a different life." She looked to the window. The ale was weak and did little to lift her spirits. "I could hardly expect to find a husband amongst the Northern."

"You crave family life?" There was a sneer in his tone.

She did not bother to look at him. "Never had one yet. Might as well have one try before it's over."

He wondered how a woman of her rank had ended up in a place like this.

"Your mother is still alive."

"And so mad she cannot recognise herself after being passed from one husband to the next." She took another drink. "After the fourth husband died, she was accused of poisoning them, until her accusers actually met her. She cannot even keep herself clean. It's probably only a matter of time until she poisons herself by mistake."

He raised his cup to her. "Well, I am pleased I chose you to provide my entertainment, Isabel. You work wonders on a man's spirits." He stood and picked up his chemise as if having second thoughts. She quickly pulled herself round. "You have the money so you dictate the mood."

He grinned, bundling up his clothing and throwing it into the corner nearest the ladder. If the talk was to continue he would have to guide it towards a more useful subject. "I thought a woman like you would enjoy being around the Northern, with their reputation."

She shrugged. "For being monogamous?" She pondered. "It's not simply a case of following the fashion for romance. Their reputation for the way they treat their wives has helped them to build up vast amounts of land. That and their military skills of course. And Bran's wizardry. Fathers know their daughters will continue to be treated well once the economics of a match have been decided. Any land given as part of a dowry will be well looked after, and its revenue probably improved. I stand no chance in a scheme so popular."

"So why not try for a home there, even as a single woman with learning. They could make use of you."

"I never really considered Drysdale to be any safer than my own home. There is always some contender arguing that Bran should not hold the land."

"Always?"

"Just about. He doesn't know the half of it due to his wanderlust. The Northern protect it for him and Pudsey won't hear of it going to anyone else when his people are so prosperous. They try all sorts of things. Brute force won't work against the Northern so it is normally more underhand. Marc was even accused of having another woman."

"So what?"

Isabel sighed as if explaining something highly complicated to a child too young to grasp the concept. "If a large part of the Northern's power is based on the stability of their marriages, the whole of their integrity comes under scrutiny. Marc and Ben were marshal and chamberlain of Drysdale while Bran was away. Susan and Marc have a very strong marriage. Undermine Marc and you have a lever to weaken the rest. Fathers would lose their faith and find other ways of gaining more land; especially with the sniff of rebellion in the air. As it is, they say that even a landless Northern knight is more likely to marry a wealthy lady than a Lord, because his prowess in battle will secure gifts of land from the appreciative powerful, and the lady knows she is more likely to have a longer and happier life. He stays faithful and the lady has no need to stray which prevents claims from bastard children decimating the land."

He considered. "Marc is still without land. He does not seem to have achieved much for a man his age."

Isabel contemplated. She saw that each man had different ways of measuring his success so there was little point in labouring over the discussion. Although, a thought did strike her. "Marc does not seem ambitious. He married Susan who brought him nothing financially although most of their children have survived, which is unusually good." Her brow creased as she thought. "Beau Repaire is in limbo at present. Pudsey holds it to try and lure your father back. If Alric was executed because it is believed he truly killed Edwin, I imagine it will not be long before another man is named to take it. It would not surprise me if Marc was that man. He could spread the knowledge he has learned from Drysdale. They would make harmonious neighbours."

He took another drink to hide his annoyance. He knew there had to be a reason that he had taken a dislike to Marc as soon as he had set eyes on him. It was bad enough fighting the legitimate claimants without upstarts like him adding to the confusion. He scanned his memory for potential heirs. Richard, barely eight years old, was paging at Drysdale. Then there was Bobby: much younger, but still a potential threat.

Isabel drained her cup. She enjoyed good conversation that stretched her brain, having little opportunity usually, but she had a living to make. "If all we are to do is talk, I must start charging a fee.

Speaking of which, all I see at present is a purse. I have been fooled by a full looking pouch before."

He looked down at his own naked body and raised his eyebrows mischievously. "An empty pouch. How disappointing for you. Especially with your ambitions for a family."

She twisted her mouth in disapproval at the innuendo, taking it as a tactic to divert her attention from finance. "Tell me what you want and I will tell you how much it will cost."

He rubbed his thumb and forefinger down his beard as if in deep thought. "I was hoping for a full afternoon's entertainment. I hadn't broken it down into a costed itinerary."

Isabel heaved herself up from the bed. He noticed the red dress was not the tight fit it had been three weeks before. She crossed to the bench and poured another drink. "What you are suggesting is expensive. It will keep me from seeing other customers. Then there is the drink. How do I know you can afford it?"

He opened the pouch and smiled at the hungry expression on her face as he emptied the holder of twelve silver pennies in a series of little jolts. Two or three dropped to the floor and rolled away from them. She resisted the urge to go after them but made a mental note of where they had come to rest.

"Does that meet with your approval?" he asked.

She nodded, trying to keep the smile from her eyes. She might make her escape before winter after all.

"Good. Now take off your clothes and lie on the floor by the window where I can see you properly."

She looked at the bare, hard floor, then back to him. "That will cost you extra."

He gave a good-natured sigh, walked to the pallet and picked up the thickest cover. "All right, Isabel. To make things easier, let's just say that I will tell you what I want you to do and you keep a tally in your head." She looked to the money. There was easily enough. She began to undress. He arranged the cover on the floor under the window and then lay on his side, watching her closely. "This is coney isn't it? Feels good."

She knelt in front of him and nodded. "From home. I haven't sold everything yet."

He sat up and pushed her onto her back. "There are plenty God fearing people who would argue that you have, young lady."

She let the comment go. It was wise not to argue about religion at the best of times. He knelt over her, the sunlight being very obliging in giving him a clear view. He ran his hands over her. He'd had worse. She turned her head and looked to the window. A few plump white clouds allowed her to hope for a warmer night than last. He opened her legs with his knee and knelt further forward, turning her chin so that she had to look at him.

"Let's start with the basics," he said. "I want you to watch what I am doing to you."

She might as well humour him. It would all add up after all. She raised herself up on her elbows and looked down the length of her own pale body to where he hovered over her. He pushed against her and smiled. "I knew you were more pleased to see me than you were admitting."

She smiled to keep the customer amused. "Maybe."

"Alric all forgotten now?"

"Maybe."

"Do you want me?"

"Yes."

"Say 'yes please'."

"Yes please."

He pushed a little way inside her. "Keep saying it."

"Yes please."

He pushed further.

"And my name."

She faltered.

"My real name."

"Roger?"

He nodded.

"Yes, Roger, please."

He lay closer against her, enjoying the feel of her stomach against his. "God, Isabel, you're wasted."

He pulled away momentarily and rolled her onto her stomach, coming at her again from behind and sliding one hand under her to enjoy the feel of her breasts. "Does that coney feel good against you?"

She allowed herself a languorous stretch and whispered, "Yes."

He lifted her a little with his fore arm. "Raise yourself up on your elbows so I can touch you more."

She obliged. He took the knife from where he had placed it under the cover while he arranged it on the floor, stroked her hair back from her shoulders and swiped the sharp blade across her throat. He held the knife high as she bled to avoid being heavily soiled himself. He stayed inside her while she struggled, the fur beneath her quickly becoming warm and sticky. When he finally stood, he turned about in the sunlight checking for blood. Just one or two spatters surprisingly. He dipped the blade in his cup of ale then drank the contents. He wrapped Isabel in the cover, congratulating himself on its generous size. Then he dressed. He picked up the coins from the floor, then swept those on the bench onto his palm and put all of them back in his pouch. He did not close it, but began a search of the room. The nooks and shelves in the walls yielded nothing.

He lifted the pallet. A silk scarf was scrunched into a large knot hole in the floor. He lifted it and seven coins fell into his hand. She was a long way from Jerusalem. He added these to his own then looked down the ladder into the dark room below.

Being satisfied that no-one was likely to enter at an inopportune moment, he picked up Isabel wrapped in her fur and dropped her to the floor below before carefully climbing down himself.

He stepped outside, glanced about, then brought several large stones, making three trips in all, and arranged them around Isabel inside her covering. He kept near the building so that he could not be seen from the bridge. He then tied the corners as best he could. He attempted to lift the bundle but found the added weight of the stones made it impossible to go any useful distance. He would be forced to drag the weight instead. It would be rough going and leave a trail to the house. As he rubbed his beard, his horse's impatient snorts gave him an idea. He brought the mare closer and heaved the bundle over her back. After checking that the stones had remained inside the bundle, and blood was not seeping out, he walked the mare a short distance beyond the shoreline and into the river. The water here was covered with a thick, foul-smelling scum. He breathed as little as possible, trying to make haste. He gave a short sharp command and threw a small stone at the mare in order to avoid entering the water himself. It reared and Isabel fell into the water, cover and all. The mare returned gladly. Roger watched the bundle. It inflated at first, then, slowly but surely, it began a slow descent to join the rest of the slaughtered remains under the surface. He walked his horse away from the river's edge and used handfuls of the cleaner grass by the house to clean her legs. He mounted and looked up at the sky. He was hungry. He still had plenty of time to make it back before dark. He would eat a hearty meal when he returned. Wilf would think he had felt too contrite to stay away any longer. It was all falling into place quite nicely. He could figure out his next step during the journey back to Drysdale.

Chapter Seventeen

In the Shade

The bailey was deserted. Catching the sun all day, the surrounding stonework emitted an uncomfortable heat and reflected a squint-making light, even now in the late afternoon. The people of Drysdale chose to carry out tasks that could be done indoors or in the cooler areas by the reservoirs. There was a strange feeling in the air which made the little community watch the alien actions and faces of the visiting knights carefully, only partially reassured by a Northern presence. Their manners, when compared to those of the Northern, were thrown into relief. They spat, they washed infrequently and they did not bother to go to the garderobe if it was more convenient to make water in a corner of the bailey. With Walter away, they had already drunk large amounts of the ale from Redgate, and when given good-natured warnings about its strength, they cursed the speaker and chased them away, inviting laughter from the rest of their company. They trusted Bran's judgement, but times were odd and twisted: the King's troubles with his sons made them wonder if *all* things would be turned on their heads.

As the shadows gradually lengthened, Wilf came down from his watch, long after his allocated time was spent. He helped himself to water and sat in the shadows thinking.

He had never felt so wretched. He wished Joss had come up with a reason to prevent him from staying. Even though, as yet, he had committed no disloyalty, having just contemplated letting the Northern down left him miserable with guilt. The damage was already done. There was no moral stone he could hide under to rationalise his decision. Joss had always said that if the Northern was to crumble, the decay would start on the inside. He had not realised that his betrayal would leave him bereft of anything else to believe in. He could not even believe in himself. He did not know this man he had become.

Thus far, the rest of the Northern were none the wiser. They put the strange atmosphere down to the anti-climax of boredom and lack of purpose after their preparation for battle; that and the indolence brought about by the heat of late August.

The slip in Wilf's ideals had cost him dear. And for what? Walter was proving himself to be a sorry soul, with little care for anyone but himself. Wilf felt pangs of humiliation when he allowed himself to recognise how cheaply his loyalty had been bought. And now Susan, poor trusting Susan, wife to a man who had saved him from death on more than one occasion, had come to him in confidence, too scared to do so when Walter was at Drysdale, and revealed that Anna truly had been raped. Bad enough when he had thought that Walter was spreading a lie, worse still for it to have happened. Susan, usually shrewd and practical, had implored with him in earnest to do something about Walter without causing more distress to Anna. He had threatened her children. Marc's brood. She had left him, feeling secure in the knowledge that Wilf and the other knights from the Northern would solve the problem in Bran's absence. And so, Wilf now waited for the one man he had finally allowed to sway his allegiance.

A call from the trees signalled that Walter had returned. Wilf watched him jump down lightly from his mount and cross the bailey to the kitchen, probably hoping there would be something to satisfy his hunger after his activities in Durham. Wilf sat still, in no mood to tackle him right now. Soon, Walter emerged, licking his fingers as he crossed the courtyard. As he reached the entrance to the Hall, he glanced knowingly into the shadows, found Wilf's gaze and gave him a level look, then stepped inside. Wilf sighed: the scales had tipped once more. Strange how even the smallest of gestures restores hope.

Chapter Eighteen

Truce

October brought a truce between the King and his sons and then between William and the English King's supporters. Just as Marc felt some relief that he would be able to return to his family, Joss ordered that he and Bran were to travel to France with a band of men to keep an eye on the French rebels and add numbers to Henry's supporters abroad. Joss and the rest would remain in England, knowing too many people had been promised too much to simply accept that the rebellion was over.

It was the sort of bright but windy day that made Bran wish that his memory was not quite so good. It reminded him of the day his mother was hanged. On such days he found the best remedy was to try to solve other people's problems, and Marc looked so dejected on being told the new orders for France, that he had the perfect excuse for forgetting his own troubles. Marc had kept himself alone, leaning against a tree which faced the harsh sunlight, his cloak wrapped about him tightly to ward off the chilling breeze. Bran envied the way he wore his heart on his sleeve with no thought of what others might think of him.

He sat by Marc, trying to make himself comfortable at the tree's roots whilst reading through a list of names Joss had given him. It wasn't the ideal place for sitting and reading and more than once he had to unroll the list again as the wind almost stole it from him. Marc sighed, fifteen again, but tortured by the separation from his children as well as Susan.

Bran bade his time. If he wanted to talk about it, he would.

Eventually, "Do you know how it feels?" asked Marc, with a rhetorical tone, as if he had shared his thoughts with Bran all along. "I feel like they've been taken from me in the night, and I've been forbidden to try to find them before some unspeakable savagery befalls them. It's driving me to distraction. You must worry about Anna too."

Bran hid his embarrassment with a shrug. He thought carefully before he spoke, sitting back and allowing the list to roll in on itself once more. "I do understand. I think about what could be happening to Anna if your instincts are right. Just because she chose to remain a sister rather then become a wife does not mean I do not care about her."

"Then how do you comfort yourself?"

"By reminding myself that Wilf is more than a match for Walter. I would rather have returned home now, but the fight is not over yet and would be drawn out for longer if we let our guard down. Ultimately, a delay now will save time later."

Marc was not convinced but he knew he had no choice. He changed the subject, unfortunately for an unprepared Bran. "Did Anna give you a reason for her refusal?"

There was a silence in which Bran gave a disbelieving shake of the head. "Just let it go, Marc."

Another silence.

"All right," Marc said eventually, then added a quick burst of speech before he could be stopped. "It's just that Susan said that Anna had told her…. and this is just the night before we left…. that she needed to speak with Walter to tell him she was not interested, and that when Susan hinted that you were interested, Anna seemed to be in unusually good spirits all of a sudden. Especially for a woman with broken limbs. So," his voice began to peter out as he noted his friend's expression. "So, I just wondered if she had given you a reason."

Bran felt his stomach muscles tauten with cringe-making embarrassment. "I really do not need to be reminded of how many people are aware of the fact that my proposal was rejected."

"Susan is never wrong about things like this. Remember, no-one would ever have guessed that Raymond and Tilly would make a good couple, but Susan saw it straight away."

Bran was beginning to regret his decision to help his friend into better spirits. "Marc, I feel bad enough without you reopening the wound to add a generous measure of salt."

Marc continued with his train of thought regardless. Bran thought he and Susan had a lot in common. "It's just that I cannot help thinking that Anna was alone when she told Walter she did not want him. She definitely intended to refuse him because she told Susan she should be alone to do it to spare his feelings. Then the next morning she rejects you and Walter is telling everyone she is willing to accept him if our checks prove him acceptable. Am I the only man to be alarmed by that?"

Bran said nothing. Once his own interests were swept to one side, Marc's argument seemed to acquire an uncomfortable gravity. He looked at his friend, head to one side. "Just keep remembering, Wilf is more than a match for Walter."

"But, you can see my point of view now?"

Bran nodded. The two men said nothing more, but gazed where the cloud shadows raced away from them towards home.

Joss watched the two of them. He did not enjoy seeing Marc suffer, but he knew it was for the best. Being too closely involved could make the mind fuggy. There were lives at stake. Bran did not seem to have taken his rejection too much to heart. Perhaps it would be more apparent on his return home. Ben had said nothing. It must be difficult for him to abide by his decision to let Anna do the choosing when he admired Bran so much.

Will approached him. "Benedict was wondering whether a letter should be sent to Drysdale and Bankside to let the families know what is happening."

Joss nodded. "I have written already with a minimum of details about the truce. I have not included information about where we go next, just in case it falls into the wrong hands."

"Of course," Will nodded. He looked across to Bran and Marc. Joss half expected a plea for leniency on their behalf, knowing his old friend's tendency to stand in other people's shoes. "They look a woebegone pair."

Joss gave a non-committal nod.

"I think you have done the right thing sending them to France: they have a good reason to be thorough in their duties to put a stop to this nonsense for good."

Joss's expression softened. "And Henry will see that Bran is more than an engineer."

Will crossed his arms and considered Bran. "I still think he will end up married to Anna."

Joss allowed himself a short laugh. "For a wordsmith, you show a surprising lack of eloquence at times."

"Simply lost for words for once," he said, and made his way back to Ben.

Chapter Nineteen

Grasping The Nettle

At Redgate, the days crawled past, turning into weeks. The early October wind sent leaves clattering and swirling in the bailey. Susan, although seemingly preoccupied swilling away dirty water whilst simultaneously attempting to prevent the wind from dislodging her veil, was focusing most of her mind on the apparent inertia of the Northern towards the crime that had been committed against Anna, even though Wilf had been informed. At first, she had felt outraged. Susan was all set to bring the rape out in the open, but Anna was against it. It had been humiliating the first time: she wanted to focus her efforts on forgetting it rather than relive it. If she had to analyse it, Anna was fearful rather than angry. There was no stretch of the imagination that enabled her to see a future of contentment. At best, it was uncertain. She had felt ill since Walter's attack and, although her wrist and ankle were finally healing, she constantly felt wary, her bones seemed leaden, her blood pounded achingly at the back of her head on trying the simplest of tasks and, strangely, her chest was painful, as if she had some inner bruising. But, hating mawkishness on the rare occasions she had encountered it in others, she tried to bury her fears in everyday routines, even trying to write herself into another idealised, poetic world, until Walter confiscated her materials. Again, Wilf was told and, again, nothing was done about it.

Still, it was not possible to stop thinking, so while she carried out the mundane but necessary tasks stemming from Susan's family life, she escaped into an imagined world instead. She found some comfort here, with most of her daydreams hovering around Bran and the way things could have been had he spoken with her just half a day earlier.

During one of their walks as he convalesced, the topic had touched again upon his perfect lady. Self-conscious whilst asking if Anna thought the lady would approve, and imploring with her not to laugh at him, he had described how he would ask for her hand. He would propose in a beautiful building: one he had built for her. He painted her a picture of vaulted ceilings; beautiful shadow-making tracework; galleries festooned with her favourite flowers; hundreds of blooms strung from the rafters; nooks and corners crammed with lilies; and, on her writing table, one perfect unopened rose. Anna had wondered whether all the flowers, no matter what their type, should be white, then, as evening drew on, the pale petals would have a soft luminescence. He had smiled at her idea, "I like that." Then he had laughed, "I like the idea of the room being in semi-darkness: that would make it harder for her to see my disappointment should she refuse me."

She had imagined it as he spoke; the silvering of the waxy petals, the mid-blue of the sky with a few early stars. "How thoughtful to build something for her."

He looked at her, "Not every woman would appreciate a library, I suppose."

"But she's not every woman," Anna had smiled.

"Do you think the single rose should be white too? I had thought red."

"Why?" she asked.

He had hesitated, then shrugged, "To make it more special."

She had not understood then, but now, in hindsight, it was all so obvious why he had allowed her to judge such a personal idea.

Remembering her past to escape her present was a dubious way of comforting herself: now that he was out of reach, her old happiness was magnified and she wondered how she could ever have been so spoilt to have been blind to it. In spite of her fertile mind, as the days shortened and the temperature dropped, she felt that a terrible finality would eventually overwhelm her. Brighter days were fast disappearing. With each earlier darkening hour that heralded the approach of mid-Winter, she felt the hopelessness of a woman watching as she was bricked up alive.

Like her younger friend, Susan had unspoken fears of her own. These knights were a different breed to those she knew or even those she had read about and the Northern seemed to be allowing them free reign. The freemen of Drysdale were beginning to look restless. They kept themselves away from the main house as much as they could and Susan wondered what would happen if they spoke to Wilf about their qualms.

She sighed, drying her cold, pink hands on her apron then returned to the shelter of the little room her family now shared with Anna. Often, to cope with the times, the two of them tried to think strategically, as if it was within their power to rid themselves of the strangers. She sought to do this now, feeling in need of reassurance.

"What would Bran do?" Susan asked, partly to start the thought process and partly to gauge whether Anna would be comfortable speaking about him now.

"He would try to figure out exactly what the problem was in order to find a fitting solution." Anna laid the now sleeping baby back in her crib. The other children were about their chores, the most worrying time for Susan even though she knew the Northern were at their watch.

"All right. So what is the exact problem?"

Anna pondered. "Walter could be a rebel, even if his father is loyal. Perhaps he has come here in the hope that the rebels may win. He may even wonder how they could possibly lose when the enemy is moving from France, Scotland and from within."

"I wish we had some information on the way things were going. I expected a letter of some sort by now."

"Would Walter allow us to see it if he were a rebel?" Anna asked, offering Susan a paw so Susan could check her wrist, which troubled her little now.

"He is an arrogant little man. But even if he is a rebel, it does not provide an explanation for Wilf's inertia."

"Perhaps there is something we do not know about. Our meddling could ruin some higher plan." Anna allowed Susan to help her to her feet so she could judge that her limp was indeed less noticeable now.

Susan shook her head. "Higher plan or not, I do not believe that the Northern would allow it to involve indifference to rape and threats to children, yet Wilf seems to be ignoring both." Susan studied. "I cannot help thinking it was Wilf who reassured Joss that he felt Walter's family were likely to be loyal from what he knew of them. If Wilf has turned traitor…"

Anna interrupted. "No. I cannot see it. Even if anyone was selfish enough to take that step, what would be their incentive? It would not make sense."

"I am sure you are right."

Anna lowered herself back onto her stool. In spite of her last words, Susan's gloom had affected her thoughts. "You don't think it will be this way from now on, do you?"

Susan shook her head. "No. We will win. And even if a previously moral man did turn traitor, why would he turn to such an arrogant, strutting little…."

Anna looked about her and whispered, "Whoreson?"

Susan nodded. "And for those in the Northern there is nothing more important than the Northern. They are very strong. The only thing driving the rebels is greed. How could the likes of Walter be the cause of the rot setting in?"

Anna chewed her lip, "Problem solving seems far easier when Bran does it."

Susan laughed, and then decided to take advantage of the lighter mood. "I don't want to pry, but..."

"Oh no!" Anna interjected. "Whenever a person says they do not wish to pry, they are about to do just that."

"Very perceptive," Susan agreed with a smile, and then decided that her seniority permitted her to carry on. "You and Bran seemed to get on so well. I just wondered why you turned him down."

When Anna thought of her last meeting with Bran it was as immediate as ever. "I was serious, Susan. I don't want to talk about it."

Susan threw her a compassionate look, and then continued regardless. "Did he speak to you unkindly when you rejected him?"

Anna shook her head. When she spoke her voice was lost in a whisper. "No." She paused, remembering. "He thanked me for being honest." She stood up and crossed the room as if to check Maud.

"Were you honest?"

Anna did not turn round but shook her head as she quite needlessly rearranged the cover in the crib.

"Why, Anna? He looked so disappointed when he left."

Anna turned back to her. "What else could I say? Would he have been any less disappointed if I had told him I loved him and fully expected him to accept that

I had another man in his bed a few hours beforehand? Accept it even if it meant I might be pregnant?"

Susan knew enough about pregnancy to speak with some authority. "It would be unfortunate if you fell pregnant after that one incident."

Anna gave a crooked smile. "Then unfortunate I am. I have not bled since the day of that one incident."

Susan put an arm round her shoulder. "I thought you looked a little sickly. Don't worry, Anna, I know how to look after you. Besides," she added, brightening, "the delay might be due to your body concentrating on fixing your broken bones."

Anna nodded and tried to lift her mood, "Funny how it never seems to happen to Isabel."

"As far as we know," Susan sighed. "Never around when you need her. A woman like Isabel, with her habit of wandering, would be a most useful person to have around right now. Perhaps she could get a message to Durham."

"Wouldn't that be saying we doubt the ability of the Northern Knights who have been left to protect us?"

Susan shrugged. "We could apologise later."

"And who would we tell? I heard some disappointing rumours about Pudsey encouraging the rebels by giving them free rein to travel southwards."

"Maybe, but he has always been a friend of Drysdale. He would take up the matter personally if he knew what had happened to you." She pondered, looking at Anna. "I have a red dress in a chest somewhere. We used it for a play."

Anna raised her eyebrows, "Why would you want to wear it? We don't want to be tarred with the same brush as Isabel."

Susan put her head on one side, "Think, Anna. Perhaps you could dress like her and get a message to Durham. The Northern guard would let you through, whereas, if you asked leave to go, Walter might step in and prevent it and we would never get another chance. I cannot go. I need to keep an eye on the children."

Anna pondered. It seemed extreme, but perhaps they would regret it later if they did not take a chance now. If she was pregnant, their time was running out. "It is worth a try."

Susan set to straight away. "It needs careful planning if we are not to be caught in the attempt. Some of those men are animals, if their boasting is true. We need to keep you safe; even if they do think you are Isabel, there could be nasty consequences."

"What difference does that make now?" asked Anna. "It is just as well I did not entertain the thought of marriage seriously. It is highly unlikely I shall marry well after this." Susan looked at her ready to disagree, but Anna rushed ahead. "Now then, Isabel always wears her hair a particular way. And if the day is windy, I have a perfect excuse for hiding my face with my hood. Who would have thought Isabel would turn out to be so useful to us, after all those years of avoiding her?"

A rider coming into the bailey put a halt to their plans. Susan rushed to the window and called her children in. She hoped Richard and the other pages were safe. It was a stranger bearing a letter. A member of the Northern went to take it, but before he could, Walter had brushed him aside to intercept it. The first knight did not look pleased at this, but Wilf intervened and took the message from Walter's hands and entered the Hall. Susan turned conspiratorially then crept out of the door to see what could be discovered.

Wilf sat by the fire perusing its contents. Walter stood over him, staring over his shoulder at the paper agitatedly. "What does it say?"

Wilf did not bother to look up. "It is my name written on here, not yours."

"Why don't you just tell me?"

"How could it possibly interest you?"

Walter glared at him. He did not like this new side to Wilf. He was proving more and more irksome. If he was going to be obstinate, he might as well be rid of him. He decided to feign a loss of interest and went to the kitchen, much to Robert's annoyance.

"Time you had a day off," he announced and manhandled him out of his demesne, quickly followed by the three pages. Robert seethed at the other side of the door, "Given the day off after all the food is prepared anyway."

He muttered his way to the stables. A young squire with a cocky look attempted to turn him away, but Walter, who had climbed onto a stool in order to shout from the kitchen window, prevented an argument developing. "Let him go, idiot. I have given him the day off." He then addressed Robert. "When you return, make for Redgate." He beckoned the squire to come to him in order to give him a message for his men, before returning to the kitchen.

Unaware of Walter's doings, Wilf read the letter again. It told him of the truce. Wilf knew he would have to be quick if he was going to regain his self respect and turn the rebels out before the Northern returned. Susan tiptoed back to the room, which seemed much smaller now with the children seated at Anna's feet. She smiled broadly looking around to make sure she could not be overheard. "Something may help our Isabel plan. Walter cannot read."

"Are you sure?"

Susan considered then nodded, and immediately began to sort through chests and shelves in order to find the red dress. She dealt out instructions to the children. Anna stood, but Susan gestured that she should stay in her seat. "Sit there and think it through," she said. "We need a fool-proof plan. This could be our only chance."

There was much to-ing and fro-ing and Anna could not help but admire her zeal once she had set her mind to doing something. A sound of retreating hooves drew her gaze to the window.

"Oh. I cannot help thinking that was a lost opportunity," she sighed as she watched Robert ride out of the bailey.

Susan grimaced. "There is probably a proverb to sum it up," she said wryly, trying not to dwell on the stupidity of allowing Robert to leave without a message from them. "Right, let's shake ourselves."

****

Wilf rolled the letter and placed it inside his boot.

"That is the first place I would think of looking," said Walter, emerging from the shadows. "Or maybe the second," he added with a disarming smile.

Wilf ignored him and moved to the doorway having noticed the Northern watch coming down before their due time. "What are you up to?"

Walter was now seated on his favourite chair by the fire. "What on earth do you mean?" he asked innocently.

"Why have you brought the watchers down so early?"

"Always do in the Winter months. It is October now. Shorter watches but more frequent."

Wilf did not believe him. Garin came into the room, angry at the orders he had been given by Walter's squire. "I have not eaten yet. Why should they have a shorter watch than us?"

"He seems to have forgotten your Winter rules," said Wilf.

Walter glared into the fire, "Shut up, Garin, and follow orders."

Garin stayed put. "I want an answer."

Walter turned to him and said calmly, "You want castrating for the crimes you have committed. If you want my tolerance to keep the upper hand, I suggest you get out quickly and do exactly as you have been told."

Garin's hand went to the hilt of his sword where his knuckles showed white as he inwardly fumed at his commander. Walter turned back to the fire as if nothing had happened. "Run along now."

Garin's chest heaved, then he turned on his heels and pushed past the members of the Northern who were quenching their thirst from the well in the bailey. To add insult to injury, they were eating early, waited on by squires, including his own. Wilf continued to watch Walter and waited for him to speak. Nothing was said. Well, if that was the way he wanted to play it.

"Are you and I still friends?" he asked.

Wilf remained silent.

Walter did not look at him. "Do you want to go somewhere more private to discuss it in more depth?"

Still silence.

"It seems much colder in here lately."

"Save your breath. The letter was confidential and it will stay that way."

"You realise that you're jeopardising everything with this sullenness."

Wilf gave a short laugh. "I jeopardised everything a long time ago."

Walter turned in his chair and looked at him. "You have changed your mind then?"

As Wilf made no answer, Walter reached and grasped his cloak, trying to pull him closer. His hand was brushed away. The seated man turned back to the fire. He spoke very quietly. "Well, that's a great shame."

"The shame is that I ever considered letting the Northern down."

"I mean it is a shame you did not think a little more carefully before I treated your men to an early break as a gesture of good will after there was no ale left for them the other night. Of course, I let them understand the offerings met with your approval. I have noticed they drink from the well at the end of every watch. Very commendable. If someone wanted to poison my men, they would be more successful if they tampered with the ale."

Wilf stared at him. He hoped it was just another way of goading him. Walter watched him as he quickly strode to the doorway again. It all seemed too simple to be true, but wanting to take no chances, he gave two raps on the open door with the hilt of his sword. Immediately the men stood and looked to him.

"Walter and his men are rebels. Think back to the men you were told to watch and see that they are arrested."

With the sound of swords drawing in unison, Walter almost doubted his own plan. His men did not wait to be met, but emerged from the surroundings with a sudden roar and clubbing of weapons against shields. Wilf stormed back to the Hall. Walter sat with his arms folded across his chest and a smile on his face. "This should be interesting."

"Shut up, Walter, and get to your feet. I'm taking you to Durham."

Walter stayed put. "Well, that's all very well, but I have no time to spare for outings. Besides, I think you will find I have a friend in Pudsey. It's not too late for you too." As the clamour increased in volume, he slowly got to his feet and walked to the doorway. "However, I have all the time in the world for watching a good dance." Wilf followed him. He could not understand it. These men should have been no match for the Northern. There was no need for it to have turned into a pitched battle.

Susan wiped the steam from the panes with the cuff of her sleeve and peered through the fuggy glass. "I cannot see Richard. I hope he has stayed away." She worried that his eight year old sense of duty would prompt him to do the honorable thing and join in.

Since he was ejected from the kitchen, and thus temporarily relieved of a sense of duty, Richard had climbed into a tree to watch the goings on. At one time, a chance break in his routine would have sent him to pester his uncle in the mews or his grandfather at the stables, but they had all been sent to Redgate now. Instead he had climbed into his favourite tree to watch the goings on below. The unusualness of the day, made him feel alert. He imagined himself as a Northern knight already and with a squinting, grown up watchfulness, he surveyed all carefully. He was confused by the early change in watchmen, thinking his own sense of timing must be wrong. The Northern men were met by several squires, bearings platters of mouthwatering sweetmeats that he himself had helped to prepare that morning. The knights eyed the offerings, unsure of whether to accept. One of the squires smiled and looked back at the Hall. The breeze in the branches prevented Richard from hearing all that was said, but it was obvious from the gestures that they were being reassured Wilf knew about the idea. The food was taken politely, but Richard, watching carefully, noticed it was laid reverently on any surface close to hand, and left uneaten. Instead they quenched their thirst with water from the well.

Richard tried to peer through the window to his family's room. He could make nothing out. The panes were misted. He wished his father was here. He saw much less of him since he had begun his paging. Life was a lot more fun when he was around. In the bailey he now surveyed, his father had swung him over his shoulder so far that he hung upside down, gripped only by the ankles. His father had turned this way and that, calling, "Has anyone here seen Richard?" He turned in circles as people called, "He's behind you." And Richard, giggling in spite of a head like lead, had yelled, "Here I am."

He had enjoyed it even though he had felt a little sickly afterwards, just as his mother had said he would.

A call from Wilf in the doorway, brought him out of his daydream. Two raps were sounded. Richard jumped and tightly gripped the branch in front of him to right his balance. Below him, men suddenly swarmed from the foliage and descended on the bailey, roaring as if in a tremendous rage. His heart thumped loudly in his chest. The northern were at a disadvantage because they were in the lower position. Richard watched carefully, sure he would learn a good lesson by following how they would regain the upper hand. Realising he had stopped breathing, he forced himself to inhale through the clamour, which seemed to have robbed him of air. He could not tell how the Northern were going to win yet. Swords rang out against each other and the men on both sides gave earsplitting yells. He looked to the window again, his spirit of adventure fast replaced by a need for his mother. He could just make out her face now at the other side of the glass. Anna was their too. Their mouths were open but they were not speaking. His mother's hands came to her face, then both women flinched and turned their heads away. His mother stooped. Richard guessed she was moving the smaller children away from the window.

He tried to count the moving men, but it was too hard at first. One time, he counted thirty-one, not including the squires, then another, he counted twenty-eight. The men he recognized were acting strangely. He knew from watching the squires in training that they were not doing it right. Their movements seemed to go from one extreme to the other: at times they fought as if under water, their weapons seeming too heavy for them to lift; then quickly and haphazardly, clutching at their throats and stomachs as if trying urgently to rid themselves of whatever gripped them from within. Eventually, it was as if every Northern man flailed in a dance–slowed-down, whether still standing, kneeling or rolling on the ground. The dirtier men began to laugh, seeing that they were dying so easily. They did not stop fighting themselves but carried on stabbing, cutting, even kicking. As one knight lay curled in on himself, his face so contorted that he was only recognisable to Richard from the colour of his hair, the one called Garin kicked him in the teeth. Three of Walter's men grinned at each other on noticing Raymond lying so rigid that his back arched away from the floor. They stood over him and raised their swords in the air with two hands, then took turns in letting them fall again and again. They counted and gave cries of disappointment or delight depending on the severity of the wound they managed to inflict each time. Eventually they stopped, having achieved their aim of cutting Will's son in two. Richard's stomach heaved. He could count eighteen dead. Only three were stranger-knights. Richard knew they had gone much too far. He had been taught that going beyond the call of duty was not always a virtue.

He began to slither down from the tree, wondering how he could get to his mother without being seen. As he dropped amongst the roots, he heard a familiar scolding cry. So familiar that it cut through the sound of the wind. He peered over the swaying grass surrounding his hiding place. Down here, things were more audible and he was able to take advantage of the amphitheatre like effects of the bailey. His mother was running from the doorway towards the men. She called as she ran, "Stop! Stop!"

Gradually, the butchering stopped and the terrible tableau seemed frozen, with all living eyes turned to his mother. Her face was flushed. Anna was outside too, but hanging back, wringing thin, pale hands. Richard began to fear for his mother. His sense of urgency increased when the twelve or so surrounding her began to laugh and step towards her, creating a semi-circle with the Hall behind her. One man grew too close and she pushed at his chest. He looked at the others and laughed, then lifted his arms and pushed her shoulders with thick, blood-stained fingers. She took a few stumbling steps backwards, her face still set and defiant. The one they called Garin came behind her, put an arm round her waist and carried her towards the Hall. His mother kicked and reached up and back to scratch his face, while Anna ran to her aid. Walter blocked the doorway, with Wilf behind him. Wilf said something. Nothing happened. Walter made a hand movement and Susan was grudgingly lowered to the ground. Richard watched her march, red-faced and angry, back into the building, Anna following quickly at her heels. He strained his ears. All eyes were now on Wilf.

Walter spoke. "Time to make a decision, Wilf."

Wilf drew his sword and faced the semi-circle of twelve. Walter withdrew to the Hall and the men took a step towards Wilf, more wary now that they were faced with a healthy adversary, in spite of the advantage of numbers. Richard thought Wilf looked strong. Three men at once approached him and were beaten back quite easily. Perhaps he had a chance. Soundlessly, as Wilf fought , Walter appeared in the doorway, a lance in his hand. Richard held his breath. Walter raised his weapon.

"Behind you, Wilf!" Richard yelled, then froze as several pairs of eyes turned towards him, sweeping the undergrowth. Wilf span just as Walter hurled the lance. He deflected it just in time, but the men saw their opportunity and fell on him while his back was turned. Three men began to ascend the bank side where Richard hid. His legs shook. He knew he had to move quickly. He slithered over the rough roots on his belly, ignoring the pain in his ribs. As soon as he had gained the bank top, he got to his feet and ran as fast as he could, keeping within the tree line. He had no idea which direction he was headed at the moment. He would worry about that once he had reached a safe place.

Back in the bailey, Wilf was on his knees. His head and arms were bloody. Weak now, he tried to blink away the redness that left him partially sighted.

"This was an easily won campaign." Walter came from the doorway and stood before him. "It was all down to you," he smiled. "Thank you."

Where Wilf's skin was clear of blood, it appeared waxy and moist. Walter stepped behind him, pushed him so that he fell face down, then pulled off his boot and removed the letter.

He left Wilf to his men, and walked purposefully to the room housing Susan's family. The door had been wedged shut. He hammered at the door, irritated that he should be barred out and irritated by the piercing cries of the baby inside.

"Open up or I'll have the place torched."

He gave the door an angry kick and went outside. Picking up a discarded shield, he took it in both hands and began to batter it against the window. Those inside huddled at the other side of the room. He went back to the door and hammered against it again, then pushed with his shoulder. It began to open, slowly at first, then he fell inside suddenly as the furniture placed against it moved aside.

Walter righted himself, seething. Susan and Anna stood before the children, ready to fight him off with any kitchenware that came to hand.

He snapped at them. "For God's sake make that baby quiet before I do."

Janey picked up the red-faced, frightened infant and put a finger to her mouth to appease her. The crying stopped. Susan and Anna remained as they were, grim-faced and determined.

Walter pointed at Anna with the hand that held the letter. "You! Read this."

Anna did not move. He stepped towards her and thrust the letter into her hands.

Anna and Susan looked at each other.

Susan spoke. "Just read it, Anna. He might hurt the children otherwise."

Anna scanned it quickly, then began to read. "The Scots are easily beaten back. We should arrive not much later than this letter," she began.

Walter stepped behind her. "Let me see," he demanded, squinting at the paper.

Anna hesitated then began again. She pointed at the page, showing him where she was up to. "Marc asks that you tell Richard to practise his Latin everyday if he finds it so hard. Running away from it will not make it easier."

Walter grimaced and snatched the letter from Anna. "What sort of rubbish is this?" He stared at the words, wondering if Anna had made it up. He recognised that the names Marc and Richard were indeed written there, but little else.

He threw the letter onto the fire, then turned to Anna. "You had better be telling the truth." He stormed into the bailey and shouted at the men. "Gather your things. We are moving to Redgate." He then returned to the room. "That goes for you too."

"Why can't we just stay?" asked Susan. "A group of women and children can do you no harm."

Walter glared at her. "If I were you, I would keep my mouth tightly shut. Do not delude yourself. I did not prevent those men from having you because I care about your modesty. I would simply prefer your husband to be around when it eventually happens."

He stepped towards the children, as if to check none had escaped. Anna diverted him. "What sort of idiot poisons a healthy water supply?" He gave her a swipe with the back of his hand, causing her to stumble and fall.

Susan went to her. "Leave her alone. She is carrying your child. Even a fool would see the advantage in keeping her well."

Walter paused and considered. "Time will tell if you are lying," he snarled. "And God help you if you are."

He left the room and Susan dabbed the corner of Anna's mouth with her apron. Anna brushed her hand away and lifted something from under her. "I didn't want him to notice this," she said, holding up a fold of the red dress.

Chapter Twenty

Experiment

Susan gathered her children about her and explained they were going to have to walk to Redgate. She would carry baby Maud, but she would need Janey to keep an eye on Bobby and Agnes incase they grew tired or ran too close to the river.

"Anna will help of course, but she is still too poorly to chase after unruly children."

"What about Richard, Mother?" asked Janey.

Susan looked at all of her brood. "I want you to promise me not to mention, Richard."

They looked at each other, but knew better than to ask why.

Susan tried to reassure them with a simple explanation. "We have to do things Walter wants us to, but, if he does not know Richard is one of our family, he may be able to do as he likes."

Bobby wrung his hands, worriedly, "Will father punish the big man for pushing you?"

Susan smiled at him, "Of course. But he has to help some other people first."

"Uvver peep furz," repeated Agnes.

"That's right." Susan nodded. "Now, let's wrap up warm. There's a bite to that wind. Don't forget hands and feet. Take water from the bowl in the house." Then she added sternly, "No-one is to drink the water outside. Something bad got into it."

"Can we take Attercop?" asked Janey, eyeing the ancient black cat, which having slept through the morning's commotion, now finally opened her eyes and was in the process of stretching in a crescent shape on the floor. Susan was going to refuse the request, but then she paused, her browed creased and she looked up at Anna.

"I'll see if I can coax her, Janey, but I make no promises. Cats have a mind of their own. Anna, would you take Maud and lead the children while I see to Attercop?"

Anna knew her friend well enough to know that there would be some logic behind her statement, no matter how idiotic it seemed right now. She took Maud from her crib, wrapped her warmly, gave orders for the children to carry what food and clothing they could, then left the building.

Outside was a hive of activity. She noticed the chair from the Hall being loaded onto a cart. As long as Walter's backside was comfortable, she thought, bitterly. It was obvious that he expected them to walk the four miles before dark with no problems. She wondered where Richard was. Hopefully, he would be able to reach Durham and tell someone they were in need of help. Even if Pudsey was remaining neutral, surely he would help old friends. She felt sick at the prospect of these people invading her home. Butterflies throbbed a little in her lower belly. She held Maud close. She wriggled, simply because, at six months, she was old enough to do so. Anna smiled at her, knowing that she would be lulled to sleep with the motion and warmth of her body once the journey was underway.

Back inside, Susan cursed Walter under her breath for depriving them of writing materials. She would ask Anna what the letter had really said when they could be sure they were away from eavesdroppers. She approached Attercop, hand outstretched and tickled behind her ears. The cat stood up and rubbed herself against Susan's arm, beginning to purr. "Come on, Attercop. We have work to do."

She took the animal in her arms, picked up the bundle containing the red dress and stepped outside. She looked at the sky. They would have to be quick if they were to reach Redgate before dark. From the corner of her eye, she noticed a heap in the corner of the bailey. She could not bear to turn her head and look properly. The smears on the flags told her the bodies had been moved aside so the large stable door had enough clearance to wheel out the cart.

Walter had been watching for her. "Where the hell do you think you are going with that cat!"

Susan ignored him and walked over to the well. She put down the bundle to free a hand so that she could raise the pail. Attercop began to struggle. "Sorry, ma'am," she whispered. She pushed Attercop into the over-brimming pail. The cat scrabbled and clawed, taken by surprise at the unaccustomed cruelty. Susan feigned a cry of pain and let the cat go. Then all she could do was hope that Attercop, if not poisoned by swallowing water or licking it from her paws, would follow to the next household, as she sometimes did. She stooped to fasten the bundle, trying to take enough time to see if the animal showed any ill-effects, but, unco-operatively, the cat streaked, hair on end, back into the building.

Susan trotted to catch up with the rest. If the water was poisoned, they would need to find a way to warn the Northern before their return, but she could not help thinking that any poison so strong and seemingly quick-acting would have made the water taste differently. Perhaps one or two men might have succumbed, but their downfall would have been a warning to the rest.

She caught up with her children and took chubby Maud from Anna in exchange for the bundle.

The day was dark and chilly with an annoying breeze that blew their hair across their eyes and mouths, seemingly more during the most strenuous parts of the road they travelled. They tried to cover ground quickly by making the journey more of a game, but before they had gone two miles, Bobby and Agnes grew too tired to be hurried.

Walter rode behind them, making sure no one attempted an escape or tried to speak to the few passers by. He studied Anna and wondered how long it would be before he could judge whether or not she was truly pregnant. If she was, it could be very useful, even if the rebels were thwarted, although he could not see that happening. If the Northern were the best there were up here, he could foresee no further problems. He looked at the darkening sky. "Hurry up will you. I have no intention of feeling my way up Redgate Bank in the middle of the night."

Susan rounded on him. "The children are too tired to go any faster and they are too heavy to carry."

Walter gave her a look of disgust. "Perhaps you need some incentive." He leaned down from his mount and grabbed the arm of Agnes and swung her onto his lap. The child began to cry with the shock of the sudden movement.

"Give her back!" Susan cried, handing Maud back to Anna.

Walter put a hand over Agnes' mouth so he could be heard. The child began to cough and squeal. "Go faster. Next time you slow down, I will hand her to Garin." He allowed Susan to take her back.

"I'll carry Agnes," said Anna.

"No you won't. Not yet anyway. There is a long way to go. We need to do something to pace it out for them." She gathered the children. "We are going to play at being Knights. Good ones, of course. Even when they are tired they have to keep going. One thing they do is to walk a hundred paces, then run a hundred. We will do it in tens because we are beginners. Anna and I will simply walk fast all the time so we have enough breath to count aloud for you. You run ahead and we will catch up with you as you walk ten because our legs are longer. Janey, you make sure they hear properly. We start from now. Run ten – one, two…"

The children ran ahead. The plan worked for the next half mile, but Agnes flagged first and became tearful, then Bobby followed.

Susan pondered. "About two miles to go. And the last quarter mile is the steepest. Anna, will you take Agnes now?" She tied a broad length of cloth over her own shoulder like a sling and lifted Bobby into it so she could carry him in front of her. She then did the same for Anna and Agnes. She looked at Janey. The seven year old was putting on a brave face but it was obvious the baby was making her arms ache already. She looked down at Bobby who grinned up at her, his old hardships immediately forgotten.

"Bobby, every now and then I am going to put you down and ask you to run to a point further ahead. While you run, I can carry Maud and give Janey's arms a rest."

He nodded and the little troop struggled on. As Redgate drew nearer, they persevered, and Walter, riding behind, could not help wondering what Marc would think if he could see his family now. The day continued to darken, throwing into relief a generous covering of frost in the undergrowth.

At the bottom of Redgate Bank, the group stopped. Most of the men were already at the house. Anna and Susan looked exhausted. There was no way they could expect Janey to walk to the top herself, let alone help to carry the baby. Walter watched Susan carefully. What would she do now? Anna limping again, was obviously fatigued, although Agnes, head lolling, was fast asleep.

Susan stopped. She turned to Walter. "When women are pregnant, the early weeks see them at their most tired. Let Anna ride on the cart. She should not have to climb this bank."

"Plenty of women do."

"And plenty are no longer pregnant within the same week. Especially those whose mothers had problems."

Walter was no fool. He realised it would be folly to test Susan's theory just for the sake of proving he was in charge. He gave a piercing whistle and urged his horse up the bank. The cart stopped.

Susan turned to Anna, "Take Bobby and Maud. It looks like there is enough room. With any luck Maud will stay asleep until I get to the top. She will be hungry when she wakes."

Anna, who felt she was only managing to carry on walking due to it being a lifelong skill, looked blearily towards the cart. "What about you?"

"I shall be fine. I'll carry Agnes and Janey can hold onto my cloak to help her up."

Anna, feeling that if she did not sit down she would fall down, did as she was told.

Susan focused on the back of the cart and set off once more. Janey cried quietly, trying to be brave. She knew they were not even at the steepest part yet. Susan ignored the pounding in her chest and the aching in her arms and simply concentrated on putting one foot in front of the other.

A cry from behind, brought her to a stop. Walter had lifted Janey onto his horse behind him. Susan glared at him, placed Agnes on the ground and approached his mount.

"Don't be a fool," he muttered, not surrendering Janey. "I said I wanted to be there before dark. Pass the child to me."

Susan shook her head.

"Suit yourself," he said and urged the horse to start up the bank again.

"Stay close enough for me to keep an eye on Janey," Susan called.

Walter frowned and shook his head. He would teach her a lesson one day, preferably when her husband returned; especially if he showed any inclination to take Beau Repaire for himself. He could not help thinking that Marc would be just as tormented seeing Walter helping his family in his absence, as he would seeing them suffering under him. He would keep an eye on Susan: she was different from the usual simpering females he was used to.

Halfway up, Susan was about to admit defeat and offer Agnes to Walter, but a black shadow in the silvery undergrowth caught her attention. She squinted into the darkness. A thin cry confirmed her suspicions. Attercop: right as rain Attercop, was following them to Redgate. Whatever had poisoned the men had not come from the well.

Fortified with the knowledge that she had learned something useful, she straightened her back, took a deep breath and began to climb once more.

Chapter Twenty One

Narrow Escape

Each day after that for three weeks, Richard managed to get a message to his mother, saying he was well. Each day she quietly left him food and extra clothing to help him ward off the increasing chill of Winter. She worried about him coping so young, but knew he was better off away from the house. It crossed her mind that he could possibly make it to Bankside, but Walter might have thought of that. It was the sensible thing to do to keep Redgate isolated from allies. She wondered about Robert. Was it possible that he had returned to Drysdale before following Walter's orders and coming here? And if he had, would Drysdale be in the same state they had left it, or would the men have tidied away the bodies? Would he have talked to anyone in Durham – raised suspicions of old friends? She stared into the fire. It was hard to figure Robert out. He seemed to take so little interest in those around him. It seemed perfectly feasible that he would have made his trip and returned without mentioning the occupation. After all, what difference would it make to him? His fortune lay in his ability to cook mouthwatering dishes. He would never be sent on his way, no matter who was in charge. But then, he was Marc's uncle. He had taken him under his wing when Marc's parents were killed. Susan's children were his blood too. Walter did not know that.

She sat up a little, shifting Maud on her lap. She liked this new train of thought. There were other things Walter did not know. He could not read; he did not know that her mother, father and brother were here at Redgate, and unlike many other communities, those of Drysdale came from far and wide so he might not assume blood links were inevitable. The door opened and the ensuing chill caused her to look across the room.

Anna had crossed the room and now stood at the open doorway, trying to discern the place on the Winter-bare hillside she had loved to think of as her own. Less than half a year ago, she had loved to hide away from the company of others. Now she hoped to use the same route to seek out old friends. Bran had said it was one of his favourite places. How long would it be until he came back again? Would he bother? Might he find a wife who presented him with less problems than she did? She tried to push these thoughts away. If she believed the situation was to remain the same it would be unbearable – she would rather be dead. Forboding pressed at them from all sides obliging them to keep alert, and yet a sense of ennui still managed to snake its way through each hour. There was so little they were allowed to do now, that, in spite of the shortening daylight hours, time seemed uncomfortably stretched with little left for them to do except hope and despair in turn.

Anna's view was obstructed by the building work between the house and the upward slope. She did not know what her father had intended to create, but was sure it was something quite different from the enormous walls now being constructed by Walter's men. Still, her father had often said they should have better defences instead of relying on having the time to flee to Drysdale if need be. She cast a critical look at the stonework. Of course, Bran and her father would have to pull it all down and start it again properly. Did Walter really think it would keep her father away from his own home, his daughter, his wife's grave? A shiver made her realise how selfish she was in keeping the door open for so long and she stepped back into the warm, closing it against the cold.

Susan still sat at the fireside, holding a sleeping Maud, the rest of the children just as indolent after their meal. Now, she looked from the fire, following Anna with her eyes as she crossed to the furthest corner of the room. The younger woman stooped forward and reached behind the chest, pulling the red dress from its hiding place in the shadows.

Susan raised her eyebrows, "Now?"

Anna did not pause as she nodded, but changed her garments, her mind made up. "If I do not go now, I never will. I am not so sickly now, but can feel the swelling beginning. If I wait much longer, the dress will not fit and my movements will be hampered. John knows to have a mount ready. And the men are wearied with drinking and watching other people work."

Susan stirred herself, her limbs unwilling to move after spending so long in the same position. She lay Maud in the crib. "I'm really not sure, Anna. Their being full of ale could have dire consequences. A drunken man would probably see any woman as fair game, but especially Isabel."

Anna sighed. They had argued it through so many times and knew there would always be risks, so now was as good a time as any. "My mind is made up. I cannot have this baby here. Bankside is so close that not to make the attempt seems folly."

They looked at each other and were watched in turn by the sleepy children on the pallet. Both women knew that if they had been men, the journey would seem a mere stroll, but for them, with little experience of travelling anywhere except Drysdale, it was a taxing pilgrimage. Susan adjusted the dress's seams so they sat more squarely on Anna's shoulders, then helped her to wind her hair quite high to reveal her neck.

"It is a shame the weather is so cold." Susan remarked, knowing Anna would need to carry her cloak at first, rather than wear it, so that the dress identified her more readily with Isabel. "Remember, if they recognize you make a lot of noise so Walter hears you. He may be displeased, but he knows you are carrying his child and should keep the men off you."

Anna felt a chill in her stomach. She took a deep breath, gave Susan's hand the briefest of squeezes then stepped out into the cold evening.

At first she needed to stand quite still in the shadows until her eyes adjusted. A few torches burned in anticipation of night, but it was still possible to see and be seen. Perfect, she thought. There was just enough light for the men to be required to guess her identity from the dress and the hair. She clutched her cloak, then realising this was not very Isabel-like, she forced her arms to relax and even swing a little nonchalantly as she made her way to the stables. She walked confidently, even trying to think Isabel thoughts as she went, but having no inkling what ideas Isabel entertained, her efforts were in vain. As she grew closer to the stables, a whistle pierced the evening and she jumped, inviting laughter from those who had seen her.

"Come over here. I could do with warming up." More laughter. Would Isabel ignore this?

"You're better off with me, love. Let that dirty bastard up you and it'll be you that's burning up."

"Get off!" A grunt sounded. Someone had thrown a punch. Thank God. They were too caught up in their own squabbling to check her out properly. She had reached the stables which John had left dimly lit. She scanned quickly and allowed herself a sigh of relief. John had stuck to his promise. As she reached up to unhook the barrier, she felt an arm slide around her waist and pull her backwards. She dropped the cloak and used both of her own hands to try to unclasp those now tightly clamped together under her ribs.

"Not a good night for riding alone, Isabel. You're better off spending some riding time in the hay with a companion" She did not recognise the voice. The arms clenched with a more bruising tightness as she began to struggle.

"I must go. I have business in Durham. I cannot be late." It was hard to breathe.

She felt sharp whiskers against her neck and turned her face away from the smell of ale on his breath. Whoever it was straightened up and Anna felt her feet leave the floor, making her unable to fight effectively, although she kicked as much as she dared – conscious of the child inside her even at this early stage.

"You do not understand. It is the Prince Bishop I must see. I dare not be late."

Her assailant kept her feet from the floor and walked her to a corner, where the hay was piled high.

"Don't you worry about him. Believe me; this won't take long at all." He dropped her so suddenly that she fell onto her hands and knees. She looked around wildly for something to use as a weapon as she was pushed forwards and her legs pulled out from under her. Straw pricked through her dress and dust from the pile gritted her eyes.

Then another voice. "Don't be selfish, Garin. Turn her round so we can all have a good look before our turns."

Garin obliged and, as Anna was rolled onto her back, a light was held aloft, making her squint and unable to identify the men now surrounding her.

As Garin fumbled with his own clothing, a voice called, "Whoa there."

Garin had other ideas.

Three men bent forward and hauled him up to his knees. He tried to free his arms, cursing.

"Wait. That's not Isabel."

"So what?" Garin complained.

"It's the Redgate girl. I don't think he would like this."

"Well, he might not find out about it." He looked back at Anna. "She probably knows better than to blabber. Accidents can happen."

Anna lay not daring to move, as the men looked at her, then at each other.

"I suppose she is wearing a red dress. Anyone could be forgiven for making a mistake."

Garin grinned. "Exactly."

The man holding the torch looked to the doorway as if expecting Walter to be standing there. Momentarily, he chewed his bottom lip. "All right, then, but hurry. He might smell a rat before we get the chance to ride her."

Anna told herself to scream, but as she opened her mouth, it was clamped shut by a foul smelling hand. She gripped Garin's clothing, trying to hold his bodyweight away from her.

"Here," said another, kneeling over her in the hay and holding her arms above her head. "Come on one of you. Get down here and cover her mouth so he can get on with it. We'll be here all night at this rate."

Anna screwed her eyes shut. Suddenly, sounding above the whispered urgings of the men, a horse screamed, hooves battered against wood and Garin was suddenly on his feet. The pressure on her arms and mouth was released. She opened her eyes to see all the men pushing their way out of the stable door.

She rolled onto her knees first then pulled herself slowly to her feet. She felt nauseous again and her knees shook.

The men cursed. "Get after him. We've been after that little shit for weeks."

Anna crept through the shadows and let herself back into the room where Susan stood wringing her hands. When Anna entered she rushed to her. "What happened?"

"They found me out. Richard saved me. He's trying to outride them."

Susan ran to the window, but finding it impossible to see, ran out into the night instead. Cries went up in the trees.

Anna turned to the children, who were wide-eyed with fear. "Stay there," she urged and then forced herself outside too: partly to see what was happening and partly to avoid being sick indoors. Much of her hair had come loose in the struggle. She was thrust forward involuntarily by a sudden spasm in her stomach and retched into the long grass by the house. She cursed herself for being so useless and tried to straighten up, placing one hand against the wall to aid her balance. She wanted to bend and retch again, but forced herself into a near upright position. She shivered against the cold and felt her hair wet where she had not been quick enough in holding it back from her face. Around her, torches weaved through the trees and men's shouts echoed in every direction. She wondered what Walter was doing and turned herself laboriously in the direction of the Hall's doorway. Her eyes fell on him straight away. She felt slightly taken aback. In spite of all the activity around him, he was staring directly at her. It seemed so odd, that she put her head to one side as if trying to make out his meaning, then her stomach muscles gave another sudden spasm and she vomited again.

When she looked up, Walter's gaze was still fixed on her. More oddly, the men, who were looking to him for instruction, were noticing his seeming hypnosis, and, thinking he was annoyed that the mother of his future child should have been left in such a state, now began to try to outdo each other in their determination to catch Richard in order that they might escape a punishment. Chaos almost ensued when a torch was dropped which ignited a drift of dry leaves, but the dampness of the forest floor did Richard no favours and he was finally pulled from his horse and carried, kicking and struggling towards Walter.

"What shall we do with him?" Garin asked of Walter.

Unable to stop herself, Susan ran over and began to beat at Garin's arms. "Let him go!"

Anna watched the scene and still Walter watched her, his mouth open, his face frozen in an unreadable expression.

Garin followed his gaze and took in her sorry state. His mouth became a thin line and he turned back to Walter as apologetically as a man not used to apologizing could. "You couldn't really blame us. As soon as we saw the red dress we thought it was Isabel. We didn't touch her though."

Walter turned to him. "What did you say?"

"Sorry," said Garin, dutifully.

"No, you idiot," Walter spat. "What did you say after that?"

Garin, still holding tight to a struggling Richard, in spite of his mother's efforts to pull and bite him to freedom, gave a shrug and said, "The red dress. Anyone would be forgiven for thinking it was Isabel. Fair game and all that."

Walter turned back to Anna and stepped closer. He took in the pale skin, the dark circles round the eyes, the damp straggles of hair and finally allowed himself to exhale. Before addressing her, he stood up straight and took a deep breath. "Get back inside and clean yourself up." He made as if to turn to Garin, then turned back to her. "And burn that dress – and when you do it, do it over there where I can see you from the window."

Anna obliged. She was freezing cold.

He turned his attention to Richard and considered. He knew he was Marc's son, in spite of Susan's secrecy. "He is more useful alive than dead for now, but urm…" he considered, "cut out his tongue."

Susan gave a cry. "No. He has nothing to tell."

Walter, thoroughly annoyed at this upset to his evening, began to rail at her. "Think yourself lucky he has got off this lightly. With a mother like you, endlessly trying my patience, it is a wonder I have not slit all of their throats by now."

He turned to go. Susan followed. "Then punish me instead. He is just a child; his allegiance could easily be moulded to suit your own needs."

Anna stood in the doorway to the family's room, hoping Walter would have it in him to change his mind in front of the men. It seemed unlikely. Even in the darkness, she could tell that his colour was high. She hoped Susan would not push him too far.

Walter looked about him. He turned to Anna, irritably, "when you have finally done as I asked, go to my chamber. I do not want you speaking with this woman again. Then you," he turned to Garin, "throw this little baggage into the gaol – no extra covers – and you," he waved an accusing torch at Susan, "stop trying my patience, or I'll take your children away from you a limb, then an eye at a time."

He then turned on his heels and strutted back to the house.

Garin watched Walter as he retreated, "Does that mean he keeps his tongue this time?"

Walter stopped dead in his tracks. His shoulders rose and fell as he sighed. Slowly, he turned back to his men. He walked deliberately to Garin, silently handed him his torch, swapping for Richard. Then he carried the child to the grating for the oubliette, which two of his men scampered to remove, dangled Richard over the hole and dropped him into it. Richard gave a cry and Susan gasped, but controlled her urge to scold. The grating was replaced and Walter began the walk back to his chamber. As he passed Garin, he hissed, "Feed him just enough to keep him alive."

Realising Garin was going to question further, he quickly held up his hand, palm towards the would-be speaker, and gave a sharp "No!" and a shake of the head, "Ask a cook, Garin," then continued on his way.

Susan looked to Anna who could think of little else to do except follow the orders she had been given and hopefully grab a bite to eat to ease her now empty belly, just in case the opportunity did not arise after crossing to Walter's chamber. All in all, things could have turned out much worse. She would never think Isabel fortunate again.

Chapter Twenty Two

Revelation

Bran shed his cloak as soon as he dismounted. Usually, he found the January Spanish sun far more pleasant than the chill of France and England, but his journey on horseback had been a long one. The men flanking the doorway to Harun's private house, recognising him from previous visits, gave him a courteous nod and opened the door. As on earlier occasions, he travelled alone. Bran knew he had already been sighted the day before and that Harun had seen to it that he had a safe passage. He had felt relatively secure travelling overland rather than oversea, feeling he had a better chance of avoiding rebels or mercenaries.

He removed his shoes then took a few steps inside, savouring the change in atmosphere. He admired Harun's architecture once more: the gleaming white floor; the alabaster pillars; the intricate ironwork of the door at the far end of the building through which he could see greenery and hear a blend of birdsong and the trickling water of three fountains. Health was Harun's main interest and the very fabric of this salubrious home boasted of it. Bran took a deep draught of cool air and felt fully revived for the first time since he had left France on his mission to build up support for the English King against the younger Henry and Louis in France.

Harun suddenly appeared, like some exotic version of wood nymph, framed by foliage at the doorway to the leafy courtyard. He gave Bran a broad smile, then beckoned enthusiastically.

"Come, come. Don't keep yourself a stranger."

Now feeling overdressed in hauberk and surcoat in such friendly surroundings, he did as he was bid. He had noticed another pair of shoes next to his at the doorway and braced himself for company, when all he truly wanted to do was to relax and allow Harun's chatter to free him of the obligation to make an effort at conviviality. Food was being brought to a table at which another man was already seated. Harun poured him a drink of water while restarting the same conversation he had shared with Bran when he left almost a year before.

"She had another child, a healthy boy, just three weeks ago. Both of them are doing well. I knew it was possible. Remember the argument with the family in the middle of it all? And now the mother is alive and well and capable of having more children. It is surely a better outcome." He raised his cup in a jubilant toast to his friend while simultaneously ushering him to a seat. He continued to speak incessantly while his food was served. "No need for the mother to die at all. I knew it." Eventually, he took a sip from his cup and pondered. "My next aim is to transfer the blood of a healthy man or woman to that of a patient to affect a cure. Now, that would be a big step forward –

women lose life threatening amounts of blood during a caesarian and people lose faith: the possibility of being given blood might reassure her."

Bran recalled an Arthurian Tale where Dindraine had offered her blood to a leprous old lady in order that she might be cured by the blood of a virgin, only to die herself in the process. "Perhaps the healthy donor might also be afraid to give their blood in the fear they might bleed to death and fair worse than the patient they are aiming to help."

Harun's brow creased, "We need volunteers who wish to help medicine and science move forward: people who will take a risk." Then he waved his hand as if erasing the negatives evoked by Bran's words, "But," he urged, "mothers who have a natural birth without an operation bleed profusely also. Many weaken and die after childbirth. Transference of blood," he sighed. "Now that would be a discovery."

Bran noticed Harun's other visitor hesitating over his meal. Child birth was not really a topic to induce a good appetite in a man, but Harun carried on happily oblivious. Fortunately, he spoke now of Bran's journey.

"I heard of your arrival in Spain a few days ago and had a room made ready. I expect you could do with a lie down." He gestured with a graceful hand to the man on his left whose demeanour was thrown into somber relief by Harun's enthusiasm. Harun ignored rank, valuing people for their knowledge not their wealth so he introduced the men without titles.

"Ralph, this is Bran. You may already know each other, both being from the same small island."

Ralph smiled with relief, able to identify Bran's allegiance to the King now that he could match a name to the appearance.

"It is good to meet a member of the Northern in such troubled times. I serve Glanville of Yorkshire: always loyal to the King."

Bran relaxed. "I recognise his name from Joss. I expect we may have come here for similar reasons."

Ralph nodded and they both turned to Harun.

Harun sighed, his face showing the disappointment of a child told to put away his toys for a while. "I imagine you wish for a show of support to finally send the rebels back to their holes for good." He flashed a smile, determined to have some entertainment from the tedious circumstances. "You may take it in turns to answer my question – be eloquent for my mind will need to be changed: I have a peaceful life here. I am left to my own devices to study, practise and, hopefully, heal. Why would I involve my community with someone else's matters of war?"

Ralph answered first. "The rebels' cause stems from greed. We can see that there are too many to be satisfied with the spoils of war, even if they win. Their share will never seem enough. Their greed is emphasised by the fact that there is no logical reason for them to overthrow the King : the law protects them better than it used to; civil peace is more prevalent, even now, than it was under Stephen, and what sane man would wish to be governed by those whose laws would be determined by individual want? Should they win, I believe men dissatisfied with their spoils will wish to apportion blame. In the past, this has led to creating scapegoats, which in turn has led to higher taxes, genocide and crusades. And here you are in the path of this new breed of crusader: a breed of man who believes it is acceptable to make or break a kingdom according to his own selfish whims. A breed of man who is a destroyer by nature and who will spread lies and make false promises to gain support when he needs it. Far better help the King deal with them now, than wait for the disease to spread."

Harun smiled. He could tell the speech had been memorized, but said politely, "I like the final metaphor." He looked at Bran and waited for him to speak.

"At the risk of sounding lame," he smiled, "I agree with Ralph." He paused to take a drink, then continued. "You are quite right: there is little incentive in venturing away from a peaceful life in order to involve yourself in someone else's war – but this war threatens our shared beliefs. Rebels would take Drysdale, simply so an oafish braggart could say 'this is mine'; - medicine and engineering would no longer have a place there. Drysdale would cease to be – and so would the connection between our communities. At present we have a kinship of ideas and trust. It is not based on nearness, a common tongue or colour of skin. This connection is about honour, common sense, proving trust can exist in the unlikeliest of places, and…" Bran paused and, beginning to grow tired of hearing his own voice, gave a sardonic smile, "if my words so far do not persuade you, remember who it was who saved your sister from being bundled into a dubious looking boat and sold into slavery two years ago in Messina."

Harun narrowed his eyes in mock disapproval, "Umm. And now Azra is so besotted by her rescuer, she flies into a rage whenever anyone attempts to speak of marriage. However, that aside," he got to his feet and walked to the closest fountain and thought, "I want to help, but I also want to be more involved with life than death. I agree that the rebels are more likely to carry on killing if they are not stopped, even if they are victorious at first. And I truly believe the older Henry is the best man to be running your land." He turned back to them. "You may cite me as an ally; you may have one hundred men to give this claim credence; I will send word to you if I hear of rebels trying to build up their numbers anywhere else in Europe; and I will spread word amongst the many neutral visitors here that the rebels are –as you call them – oafs, who would unwittingly destroy the land they wish to claim. If things reach crisis point, I will review the number of men promised. And that, my friends, is the best I can do. If my good fortune should ever leave me, and I am to be set upon by Christians, I hope I can trust in your support as much as you can trust in mine now."

Both men smiled their thanks.

"Now," Harun took a deep breath, and lifted his cup to his visitors, "let us speak of more pleasant topics. Bran, how were your family on your return?"

"Well," Bran said, in a rather non-committal way, for a man who had just been granted a huge favour by his questioner.

Harun sniffed a story. "Umm. Not like you to be so reticent. You know you can trust Ralph."

Ralph smiled at Bran apologetically for being used as a tool to force open his private life.

"There has been so much to do with the rebellion that time seems to have slipped by with little room for social niceties."

Harun cut to the chase. "How is that little girl with the brilliant mind? Joanna was it?"

"Anna," corrected Bran. "Not a little girl anymore."

"How is she?" Harun pressed on.

Bran found himself unable to suppress a smile, knowing exactly what Harun was getting at. "She is now a beautiful, intelligent, well read young woman with a startlingly analytical mind," he took a deep breath, "who is all set to be married when all of this trouble is over."

Harun studied him. "Betrothed to you?"

Bran shook his head "No."

"Jealous?"

Bran decided to call his bluff, knowing a denial would only lead to more teasing. "Of course."

"Has her father approved the match?"

"Unofficially. We will look deeper into his family history once the rebels are beaten for good."

"I am surprised you did not come here with a request that I help to prolong the campaign. She may go off him in time."

Bran gave a quiet laugh. "She's not that shallow."

"Ah, shame."

Ralph, who had been waiting politely for a long awaited lull in the conversation, quickly interjected. "Do I know the lucky gentleman?"

"You may. He is the son of Walter who holds Helmislay."

Ralph washed his hands of orange juice and pondered. "Walter Espec?"

Bran nodded, surprised at his own ability to appear so detached from a topic he had tortured himself over ever since he left Drysdale.

"Are you sure?"

"It is how he introduced himself, and Ben had a letter beforehand from his kinsman expressing his interest." He noticed Ralph's confusion. "Is there something amiss?"

Ralph looked at him. "I know the older gentleman quite well. He holds the respect of people from all ranks. And he did have a son."

"Did have?"

"His only son was killed quite young. We were of a similar age and he had been a boy in good health so I remember the day my father told me as a particularly sad one - and so unfortunate. It was a simple fall from his horse, but the way he fell broke his neck."

Bran began to feel uneasy. Harun intervened. "Is it possible that there is another Walter of Helmislay?"

Ralph nodded. "Certainly, but not one purporting to be the son of Walter Espec." He pondered. "There was another Walter, a cousin of the dead boy, and," he raised his eyebrows as he felt one piece of the puzzle almost fit into place, "Espec treated his nephew as most men treat their sons...." He seemed to come to and shook his head. "But he could not be your Anna's betrothed."

"Why not?" asked Bran.

"He died in Italy eight months ago. In fact," Ralph sat up straighter and looked at Bran, "he did mention he was considering marrying – and he mentioned the Northern. But he was a modest young man and would not speak of it in any deeper detail at such an early stage." Both Harun and Bran began to feel the import of what Ralph was saying.

"Is it possible you are mistaken about his death?"

Ralph shook his head. "I wish it was so: he was a good friend. I was entrusted to accompany his bones on his final journey home."

Bran frowned, trying to piece together a puzzle with disparate parts.

Ralph said sympathetically, "I fear your Anna is being used to aid the rebels' cause."

Bran considered. He remembered what Marc had said about Anna's decision while he spoke of his fears for his family. He remembered how ill she had looked at their final meeting before he left. He remembered how Walter had been allowed into her room so he could speak with her privately. It was all beginning to make a horrible sense.

"Are there people left behind to protect her?" asked Harun.

Bran looked at him and nodded, his face a picture of guilt. "I feel I may have allowed my pride to blind me to Anna's troubles."

"Your pride? You mean she refused a proposal?"

Bran nodded.

"Well, my friend," Harun deduced, "I need no more evidence. A man of your means and stature? She must have made her decision under duress."

Bran stood, his sense of urgency heightening in spite of the knowledge that a guard from the Northern had remained behind. "I have to leave now."

Harun and Ralph stood, and the latter spoke, "If I can help in any way, just command me. I feel to help Anna would be to disadvantage the rebels."

Harun held out his arms in a gesture intended to calm them down. "Remember the best campaigns are carefully planned. Besides, I have a ship almost ready to make a voyage. I can send a message so that we can sail in the morning. Surely it is better to plan tonight to ensure success, rather than to rush into another journey while you are still saddle sore."

Bran had been weary but now his fatigue was dispelled by an equally crippling urgency.

He sat again, unconsciously stroking his forefinger across his lips as he thought. "Ben will need to know, he is still in Scotland, and Marc will expect to be informed when his own wife and children are at Drysdale too."

Ralph offered more precise support, "Perhaps I can make my way back to Aquitaine with the hundred men you promised, Harun. I will inform your friend, and should he feel the need to leave for England immediately, I can remain to negotiate with this show of strength."

Bran smiled his gratitude. "I will write a letter so he accepts your word."

"It may take some days to gather the men together and reach France, but those days can be well spent in sharing your cause with them so that they see the sense in remaining loyal."

"Is there no way we could sail tonight?" asked Bran.

"Trust me, friend," Harun smiled, "you look exhausted. Have a good night's sleep and plan more effectively in the morning." He clapped his hands and two men emerged as if from nowhere and showed Ralph and Bran to their respective quarters for the night.

On stepping over the threshold, Bran paced the room, his thoughts in tumult. The place was cool and well aired. Incense burned in holders suspended from the ceiling and a cooling draft helped the aroma to explore the room. Fine muslin billowed at the large open doorway which faced onto the same shady courtyard where he had spoken with Harun and Ralph. The room was designed to calm the occupier, to maximize relaxation, but Bran was tortured by this recent revelation.

How could he have been so blind? If anything had happened to Anna he would never forgive himself. To think, he had been so arrogant to assume she had cried out of respect for his feelings. He undressed and stepped into the bath that had been prepared for him, taking little comfort in it. He only hoped the Northern who had remained behind were already alerted to the intrigue. Perhaps Ben already knew. He tried to continue thinking along those lines, knowing he would be on the rack until morning otherwise.

Being deep in thought, he did not emerge from his bath until the cooling water urged him into action.

He glanced around for something with which to dry himself only to find himself face to face with Azra. She held out a cloth sheepishly, at arm's length.

Bran took it quickly and wrapped himself with a hasty coyness, which made her smile.

He had been so deeply immersed in other thoughts that it took some time for him to think of appropriate words to approach this inappropriate situation. This was not going to be easy. From years before, Joss's words came echoing back to him. It might seem like the easiest remedy is to be honest when refusing unwanted advances, but if honesty was not delivered sensitively, even the closest of friends could become the deadliest of enemies over a dishonoured sister.

Bran dried himself as nonchalantly as possible to buy himself some thinking time. He decided against asking how long she had been in the room with her, knowing it was likely that he would feel even more uncomfortable if he heard the answer.

"It is a long while since I last saw you Azra."

She smiled and poured some oil into her palm and looked at him, head to one side. Her hand, still cupped, was held towards him. Bran gave a quick shake of the head. She shrugged, unfazed, and seated herself on the edge of the low bed. Unusually, her legs were bare. She allowed the white silk to fall away from her thighs and began to massage the oil into her own skin instead.

As he watched the movements of her hands, he asked, "Does Harun know you are here, Azra?"

Without stopping, she looked up at him with a smile and gave a slow shake of the head.

Bran withheld a deep sigh and pulled his chemise quickly over his head and shoulders and then walked to the muslin covered doorway which opened onto the courtyard. Harun was not there. He returned, crossing the room and stepped through the door to the shady corridor beyond. He could hear voices. He looked back to the bed. Azra was now standing up and looking rather less self-possessed.

"Should I leave you alone?" she asked.

Careful to word things so as to hurt neither her feelings nor her pride, he nodded and said, "I think Harun would expect it, don't you?"

She looked down at her hands. Bran stepped back inside, but was careful to leave the door open. "I must spend the time until morning thinking and planning. A lady very dear to me needs my help. I do not want to let her down."

She nodded. Without looking up, she asked, "Do you wish to marry her?"

"If she will have me."

She nodded, making a closer examination of her fingernails. "I will leave you to think, Sir." Then she left, closing the door.

Bran listened to her receding footsteps, and then closed the shutters to the courtyard leaving the room in a sudden darkness. He felt like he had just had a narrow escape. Carefully, with only the glow from the incense burners to guide him, he poured himself a cup of water, then lay on the bed thinking. Despite his racing thoughts, he soon fell into a deep sleep.

Chapter Twenty Three

Ambrosia

The scent from the orange groves permeated his dreams: nevertheless, he was at Redgate again, looking down at a startled, large-eyed Anna, who had been making the laborious climb to the grassy seat beneath the canopy of chestnut and lime. When she recognised him, she smiled and took his outstretched hand. Once on his level, he stroked the hair from her face.

"You're all healed again," he smiled.

She nodded and slipped her arms round his waist, resting her head against his chest. He kissed her hair and stroked her shoulders. She raised her mouth to his ear and whispered, "Could you bring yourself to want me still?"

He kissed her brow, her mouth; lifted her closer to him and carried her to the glade; telling her, "I have always wanted you. That will never change."

They stood now, embraced by tree shadows. A breeze sighed through the boughs. He kissed her mouth. He felt he could not kiss her for long enough. Stroking and caressing, her hands found a way to his bare skin through his clothing, giving him a sense of urgency he knew he would need to curb.

He laid her down, feeling his skin against hers, but instead of grass beneath him, he now felt silk. They were in a bed: a beautifully wide bed; and she was naked under him in the near darkness. He wanted her so badly. What would Ben say?

Almost afraid that she might change her mind, he lay to one side and asked gently, "Are you sure this is what you want? That I am what you want?" He felt her fingertips brush against his stomach.

"I trust you."

He smiled in the darkness, kissed her face and murmured into her hair, "You know you can. I want you as wife – always."

Right or not, this was a good dream. He would make the most of it. He slid his palms beneath her shoulders and she turned her head to one side as he kissed her throat, her breasts, her stomach. Sensing her breathing change, he slowly trailed the tip of his tongue in a line down her stomach to her hips. She stroked his hair and sighed. He gently rolled her over, easily raising her to her knees, and knelt behind her. She lifted her arms and reached back, placing her hands around his neck with her back arched in a delicious invite to his hands. God, he was so hungry for her. He held her close with one arm and swept the other palm gently against her breasts, then down to her abdomen. She breathed his name and he played his fingertips lightly between her thighs. She brought one hand down to shadow his fingers with hers. He could feel her heartbeat strong and fast. Shifting a little, she reached back, clutching at his hips, urging him closer. He brushed against her.

"I want you, Bran."

He leaned over her shoulder, gently turned her cheek so he could reach her mouth with his. "I do not want to hurt you."

"You will not. Please." Was she telling him Walter had lain with her? It mattered little now. Regardless, he wrapped his arms around her, kissed her hair and spoke as if it were her first time. "Just say if I hurt you. There are other ways."

The darkness deprived him of sight, beautifully heightening his sense of touch. She gave a gasp. Gently, he pulled away and eased her onto her back. He wanted her to enjoy their love-making, not tolerate it. "In a little while, when we try again, there will be more pleasure than pain."

She kissed his cheek then slid her hands down to his hips. "Please don't stop again."

He held her close as they move together, bathed by the scent from the orange groves. He would have to be careful. Wouldn't he? He put his hands on her waist. "We must stop, Anna. Wait."

She kissed his mouth then asked, "Why? It is just a dream. Just a beautiful dream."

He considered, then held her close again. She was right. It was just a dream after all. He pulled her closer still, enjoying the feel of their nakedness.

"Oh, Bran. It is just a dream. Don't stop. Let it be."

Just a dream. "I won't stop." God, yes. Just a beautiful, beautiful, beautiful dream.

And in the morning, when Harun, out of respect, chose not to send a servant but to rouse him personally, he found Bran naked, in a twist and tangle of bedclothes, fast asleep in the arms of his sister, Azra.

Chapter Twenty Four

A New Year

"I cannot make out the hand."

Walter snatched the letter from her, threw it down on his chair and gripped Anna's jawbone between his thumb and forefinger. She gasped as he tightened his grip, feeling the sharpness of his fingernails, and tried to back away, but he simply followed her and backed her against the tapestry which hung before the closed door.

"Do not irritate me, Anna," he hissed through clenched teeth. "You know what happens when you irritate me. I know this was written by your father. "

He released his grip quite suddenly, twisted to retrieve the letter and turned to her again. "Now, enough time wasting. Tell me."

Anna worked her jaw a little and subconsciously placed her hand on her swollen belly. Perhaps she should be more careful. There was nothing in the letter which could help Walter anyway. The Northern would not include anything of great importance which might jeopardize the campaign. She took the letter from him, wishing she could contain the shaking in her hands. The baby kicked erratically. "William's truce appears to have been short lived. The rebels still try to overthrow the King's forces, but they are at odds with each other and will prove to be easily thwarted."

She paused, wondering whether to read the next part. "My father simply hopes that I am well again since my fall."

Walter stood looking over her shoulder. He jabbed his finger at a place lower down where he recognized Bran's name. "Here. What does he say about the Jew?"

Anna took a deep breath and read, "I do not know what caused you to reject the proposal from Bran. It proves that fathers are no judge of their daughters' tastes. Perhaps you regard him as too much of a brother. Whatever your reasons, you have my support and I am sure that, one day soon, you will have his also. Speaking of support, at present he journeys to Spain to raise support from old allies there. I hear many a lady plays pilgrim in the hope of making him a husband…."

Walter snatched the letter back, rolled it and tucked it inside his gown. "We will see if Susan's version coincides."

Another kick inside prompted Anna to take a seat.

Walter sat looking at her now, unable to prevent his eyes from straying to her belly.

"How long to go now?" he asked.

"Just under four months," she replied, yet again. She sat on a stool, leaning her back against the wall, wondering how Bran's potential wives might look. In this new position, the child began its acrobatics once more. She looked down when she felt, what seemed to her, a massive movement as the baby turned over. Walter's jaw dropped at the movement under her gown.

"Was that the child?"

Still looking down, Anna nodded.

"Does it hurt?" he asked, forgetting to keep his customary distance.

She shook her head. "No more than it would hurt you to push your tongue against your inner cheek." From the corner of her eye she noticed Walter's hand come up to his face and guessed that he was experimenting. It was quiet for a while.

"Are you scared?" he suddenly asked.

She considered. "I try to push it out of my mind." She looked at him. "If we both survive the birth, I would ask that you wait until the baby is weaned before you kill me."

He said nothing. In truth, he hoped the birth would be difficult, but that the baby could be saved. The child was enough to serve his purposes. Still, he pondered on this issue of weaning. He had not even considered how it would be fed if its mother was dead. He could not rely on Susan's milk still being enough in a few months time. Perhaps she was right. Prolonging her life would prolong the child's. There would be too many people vying for the same land when this rebellion was won. At least a child to the only heiress would secure his claim. Not that he would always be satisfied with a manor of this size. His father could possibly help his claim for Beau Repaire. And he was young enough to find other women. His mind turned to Marc again. He wondered how long this campaign would last. The men were bored. It was tiresome constantly trying to keep them away from the women. Perhaps he should have entertainment brought in from elsewhere. No, probably not. Knowing his luck, the Northern would return just as his men were getting their legs over. Not a good idea.

The fire crackled and the two of them remained lost in their own uncertain thoughts.

A sudden loud knocking at the outer door made Anna jump.

"Open it," Walter ordered her.

Anna did so. Susan stood in the cold, holding a stack of furs.

Anna ushered her into the warmth.

Walter looked at her and smiled. He already knew what she would ask so simply asked, "Why should I?"

"If you had meant for him to be killed you would have done it weeks ago. If you are going to kill him, you won't leave that pleasure to the weather. He is already half starved and too exhausted to keep the cold at bay any longer."

Walter simply looked at her, eyebrows raised. In spite of her matter of fact performance, it made Susan queasy to talk of her son so candidly. She stood awkwardly under his gaze, her knuckles white as she gripped her cargo tightly to her. He turned to Anna. "Go and make yourself useful elsewhere."

Anna glanced at Susan. She hoped she would be safe on her own, but did not dare disobey Walter. She had done so before and rued it. Susan gave her a smile to reassure her all would be well and Anna left them alone.

Walter sat up a little straighter and peered at what Susan was carrying. He beckoned. "Let me see what you have there."

Susan held out her arms. Walter peered and beckoned again. "Come closer."

Susan already knew where this was leading and if Richard did not look so poorly; so painfully ill and pale; and the weather was not so piercingly cold, she might have turned on her heels. But she knew Richard would die if no one helped him. Even with the extra tidbits she had been surreptitiously feeding him, his appearance was changed dramatically.

At first, she stayed put and looked at Walter. He shrugged and turned away from her, saying, "Close the door on the way out."

She stepped closer to him and he turned to her, smiling once more. He placed one hand on top of the pile of furs and one below and lifted them from her. He stroked their texture with his fingers and rested them on his lap. He rubbed his jaw between his fingers and thumb, still perusing the bundle. "How highly do you value your son's life?" he asked.

"More highly than my own," she replied.

"He deserves to die. Had he escaped, there would have been much bloodshed. It is fortunate that I had much on my mind that day."

Susan was restless. She felt that every passing second might push her son beyond the point of recovery. She had lain tormented all night and would have come to Walter then but she had been afraid that he would be so dismayed at being woken that her pleas would fall on deaf ears or anger him into hurting Richard.

Walter handed back the bundle. "I find you a practical woman: a woman who prefers to get things done. I admire that. I watch you a lot. Like the day we left Drysdale. That play you performed to see if the cat would be poisoned. A nice idea."

She said nothing.

"You may take your furs to Richard."

She sighed with relief and turned to go. "Ah ah." He waved her back. "Of course, I need something in return."

Her heart sank.

"I find I worry about my unborn child."

"I can be of help there. My mother too. We are both experienced midwives."

"Very kind of you to offer your services, but I was not thinking that far ahead. I find myself wanting a woman, but not wanting to risk the health of the unborn child."

Susan knew she could say that the baby should not suffer if the man was gentle, but she did not want to leave Anna vulnerable to his advances.

"And, do you know, Susan, in spite of your many children, I find you very attractive." He turned back to the fire. "Give the furs to Richard and I will come to you tonight. If you do not comply, Richard loses his covers."

"What about the children? We share the same quarters."

"Then think of a reason for them not to." He turned back to her. "Hurry up, before I change my mind."

Susan bit her tongue and did as she was bid. She would think of a way round this afterwards.

Chapter Twenty Five

Delicate Cage

The panels of intricate open trace work in the ornate doors, an indication of freedom, mocked Bran where he sat on the bed, unable to fathom a way out of what was happening because he had no idea how he got into it in the first place. In spite of Harun's angry pacing and Azra's fumbling haste as she shame-facedly dressed herself before her brother, he felt completely isolated; the full weight of what this would mean pressed more heavily with each and every lumbering second. It was bad enough to have sacrificed his mission to gain support for the King; but worse still to have failed because he was accused of lying with his host's sister.

It seemed to take Azra a lifetime to dress. When finally clothed, she looked across to her brother trembling. She had never seen him so infuriated. When he turned to her, his glare robbed her of breath. He pointed to a chair by the doorway. "Sit!" he snapped.

She did as she was told and looked down at her own clasped hands in her lap. Harun turned to Bran. Quietly, he muttered, "I would appreciate it if you would clothe yourself." His voice was quiet but over brimming with scorn.

Bran, still feeling dazed, glanced about the room for his clothing. All but his chemise lay across the stool near to the place he had bathed the night before. The chemise lay in a crumpled heap at the foot of the bed near his ankles. He reached for it, pulled it over his head, then crossed the room and continued to clothe himself, completely lost for words. All the while, there was no sound in the room save birdsong and the trickling of the fountains from outside. He stood, unsure of what Harun was expecting. An explanation? He looked from Harun to Azra and back again, took a deep breath and said quietly, "I do not know what happened here, Harun."

There was silence as Harun gave him a long, level look. Bran took it that this was better than an outburst and continued. "It was dark. I lay on the bed and slept. When I awoke..." he paused, realising how implausible this all seemed, "Well... you were here when I woke."

Harun, although looking at Bran, addressed Azra. "Go to your chamber. Make sure you are alone. If your sisters are there send them away. I will come to you shortly."

She did as she was told. As she left, she called tearfully, "He promised he would make me his wife." Bran closed his eyes at the humiliation of the whole house hearing her call. He and Harun were left alone.

Harun walked to the double doorway and stood facing away from Bran, one arm across his chest, the other rubbing his chin. To Bran behind him, his friend looked as if he was shaking his head. It seemed a long time until he spoke.

"Do you know how many times I have had to deal with a situation like this?" he asked.

Bran made no reply, unsure if the question was rhetorical.

Harun continued. "Not once." He turned to Bran. "And I had no suspicion that I would need to protect my sisters from you."

Bran took a breath to speak, but Harun held up his hand and interrupted him. "This must be sorted out," he said quietly. He shook his head as if to clear his thoughts. "Do you realize what a dishonour this is? Why on God's earth did you do it? Have I not been a good friend? If you were so desperate for a woman, I could have provided you with one – several if you had wished – I simply thought it was inappropriate when the whole point of staying one more night was to rest."

Bran held up both of his hands under the torrent from his friend. "I neither wanted a woman nor had any inkling that I shared my bed until you woke me, Harun. Why on earth would I lie? You know how determined I am to leave here as soon as possible. You guessed my feelings for Anna without me having to tell you. Do you really think I would risk everything – the security of the King? Anna's safety? My reputation? My friendship with you?" He shook his head, at a loss how to convince his friend further. "I know this will sound dishonourable, Harun, but I have no recollection of lying with Azra. I do not even know how she came to be in the room."

Harun gazed at him, disbelievingly, "I think we are beyond wondering what happened as opposed to why it happened."

Bran sighed, "Have you such a low opinion of me that you think I would lie with your sister and then walk away, heartlessly, fully intending to attend to my lady's troubles at home?"

"Should I have a low opinion of my sister and allow her slandered reputation to colour the rest of her life?"

"I wanted to leave last night, remember? What was Azra doing in my room? All I could think of last night was Anna. How every hour I am away from her she could be deeper in misfortune."

Harun narrowed his eyes as a thought struck him. "You know she is besotted by you since you saved her from that boat."

Bran sighed, "Only because you told me."

"Perhaps you hoped this incident would go unnoticed and Azra would keep your secret."

"I am telling the truth." He stood up and walked towards Harun, reaching for the doors and closing them. "I closed these doors myself," he pointed across the room, "that one was already closed." The room was now in shadow, in spite of the light forcing itself through the trace work. "It was dark inside. I could barely see." He walked to the bed. "I lay on the bed, turned and took a drink of water." He stopped and looked at the shelf. "There was a cup here last night, I swear. Then I lay back hoping to think of an efficient plan for informing the various branches of the Northern of what was happening, but I did not get far. I fell into a deep sleep." He looked at Harun a little sheepishly, "Granted, I dreamt that I lay with a woman, and granted I mentioned marriage, but not only was the lady not Azra, she was not real."

"So, I must believe you and brand my sister a liar and a whore."

Bran looked to the ceiling hopelessly. "Believe the truth rather than making it a competition between the two of us. Why did she come to my room? How could I have summoned her? Where has the vessel gone since I drank from it?"

There was a knock at the inner door. Harun's brow creased at the interruption, but he answered it. Ralph stood in the doorway, apologetically. "I heard your voices and could not help but catch the gist of what you were saying. It pains me to hear two old friends arguing so."

Harun studied. "Stay here. I am going to speak with Azra alone to hear her side of the story." He left the room.

Ralph stood awkwardly. "Things have changed so much in such a short time."

Bran's mouth became a thin line. Harun's leaving eased some of the tension and he rested his elbows on his thighs and stared at the floor before him, his face a picture of misery. "I just cannot figure it out. There is no logic to it."

Ralph shrugged. "She is a beautiful young woman. You were tired. The room was dark. It has been a long campaign. I confess if she had come to my room I would have welcomed her most gladly."

Bran looked up at him with a furrowed brow. "I did not welcome her, Ralph. I did not want to disappoint Harun, but she was in my room before I arrived. I did not know it until I stepped from the bath. It was a complication to me, not a temptation. I threw on my chemise and went to the door as if I was looking for Harun and she left. That is why I closed all the doors, although I would have preferred fresh air." He turned his palms upwards, shaking his head and looking to the bed behind him. "And when I woke, we were both here, naked."

He looked to the floor again, finally allowing the full consequences to sink in. "I should be preparing for a voyage now. Taking steps to safeguard Anna and Drysdale. Maybe even Bankside too." He allowed his head to drop to his hands. "Oh, God. What will Joss say?"

Ralph seated himself on the bed too. "Will he believe you?"

Bran lay back, staring at the ceiling. He pondered a second or two. "Yes, but it is likely he will feel it necessary to sever my ties with the Northern."

"Truly?"

"Yes, truly. There are men turned away every day because they cannot live up to the standards. He cannot allow me to cast doubt on his judgement and bring disrepute to the rest of the order." He closed his eyes. "What will become of Drysdale? And as for marrying Anna – I can no longer look her in the face."

He sat up slowly, finally beginning to feel personally slighted rather than a victim of circumstance. "Well, Azra, if this is how you show you love a man, I am glad you did not take a dislike to me." He stood up as the door opened and Harun stepped back inside.

"I am eager to hear your sister's side of the story."

Harun held up his hand. "I have not spoken with her yet. Forgive me for taking the perfect opportunity to eavesdrop." He rubbed his chin. "Half of me is pleased with what I have heard because there seem only disincentives for you lying with Azra and I want to believe my old friend. And yet, the other half of me is angry that I am expected to disbelieve what I saw with my own eyes."

Bran pressed forward, encouraged by the merest hint of an advantage. "But what exactly have you seen, Harun?"

Harun held up his hand again. "I shall go to Azra now. I would like you to wait here. Obviously, the outcome will have serious consequences for all of us. Yesterday's agreement rests on it."

He turned and left. Bran and Ralph sat in silence for a while. Bran was so downcast that Ralph eventually attempted to comfort him. "All may not be lost, Bran. Even if she stands by her story, I will offer to marry her."

Bran looked at him. The colour rose in Ralph's face and he shrugged. "A man could do a lot worse, and besides," he reasoned, "if action is taken quickly, reputations may be repaired."

Bran pondered. "I would still rather that the truth came out first. Then propose to your heart's content."

Both continued to sit in silence, each lost in his thoughts.

Chapter Twenty Six

Another Woman's Poison

Susan looked up at the early night sky and shivered. No cloud. Anxiously, she pulled her cloak more tightly about her and gazed down, yet again, through the frost-glittered grid of the oubliette. Richard had eaten well today, but she still could not bring herself to turn and leave him all alone on such a cold, dark night. And the nights were so much longer at this time of year. She wondered what was happening at Bankside. Were they in a similar predicament? Would Will's angels be safe or vulnerable being so unusually beautiful? Adela had probably left by now, moved to one of Joss's stronger homes.

Richard, cocooned in furs, peered up at his mother's silhouette against the night blue sky. He could see her breath quite clearly and imagined he would see his own if it was not so dark down here. He was the warmest he had felt for a long time. The furs were perfect. He had managed to wrap himself so carefully that no blade of cold penetrated the folds. He had relished every mouthful of the food his mother had brought him, managing to satisfy what had seemed an insatiable appetite, and he still had enough to make another meal at daybreak. His eyes were beginning to feel heavy. He recalled the promise he had made to his father in the summer: look after mother. He called up to her, "You should go inside. I am warmed through now. There is no need for you to stay in the dark." He hated to lie to her and say he did not need her. He had been so afraid the night before, thinking he might not be able to fight off the cold any longer.

Her bare fingers moved where they clung to the grid. He imagined the cold would make them stick a little as she rose to her feet. "Be brave, Richard. You have done so well. The weather can only grow warmer from now on." Then she turned and was gone.

He felt a pang of loneliness, but closed his eyes against his tears, knowing that at least there was a chance he would sleep well tonight.

Susan's heart ached as she crossed to her family's room. When she reached the doorway, Walter's voice shocked her out of her dismal reverie. She could just make out the sheen of his eyes in the shadows. "Send the children to Anna. She knows to expect them."

Her heart sank as he followed her into the warmth and subdued light of the room.

She had hoped for more thinking time. The misery she felt at betraying Richard by leaving him alone in the dark magnified at the thought that she was going to be forced to betray her husband and the rest of the family. For a while, she could bring herself to face neither Walter nor her own children and she busied herself more than was necessary with the clasp of her cloak, then damped down the fire for the night, then tidied away some of the leftover herbs she had prepared for Richard's drink. Only then did she take a deep breath and turn to the children. They were all seated on the pallet, save Maud, who lay in her crib an arm across her eyes. Walter sat silently on a stool in the far corner watching her closely.

"You are allowed to visit Anna tonight," she announced. "Fetch your warm clothes." The children looked at each other, a little bewildered, used to settling down for the night once it grew dark. Janey pondered as she wrapped herself in another layer. Why were they doing things differently tonight?

"Is Richard well?" she asked.

"Yes, Janey, much better."

Walter noticed Janey's brow crease just like Susan's. "Then why are we going out in the dark?"

Susan picked up Maud from the crib. "I am to have a meeting and it is only for grown ups."

All of the children, save Maud, looked at Walter. He felt the scrutiny of their collective gaze. Without looking at him, Susan continued, "I have to feed Maud first or she will be hungry and cry all the time she is with Anna."

Walter said nothing and watched the mother and child closely, while Janey took over the duty of getting the other children ready. It wasn't long before Maud slept at her mother's breast. Resignedly, Susan rose and tenderly wrapped the infant in a warm blanket. She passed the child to Janey, kissed the older daughter's brow and asked her to keep the covers tight so there was less chance of the cold waking her. Bobby and Agnes received their kisses and trotted at either side of their sister, through the darkness towards the light from Anna's now open doorway. Susan waited until they were all safe inside, threw a last glance towards the oubliette, then closed the door.

She stood for a while, still facing the door, reluctant to turn and see Walter now a part of her familiar surroundings. It was silent, but for the slight creak of the stool that told her Walter now stood. She had never felt so miserable or so unable to find her way out of a problem. She wished Marc was here. Walter stood behind her now. Her flesh crawled at his closeness. If this only involved her, she would fight: stab, poison, bite her way out of this. Marc had taught her so many ways to repel a man. But what of her children then? And, even if she killed him, what would become of them without Walter to protect them from the other men? He stepped closer and put his hand next to hers where she leaned against the door. She knew there was no way out now and closed her eyes against the reality of it all. He stood so close that his breath brushed her ear. Oddly, she wanted to seem brave, even nonchalant, but her body let her down. Having to ignore the instinct to run made her heart pound and her limbs tremble. It was only pride that kept her on her feet. She felt his arm curl around her waist and the pressure of his hand on her shoulder, turning her to face him. He lowered his mouth towards hers, and she turned her face away. He looked at her; noticed the closed eyes and the one escaped tear. He knew he could force her. In fact he was quite adept at taking women who tried to fight him off. But Susan did not fight, even though he knew that by nature she was a fighter. They both stood, unmoving. Susan opened her eyes and looked beyond him into the fire. He pulled the fine white cloth so that it no longer covered her hair. He perused her: the hair no more special than brown, apart from its sheen; the eyes not startling in their colour or shape, but in clarity; the face not remarkable, except for the smoothness of her skin, the almost unnoticeable hint of rose at her cheeks and the quiet defiance in the gentle tilt of her chin. He stood a long while in silence before finally allowing his arms to release her, moving to one side and gesturing that she should step into the room. He lifted the latch to the door, said quietly, "Another time. I shall send the children back," then stepped out into the night.

As he marched through the darkness, he felt an inexplicable anger. It made him surly with the children, making them afraid and Bobby and Agnes cried aloud. When Anna tried to calm them, he struck her so hard that she fell, only Fortune's guiding hand making her fall across the bed rather than the fire. The children cried all the louder and Maud awoke, adding a dismal wail to the general hubbub. He chased them out into the night, only allowing them time to clutch their outdoor clothing before running home to their mother, who met them halfway and gathered them to her. He slammed the door against them all. Anna still lay on the bed. Used to his anger, she dared not move only to be struck down again. He glared at her. Her nose and mouth were bleeding. He would show that damn woman he could not care less. Ignoring Anna's pleas to be careful, he dropped to his knees at the side of the bed, gripped her legs, pulled her under him and took her instead.

This was her fault. She must never know how he had just felt.

Damn her.

Chapter Twenty Seven

Addressing Weaknesses

Anna lay in the darkness on her side trying to imagine herself alone. Walter had walked out of the room as soon as he had done with her, but had returned soon after with a pitcher of ale. He sat facing the dark window now, drinking quickly and noisily. She hoped this unaccustomed agitation was a sign that things were going badly for the rebels. Perhaps this child would be born in peacetime after all. She lay as still as she could, resisting the urge to dab at her nose to see if it still bled and closing her eyes against the spasmodic pains when they came.

Eventually, she could hide it no longer. She must shift her position. As she turned, Walter's arm froze in mid-air momentarily, then continued on its path, raising the jug to his mouth. With the next pain her eyes screwed shut and her jaw clenched. When it finally passed, she opened her eyes and tried to breathe freely again. Walter was looking at her from the corner of his eye. She felt sick. Her skin was pale and clammy. Walter placed the jug on the windowsill and stood over Anna, his hands on his hips. He walked to the window, saw a light still burned in Susan's room and walked out into the night air.

He gave a few short raps.

"Anna needs you," he shouted, then turned on his heels. Susan peered beyond him to his half-open doorway. She could roughly make out Anna's shape on the bed. The children had told her tearfully that he had struck Anna hard and that there was blood. She had only just managed to console them enough to allow them to finally get some sleep. She turned to them now. They dozed in a tumble on the bed, apart from ten month old Maud, who lay on her side on a blanket of her own, thumb in mouth and only just audibly snoring. Susan stooped and gently brushed the baby's one fine brown curl behind her ear, for tenderness' rather than practicality's sake. Maud gave two sucks on her thumb at the touch of her mother's fingers, then sank back into a peaceful sleep.

Susan walked back to the window and scanned the other doorways, wondering whether to disturb her parents to ask them to keep an eye on the children. All seemed quiet. Hating to leave them alone, she snuffed out the candle and quickly left the room, quietly securing the door behind her.

Walter was looking at Anna impassively. When Susan entered, he seated himself in a corner. Susan ignored him completely and cast about for clean water and a cloth to cleanse and cool Anna's face. She did not ask what had happened. Anna curled in on herself with the next bout of pain. Susan squeezed her hand and stroked her brow, then, shielding Anna's body with her own, she looked under her clothing to check for bleeding. She saw the evidence left by Walter, but no blood.

Anna held onto her hand. "Will it come too soon?"

Susan shook her head. "There is no bleeding, but it is very important that you rest until the pains are over, and even then, rest as much as you can."

For the first time, she turned to Walter. "It is important that she eats well and rests. She should not even have to stand to prepare your food. Robert should be doing that anyway."

She hoped she would learn something of the whereabouts of Mark's uncle but the comment fell on stony ground.

Walter, who had been staring silently out of the window, now turned to Susan and gave her a level look. "I suppose you take me for an idiot."

Anna felt a pang of panic at his tone, but Susan simply shrugged and said, "It is not your intelligence that concerns me. There are plenty of other reasons I find you abhorrent."

Walter continued to glare at her. "It would suit you to stay here with Anna so you could continue plotting, would it not?"

Susan gave a slight shake of the head. "It need not be me who cares for her. Janet would be just as capable." She gave him an arch look. "Or you for that matter, if you are concerned for your unborn child." She looked to Anna and stroked her brow, then turned back to Walter. "The alternative is that the baby arrives far too early….if it survives, which is highly unlikely, it will be too weak to feed….my milk will be insufficient now that Maud is almost fully weaned and Anna's body will not produce enough at first. If that is the road you want to go down, we need to bring out the birthing table and to find a suitable wet nurse."

Walter took another swig then stood abruptly and left the room. He left the door swinging open and the cold night air soon made its claim on the room. Susan followed him with her eyes, wary for her children's sake. He stood half-clothed in the early blue of morning. He talked to himself and paced a little, occasionally lifting the pitcher to his mouth again, then wiping away spills with the back of his hand. It was cold with the door open, but Susan knew better than to follow her urge to close it on him. Besides, with it open, she had a clear view of where her children slept. She stretched and picked up Anna's cloak from the foot of the bed, draping it over her. She looked about her for something else, knowing from experience that bracing muscles against the cold did little to alleviate the cramping pains involved in pregnancy. She did not want to use anything belonging to Walter. The corner of a fine piece of patterned fabric revealed itself amongst the folds of Anna's cloak as Susan teased at them, trying to keep her warm. She pulled at it, revealing more and more cascades of silk. Anna watched her as she smiled in admiration. "This is beautiful."

"Bran gave it to me."

Outside, Walter was growing more and more agitated. The more he drank, the more his thoughts assailed him, thick and fast. He knew he had to face his weakness. Up until now he had had control. He had thought it would not matter. But it did. Trust it to be now, when his father was due any time. And worse still, his mother: a harder taskmaster by far.

Yes, it was time to show how strong he really was. How fit he was for the roles that lay ahead.

Susan quietly consoled Anna, reassuring her that it was not too late for all to go well still. Frequently, she glanced to her family's window. Presently, it was a little brighter when she looked. Janey must have stirred the fire to warm the room before the others rose. She would be wondering where her mother was. She wondered how long Walter would be. Part of her hoped it would not take long for him to drink himself into such a stupor that he was no longer a threat. But another part of her could not help thinking that the longer she sat waiting, the more likely it would be that her children would venture out on their own to find her. Maud would need changing. She pictured her creeping across the matting, head raised as she reached yet again to see if she could actually pick up the embroidered flowers on the bed's coverlet with her fingertips this time, saying the only word she could so far – dada.

At length, Susan rose. She could bear to leave them no longer. "I shall be back shortly," she reassured Anna and left the room. Deciding not to risk a refusal, she ignored Walter en route to her children. Walter glared after her, then went back to Anna. At the doorway he froze. She lay under a length of patterned silk. He knew it was a gift from the Jew. His anger erupted and he threw the now empty pitcher at the wall behind the bed.

Susan and her family flinched and looked towards the noise. "Janey, wash Maud for me and wrap her in clean cloth." Maud laughed at the sudden unexpected change of hands and Susan hurried back to Anna.

Instinctively, Anna had curled as well as she could into a ball and closed her eyes tightly against the flying pieces of broken pottery. Susan arrived to see Walter pulling Anna roughly from the bed by the wrists. As he did so, he noticed with satisfaction that Susan's face had blanched. Yes, ridding himself of these weaknesses was long overdue. Susan tried to intervene but was felled by a side sweep from Walter's boot. He dragged Anna into the courtyard. By now, lights were being lit, only slightly illuminating the early morning grey. Garin and a handful of others stepped out to see what caused the commotion. Those at watch stayed in their positions, but strained to see what happened in the bailey, rather than staying focused on the outer perimeter. Walter was half marching half dragging Anna to the oubliette. Momentarily, he released her to heave open the grate, then caught up with the terrified Anna, who tried to scramble away on all fours while he had no hold on her. He lifted her, roughly clamping her swollen waist with one arm, then dropped her, feet first, into the darkness.

Susan's composure left her with a scream of "No!" and her hands came to her eyes involuntarily. She ran to the grating as he dropped it back in place, attempting to see how Anna had fallen, but he span about and swiped her with the back of his hand, making her stagger and fall back into the cold grass. Her children cried and she realised she would need to help them first. She felt her lip thickening already as she called, "Lock yourselves in!"

Walter quickly looked to the men, exhilarated by drink and his rushing blood. "Fetch them all!" he shouted. The men did as they were bid, easily catching up with the children as they tried to scatter themselves in the tiny room. Susan struggled to her feet, flailing wildly at the first man she met, who held a squirming Bobby fast by one wrist, while Agnes was pinned against his ribs with his forearm. Easily, he shrugged Susan off, without the need to relinquish his hold on her seemingly tiny children. They cried pitifully and reached out for their mother as the man who carried them strode across to Walter, who now waited at the re-opened grate. Walter simply flicked his head to indicate the children should be dropped inside. Susan found that awful anticipation would not allow her legs to carry her closer. As they fell, her knees buckled as she watched the shock of a sudden drop etch itself on their tear-stained faces. They screamed as they fell and screamed all the more once inside. Their mother found herself grasping at very thin straws of hope. At least their cries meant they had survived the fall.

Janey was being dragged by her hair, having bitten her way out of her assailant's arms. She was thrown after her younger brother and sister. Susan looked back to the house. Maud sat on her bottom on the mat: face red and contorted by pitiful wails. Her mother ran to her, scooping her into her arms to soothe her, while turning to swing the door shut with her foot. But too late. It was kicked open again, allowing her just enough time to spin away to prevent the door's edge from making contact with Maud's head. The child gave terrified sobs as her mother held onto her whilst being dragged to where Walter stood waiting.

Susan's parents and brother emerged from their quarters, armed with the only implements they could put their hands on. Thomas was struck first then killed with the scythe he had wielded seconds before. Grey-haired Janet was knocked to the ground and then, because the same scythe was conveniently close to where she fell, her head was split by Garin. Maud wailed while Susan tried to hide her face. Her brother, full of fury and armed only with a hoe, ran at Garin, who stopped him in his tracks by throwing his dagger. While he lay dying, Garin placed one foot on his stomach and retrieved the knife from his chest, wiping the blade on his tunic before returning it to its sheath.

Susan held Maud close, as much to seek comfort as give it. She forced herself to look at Walter to gauge what he had in mind for them. He stood, hands on hips, the ale creating a grotesque mask of his usual arrogant expression. He looked back at her, head on one side, wearing the look Marc had described to her on the day of Alric's execution. The look that said, "Just try me." He walked across to her and held his hands out for Maud. Susan turned her back to him. Three men blocked her way and Walter gripped Maud beneath the arms. Susan struggled, determined not to relinquish her hold at first, but Maud squealed in pain and she let go, afraid what might happen if Walter continued to pull at the child with no regard for her injuries. He passed the child to Garin. Susan, unable to speak, looked from Walter to Garin, stepping towards him, her bloodied hands outstretched, desperate to soothe her terrified child. Garin seemed confused and looked to Walter then the other men as if for guidance. Susan began to shake and instinctively covered her mouth with her hand. She never cried in front of others. Maud's pitiful wails began again.

Walter grabbed her mother's hair from behind and she was dragged, stumbling back to the room which had housed him and Anna. Unlike the evening before, Susan now fought and bit, in spite of several sound swipes. She had to get back to Maud. When she had sunk her teeth into his cheek for a third time, he turned her over onto her stomach before continuing to fumble with his own clothes and hers. When, after pinning her down at last, he realised that the ale was going to prevent him from carrying out his intentions, he took his dagger from its sheath, put his palm over Susan's forehead to force her head back and then swiped the blade across her throat. He rolled off her and knelt by the bedside, fascinated by her hands clawing at the bedding as she fought for breath. As if going on like that would help her to breathe. He took in the crooked veil, the bruised and bloodstained skin, the fearful expression in her eyes. This did not look like Susan any longer.

When at last she was still, a half moon of blood emerging from beneath her face and seeping through her brown hair, he got to his feet and went outside. The men, at a loss as to what to do with the screaming infant, had laid her on the wall next to the opening of the oubliette, leaving it to God to decide whether she plunged in or not. Walter took in the kicking legs, the contorted wet face and the tiny hands forming little red fists. The men watched as he approached the baby and drew his knife once more. Garin stepped forward. "Just let her fall. That way it's not our fault."

Walter sneered at the larger man and drew the blade across the child's throat. His men stared at him and then watched the child whose cries were suddenly and horribly transformed. Incredulity distorted Garin's face. He turned back to Walter, finding the shock of what had been done so unceremoniously left him short of breath. "Finish it," he gasped. Walter ignored him and seated himself on the wall next to dying Maud. Garin stepped forward quickly, took Maud's little head and shoulders in his big hands, closed his eyes and broke her neck as quickly and cleanly as he could. The other men exhaled, relieved at what Garin had done, but unwilling to have been the one to cross Walter. Garin carried the lifeless child back to the family's room at a loss for a better idea. Walter watched him. He would pay him back for that.

He turned to the other three. His head was beginning to buzz. "Take the places of three on watch, and tell those three to ride to Bankside with a message to be rid of the families of the Northern. There will not be a problem. They have been itching to do it for months."

"Should they damage their mail and tip the sharp edges with wolf bane?"

"Those worthy of wearing mail will already have been dealt with. It's up to them how they want to deal with the women."

"What of those here?" asked another, nodding at the opening of the oubliette.

Walter shrugged as he turned. "Leave them to starve."

He went to the room where Susan still lay, rolled her in the top layer of bedding and dragged her outside. Then he returned, slamming the door behind him. The silk lay on the floor, remarkably untouched by Susan's blood. He kicked it to move it aside, but it hardly budged. He stooped to grab at it, but simply fell, rolling onto his backside, the ground unsteady under him and his bladder uncomfortably full. From where he lay, he kicked and swept at it but it simply billowed a little then gently floated back to earth, barely inches from where it had started. After a further fruitless swipe with his foot, he rolled onto his back, where he rocked sickeningly along with the rest of the world, a warm wet patch spreading across his breeches.

Let them try to accuse him of being weak now.

Chapter Twenty Eight

Short and Sharp

When the group inside the tithe barn heard the bar being raised, their eyes shifted to the doorway. The enormous double doors had a smaller single door cut within them and, through the very slight gaps in the woodwork, the wary women watched the moving shadows of those about to enter. Once, the hay might have made a good hiding place, but it had been swept to the other end of the long, low building; piled high until it almost touched the vaulted roof. The women had been corralled like beasts into this third of the building by the door. They had no idea of what was happening outside except that they could guess when it was frosty due to the icy air inside, and when the sun shone as the roof creaked gently when the woodwork acknowledged the subtle change in temperature.

Common sense allowed them a little more knowledge. Common sense told them that if all was well with the members of the Northern who had remained as protectors, they would have been freed by now. Leona prayed that those at Drysdale, Raymond amongst them, were faring better than they. For once, Adela rued her quirk for spontaneity. Had she been in the habit of letting her family know of her travelling plans, instead of relishing unexpected arrivals, perhaps her brothers would have come to her rescue by now. It just showed how times had changed for the worse.

Silently, the women got to their feet and re-formed in order to hide Will's younger girls from the immediate gaze of those who would enter. When the door was opened, the day revealed itself to be bright. Five men in mail stepped in, eyes large with the contrast from light to dark. The two groups stood facing each other for a moment, one as inscrutable as the other. The tallest stepped forward, removed his helmet and gloves and looked more closely at the women before him. When his gaze alighted on Adela, unusually dark amidst Will's golden family and chestnut Tilly, he narrowed his eyes and beckoned that she should step forward. She did so, unwilling to give the men an excuse to look for more vulnerable figures.

The tall knight pondered. "Say something."

Adela raised her chin, took a deep breath and replied, "Something."

The knight gave a snort and turned to smirk at his four companions. "Hear that?" he asked. He turned back to Adela. "Some sin." He grinned at her clownishly. "The French woman who made him marry again." He looked her up and down and stepped towards her. "And I can see exactly how. I bet he gets some sin on a regular basis."

Abruptly, Adela's small fist flashed through the shadows, sliced up at the knight's nose, then was back by her side before he had time to realise he had been struck, let alone that she had drawn blood. When the men behind him laughed at his expense, he drew his sword and took a more determined step towards her.

Leona willed her to be less provoking. It would be bad enough without angering them and so more likely to hurt or kill. Adela held her ground, head held high. "You are heavily armed to attack an unarmed woman, Sir."

He held her gaze while the other men watched this mouth-watering woman with interest. Ostentatiously, he threw his sword to one side. "Believe me, Sweetheart," he leered, keeping a wary eye on her hands lest they should strike again as he moved closer, "you are about to feel just how well armed I am."

As he bent his knees and stood poised to jump at her and pull her to the floor under his bodyweight, the point of a blade flashed from above, cutting precisely at the point where his hairline did not quite meet with the back of his collar. In the blink of an eye the metal had severed between two of his upper vertebrae and on through the back of his throat, then disappeared again into the shadows of the vaulted roof. The remaining knights drew their swords and raised four pairs of eyes upwards. Simultaneously, four pairs of eyes were slashed precisely across. Instinctively, they lowered their heads and covered their faces. Will, Ben, Joss and Marc swung from the vaulting and dropped soundlessly to the floor. Shielding how they did it from the women, they ended each man's life, turned, placed a finger to their lips, and then slipped out of the building, returning the way they had come. The ladies watched as the men silently helped each other to swing back into the roof space, and then walked cat-like to the place they had entered unseen.

They strained their ears, but there was no clamour, no commotion, no clashing of swords, no cries of pain. Less than an hour later, Will returned and held his wife and daughters close. "You are safe now. It is all over. I am to stay with a small band of men to watch over Bankside while Joss, Ben and Marc take others and check on Drysdale and Redgate." Tilly followed as he led them back to the main house, wondering how soon it would be before she heard from Raymond. There was no sign of the killing.

As they left, Joss entered. Adela, still stood proud, head held high, unwilling to seat herself until she knew what was happening.

"Did you know we were here?" he asked, as he walked to her.

She shook her head and put her arms round his waist, not saying a word. He held her close. She was shaking. He buried his face in her hair and closed his eyes. "Oh, Adela. That pride."

Chapter Twenty Nine

Just Too Late

In the steep-sloping semi-dark of the woodland surrounding Redgate, they allowed the occupiers' warning whistle to go up in order to locate the rest of the enemy's watch more readily. Twelve were taken and several more ran into the courtyard below them, squires hastily arming the handful of remaining men. All of them strangers. Ben saw no sign of Anna or Susan and took it that they were still under the protection of the Northern at Drysdale. But why mount a watch here?

In moments, Joss was amongst them, disabling all while Marc kept a wary eye out in case of further hidden threats. All lives were taken. It was a given that none should be spared after discovering the butchered bodies of their men at Bankside. Mutilating bodies to that extent was unforgivable: killing simply to provide a warning to the enemy. Well, Joss had concluded, let them see how we react to warnings. He was tired of altruism rendering them vulnerable. He would simply punish now rather than later. The bodies were dragged into the tree line so that they would not be easily noticeable should further rebels pay an unexpected visit. Ben began to search the buildings, followed by Joss and Marc, as soon as the obvious dangers had been dealt with.

No doors were barred. All opened easily. Joss entered the living quarters next to the stables. No people but plenty of mess: pitchers half emptied of ale, half eaten bread, even boots left unworn in the hurry to answer the call to arms. He came back to the paler grey of the courtyard. Ben stood staring at what had been the site for Anna's library. The building materials had been used to construct a wall instead. Ben shook his head at the shoddy workmanship as much as the audacity of the enemy behaving as if they already owned the placed, then turned to join the others in the search. He turned to his left where Marc stood by a still closed doorway. The younger man stooped down.

Somehow, in spite of the bundle being wrapped in a cloak so as to obscure the figure within, Marc knew what he would find before he pulled back the folds. His hovering hand hesitated. He became aware of Ben walking towards him, braced himself and turned down the cloth. Her hair. She lay face down. He turned her to face him. Her mouth was red-black with dried blood, her face grey and bruised, the front of her dress blood-washed. She looked so unhappy; her face frozen in a despairing effort to live. She would not have gone without a fight. Marc knelt by her then pulled her close. Her skin was as hard and cold as stone against his cheek. Ben put a hand on his shoulder. He knew there was nothing that could be said to console him.

"How long do you think she has been here?" he asked of Ben.

Ben considered the stains on her dress and offered quietly, "Hours rather than days."

Marc closed his eyes momentarily then gently laid her down again. "Help me find my children, Ben."

Behind them, the door creaked on its hinges as Joss's search progressed. He hesitated on the threshold prompting his two companions to look his way. Beyond him, sprawled on the floor in his own filth, lay Walter, reeking of ale. His breeches were still undone. It was only this and his smell that told the men that he was not also a victim of an attack.

Marc glared, immediately noticing the blood on his clothing and next to the bed.

Ben picked Walter up by the collar and dragged him to the water trough, saying, "We must sober him up first. He does not deserve the relative ease of dying while in a drunken stupor."

As he looked down at the sodden Walter, he shook his head in disgust. Glanville's man, Ralph, was right. Walter had stolen the genuine young Espec's letter of commendation. Maybe he had him killed too. All it had taken was a chance meeting to turn the whole affair into an opportunity for the rebels.

Ben scanned the other doors. Anna. He had left her all alone with this. He had thought it too strange when she had refused Bran. What an old fool he was. And now Bran in trouble too. There was no telling how long it would be before they could offer him their support in Spain.

Joss gave a call from another building. Ben and Marc crossed to join him leaving the drunken Walter where he lay. Joss pushed the door further open to allow more light to enter the room in which he stood. The bodies of John, Tom and Janet lay in an untidy heap.

Marc tried to hide his growing agitation; to remain the clear headed soldier. "Look carefully for the children," he urged, then, even realising as he said it how ridiculous it must sound, added, "They are small. Maybe they are hidden." The two older men stood back, allowing him to satisfy his curiosity, although they could tell the room held no other surprises. Joss left and looked into the neighbouring quarters while Ben and Marc arranged the bodies of Susan's parents and brother in a more dignified manner. After doing so, they crossed to the Hall. Marc did not know whether to feel relief or panic. Joss was in the only room that had not been checked. It seemed unusual for him to take so long over a search and, taking care incase there were enemies remaining after all, the other men cautiously approached the room that Joss had entered last. They found him, knelt over the pallet, still as a rock, his forehead bowed over his fingertips as if in private prayer. It was Ben who eventually asked, "Have you found something, Joss?"

Joss nodded and looked over his shoulder at Marc. Although the light was growing ever dimmer, his eyes shone clearly. When he spoke, his voice was hoarse. "I made the same mistake all over again." He shook his head and looked down once more. "Will you ever forgive me, Marc?"

Marc took a step forward to see over Joss's shoulder. There lay Maud, body unnaturally still and crooked, a small quantity of blood on the bedding next to her. Joss stood to allow the younger man to be closer to his daughter. Marc removed his gloves and stroked his baby's brow but looked at her fists, finding it unbearable to look at the horror frozen on her face. "This is not your fault, Joss." It was as if he knew what they would find and had already rehearsed his vindication of the older man and the orders he had given that summer. The men stood in silence out of respect for the suffering this child had borne. For a long while Marc simply played with the cold little fingers and then he spoke again with an authority which almost subdued the tremor in his voice. "You must grant me permission to kill the man who did this. No trial by jury, but by combat. Allow me that." He turned to see Joss's reaction.

Joss nodded and left the room. He sat on the wall of the well, and aimed a kick at Walter's ribs. Walter moaned but stayed on the other side of consciousness. Joss kicked again. Ben came outside. They were losing the last of the light. "Anna! Richard!"

In the shadows of the oubliette, the children had quickly grown quiet, too terrified to even cry or ask about their mother and Maud. Anna had heard the child cry directly above them and then the cries had stopped. She prayed silently that this was because the child had been handed back to Susan for soothing. Bobby sniffed and rubbed his throbbing elbow. Richard wrapped the fur about him, hoping the night would be milder. Anna lay uncomfortably but felt she must stay still for Janey's and Agnes' sakes. Her pains had worsened so that she found it difficult not to gasp in spite of her best efforts. She tried to push the anxiety away, the consequences of what might happen to them down here, even had she not been pregnant, too awful to contemplate. She and Richard had had the presence of mind to try to break each child's fall, but even then it was a long drop. Anna had been the first thrown down and, although landing on the pile of furs quickly scraped together by Richard, had felt a severe jarring and been winded. She would have lain still, allowing herself the luxury of worrying about the unborn child, but the plight of Susan's children dictated that she should ignore the dizziness and get to her feet to help break their fall. Richard was remarkably calm and practical for an eight year old – much like his mother. He pointed out that there was enough food and water left over for them all to be able to take the edge off their hunger round about midday. He also felt more likely to escape and get help, now that he had people to help him to reach the possible footholds higher up the damp walls.

"Father always says if there is a way in, there is a way out," he reported. There was no way optimism could squeeze through the nausea and shivering pains she was experiencing, but she admired his spirit. Her pains were becoming so intense, with less of a lull between them, that she felt like she must move, even at the expense of waking the children again. It was so dark down here she knew that, even if she had the privacy, she would not be able to see if she bled. Things did not feel right at all. As she struggled to her feet, no longer able to ignore her discomfort, she felt a long rush of warm wetness leaving her. She tried to figure out how early it was. Was it February yet? The month she was born. Silently, in spite of a cramping that bent her double at times, she paced as much as she could between the children. Soon, this also became too much and she slowly and clumsily lowered herself to the floor once more. She felt incredibly restless, but just before dark, she found she had managed to doze a little. Voices above broke her sleep and Richard stirred. Unwilling to accept there was something else to contend with, she closed her eyes and allowed the dizziness to overcome her again. Half conscious, her mind rambled. She could not ignore the pains. How long had it been now? Twelve hours? A day? More than that? She wished Susan was here. In the darkness, Richard slipped his small cold hand into hers.

"We shall be all right now, Anna. That will be father come to save us."

Was she dreaming? How long had she lain here? It seemed the only thing she could be sure of was her uncertainty about everything. She felt movement. As if she was being raised upwards. Was she dying? She had heard tales of those who had been desperately ill and felt they were moved towards a bright light. She felt that now, although the light flickered weakly, only just illuminating the bearded face that she moved towards, as if through a tunnel. Enough for the face to seem familiar. Her Lord? The face smiled and spoke. "Thank God, Anna." Of course, she would thank him. She felt warmer already. Then recognition. Her father.

"Good work, Richard. You secured the ropes well. Now your turn." Ben eased his daughter's body through the awkward opening and dropped the rope back to Richard. He held her gently and carried her through the yellowy glow of torchlight, to the relative warmth of the Hall, choosing to avoid the rooms where the bodies of their loved ones lay. At least now they could use the oubliette for the still ale-soused Walter until they could question him on his real identity. In the Hall, a makeshift bed was devised and the fire revived. Ben frowned down at Anna's cracked lips, her bruised face and blood matted hair. He gently pulled her bloodstained gown so that it covered her legs once she was laid down on her side.

"It seems she has been subjected to brutal attacks over a sustained period…with rape likely too."

Anna opened her eyes with another pain so severe, so different, that it brought her back to consciousness with a loud cry. Then she felt another hand take hers and another voice addressing her father. "She is with child." Then gentle fingers stroked the hair from where it clung to her brow and Bran lowered his face to hers so she could see him better in the firelight. "Do not be afraid, Anna. I am back to help you and Harun is with me." Behind Bran, her father's face twitched almost comically between disbelief and thankfulness.

"My God, Bran. How on Earth did you get back to us?"

"It's a long story. First things first."

Bran focused now on Anna and Harun moved closer to the table.

Ben and Joss drew back.

Anna was swept in and out of consciousness, almost relieved when blackness smothered the pain. It was morning when she seemed to wake from a nightmare to see Bran had finally moved away from the table to the firelight. He looked back at her over his shoulder. Anna's head was turned towards him. All but Harun looked to him as well. He carried the child back to her. Before he reached her, she knew something was wrong. If not, he would have said by now and put her out of her misery. He gently shook his head and lifted the child a little in a gesture which asked whether she would like to hold her tiny daughter. Anna's mouth became a thin line of misery, but she nodded and held out her arms to take the tiny, doll-like bundle from him. Bran knelt by her and held them both close so that she might be private and yet comforted in her grief. She was shaking and her skin cold. He reached for his cloak and tried as best he could to warm her shoulders. "The shaking will stop soon, Anna," he whispered. "Your body is righting itself after the shock."

The room was quiet. Harun prepared herbs so that she would have some relief from the pain as her womb contracted back. Ben and Joss seated themselves resignedly, this particular part of the battle lost.

Harun looked at Ben. "Anna will be safe now. She must have complete rest."

Both Ben and Joss relaxed a little. Terrible for a child to be lost, but at least Anna was still with them.

Anna said nothing. There were no words to describe how she felt. She rearranged the cloth gently about the child's innocent face, taking long, deep breaths until she felt she could speak. "Sorry, little one," she whispered.

Chapter Thirty

Recompense

Will's boot made contact with Walter's mouth and the younger man's face, already creased since his elevation from the dark oubliette into the daylight, crumpled further. Will circled him, itching to have another kick. He held back.

"Are you proud of the havoc you have caused? Little man managing to create a big wave?" He squatted down and looked into the younger man's reddening eyes and hissed, "I hear you laughed as your men made umbles of my son." He grasped Walter's jaw tightly. "Look at you! Soaked in your own piss! You worthless …." For once, Will's eloquence failed him. He threw Walter's head back.

Walter breathed heavily. Lying on his side, he sputtered, "I demand a fair trial."

The hackles of every man within earshot rose. Will glared down on him, "Demand? Fair? That is precisely why we brought you back to Drysdale." He grimaced, stooped and dragged Walter by one heel up the stone steps into the Great Hall. He left him at the centre. "Trial it is. Lord Drysdale is eager to hear your defence."

Walter turned a bleary eye to Bran. His brow creased. "This is not fair. The Jew is bound to be biased in this case. I took his woman."

He looked at the faces about him. They had given Alric time to think over a confession. What was taking his father so long? Could he not see what they were doing to him?

Bran was seated in front of him. Ben, also seated and writing, looked up, his face inscrutable. "That's one accusation accounted for. You admit to the rape of my daughter."

A querulous frown etched itself on Walter's dampening forehead. "She bore my child," he complained. Ben momentarily rose to his feet and Walter said no more.

Ben glared at him, holding each side of the desk, white-knuckled, then gradually lowered himself again and wrote while addressing him. "You killed the child while still in the womb through willfully causing serious injuries to the mother. Indeed, attempted murder of Anna of Redgate is to be added to the list of charges. If it had not been for our friend from Spain," here he nodded towards Harun, who was seated at a distance, "both mother and child would have perished." Having regained his composure he looked to Bran.

To those who knew him, Bran was anything but composed. He glared at Walter with a look so black that Anna, watching from the shadows, thought that he no longer resembled himself. Today he was more jackdaw then falcon. He rose and stepped towards the younger man who still lay on the floor.

"Who would you have hear your case, Roger?"

The younger man flinched, then put his head to one side. "My name is Walter. Walter Espec."

Bran ignored his lies. "Feel free. Look about you. Any man here has the authority to deal with your case."

Roger stayed at floor level, feeling that if he should stand to look about him, he would surely be kicked to the ground again. He glanced about him, but said nothing. Anna watched him. He made her feel sick to her stomach. For everything he had done to her and, more so, for the way he had killed Susan and Maud; when he was drunk. For the way he had killed the young men of the Northern – poisoning them first. For the heartless disregard for Janet, Thomas and John. And now it seemed there were other lives too. Espec had been dead for almost twenty years, but his nephew, also Walter, had indeed wished to be suitor to Anna. Simply by being in the wrong place at the wrong time, this young man was murdered in order that the opportunist, Roger, might take the letter of recommendation composed by Espec's nephew and use it to infiltrate the Northern. She glared at him; the murder of her daughter, her lifelong friends, poor Maud, all engraved on her heart; and felt the tears in her eyes springing from a furious hate as much as sadness. She edged forwards, watching the proceedings closely. Strangely, for one who had never been able to rid herself of empathy for the convicted and so had never watched an execution, she found herself greedily lapping up Roger's agitation. She had never seen this side to her father and Bran, and certainly never Will.

Bran was asking more questions. "Well? Who is it to be?" He watched as Roger wheeled from palm to palm, turning to see whether those who surrounded him were closing in. Bran watched him as he turned, asking, "Will? Is he your choice? The father of the honourable knight you dishonourably poisoned before having him hacked to pieces. The father who prevented his wife from seeing her dead son for a final time, and who hopes she will never ask why."

Roger turned away from Will, only to find his wary look meet the black eyes of Joss.

"Joss? An interesting choice. I'm sure he would relish the role of judge. Men you sent into Bankside would have raped his wife had they not been prevented just in time. Forty members of the Northern all treacherously murdered in cold blood, at the height of rebellion when they were needed most – the King himself would not decide a harsher penalty than this gentleman."

Roger was growing more agitated. Bran continued. "Ben perhaps. Anyone of us here can take over his role as scribe. His daughter assaulted and close to death; his otherwise healthy grand daughter still born because of your ill treatment: a man who cherishes life, especially that of his daughter, having watched his wife suffer for so many years in her heartfelt efforts to bear him a child."

Roger stopped turning. He sat, arms draped over his knees, head down, knowing he might as well wait until the list of wrongs was aired. Bran did not stop.

"Perhaps you think you might as well be judged by me. What reasons do I have to hate you?" He paused. "It is true you hurt a lady I love." Joss let his eyes rest on Harun, who shifted uncomfortably. "You threatened her with terrible consequences for others, knowing her unselfish nature would make her comply – then carried out those threats regardless, even to the point of slaughtering babes in arms. You invited yourself onto my land, having promised a meagre slice of it to the pitiful men who would fight by your side. Men who no longer wish to be associated with you, either because the rebellion is breathing its last, or because they now see you for the animal you have always been, Roger, son of Edwin."

Roger raised his head. "I know of no Edwin."

Bran beckoned someone from the shadows and Garin was led in by two men.

Roger glared at him. Garin did not return his gaze.

Bran asked. "What can you tell us of this man?"

Garin did not hesitate in his response. "This is Roger. A liar by nature. His father is Edwin, once Lord of the land now overseen by the church – Beau Repaire. He is a rebel, as I was. He assumed the identity of an honourable knight he murdered in Spain to avoid detection. He was going to use his younger half-brother, Alric, to help us infiltrate your ranks. Alric would confess to the murder of his father and then his execution would be stopped with a timely attack. But when the time came, Roger told us there was no need to risk losing a battle as things had gone so favourably after the lady's fall into the stream. We were told to leave Alric to the executioner." Garin paused, unsure of what to say next.

Bran threw a grimace in Walter's direction. "We have had long talks with Garin. He has told us much."

Roger quietly seethed. "He has never met Edwin. Nor could he. Edwin was murdered by Alric years ago. Isn't that why you hanged him?" He cast a contemptuous glance back at Garin. "I marvel at the people you would take testimony from. Did he tell you it was he that broke the child's neck?"

He looked at Marc for a reaction, but saw none.

"Yes," answered Bran. "He broke the child's neck to put her out of her misery after you had cut her throat when you were so drunk you could hardly see."

Roger remained quiet, realising the men around him knew more than he could fathom right now.

"Garin has not met Edwin, but this man has." Bran faced the shadows once more and beckoned. Robert stepped forward, looking markedly leaner than when Roger had seen him last. Bran watched Roger's expression; realising recognition was taking some time. "Had you forgotten about the household's cook, Roger? What a sorry lord you would make – forgetting those individuals who make up your community. Half of my people – hard-working, honest, God-fearing, knowledge-seeking people - were either killed for interference when they questioned what was happening or allowed to starve under your occupation. Robert witnessed it all. He watched your armed soldiers slaughter the elderly Janet, her husband and son. He watched you attack his nephew's defenceless children, separate their mother from her baby daughter and cut both of their throats. And Roger," here Bran stooped slightly to see the younger man's face more clearly, "he watched your father, Edwin, and a handful of his men coldly questioning the wisdom of coming closer to help you, knowing we were coming to reclaim our land." Bran straightened and turned back to Robert. "Tell him Edwin's decision."

Robert obliged. "He said, 'We shall move away and disassociate ourselves from the deaths here. Let the Northern use Roger and his men as they see fit so they feel vengeance has been done with a series of executions. Meanwhile, move back to Alnwick, exercise a little patience, then return again. This rebellion is a long way from over."

Roger's breathing had deepened. "This is all very easy: making up charges based on the words of men who are easily bought. Now that whore has changed her mind about who she wants to marry, you conjure up charges to be rid of me."

Ben sorted through some of the rolls on the desk top, selected one and stood, unravelling it as he approached Roger where he was still half-sprawled. "Tell me whether you find any of these words familiar. This is just a part of a very interesting and incriminating account. 'I had not thought to kill Susan and the child until I saw them together..close…very close. I suppose the way most mothers would be with their children. I realised it was something I had never had. I spent so much time trying to make it her decision that she would have to come to me – just to get at him, and then, when she was there for the taking, in their room, with his children, and she was crying because she had resigned herself to it – I found I could not, and I turned away – just left it. And then I thought, 'She's dangerous.'"

Ben looked up from the roll. "Any of this bringing back memories, Roger?"

Roger shook his head and gave a petulant, "No," but in truth something niggled on the very edges of his memory, just out of reach.

"Remember anything about last night?"

Roger avoided Ben's eye. In truth, he had a large gap in his memory which he had put down to the strength of the ale, even though it was days since his hangover had left him. He could not remember travelling from Redgate at all.

"This is your confession, Roger." Ben held up the parchment so Roger could see it clearly if he cared to look. He gave a quick glance. "You spoke, I wrote. And then you signed it just here." Ben indicated with an inky finger.

"Impossible!" Roger snarled. "I would have remembered."

"Not necessarily," Ben shook his head as if simply refuting an assertion that it would snow again before Spring. "You see, you might have finished with Susan, but she was not finished with you."

A chill fingered the pit of Roger's stomach. Was she ghost now, come back to haunt him? Would Isabel join in? He said nothing.

"Susan was always an expert at her simples. She read widely. You already told us in your confession that you admired her superior mind. Years ago, when we were investigating another death, we asked Susan to join us, knowing her knowledge of poisons could be of great help to us. She told us of the properties of the flesh of the yew berry; how it can affect a man's mind so that one can hold a conversation with him, only for him to forget it later. How did she put it now? Yes – as if you have woken him from a deep sleep, conversed with him, then let him drift off again, so that when he wakes, he will not recollect it. I remember at the time, we referred to it as a truth drug."

He rolled the parchment once more. "We had long talks with you last night, Roger." He waved his hand towards the desk top. "There are four more rolls here, all containing your signed confessions – although Garin's and Robert's were enough to confirm our suspicions."

Bran gave his decision without asking for Roger's further opinion, "Your fate will be decided through trial by combat with Marc- the new lord of Bradley Hall, since you killed Raymond, his predecessor."

Roger could have argued, it being the defendant's choice as to what form the punishment should take, but his stubbornness was such, that he threw away the opportunity and tossed at Marc the only thing he felt he had left – the old look that said, "Come on then, try me."

Marc gave no reaction except. "I leave it to you to choose the method and weapon."

Anna moved forward, her movements drawing Bran's eye.

"Would you like to say something, Anna?"

She looked at Bran as if verifying whether she was truly permitted, then looked down on Roger. There was much she wished to say. In her head it was clear as crystal. She could not wait to witness Roger's suffering as Marc and the Devil took part in a savage Tug o' War for his soul. But she said nothing, knowing her anger would trip her tongue. Instead she shook her head and shrugged "no" then turned from the proceedings, as if she had done no more than come across Attercop lapping milk from a good bowl.

But when the fight began, shortly after Garin's hanging, she made sure she had a good vantage point. Roger would not speak further, so, no weapons having been specified, Marc fought without. As she watched from where she leaned against the frame of her chamber window, despite her heart beating quick and heavy at he horror of it all, she savoured every spray of blood; each deadening of another limb; Roger's growing inability to regain his feet, then his knees. As she watched him being killed – far more slowly than was necessary – she could not help thinking of all he had done to so many people who had not deserved it. After minutes, Roger was no longer recognisable: his swollen eyes all but closed. As Marc kicked him in the stomach, while his shoulders trembled with the exertion of trying to remain on all fours, she could only think that he deserved it. She hoped Beelzebub would continue the punishment where Marc left off.

And the man that had created him deserved no better. One day. One day soon. Edwin would get what was coming to him too.

Which was precisely what Marc was thinking, as he finally dealt the fatal blow.

Chapter Thirty One

Limbo

The relief Anna had felt on the return of her father, Bran and the Northern began to waver in the days following the executions and the burials of her beloved friends. It soon became apparent to her that her seemingly new found strength had been born of relativity. She had supposed that at the return of the Northern, the suffering would stop. But it did not. She had spent so long worrying for the safety of the child, following her every move, that now she felt utterly empty – even lonely. At night, it was hard for her to sleep. She lay awake thinking it would have been more natural if she had died with her baby, like so many other women. Then the nightmare feeling that she was not really, utterly, completely alive would magnify over the long, dark hours until her heartbeat would flutter and pound irregularly and her fists would clench and the muscles in her feet cramp, forcing her to get up and pace until she was too exhausted to do anything but lie down again.

Bran suggested she remain at Drysdale, at least until the Summer. Secretly, he hoped this would be enough time for her library to be completed. It would be something new to occupy her. Anna felt that she owed it to others to become strong again. Quickly. But she was so, so tired. And early March held all in an icy grip. Time itself seemed frozen. Winter had no idea that it was supposed to be gradually making room for Spring. Harun had borrowed extra layers of clothing, completely taken by surprise at by the severity of the North of England's cold.

On one of the coldest days, Anna wrapped up as warmly as she could and ventured down into the whitened courtyard. She noticed that Bran was deep in discussion with Marc about some plans for building work at Redgate. The pages were being put through their paces by two squires, not yet recognisable to Anna. She watched them as they wrestled, or fenced or rode at ring and quintain. Was it too much to ask that she could be trained like them?

Bran was explaining how Roger's wall was to be dismantled and the materials used to build the library as planned. Having caught sight of her from the corner of his eye, he was careful not to mention her name incase she became curious about the building. Marc perused the plans, which were much the same as they had been when Bran had drawn them up on the day he had arrived back from Spain. Bran watched his friend carefully. Often now, the deadening behind his eyes rendered him unrecognisable. He could only guess at the torment his friend must be going through. Thinking back to how he had attempted to persuade Joss to change his mind before they left for the Borders, it was as if he had always known something terrible was going to happen. If he had been the old heart-on-his-sleeve Marc, Bran would have spoken with him in an attempt to share the grief – to provide some solace – but there was no way he could broach things with this seemingly anaesthetized version of his friend.

As they studied the plans, he glanced towards Anna, noticing her pale appearance, in spite of her being swamped in a heavy cloak. She stood in the one patch of narrow sunlight, near Drysdale's walls, watching the pages from a safe distance. When he looked back to the plans, Marc was studying him.

"Has Harun spoken with you about Azra yet?"

Bran shook his head.

"I suppose it won't go away – in spite of everything we have been through here."

Bran's mouth became a thin line and he shook his head again. "He arranged for her to arrive a few weeks after us so there would be time to send a message to delay if the journey would be too dangerous. We organised an escort to travel with her from the port to ensure a safer journey."

Marc rolled the parchment and mounted. "When the time comes and you send word to Ben at Redgate, I may return with him. I am in the mood for speaking my mind. Unfortunately, the people I would have hear me are out of earshot just yet."

"He's not a bad man; just protecting his sister."

"Well, they had better be ready to justify themselves to Joss. I hear he is livid."

Bran did not conceal his disappointment, "Oh."

"He is not angry with you. He takes an insult to one of his confidantes as an attempt to undermine the Northern." Marc looked at the plans again. "And, of course, he thinks that even just half a day's less delay could have saved more lives."

Bran thought that was probably true. He turned to Anna again, thinking of the death of her premature child.

Marc followed his gaze, noticing Anna's haunted appearance. "Let us hope it is solved quickly. She needs someone who can flush the horror out of Drysdale and Redgate. Make it feel like her home again." He looked back at Bran and gave him a frank look. Bran, knowing the look full well, braced himself. "The same quality that makes you the Northern's best diplomat and ambassador leaves you wanting when it comes to sharing your feelings with those you are close to."

Bran looked up at his friend. "That sounds like the sort of comment Susan would have made."

Marc smiled. "So she would."

"I would have asked Anna sooner, only I thought she was too young to know her own mind. In the end, she had no choice in the matter." He looked to Marc again. "Marc....I" He stopped and he shook his head apologetically. "I wish I could say something that helped you to see some sort of sense to your loss."

Marc shrugged and looked down at the rolled plans, as if ensuring their fastening was secure. "Talking about her like you just did – that was – that felt better. When people avoid mentioning their names, it's like they never existed."

Bran handed him letters for Ben. "Will is sending Tilly to Drysdale to help look after the children. You know they'll be safe here now. And Joss had already sent word that there have been several sightings of Edwin up near the Borders."

At the mention of Edwin, Marc's eyes changed and his thoughts seemed to take another turn. He urged his mount forward with no further words and began the short trip to Redgate, a handful of masons and labourers following his lead. Bran could not help doing some dwelling of his own. There were several people with deep personal grievances against Edwin. He had always dreamed that he would be the one to be rid of him. He had his parents' and Catherine's deaths to avenge. But what about Ben? And Joss seemed to have issues that were never spoken about. When the time came, would Bran be big enough to step back and allow another man the personal pleasure of killing Edwin?

Bran was so lost in his thoughts that when he heard Anna's voice at his shoulder, he almost gave a start. She must not have noticed because, with no explanation, she repeated, "Will you teach me how to fight?"

He did not take in what she said at first. "Fight?"

She nodded and looked back at the pages as if to illustrate her request. As she was turned away from him, he took a closer look at her pale face, dark shadows cradling her eyes. He reached out to feel her hands. "You are very cold, Anna. Shall we go inside to talk about this?"

She allowed him to lead her back to the warmth of the hall, talking all the while. As she spoke, Bran noticed there was a tremor to her voice and he felt trembling through her linked arm. "I need to do something.

Something to be rid of this feeling of..of.. weakness. No. No. That's not the right word. Uselessness."

As they stepped into the Hall with its busy to-ings and fro-ings, she stopped. Bran glanced about for a vacant window seat where they might talk privately, although he knew it was a pious hope to be left alone at this time of day if he made an appearance in the Hall. He noticed Harun sitting playing chess against himself in one corner.

"It's too chilly to sit at the window," decided Bran. "Come to the trace room with me. It catches the sun at this time of day."

Pretending to be too caught up with Anna to have noticed the two men visiting from Durham with questions about extending the Cathedral near Cuthbert's shrine, he led her outside again, taking her around the periphery of the courtyard to avoid the activities of the pages. He guessed both Harun and the engineers would feel slighted by his behaviour, but Anna was more important. Besides, Marc's words about diplomacy had given him an idea he needed to think through. He was secretly proud that he had never left a situation feeling dissatisfied about the outcome when he was in the role of diplomat, so it seemed evident this was the cloak he should wear when speaking with Harun. But first, he needed more time to straighten his thoughts. He wondered if Ralph had been serious when he showed an interest in marrying Azra himself. He had seemed to be. But, perhaps it was no more than a show of allegiance. Still, he felt hopeful about Ralph's inclusion in Azra's escort. He held Anna's hand as they picked their way through the driest parts of the wet patch in front of the trace room door.

"One day I'll solve this problem," said Bran.

Normally Anna would have smiled and said something like, "Just move the door," but today she hardly seemed to hear him.

It was warmer in the trace room. A brazier had been lit in the centre. Bran took two stools from near the walls and placed them closer to the fire. As soon as the door was closed, Anna began to speak again. It was as if she could not say what was on her mind quickly or precisely enough. "I need to do something to stop me from feeling so helpless. So self-pitying. I am fortunate. I need to do something useful. I cannot lie in bed when those who lost their lives would be doing something useful. Getting on with it. I need a purpose. To be doing something to help fight off this need to hide away and do nothing. Something to help me fight off this permanent chill – this permanent fear. It's all over now."

Bran watched her carefully. She was still shaking in spite of the warmth from the fire. He felt her brow, which caused her to stop speaking momentarily, then he slid his fingers under her hair to the back of her neck. Her skin felt clammy.

Anna continued, as if his examination was mere routine. "Like a page," she suggested. "I could learn. I know I could never be as skilled as they, but at least it would make me feel…make me feel," she grasped around for the right words, "like I had a purpose. Like I could hunt as well as be hunted."

Bran took her hands, which she now wrung within her sleeves, he guessed from a subconscious effort to warm herself.

"I am going to treat you exactly like one of Drysdale's pages."

She looked up at him surprised. "You will?"

He nodded. "When did you last have a good night's sleep?"

She looked at him. Her mouth opened as if to answer, but none came forth.

"And when did you last eat a hearty meal?"

She considered him and her brow creased, almost querulously. "I cannot recollect right now. It doesn't matter. As I strengthen myself, my appetite will grow."

Bran raised an eyebrow. "If I forced a page under my care to take on his daily training when he was as ill as you are, his father would take him away from here, and rightly so. I think you know this too. It is one of the symptoms of your illness to think otherwise. You do not know how ill you are, Anna. You have lost as much blood as a warrior knight who has been almost slain in battle. Just like that warrior, you have survived to fight another day. Your wound is serious and must be given time to heal."

Anna subconsciously lay her hand across her abdomen. "Then you will understand a warrior's need to feel strong again."

He nodded. "But as your overlord, I insist you do it my way."

She seemed to consider it. "Why do I lose my train of thought so easily? I sometimes feel so strongly about things, and then, just as I am thinking of a list of reasons why, I forget the subject I was analysing. Why is that?"

"Because you are exhausted. Your body wants to spend all of its energy making new blood, healing you so your bleeding stops and makes it efforts more fruitful." He took an inner swathe of his cloak and wrapped an extra layer around Anna's shoulders so she could benefit from his body heat. She allowed her cheek to rest against his shoulder. Bran cradled her, almost glad of the cold which gave him an excuse to hold her so easily. "And when *you* think, Anna, you put everything into it. The body gets tired from all of that headwork. Do you feel dizzy when you think a lot too?"

She nodded. "Like my body is being swung in circles, one way then the other."

"Allow yourself to rest. Give God and Nature a fighting chance."

He felt her nod. "I suppose God and Nature intended that all I would be thinking of now would be my child. Now she is not here, my mind stumbles from one thing to another making little sense of it all."

Bran held her a little closer. "That was anything but a stumbling thought, Anna."

They sat quietly for a while. When he allowed himself to glance at her face he saw she had closed her eyes, but her breathing and the unusually thin line of her mouth told him that she was making an effort to hold back tears. The sounds of shouts from the pages gave their silence some sense of normality. Eventually, she asked. "When you marry Azra, will you live in Spain or will she come here?"

Again, her question took him by surprise. God, she must think all men were cut from the same cloth. He felt he owed her an explanation. "I don't know how much you have heard about that, Anna. But .."

She tensed and shook her head. "You do not have to explain anything to me."

He took her hand. "I want to all the same."

She waited. "I have no feelings of love for Azra. I cannot even respect her as a sister of my friend after what she has done. I know the truth must sound like a feeble attempt to justify terrible behaviour, but it is the truth nonetheless. I was tricked by Azra – most likely drugged. Her scheming could have prevented me from getting back to you in time to save your life – perhaps the delay could have made a difference to Susan and Maud." Anna felt his heart begin to pound as the enormity of what Azra's actions had meant unravelled. "I have no intention of marrying Azra. Even if it means I must give up Drysdale and my place in the Northern. I would rather be dead."

Anna sat up and he turned away, embarrassed. She took his hand. "It must be so hard for you to find a place where you are allowed contentment." He took her words to mean that he had not proved himself to her yet. She squeezed his hand. "I do not doubt you. And my father and all others in the Northern never will."

He looked back to her and saw she was in earnest. "Thank you. It is important to me that you know I would never lie to you."

He thought back to their conversation from almost a year before. "I once said I envied your ability to be happy anywhere. It showed you were happy in your own skin – the true way to contentment." They were quiet for a long while. He knew Roger's attacks had been so humiliatingly invasive that it was hard for Bran to try to think of a sensitive way of letting her know that he understood how that inner peace had been wrenched from her. He wished he could heal the memories of that intimate violence in the same way that he could cure her physical pain. He could not find the words and felt crippled with inadequacy. He stroked her hair and looked down at her face. Her eyes were closed and this time it seemed that she slept.

He gazed down at her a long while, enjoying their closeness. As the winter light faded and Robert's voice cut through the silence as he rebuked the pages for being late for kitchen duties, he stirred himself, lifted her gently and made his way back to his room. As he passed through the Hall, all who saw them knew to fall silent so as not to wake her. Harun watched from the fireplace.

Chapter Thirty Two

Day Dreams

The first thing Azra noticed about this new land, further west than she had ever been, was its greeness. Green of varying hues. And it would keep on changing, according to Ralph, her guide, because it was only Spring. In some places, like the fallow fields they passed with their grazing sheep, it was a thick, lush jewel green; in others, a netting of new buds gave a hazy obscurity to the edges of the forest. During the voyage, she had imagined how it might be. Of course, at the centre of it all were she and Bran, always perfect, but the backdrop, she now realised, had been pictured all wrong. She had seen him against intense blue skies, pale stonework, orange groves and palms. There was not much of that here. Even the creatures were different. She recognised the deer, red and fallow, from books, and from those she had seen in parks created by Englishmen in Europe. The birds were different too: some jet black with bright orange beaks; some far smaller in various shades of brown; some with red breasts – all in full and strange song.

The sun was out, but not warming to Azra. It was much cooler than Spain. She wore far more layers than Ralph and the other English horsemen who made up her escort. Ralph came to her often, giving her details of what had happened on the journey so far, and what they could expect. He seemed an amenable gentleman. Not like she had been led to expect form the stories she had heard about Englishmen. That did not include Bran, of course. He was exceptional; a man based on no existing mould. Every time she thought of him her stomach gave flutterings of pleasure: especially since that night they had shared naked. She imagined the smoothness of his skin; how he had touched her; kissed her; moved with her. Often, alone at night, she ran her hands over her own skin, wondering how she must have felt to him. Surely, when he saw her he would want her again, without any persuasion this time. She remembered how he had reassured her, held her close and moaned. Surely.

The journey itself was not quite as she had anticipated. During the voyage, rather than spending long evenings looking out to spectacular sunsets, the days had been short and chilly; the water roughly nauseating, forcing her to spend much time wrapped warmly below deck. She would curl up on her pallet, pretending to read when she heard Ralph come to check that she was well, but as soon as he was gone, she returned to her fantasies once again. These alone were far more warming than the strange tasting soup her guide brought to her. She thought ahead…. As their ship came into the port, she would go up on deck to see Harun and Bran standing on a jetty, framed by an ocean dancing with sparkles, both smiling, both looking pleased to see her, Bran taking it upon himself to be the one to help lift her down a trickier part of the gangplank as she disembarked, holding her a little more closely than was really necessary so that she might know he wanted to feel her closeness again. In her dreams, Bran never disappointed. He always said the right thing; did the right deed; looked his most attractive.

But, in reality, Drysdale was a long way from the sea and they had had to wait a good few grey hours in the rain: preparing a safe route; arranging to meet and have talks with people along the way in order that they might travel safely as there was still a threat from rebels.

And all because of the waiting, the rebellion pleased her a little. It fuelled her mind and heart with more dialogue and plots - perhaps she and Bran could be involved in a rescue – but not like the one involving Anna. And with the inconvenience of the rebellion, wouldn't Bran rather come to Spain to live with her rather than stay in this cold and hostile place?

Once the journey over land was underway, Ralph contented himself with riding by her side rather than attempting to socialise, which pleased Azra as it had been rather annoying to be interrupted in her daydreaming. Now, she could concentrate on reworking her ideas so they embraced the English landscape. Her best version was where she arrived at Drysdale to find Anna was happily married to the rebel who had proposed, much to Bran's disgust. She was not the woman he had imagined. And when he spoke of his disappointment to Azra, she would be magnanimous – at least, now she would be – her original version had been harsher when she had felt stabs of jealousy whenever she considered what they might be doing in her absence. But not now. Not now she had had time to think it through logically. Especially after what she had learned since they disembarked. Anna had lain with another man and borne his child, while Azra had lain only with Bran. And Bran would gain a brother who could teach him much, while here it seemed that Bran was the one who did all the teaching. And in Spain, Bran could live in a protected environment, while here, he was constantly under attack. Surely, he would see Azra as the more favourable bride. Surely, it made more sense for him to choose her, especially as he was a good friend to Harun and would not want his family to be dishonoured. She wondered if he would decide to propose more formally, choosing the perfect time and place, or whether he would assume his original remark about making her his wife would suffice and jump straight to preparations for the wedding. Would he encompass all beliefs and traditions in the ceremony, or would he convert and follow the rituals she knew and dreamed about? She was prepared to be flexible. It could be her first way of showing her wifely duty to him.

Ralph glanced occasionally at the self-possessed young woman by his side. She seemed aloof in some ways, but he admired her all the same. Maybe she was coming to acknowledge her mistake with Bran. And if she did not yet, she soon would. And when she did, he would be there to sympathise and commiserate; to offer her a shoulder and anything else she might accept. Surely then, the first thing she would want would be to put the whole embarrassing episode behind her, return to her own, far warmer country and marry a man who was willing to live with her there, amongst her own customs and familiar faces. But for now, he realised he would have to be patient. He had learned enough about her to know that she would have to see things for herself rather than be tutored. He could satisfy himself that Bran had no interest.

In Drysdale, after the outrider had sent word that Azra was on the way, Bran assumed the role of diplomat. He arranged to meet with Harun in order that all interested parties meet to discuss the issue at one particular time, rather than treating this like a visit from an old friend with no boundaries set on time, or goals to be achieved. He resented this woman; this girl; and the more he thought about the knock-on effects of her actions, the angrier he became, almost to the same extent as he felt for Edwin. When working abroad, he tried to ascertain as much as he could about the character traits of those he would arbitrate between, knowing that, in spite of their protestations to the contrary, personalities could affect the way they viewed the politics which seemingly ruled their decisions. He had spent many an hour, while Anna slept, wondering what made Azra do what she did. In the end, he could only conclude that mind over matter had affected the way she had felt about him. As Anna had reminded him, he had been deluded about the master mason's wife. The difference was that once Bran recognised the truth, his illusions vanished whereas Azra, probably fuelled by Harun's insistence on honour being restored, was allowing her delusions to dominate reality. What Bran needed to do then was to show Harun that there would be no honour in a marriage between them and to shatter Azra's dreams. The hard part was to do this without bringing dishonour to Anna, The Northern or Drysdale.

The more time he spent with Anna, the more selfish, petty, deceitful and scheming Azra seemed. He knew he would have to stay neutral in order not to offend his friend during the proceedings, but a large part of him simply wanted to tell Azra exactly what he thought. And of course, there was the danger that some may assume old Jewish – Muslim hostility might be at the core of his argument. But that was nothing to do with it. Her fantasies had wasted time and he had arrived too late at Redgate. It was such thoughts that filled Bran's mind on the afternoon of her arrival. He had had forewarning and left Anna's bedside to watch from the window. He was glad she slept. It was awkward for him, his feelings for her being even stronger than they had been before his proposal. He watched as Harun greeted his sister and helped her down, then led her by the arm into the Hall. The proceedings would not start until the next day and Bran had thought of several ways of taking the wind out of Azra's sails in the mean time. First, he would show himself to be an impolite host and not greet Azra on her arrival. She would not see him until it was time for the household to eat, and even then he would treat her no differently from the other company. Secondly, he would fuel her imagination with darker thoughts. The room he had had prepared for Azra was unpopular with guests because, when the fire was lit, it had many shifting shadows in hidden corners. Coupled with this, on the slope a few yards from the window was a tree, whose branches had managed to bridge the gap from trunk to stonework. Even in the slightest of breezes, a tapping at the window could unnerve the sleeper within. And allowing little sleep to those whose case rested on lies had often proved to be a good way of allowing them plenty of rope with which to hang themselves. And thirdly, he would leave his meal early rather than spend time on social niceties, as he had been doing anyway, in order to spend time at Anna's bedside. Azra would see how little she figured in his plans.

He seated himself, determined to wait a good long while before going down to greet the company. He knew Tilly would show the guests where they would be sleeping for the night. He rested his head on the back of the chair and tried to relax while he thought. He must get this right. Joss had once told him he did things intuitively well, but Bran wanted to take no chances.

Anna opened her eyes and watched him quietly. He looked so weary and troubled that her heart went out to him. The late sun cast a glow of amber across his shoulder. She could hear the voices of the guests and the trestles being prepared in the room below. It must have stirred Bran, because he rubbed his eyes a little and combed the hair away from his brow with his fingers, then turned his head towards her. Not knowing whether he could see her clearly in this light, she smiled. He gave her a gentle smile back.

She did not move but spoke softly. "You need some rest."

He wished he could tell her that all he wanted was to lie next to her, to hold her while he fell into a contented sleep. But he had to solve this problem before he gained the right to share such tender thoughts with her.

"Would things be easier for you if I returned to Redgate?" she asked.

He put his head on one side and considered her, shaking his head. "I want you here with me." They said nothing more, but gazed at each other a while.

Anna stirred herself and Bran moved to stand up to help her, but she raised her hand to stop him. "Stay, please."

She shifted to the edge of the bed and stood up gingerly, her head buzzing slightly after having slept so soundly. She crossed the room and stood before the window, looking down at him. He allowed his head to rest against the back of the chair once more and gazed up at her. Still beautiful. He realised he no longer compared her looks to Margery or Ben, but simply saw her as Anna. She gazed back at him, and he was comfortable under her look. She was right; he was tired to the bone, although rather, it was a tiredness of the mind and spirit rather than the physical. A lot rested on the next few days.

There was a lot she wanted to tell him. But now was not the time. Perhaps the words she allowed herself to speak were uttered as no more than a whisper because they seemed so inadequate compared with how she truly felt. "I wish I could solve it all for you."

He sighed and gave a tired smile. She tenderly stroked back his hair and stooped to kiss his brow. He closed his eyes and allowed his lips to lightly trace the line of her throat.

A knocking at the door interrupted them. He stroked her cheek then stood and helped her back into bed. The knock came again then Tilly's faltering voice said, "Sorry for this rudeness, Sir. I have been sent to take over from you that you might greet your guests."

Anna saw Bran's jaw tighten at the ill manners that prevented him from doing as he wished in his own home. He kissed her hand then went to open the door. A sheepish Tilly hovered at the threshold. He smiled at her and beckoned her through. "It's not your fault, Tilly. I am sorry you have had to put up with this…" he searched for the right word, "awkwardness."

Before leaving the room, he looked back at Anna. "I'll have your meals brought up," he said and left.

Chapter Thirty Three

Start As You Mean To Go On

At the bend in the stairs, Bran hesitated. From here he had a good view of the assembled company. Judging by their shifting unease, it was obvious evening prayers had been over for some time. Harun, Ralph and Azra sat on the dais, seemingly more isolated from than elevated above the rest of the company. The silent musicians sat awkwardly in the gallery, unwilling to commit themselves to playing until they knew the nature of the gathering. The food had not yet been served, and when it was, Bran knew there would be little fresh meat; the herds they had been licensed to hunt being deliberately left alone until the Summer so they could breed in peace and gain weight. Still, it was not in Robert's nature to serve a disappointing meal.

Scores of tallow candles were lit and amongst them, the guests sat awkwardly. Perhaps they wondered how much longer they would have to wait under the other would be diners' scrutiny. His heart went out to Ralph, who made several unsuccessful attempts to engage Harun and Azra in time-passing conversation; so much so that when one minstrel approached Bran on the stairs, redundant viol in hand, he decided he should acquiesce and let the music begin. The player looked relieved and turned to go, but Bran had an afterthought and stopped him, "Wait. Try to avoid love songs."

"Oh," the player looked disappointed. "Most of our songs are love songs." Then his face brightened and he offered hopefully. "They are not obscene like those French ones. Not a prick nor a…"

Bran hastily held up his hand and shook his head. "Nevertheless, let us compromise. When you play a love song, do not sing the words – except," a thought struck Bran, "except when you see I have finished my meal. I shall wipe my hands and mouth. Then play your most tender love song. I shall not remain to hear it."

The player trotted back to the gallery and quickly passed on the instructions so that this particularly generous knight might not be disappointed in their performance. Robert took the music beginning as a sign that the pages should begin to serve the food.

Bran slowly began his descent into the Hall. He nodded curtly at his guests, then, ignoring the vacant chair between Azra and Harun, seated himself by Ralph and began questioning him on the nature of the voyage to ascertain how visible any rebel activity had been en route. He could see Harun's stony profile as he spoke. If he really cared about his sister, he should already be having second thoughts.

Bran had little appetite. He ate his meal without comment, aware of the eyes of his household trying to judge his mood. When he had finished his main meal, he called Richard over. "Have the Cook prepare two meals, then take them up to Anna and Tilly in my chamber."

Richard nodded politely then scampered off to fulfil the request.

At long last, Bran allowed himself to turn to his guests and study their faces, under the guise of host. Harun's expression was no less than thunderous; Azra was picking at her food, head bowed; while Ralph sat, every muscle in his body rigid with the tension of the situation.

Bran spoke, not unkindly. He found there was only so much torture he could allow himself to inflict upon his guests. "The musicians will continue to play should you wish to dance. And," he nodded at Ralph, "I hear my friend here is an excellent chess player. Perhaps you could have a game before retiring to bed. When Richard returns from seeing to Anna in my chamber, I will ask that he sees to your needs this evening and lights your way to your sleeping quarters. I have had fires lit in each room. You must be used to warmer temperatures."

Azra looked at him, her heart stinging at the mention of Anna and his chamber in the same sentence. Tears came to her eyes.

Harun gave Bran a level look. "Of all my visits to your house, I have never known it be as cold as this."

Bran had little patience for a young woman who cried so easily at a situation that was no one's fault but her own, when those he lived amongst had suffered their horrors with remarkable stoicism by comparison, but he kept his voice even and light, "Perhaps tomorrow will see things warm up a little. I am afraid the recent troubles here keep our minds away from entertaining. Those dear to us have suffered under some horrific circumstances."

Conveniently for Bran, there was an appropriate lull in the music; he wiped his mouth and hands with a cloth. As instructed, the musicians began a lilting love song, about a lady and a knight kept apart by circumstance. Bran sat back and took in the tune and the words, tapping his fingers on the arm of the chair. Occasionally he felt Azra's eyes come to rest on him again. He stood and shrugged off his cloak, making some people think he was going to dance, which prompted them to do the same. But Bran did not dance. He nodded courteously to his guests, apologised for absenting himself so soon, then quickly climbed the stairs to his chamber. En route, he met with Richard.

"Do you remember the rooms the guests have been allocated tonight?"

"Yes, Sir."

"Good. It is very important that Azra is in the far room and Ralph in the room next to that. As for tonight, let them drink as much ale as they like and if they sit without dancing, take the chessboard to them. In fact, make sure there is a board kept to one side just for that purpose. Most people will probably choose to dance anyway."

"Yes, Sir."

"Your father will travel here in the morning with Ben from Redgate. After your extra duties here tonight, you will have earned the right to spend your time with him as he wishes."

Richard smiled. "Thank you, Sir." And they parted ways.

By the time Bran entered the upper chamber, Anna and Tilly had almost finished the meals they had been brought. Bran seated himself by the window once more. The young women looked at each other, Tilly having just questioned Richard on the goings on downstairs. She raised her eyebrows at Anna, scraped the last of her soup from its bowl, then stood, making an excuse that she had promised to help in the kitchen as soon as her duties with Anna were over. She took Anna's leftovers and exited as quickly as she could.

As soon as the door closed, Bran sat a little straighter in his chair and turned to Anna, unable to stop himself from smiling. "She seems to be in a hurry."

"I am afraid she has taken a great dislike to Azra over this whole affair. She feels she was given a suspicious glare on her arrival. It seems every female is a threat to her. I suppose it irks Tilly when she misses Raymond so. She is unashamed in her hurry to have your guests see that she has left the two of us alone."

"Ah. Does that not throw some dishonour your way too?"

Anna considered. "A little dishonour is the least I have had to cope with lately, and if it helps you out of this situation, I would take much more."

He leaned forward, his elbows on his thighs, and threw a little more wood onto the fire.

He looked at the dancing sparks as he thought. "I need your help. You know more than I how women think. This one seems obsessed when she has had no invite – even though she has obviously been rebuffed.

What can I do without ruining my own reputation and that of the Northern? How can I simply make her see that her feelings are misguided?"

Anna seemed to scan the rafters for an answer.

As she thought, Bran offered a little help. "You know, Ralph is quite taken with her. It is obvious. He had really put in an extra effort with his appearance this evening, in spite of the long journey. Perhaps he would have proposed in Spain if events had not got in the way."

Anna shook her head. "While she is obsessed with you, he will remain invisible to her."

Bran's mouth became a thin line of disappointment. "So my putting her in the haunted room with Ralph on stand by next door to rescue her may not work."

Anna smiled and shook her head. "She will only wish it was you."

He looked back to the fire.

"There is something that might work. Women hate to feel scorned; it is just a matter of finding which method will sink in."

"Do you think you know the method?"

Anna considered. "Perhaps."

On the floor below, the music had taken on a far happier and decidedly bawdier tone. The ale flowed freely, although the three main guests touched none of it, being wary of its reputation. Ralph and Azra had had the chessboard placed between them, but Azra was determined not to enjoy herself. Harun decided it was probably for the best if he and his sister moved to a quieter corner and discussed what the plans for tomorrow seemed to be. This left Ralph at a loss as to what to do, not being a confident dancer even amongst more convivial company. He bowed to his companions, wished them a good night, then allowed Richard, now candle bearer, to lead him the way to his chamber.

Harun had pulled up two stools. He wasted no time in discussing the issue. "You said Bran seduced you? Do you still hold to that?"

Azra glared at him. Her pride was already scratched raw at the evening's proceedings and now her brother was questioning her credibility. "Yes."

"Tomorrow, Bran has decided on a formal way of us discussing this matter of a marriage between you. That can only mean he wishes not to go ahead."

Azra's face fell.

"I shall argue your case to uphold your honour, but even if he eventually agrees, it will not be straight forward. There is the matter of religion. Your children would need to be brought up according to our faith, preferably away from this barbarous isle. And then there is the matter of Anna. He proposed to her before he came to Spain. It is rumoured here that she refused him only because her loved ones were under threat of death."

Azra sighed impatiently, her fantasies now seemingly as substantial as gossamer in a storm. "So, my fate is to be decided through rumour. I am only concerned with reality. It is true that he lay with me. It is true that he said he wanted me as wife."

Harun's brow creased and he waved his hand to stop her remarks. "Less of the scolding, Azra. Regardless of what Bran has done against you, you had a part in this too. You should never have gone to his chamber, talking of marriage or not. Other brothers would have dealt you a far harsher penalty by now."

Azra quietened but remained sullen.

"Fighting your cause will mean losing a close friend if he still refuses. I am not in the habit of making enemies and have previously trusted Bran. Indeed, I have had a great deal to thank him for over the past ten years. So I need to know that you are telling the truth. I need to know there is no truth in Bran's version of the story – that you tricked him."

Azra's back straightened once more. "Am I so unworthy that I would need to trick a man into wanting me? He has lain with me. Now I must marry him or I will have no hope of entering a decent marriage with anyone."

Harun sighed. His sister's prickliness showed she had a lot of growing up to do.

"Let us just say that there is more than one way to dishonour your family, Azra. What has happened reflects on me and your younger sisters too. I have seen Bran arbitrate between parties that I felt could never compromise, but he has managed to reach that goal. If he convinces me that you are the one who is lying, never expect me to trust your word, or to provide you with a roof over your head, again. Think on that tonight."

Azra stood up haughtily and took advantage of Richard's zeal in seeing to his allocated guest's needs so quickly after lighting Ralph to his bed. She kept her back straight as she left the room and mounted the stairs, but was glad of the darkness of the passages, which hid her fear of Harun's unexpected and chilling words with their threat of her being disowned.

Richard led her through a door and lit more candles within, then put more wood on the fire, as Bran had ordered. Azra had no lady to wait on her so Richard offered, "If you wish for help in preparing for bed, I can have Tilly come to you."

Azra wanted nothing more than to be left alone. "That will not be necessary," she answered and Richard left her to it.

As she undressed by the fire, she glanced about her. In spite of the candles and brightly coloured tapestries, there was a gloomy, almost foreboding aura to the room, with its shifting shadows cast by the variously sized flames from hearth and tallow. The eyes of the figures on the hangings seemed to follow and wink at her as she moved from one part of the room to another. She tried to ignore the wavering edge of the tapestry in the corner by the chimney, telling herself it was just the breeze from the window that moved it so.

She decided to extinguish most of the candles, but to leave the two longer ones on the board above the hearth, incase she woke in the night wondering where she was. And the flames from the fire would lend some light too. She turned over, pulling the covers over her ears. Had she had less on her mind, she might have appreciated the softness of the linen sheets and the warmth of the miniver in which she was ensconced, but Harun's words had crept further into her consciousness and were starting to allow prickles of anxiety to tear through her hitherto protected little fantasy world.

At the edge of her vision, the tapestry moved again, doing little to help her relax. Usually, in moments of self-doubt, she simply imagined how it had felt to lie with Bran, how warm he had seemed; how tender his voice. But tonight when she summoned him, remembering he was in his chamber with Anna, at this very moment, racked her with stomach-churning jealousy. The wind began to pick up and the shadows moved more erratically, now accompanied by a strange howling at the chimney and what she hoped were the ill-fitting windows somewhere behind her. Deciding it was best if she faced her fears, she rolled over under the covers to face the unseen. She kept her eyes closed at first, then braced herself and quickly opened them. She gave a start then sighed impatiently, irritated with herself for being alarmed by what was simply the reflection of the fire's flames in the polished pewter that stood on a chest by the door. A door closing elsewhere, momentarily stopped her breathing once more and she listened to see what would follow.

Apart from the sound of the wind, which had grown so strong now that it sent occasional billows of smoke back down the chimney and into the room, she seemed to be able to hear muffled voices. Her heart beat heavily. Soon, she came to realise that the volume of the voices rose and fell with the wind at the chimney. Did one of those voices belong to Bran? Suddenly more curious than afraid, she sat up in bed, wrapped herself in her cloak and crept to the door to ensure it was locked so that she might not be discovered eavesdropping at the chimney breast. She drew closer to the source of the sound, trying to make out the words. She thought she could make out Ralph's voice, but not what he was saying. And then Bran. His voice was deeper and resonated further.

"I do not want to be deliberately cruel, but she is sadly deluded if she thinks I could love her."

Azra felt a barb to the heart, then a little hope. Perhaps he was not speaking of her but of Anna. Of course, he could not show any affection for her while he was nursing Anna back to health, and he was so considerate, he would not risk a relapse by letting Anna know that his feelings had changed.

His voice came again. "I have no feelings for her at all. Well, no positive feelings. I know, I know, it seems cruel. But how can a man tricked into lying with a woman be expected to feel any differently? I am so angry with her – a little girl tampering with the fate of others. They might have lived you know, had I got back sooner. And she must have planned it – to have the drink ready. And to ignore what I said about Anna so she would leave my room."

There was a pause in which Azra felt the weight of his disappointment in her return with a jolt. He was speaking of her then.

"There are so many important issues to be dealing with - the rebels are still a threat, even though the King seems to have made his peace with his sons. Really we should be on our way to Alnwick tying up the loose ends at the Scottish Borders, not being sidetracked by the infantile ramblings of a love-sick girl."

Azra felt the blood come to her cheeks. "Infantile! Love-sick!" she whispered angrily. Ralph's quieter voice responded. She could not make out the words, but guessed he must have said something in her defence because of Bran's rejoinder.

"Believe me, Ralph, I am being as sympathetic as I can be under the circumstances. Joss sent word that he is all for having her put on trial, and of course Marc is in agreement with that because he feels Susan and Maud would have lived if Azra had not caused a delay in the message reaching him in France."

The blood began to beat heavily in Azra's ears. Harun had already told her how barbaric the sentences had been that he had witnessed himself.

"I am sorely tempted, but Harun's friendship means much to me. I have only gone so far as to agree to take the truth drug we gave to Roger. If Azra wants to show she is telling the truth, she should agree to take it too. That should end all the confusion."

Azra straightened, her breathing had deepened and she felt the sudden need to take the weight from her feet. She crossed the room to the bed and lowered herself again. A truth drug. Harun had mentioned it but she had not thought it would ever be considered in her own case. She had thought it would simply be a matter of collecting her husband and returning to Spain, where they could live out their sunny days in happiness. What would Harun say? More importantly what would she say? Would she have any control once she had taken the drug? Would she be able to hide the whereabouts of the cup Bran had drunk from, or that she had never been further than a few yards from his room all along, so that she could watch from an adjoining door, half hidden by a screen, and judge when he had fallen into a fitful sleep. And My God! What would Harun say as he heard her speak? After all of her haughty demands that he ought to believe his sister.

She sat, wringing her hands and chewing her lip. She must find a way out of this, before she was left with neither husband nor family.

A tapping at the window made her jump. The voices had stopped and Azra heard Ralph's door being closed. She breathed deeply and tried to calm herself, in an effort to think of a sensible way out of this. Perversely, now she was desperate to find a way out of tomorrow's meeting with Bran, she began to feel angry. How could he have let it go so far? Surely, the stupid man had a tongue in his head. He could have told her sooner, instead of sneaking to other men's rooms and spreading horrible rumours about her. And that horrible journey. The cold. The inhospitable English. Surely he could have made things plainer and saved her the humiliation of coming here.

She felt self-pity begin to twist her mouth and prick at her eyes and threw herself down on the bed, allowing herself to sob. Usually, when she sobbed, her younger sisters would be there to comfort her, but tonight all she had was the incessant tapping and howling at the window. Anger still outweighing all other feelings, she stood up impatiently, strode across the room to the wavering tapestry and pulled it viciously from its hanging. She screamed at the black figure which suddenly seemed to reach for her, brought into strong relief by the moon silvered sky and the scudding of the clouds behind gnarled grasping fingers.

The tapestry had fallen dangerously close to the fire, but Azra did not notice, unable to take her eyes from the massive nodding shape at the dark window, which now, since she had backed away several paces, seemed to have acquired several orange flaming eyes. She jumped again as the latch at the door rattled. She turned sideways so that she could glance at window and latch in quick succession, only now noticing that an ember was beginning to smoke on the stricken tapestry at the hearth.

Ralph called from without. "Azra! Azra what is it?"

Oh, thank God. Someone who could think straight and help her. She ran to the door and unlocked it. An undressed Ralph ran into the room, looking to left and right. He quickly spotted the now smouldering tapestry, dashed to the pewter jug, carried it back to the hearth and poured the contents over the burning fabric. After moving the rest of the hanging to a safe distance, he looked to Azra, who still stared like a stricken hare at the uncovered window. He could not see what frightened her and so went to her side. She shook so much that he felt he ought to hold her and walk her to the bed. Her heart was beating quickly and erratically. He looked over her shoulder and saw the shape of the boughs and the sinister way the reflections of the candle flames had endowed the trunk with glowering eyes.

"It is nothing Azra. You are safe. It is just the tree that taps and the wind that howls. Shh. You are safe now." He stroked her hair and held her closely. She sniffed, "I want to go home."

"But you have important business here – with Bran."

"I don't care. I no longer care for Bran. I want to go home now."

Ralph looked up at the sound of footsteps in the doorway. There stood Harun, awakened by the activity. He stood, hands on hips, his face a picture of disbelief. Azra stirred and looked up at him. Although her eyes were blurred with tears, she could see her brother's outline clearly. His posture did not bode well. It was only then that she and Ralph became more aware of his nakedness.

Ralph cast a self conscious look down at himself. "There was a fire," he offered weakly.

"Am I to be made to look a fool every time I turn my back on you?" Harun demanded.

Ralph and Azra were not sure which of them Harun addressed, so Azra repeated with a sniff, "I want to go home. I don't like it here. Bran can marry Anna. I no longer care."

Harun put his head to one side and glared. "You seem to have had a severe change of heart since our conversation this evening. And how does Ralph fit into all of this? I have trusted you to protect my sister on the journey here, but it looks like I sadly misjudged."

Ralph relinquished his hold on Azra and attempted to cover himself with the bedclothes.

"Azra was startled in the night, Sir. Protection was the only thing on my mind."

Harun looked less than convinced.

"It is true, Harun," Azra said, taking up his cause, just as he had done for her while she listened at the chimney. "He stopped the tapestry from burning on the hearth. And he has been far kinder to me than Bran has been."

Harun came into the room and lowered his voice to a growl. "Do not dare to tell me of truth, Sister. You have made a fool of me. You seem to change your heart and mind with alarming regularity. Do you know what it has cost me to support your accusations?" His voice shook with anger. "We will go home, but not before I try to restore my own honour amongst these good people." He stood over her, glaring. Ralph braced himself ready to prevent him striking her, he seemed so angry, but Harun wheeled round again on hearing a voice in the doorway.

"An interesting development." It was Bran. "Am I now to suppose that it was more appropriate for Joss to remain in Alnwick, where he was needed most, rather than make his way here on a wild goose chase?"

Harun looked mortified, then turned back to Azra, livid. "See what your scheming has done? I am disgusted." He held up his forefinger and thumb so that they almost touched and held his trembling hand scarcely an inch from Azra's eyes. "This is how much respect I have for you. Think yourself lucky I allow you this much. It is only this that stops me from allowing the temptation to kill you from winning me over."

Azra began to cry again. Harun snorted in disgust. "And stop snivelling." He looked down on her and Ralph. "Look at you..you..you whore!" He raised his hand as if to strike her and Ralph quickly stood between them.

"Stop. Can't you see she has learned her lesson? There is no need to humiliate her further."

Harun glared. Bran thought things were turning out rather fortuitously and decided to remain silent.

"Humiliate her? Her? She has driven a wedge between two friends, two communities!"

Harun's shuddering anger made Azra quake. "Do you realise the implications for this community? For the Northern? Their friends and family? For Bran, as a near outcast in his own homeland even before this blow to his reputation? God forgive you your selfish lies and the lives that were taken as a consequence!" He clenched his fists. "I cannot stand to look at you. You foolish, selfish….Ah! Words fail me."

Azra lowered her face. He span away in disgust. "I have finished with you. Once we are back in Spain, stay out of my sight. The more I think of what you have done, the more I cringe with embarrassment that you share my blood."

Bran spoke from the doorway. "Perhaps there is a way out of this that would restore some honour."

Harun gave a dubious snort, but remained quiet, thankful that there might be a chance to hear any positive comments from the old friend he had insulted so deeply over this whole affair.

Bran looked at Ralph, and, realising he was not best attired for serious talks, entered the room and handed him his own cloak so that he might at least cover himself and look more of an honorable suitor – although from Harun's demeanour, he felt his friend might think any solution, no matter how it dressed itself, was welcome right now.

"Well, Ralph?" Bran prompted, not wishing to sound like he was putting words into Ralph's mouth.

Ralph put on the cloak with an air of gratitude, and braced himself to look Azra's brother in the face. "Events rather pulled the rug from under me when I was in Spain. I had had two tasks in mind when I visited your home. The first, as you rightly surmised, involved requesting help to bolster Henry's troops, should he have needed it. But there was a second, more personal issue I would have liked to broach, had…circumstances… not taken over." He paused, self-consciously. Harun gave him a level look.

"For several years, I had always thought that I would like to make Spain my permanent home. The rebellion here added fuel to that idea. You have always made me feel welcome in your house, and," he added hastily, "although I have always thought honorably of your sister, as she has grown into a young woman, I have also realised that my feelings for her have grown quite strong."

Harun continued to give him an inscrutable look. Ralph was aware that Azra had now raised her head and was looking from her brother to himself. He paused, finding it difficult to judge the best way to continue. He had found it hard enough to compose what to say to Harun when he thought he was going to have time to broach the subject during his last visit, but now, after midnight, wearing his host's robe in his potential intended's bed chamber, the task seemed more than irksome. He took a deep breath.

"I have managed to establish some business links in Spain and have accumulated a modest wealth here in England. I had hoped that I could make Spain my home, and with your consent, and Azra's acceptance, marry and settle there. Raise a family…"

He petered out, realising he was rambling now.

Harun interrupted, "Are you saying you wish to marry, Azra?"

"Yes, I am."

"Even though she has tricked and wheedled her way into this man's bed and behaved in such a shameful manner?"

"Well, yes. I am sure she will not want to repeat this evening's embarrassment."

Harun looked to his sister. "Have you learned your lesson?"

Azra nodded and whispered, "Yes."

"Then take her. The sooner the better. And more fool you. Stay with her tonight if you wish. She probably will not complain."

Ralph shuffled awkwardly and looked down at Azra. "Do you want to marry me?"

Azra looked at him. He was rather amenable, and had tried to protect her rather frequently, she now realised. "Yes."

He smiled. "That's decided then. But, I shall sleep in the next room. If you grow frightened in the night, just call for me."

She thanked him quietly and he left.

"You do not deserve such kindness," Harun remarked and looked to Bran for affirmation, but Bran had left the company and returned to his chamber.

He entered quietly so as not to wake Anna and stepped quietly across the room to the bench near the fire, which he had made his bed since his return from Spain.

As he settled down, easing his back against the woodwork, he heard Anna stir, then her sleepy voice. "How did it go?"

"Wonderfully. You are a credit to Redgate."

"Has she dropped her accusations?"

"Yes, and has agreed to marry Ralph on her return to Spain."

He heard her sit up in bed. "Truly?"

"Truly."

She lay down again, making herself more comfortable. "Susan deserves a lot of credit," said Anna. "Simply through the power of her suggestion that yew berries might make a truth drug, two liars have been brought to task."

"Um," agreed Bran. He thought awhile. "It's good to be able to speak of her without sadness at last."

"Yes." Anna made herself comfortable amongst the covers, hoping that tonight might be the first night she was not troubled with painful cramps in her abdomen. "Yes, it is."

"Can I bring you anything to help you sleep?"

"No, thank you. I feel most restful." She stretched almost languorously. "You can lie in your own bed soon."

They both smiled into the darkness.

Chapter Thirty Four

Rising Tide

Azra's shame-faced exit was not devoid of advantages for the Northern. Harun was so contrite that he offered to send further troops to aid in the fight against the rebels, and to send them now rather than wait for a crisis point. If anything, the friendship between he and Bran was strengthened. Apart from the stony look from Joss which reduced Azra to hot, shameful tears the morning of his arrival from Scotland; there was no harm done. And Ralph was positively beaming.

Harun took great care over his examination of Anna before he left, perhaps to show how sorry he was for the extra burden his sister had put on her at a time of great personal suffering. Physically, she was healing well when it came to her womb, but it was only with Harun's examination that the discovery of other, older, untended injuries was made.

Harun was gentle in his bedside manner and moved away from Anna that he might speak with Bran without causing her alarm.

"Did you know about the other injuries?" he asked.

"I noticed her wrists and ankle must have been broken at least one more time since her fall into the stream. I guessed because of Roger's ill-treatment."

Harun stroked his chin and nodded. "I would guess he has deliberately done this to hurt her – to control her – or perhaps it has happened during one of the times she was raped."

Hearing it summed up so, gave a close up feeling of the horror that Anna must have gone through over the past few months. And all this while she was pregnant. The only surprise was that she had not lost the child sooner. Harun looked at his friend and Bran realised he was not finished in his appraisal.

"There's more?"

"There is a scar from burning which goes from her throat, along her collar bone, towards her shoulder. It must have been very painful, being so close to bone, whether from boiling liquid or from fire. The hair hangs shorter at that side. Perhaps it was burned at the same time. Unless he used oil then she cut the hair away herself as it would not clean."

Bran's understanding of the sort of torture Anna had been through had only scratched the surface so far.

"There is still some discolouration of the skin where bruises have not yet healed. Even after all these weeks. Especially on her back, legs and arms. But this is not surprising with the amount of work her body is doing to heal at present: it is the burn which concerns me more. It needs immediate treatment; it has not healed well so far. Skin that is past the point of repair does not remain in that state; it worsens and spreads."

Bran gave a self-deprecating sigh. "I should have seen this."

Harun shrugged. "The flesh is not pretty. It may be that she has been hiding it from you, fearing it might affect your feelings for her."

Bran felt no better for this. "I shall arrange her treatment immediately." Admittedly he had noticed a change in her mood lately. He had imagined that once the Azra issue was sorted, they could be as they had been that day in the forest, but there were times she was a little distant with him.

Harun lowered his voice further, "You know if left it could be life-threatening?"

Bran nodded. "I'll make her well. Roger hasn't beaten her yet."

As Bran reached up to the higher shelves to collect hyssop, cowslip and waybread, Harun drew a little closer to him. "I would make sure she has plenty of this too." He handed Bran peony. Bran looked at him. "As her physical pain decreases, expect her melancholy to take a stronger hold. She has a lot to forget."

Bran took the proffered plant. How could he have been so blind to her needs: presuming Anna's mood would improve so simply. "I had guessed at it from some of the things she has said lately. And occasionally she has bad dreams. I cannot say whether she remembers them on waking, but they do colour her mood for the first few hours of every day. I suppose this gloomy weather does not help. It still feels like Mid-Winter."

"Try to give her distractions, but at the same time, talk to her about things that have happened when she feels she can. Some doctors recommend complete mind rest until the melancholia passes, but in my experience it gives way to a deeper depression – even madness."

Bran looked at him. "That won't happen to Anna. She enjoys distractions."

"I am sure you will look after her well," his friend concurred, and left him to continue his nursing of Anna alone.

As Bran approached the bed to judge whether his choice of medicine was the right one, he noticed that Anna had covered the wound with her hair.

She smiled at him a little nervously. "Is everything all right? I feel much better than I did."

Bran smiled. "Nothing to worry about," He seated himself on the bed. "Harun has been chastising me for overlooking some of your injuries."

She looked down at her hands. "I have no complaints," she shrugged.

"I know." He paused, prompting her to look up at him. "May I?"

She raised her eyebrows and grinned, "May you what?"

"Examine where Roger burned you. I need to see which ointment or poultice would be best."

Anna's smile faded. "It is nothing. Time will heal it."

He covered her hands with his. "Please trust me."

Reluctantly, she turned her head to one side. Gently, he moved the fabric of her chemise from her shoulder and stroked her hair away. He shifted a little on the bed, allowing the light to fall on the ruined flesh. There were tiny fragments of blackened fabric still clinging to the wound where they had become one with the flesh. He said nothing but made a practical examination. He would give her something to help numb the area first and remove what he could before applying the paste. He gently covered her again and took her hands once more. Her head was still averted.

"He treated you most brutally, didn't he?"

Anna's shoulders gave the slightest of shrugs. "I'm still here."

He cupped her face in his hands and rested his cheek in her hair. "And I am most glad that you are, Anna."

She slipped her hands around his shoulders and held him close, and he understood now that it was so that he might not sit back and see that she was crying, just as it had been the morning they left for the Borders. He was swamped with guilt that he had missed her misery because of his injured pride and wrapped his arms round her, his voice broken into whispers, "God, Anna. Forgive me. Leaving you all alone like that. Let me make it better. Forgive me."

She lifted her head from his shoulder, wiped the tears quickly from her eyes with the back of her hand, shaking her head. "None of this was your fault. I should have said something. The lives I could have saved...Tilly must be heartbroken and yet she has not mentioned Raymond once. And Susan...and... God...and...poor little mite...poor little.." Her mouth became a thin line as she tried to hide her misery. She covered her face with her hands.

Bran pulled her close again. "No, no, no. Shush, Anna. No blame lies with you. Push it away, Anna. Susan would want you to, I know she would." He rocked her gently. "He's gone now. Don't burden yourself with his vices. Shh. It's not your fault, Anna."

Later that evening, he wrote to Joss agreeing that he would stay and look after Anna as his older friend had suggested weeks before, rather than join him in making the final arrests further north. He gave her newly discovered injuries rather than her mental health as the reason.

After sealing the letter, he gazed out of the window. It framed a gloomy sight. In spite of the darkness, the wind and rain made themselves known through a fitful clattering at the panes. He hoped the weather would break soon. Such gloom well into April was enough to depress anyone. He crossed the room quietly and looked down on Anna. Her sleep seemed deep and her breathing even. Now her bleeding had finally stopped, he hoped her body would put more energy into healing her quickly. Perhaps this restful slumber would last the night and the nightmares of the past week would begin a retreat.

He stretched and made his way to his makeshift bed by the hearth, as he did every night so that if she woke, she would not find herself alone in the dark.

Chapter Thirty Five

Telling Her

Just as it had seemed to Bran that Winter would keep its icy grip on the land for the whole of April, the sun came out. His spirits had been raised even before he opened the shutters slightly that morning in order to assess the day and, although still early, he had decided to get up and work so that later, he might entice Anna out of doors.

For the first time that April, the morning was still and golden. The remains of a thin mist draped across the tranquil lakes beyond the window of the trace room, disturbed only by the occasional swoops of swifts eager to pick insects from the surface.

Bran's muscles complained from having been at his stool since first light. He was pondering over the tracery of the window for Anna's library. Now and then, he raised the charcoal to the paper, but then drew it away again. He was uninspired, his mind elsewhere. He didn't want to waste his materials with an attempt at a half-hearted design then change his mind.

Finally, he sat back, rotating his shoulders to rid them of their stiffness. He put his hands on his thighs, casting one last look at the sheet, as if the answer was hidden just beneath the surface. No change.

He wondered if exercise would help his mind and prepared to stand up. It was only then that he noticed he had an observer. He sat back again listening for the slight rustle of cloth from the doorway that had first drawn his attention. He watched, head to one side. Eventually, Anna, knowing she had been discovered, stepped inside awkwardly.

She looked at him apologetically, wondering if he was annoyed by her intrusion into his private space.

He smiled. "Good morning." He turned back to his work, as nonchalantly as possible, as if seeing her outside for the first time in two months was no great surprise. She leaned stiffly against the door frame, wondering whether to stay or go. He glanced across at her and smiled.

"Come in and keep me company. Have a seat."

Her gaze followed his hand which indicated a bench near his desk. A band of sunlight fell across it. She seated herself and looked around the room, while Bran looked back at the paper. She sat upright, looking about her. The sleeves of her dress had once been fashionably close-fitting, but now hung loosely, revealing her long white wrists. While she looked away, taking in the reflections from the lake as they shimmered across the walls, he stole a glance at her face. She seemed ethereal somehow: her complexion pale with so many weeks spent indoors. The purpose of his paperwork seemed to be eluding him. Time and again he was about to draw but stopped short of the paper. Then it came to him. He imagined he was looking up through the branches of the chestnut that looked over Redgate. He would use a simplified version of that pattern of branches. He became quite lost in the drawing, until, gradually, he realised that Anna, spectre-like, had crossed the room and was looking out of the window behind him.

He kept working, watching the shadow-strings of her hair moving across his hand and the sketch. Gradually, she turned from the window with its view of willow, lakes and engines, and turned to look at what he drew. He sat back so she could see, as if awaiting her approval. She put her head to one side and pondered. Some of her hair had escaped the braid that she had tied and a warm breeze blew it across her eyes. He smiled and drew it back from her face and over her shoulder, sitting back a little so he could gaze at her unnoticed. Reflected lights from the lake danced over her.

"It's pretty," she decided. She looked at him. "What is it?"

He laughed. "A window."

"Oh." It seemed too beautiful to be a window. "It must be for a very special building."

"It is." He raised his eyebrows mischievously. "A building for a very special person."

"Is it for the Prince Bishop? Puiset's additon to the Cathedral?"

"No, not this one. But that reminds me. Puiset, or Pudsey as they are calling him, wants me to visit at some point over the next week. His building work for the extra chapel hasn't been successful. He may need to start again."

Her heart sank a little at the thought of Bran leaving when there was so little to occupy her with her father being away.

"I wondered if you would like to come with me."

She looked at him a little startled.

"If you want to. You could choose which day you would prefer to travel."

She smiled. She could think of nothing better than escaping for a while, so long as Bran was there to keep her cushioned from the rest of the world. She nodded. "I would like it very much." She considered. "Is it allowed?"

"Allowed?"

"Saint Cuthbert didn't really like women, did he? Perhaps Puiset will disapprove."

He smiled. "Puiset wants extra room around Cuthbert's shrine. That's what I will be helping with. I don't know who began that rumour about Cuthbert, but," he added, with a mock air of indignation, "if Puiset wants his building to stop falling down, Puiset can put up with the idea of me having a lady companion. Besides, he is in no position to protest at present – after his interpretation of remaining 'neutral' over the rebellion."

"Shall we go and come back all in one day?"

"If you wish it, but it seems a shame when we could take our time and we have comfortable rooms at our disposal."

She smiled and blushed a little. "I haven't been to Durham since I was a young girl."

"Then it's time you were reacquainted with town life."

"Do you think my father will mind?"

"You going to Durham, or you going to Durham with me?"

She shrugged, embarrassed at the implications. He sat back from her a little to ease her discomfort.

"Ben has often asked me to keep you close. I think he would rather you went with me than stayed here. He is due back within the next few days. If you wish, I could have Marc arrange some protection while we travel."

She gave a slight shrug. "Whatever you feel is right."

He watched her. Her hands were clenched anxiously at the desk top.

"It's a beautiful day. A day prescribed to raise the spirits."

Anna nodded and, without looking from the window, said, "I do think I am ready for more exercise."

"Let's walk now; build up an appetite while the weather is good. You have seen my favourite place at Redgate, so if you can promise not to tell, I shall show you where I go to escape and think in Drysdale."

He had caught her interest and she turned to look back at him. "I imagined this was your favourite thinking place."

He put his head to one side, considering. "Favourite place to work, yes. But there are times I just want to have the time to give my mind free rein – to think of things more pleasurable than siege engines, drainage systems or battle plans."

He reached back for his cloak which hung over the sill of the open window, flung it over his left shoulder, then linked her arm and escorted her from the room.

"We shall walk down to the river first – I find that throws people off the scent – the secret place involves a climb. And don't worry," he added, noticing the sudden doubt in her eyes after so many weeks spent resting, "I shall carry you if necessary. I have always wanted to show you this place."

She smiled at how well these words suited her. "I look forward to it. There is so much to see here. I love Drysdale."

Uplifted by the fact that she blushed when she said this, he immediately held to his promise by carrying her as he stepped carefully around the puddle outside the trace room door.

They strolled leisurely between the lakes, stooping now and then to avoid draping fronds of willow. Water falls of varying sizes broke the silence and the high pitched elongated whistles of swifts warned them before sudden flights swooped at them daringly then swerved away. On reaching the top of a slight incline, Anna turned to survey Bran's home and the grounds with its fantastic mix of natural and man made wonders. He stood a little behind her, hoping she would prove to be fit enough for the journey. She closed her eyes and raised her face to the sunlight, smiling. If she was his, he would have held her, kissed her neck, told her how beautiful she looked. He could smell violets on her skin and in her hair. Tilly must have prepared her a morning bath.

"What was it that made you decide to come outside today?"

With her eyes still closed, she put her head on one side as if pondering. "It's hard to say." She turned to face him.

He waited, allowing her time to unravel her thoughts. She held his hands while she considered, more like her old self. As if her fortune lay in his hands, she studied them and spoke. "Today seemed different. Partly because of the sun coming out; partly because I didn't feel so sad inside when I awoke." She glanced up at him. "And partly because you weren't there and I wanted to find you."

A look passed between them and took them both aback. He hid his face from her by looking at their hands while he cupped hers in his.

"I'm glad you did, Anna," he whispered.

She stood back from him and gave him a smile. The heavy feeling of dread; the feeling that she might never be normal again was not such a barrier against her chest as it had been of late. She breathed in deeply and sighed, trying to savour the knowledge that she was simply out in the fresh air. She felt the way a condemned man would if he was allowed to take a step out of his prison shortly before being returned to his executioner. "How long can we stay out?"

"As long as you want. All night if you wish. I'll pitch a tent and bring us blankets," he grinned.

She raised her face to the sky and breathed deeply, as if light was an elixir to be drunk. He took her hand. "Come with me," he smiled. "Where I am taking you is where the light lasts longest."

He led her a little way from the river and helped her to crest the hill which gave the one natural waterfall its momentum. Here the trees thickened, but at one point, a thick branch stretched a muscled arm across the stream. He walked ahead of her, sat on it facing her as she approached, and grinned. "Are you up to edging along here with me?"

She considered the branch. It seemed broad and strong enough to allow a safe passage, but falling would mean another dip in the fast running water. Not a thought she relished after the series of events it seemed to trigger the last time it happened. Although she eventually nodded, she absentmindedly rubbed the wrist that had been broken.

Bran stood on the branch, held out his hand to her and helped her to step alongside him. She found the perch far less precarious from here, there being a fretwork of secondary branches, which gave the effect of a safety net.

"Trust me?" he asked, facing her and holding onto both hands while beginning to step backwards along the trunk.

Anna cast quick glances to either side and again nodded somewhat nervously.

"Look at me," he said. She did so. "You see, it is no more precarious than the rope bridge over the narrow end of the lake by the house – in fact, it is sturdier." He broke into a grin. "I have done the calculations."

Two thirds of the way along the branch, he stopped, lay down his cloak and helped her to sit on a relatively flat part of the bough, which conveniently sent up another thick branch to act as a backrest. She had to confess it seemed sound enough and made a comfortable and airy seat. Anna sat back and took a quick breath, as she finally allowed herself to take in her surroundings. "It is like we are floating." To the right, the river and land fell away, leaving only an expanse of sky and moor land.

"Do you feel better for being here?"

"In your favourite place? Yes." She allowed herself to relax into him and sighed, "I can see why you love it here."

He leaned forward to see her better and found he could only gaze like a fool. He wanted to kiss her, but he would wait. Perhaps she would think twice about travelling to Durham with him. "You see? No need to be afraid of the dark any longer."

"I think I am on the mend." A sudden thought occurred to her, "I don't think I want to learn the quintain any longer."

He assumed a look of disappointment. "Shame. I had a wager that you would be my most high achieving page ever."

She smiled.

He helped her to her feet again, noticing her back seemed to pain her as she rose. "I'll treat your back after our walk. It may take some time to readjust to everyday life."

On their return, just before they ate, Bran sent word to Marc that he would be leaving with Anna for Durham the day after next and that he would appreciate a small party to ensure their safety by following them at a discreet distance. He read through the message and underlined "at a discreet distance" before sealing it and sending it to Redgate where he was looking after things in Ben's absence.

Anna's appetite had returned and she smiled so much more. Before night had fallen, Marc and a small band of Squires had arrived at Drysdale. Bran could not help thinking that they seemed overly keen to see them on their way. On their arrival, Marc grinned at them both as they sat on a bench reading, enjoying the last of the evening sun. He wasted no time in finding an excuse to speak to Bran alone. He pretended he was not too clear on his orders. "Have you told her yet?"

Bran gave a sigh. "No, not yet. Just leave me to tell her in my own sweet time."

"All right. I might seem impatient, but it's just that I know how happy this will make you. Of course, I insist on coming with you."

"There's no need, Marc."

"Oh don't worry. I'll make sure you have some privacy. It's not just nosiness. You're a prime target and you need protection."

"Even for a simple jaunt to Durham?"

"Especially for a simple jaunt to Durham - that would be when you least expect it."

"Um." Bran was not convinced.

"Will, Leona and Tilly will stay here ready to meet Ben should he arrive early - not that he would disapprove of course," he added, seeing Bran's annoyance.

Marc ferreted around in one of his pockets. He pulled out a corked glass bottle which made a sloshing noise when he shook it. "I know if Susan was here she would insist that I give you this." He passed it to Bran who looked at it questioningly. "Scented oil for Anna's back."

"Aha." Bran shook his head at his friend's enthusiasm for this trip.

Marc grinned. "For medicinal purposes only of course."

"Of course," Bran said wryly, trying to hide the bottle discreetly inside his cloak, before Anna noticed. He looked so uncomfortable that Marc stopped his teasing. "Anything else? Aphrodisiac? Truth potion?"

Marc smiled at his sarcasm. "You'll wish you said something months ago."

Bran gave a sigh as he turned to go back to the company. "I thought I did," he muttered.

The group of friends gathered outdoors. The day passed to evening in a happy haze of chatter and eating, helped by the ale and the early arrival of Will and Leona. As the last of the sun began to disappear over the tree tops, a sudden gust of wind ran amongst them. It blew some papers from the trace room and brought a sudden downpour with it. The company joined forces in dismantling the table and rescuing half full cups. Anna ran to retrieve the papers that had blown onto the grass, picking them up quickly and placing them on the desktop where she weighed them down with her penknife and the pot of ink gall. By the time she looked out from the trace room doorway, the rain fell heavily in great golden drops. She decided to be hung for a sheep as a lamb and stepped out. The drops were beautifully refreshing. There seemed no need to rush. She held her palms upwards, enjoying the weight and coolness of the rain against her skin.

Within seconds her hair was wet through. Bran quickly ran for his cloak and as he approached her, the sun re-emerged between a gap in the trees and sent rainbows of colour across the courtyard and Anna, who stood looking at her arms and the colour-filled air around her. Red, indigo, yellow and green hovered at her fingertips. Bran stopped mid stride, almost forgetting the purpose for the cloak he held in both hands.

"Do you see it too?" she asked, smiling and turning her hands, moving them about through the colours. He gazed at her, nodding. Within seconds, the sun dropped from sight, dragging its rays behind it and leaving them standing there like fools in the pouring rain. He put the cloak about her shoulders, then walked her back to the house unaware of the looks from his friends, who were spying from the doorway. Just before they reached earshot, Will whispered to Leona, "How much of a sign does that boy need?"

Leona shushed him gently, saying, "Give it time to unravel. It could be too soon." But she was smiling.

Chapter Thirty Six

From East To West

Bran was seated on the windowsill, reading some legal papers he had had written up so that Marc could hold the tenancy to another of the manors more securely. Times were still doubtful so it was better to be safe: the Bradley estate was perfect for Marc: set midway between Redgate and Drysdale as the crow flies. On seeing Anna, he jumped down from his perch, crossed to join her and pulled out a stool for her to be seated.

She surveyed the table, her mouth watering. "This looks delicious. Is it all for us?"

"It is," Bran nodded and began to serve her, having told Richard that he could break his fast with his father this particular morning. "I want you to be as strong as possible for this journey. Your father would never forgive me if it turned into an ordeal for you."

She smiled and took the generous helping he had prepared for her. "I'm sure it won't." Chewing thoughtfully, she asked, "Will I really be allowed in?"

"Yes," said Bran, "although you will need to stay at the back." He looked at her apologetically. "They even have a line drawn to make sure."

She thought a little and grinned. "I'll think of it as a line that keeps them within rather than me without."

"If it makes you feel any better, it's a miracle Hugh Puiset is letting me into the building at all. He doesn't want to risk me working from plans without studying the existing structure." Mysteriously, he added, "If he only knew."

Anna stopped and waited. "Knew?"

He mused a little, and glanced at Anna, wondering whether to tell her more. "Can you keep a secret?"

"No," she smiled.

Bran grinned then looked around him and leaned forward like a conspiratorial little boy. "My Great Grandfather was the master mason on the original building work."

Anna's eyes widened.

"I see you're suitably impressed," he smiled.

"Of course. That's marvellous! I always thought it rather odd that the man responsible for such a major building would not be named. I'm assuming you mean your Great Grandfather on you Father's side." She thought a little more. "But weren't your family based in Italy originally?"

Bran nodded. "Yes. My Great Grandfather settled here for a while, but travelled far and wide, which must have influenced my Grandfather, who settled in Italy and brought his children up there. My father returned to England before I was born, having heard of my Great Grandfather's contribution. That's why he took the uncommon step of visiting and staying in the North rather than the political centres like Winchester and London. Although we do have family buried at

Cripplegate." He took another morsel of hare before continuing with a feigned nonchalance worthy of Will. "Never talk about it of course. Might annoy the Christians."

He stood up and held out his hand. "Come with me. There is one very important thing you will need for your journey."

He led her to the doorway where they both looked to the courtyard. There stood the young page, Ross, holding the reins of a beautifully polished and prancing mare. Anna didn't understand at first. Bran helped. "What do you think? She looks flighty and headstrong but she's as meek as a lamb."

"Am I allowed to ride her to Durham?"

"Yes."

She walked over to the mare, which now stood quietly, coat gleaming.

He walked with her, watching her response.

"What's her name?"

Bran shrugged. "She doesn't have a permanent name yet. That's your decision. We've been calling her The Mare."

She looked up at him in confusion.

"She's yours."

Anna approached the animal. She reached to stroke her flank. The chestnut coat, smooth and warm, gleamed like a polished nut.

"Yes," said Anna, nodding. "She should stay without a name. Keep her safe."

"Do you like her?"

Anna continued to stroke the mare's coat, smiling. The mare pushed its brow against her palm. "I love her. Thank you." She turned to him. "I know I should say that it is too much and that you shouldn't have, but she's beautiful. Thank you."

"There's one more thing." He led her towards the house where a smiling Tilly stood on the step: a length of rich, green and ample velvet draped over her arm. "Every lady who goes riding needs a riding cloak." Tilly and he held it up for Anna to see. She stared at the deep luxurious cloth. He watched her carefully, really not sure how she would react. He did not want her to think that her existing clothes were not considered good enough. She reached out to feel the material. At the edges she noticed a flash of orange and ran her fingers under it to see it more clearly. Some of the patterned silk he had brought back for her over a year ago had been used to line the edges of the cloak. The work was beautifully done. She guessed, rightly, that Tilly had done it and thanked her with a kiss on the cheek.

"Janey helped me."

Bran was careful of her reaction. He now knew that Roger had used the silk as an excuse to hurt her: suggesting she wear some of it like a shawl as she suited the colours, then setting it alight when she did so. She looked up at him.

"This is beautiful. I don't think I have ever worn velvet before."

"Will you try it?"

He held it so that she could slip her shoulders inside.

Blushing, she asked, "Does it look well?"

He gazed at her, smiling.

Tilly nodded. "It suits you well."

Behind them, two squires, Adam and Stephen, led both of their coursers to the mounting block, Seer making his own way there, eager for a ride out.

Bran took Anna's arm and helped her before mounting his own horse. The little group of observers waved them off from the courtyard, while Will and Leona watched from their chamber window. Leona waved at Stephen, hoping her youngest would conduct himself well. Marc waved up at them, discreetly indicating the open door of the trace room. Bran planned to come back via Redgate where Anna could finally see the library and Bran wanted her desk and papers to be in place by then. Will waved and nodded, then went back to bed, sitting up with his back against the wall. He watched his wife gazing wistfully after the couple.

Very quietly, he said, "Leona."

She turned to look at him and smiled.

"Come over here again. Let me show you how much I love you."

****

It was half a life-time since she had been to Durham, so her heart still lurched when she and Bran approached the Cathedral from Framwellgate Bridge. Although it was busy and noisy with traders, Bran found a spot from where they could survey the building. It observed the City from its perch on the peninsula like an alert yet comfortable lion, ears pricked and tail straight up. The Castle walls seemed to embrace it protectively from here. The sun had come out during the journey, creating a pure blue backdrop for the golden stonework with its dark arches and towers. Anna took in every detail of every pane and stone, including the rather lopsided scaffolding just visible at the East end, which lay furthest away from them. "It's magnificent," she whispered.

They first caught up with Marc and the squires to be shown their lodgings. Anna was whisked away by a rather businesslike woman with a rosy face and a body as wide as it was tall. It looked like they would be staying here for the night after all. The woman explained the rules about females in the monastery and after a short while, Anna was left to unpack her things. She had very little to unpack. The windows gave her a view of the internal courtyard and offices. If she peered carefully she could see the route leading down to Saddler Gate and the town to the left or the river to the right. She saw their mounts being led out of sight and shortly Bran arrived in the courtyard and stood looking up at the windows, vaguely in her direction. She was glad to see a familiar face and went down to join him. On reaching the ground, she saw that he was being greeted by a man who looked to be welcoming him with open arms. He greeted Bran enthusiastically in French, so she could hear what was said before she reached them.

"Drysdale! The man who can solve all of my problems I hope. Have you been to your lodgings yet? Sorry I could not greet you personally."

Bran turned to Anna and introduced her. "This is my Goddaughter, Anna."

He turned to her and clasped her hands warmly.

Pudsey continued to boom at them good-naturedly whilst steering them to the east side of the church, which looked decidedly shabby and war torn compared to the rest of the building.

"I am almost beaten into giving up on this project," he said to Bran. "I fail to see why our calculations aren't successful."

Anna watched this charismatic man as he went into more detail and guided Bran to a table which held the aforementioned plans. She now knew why he wasn't dressed in the splendid attire she had expected of a Prince Bishop. He wore a rather plain robe which was spattered in ever increasing amounts of grey dust towards the hem. As they spoke she looked about her. Several novices worked across the way in their garden. Groups of people she took for pilgrims stood in the Cathedral grounds, some chatting cheerfully, others assuming what they thought to be more pious expressions. A group of young women chattered and giggled in a huddle, throwing glances in Bran's direction now and then. She looked back to Bran who leaned over the table and absentmindedly stroked a finger across his lips, oblivious to the looks they gave him. He looked up at Pudsey and said something she could not hear, but she assumed from his nodding and Pudsey's smile that he was confirming that the plans seemed sound.

Bran walked to the area where the rubble lay. It looked like they had made a promising start as some of the masonry was quite high in places. Bran went beyond these ruins and surveyed the ground from a distance. Where the ground sloped away he stooped to inspect things more closely, even taking a sharpened pole and shoving it into the earth. Pudsey watched with interest.

After some time had passed and Anna had seated herself on a grassy slope, taking care not to muddy her cloak, Bran stood up straight, gave a deep sigh and turned to look at Pudsey. As he passed Anna to talk with the Archbishop, he whispered, "He's not going to like this - come with me."

Awkwardly, Anna got to her feet and followed him, keeping a respectful distance.

Bran gave a disarming smile. "Before I tell you what I think, may I take you both for a little walk?"

Pudsey looked at Anna and smiled. "Can we trust this man?"

Anna thought Pudsey could learn a lesson or two about trust himself, but grinned and said, "Always."

"Lead on then Drysdale."

Bran picked up the plans before setting off.

He crossed the green and took them through the alley to the edge of the peninsula that dropped suddenly and steeply to the river. Here Bran looked up at the Western part of the cathedral with its two thin towers and ornate carvings about the windows. His companions found themselves doing likewise. Bran approached the base of the building, saying, "This part of the peninsula is solid rock. The whole Cathedral, standing strong and firm, is built on solid rock." He stood up straight again. "The east end of the peninsula is a completely different geology there. It tilts too."

Pudsey looked dubious. "But we need more room. The most sensible place to expand the building is where there is space at the east end."

Bran took his hands from his hips. "Not if it keeps falling down. Besides, I think you have room here." He indicated the area where they stood.

"But this is close to the edge. A sheer drop to the river. Within a few years erosion might send the whole chapel tumbling down the bank side."

Bran stood firm. "Not if it's built on rock, which it will be," he said, stamping his foot as if to prove the immovable nature of the substance beneath his feet.

Anna watched the two men with interest. Pudsey rubbed his chin dubiously, unaware that he was leaving a dusty streak across his jaw. Bran could see that he was not convinced and gave another invitation.

"Can I try your patience a little further?"

"Certainly."

"Is the river crossing manned?"

"Yes."

"Then can I attempt to persuade you with a little boat ride and a further short walk?"

Again, Pudsey looked at Anna, who was trying to hide her enthusiasm for this adventure. The Prince Bishop waved Bran ahead of him. "Come on then. Let's get it over with."

They followed the pathway which took them down a gentler bank to the riverside. Here, between a gap in the trees, was a little landing area with a boat moored to it. The man responsible for a safe crossing was half asleep, leaning against a tree with his hood pulled over his eyes. He did not expect many customers with the river having two bridges now. On hearing footsteps, he jumped up in surprise. He had even more of a shock when he saw the Prince Bishop, with a woman and someone that looked like a foreign man, waiting to use his bark. With a little wobbling, they all managed to seat themselves comfortably. Bran sat facing Anna. He smiled and sighed, lifting his face to the sun. "Ah, what a magnificent view," he announced. Pudsey and Anna looked up at the Cathedral.

After the short crossing, Bran asked the man to wait for them as they would not be long, and he helped his guests to disembark as elegantly as was possible.

From here he led them up a slightly muddy path, through a little gap in the wall which surrounded the river, then along this same wall as if walking into town. Soon, it became apparent that this road faced the Cathedral from the opposite bank. Bran suddenly stopped and opened his arms as if to embrace the view.

"Beautiful!" he proclaimed. "Almost a fitting monument to our God."

Pudsey, who was also appreciating the view, raised a cynical eyebrow and commented wryly, "Almost?"

"It could be so much better." Bran unfolded the plans he was holding and held them so that his two companions could see the drawings and the real thing side by side. Pudsey looked from one to the other several times, trying to envisage the finished result. Eventually, he turned his back on the Cathedral, one arm crossed against his chest and the other hand rubbing his darkening chin once more. Finally, he put his arms to his sides and asked earnestly. "Can you honestly tell me that building the chapel there will mean that it will never fall down?"

Bran replied. "I can give you my word that it will last as long as the main building, so long as there is no subterfuge and it is not deliberately destroyed. And even then, the Scots have never been able to take the castle next to it."

Pudsey turned back and considered the view. "I suppose that it would follow the pattern of the monks' procession - a Galilee Chapel."

"And a place for women to worship." Bran said, smiling at Anna. "They could enter it from the back of the main building where they are forced to stay at present."

"And the cost?"

Bran knew it was nearly over. Money was being discussed. "It will be far more economical to build successfully on rock rather than continue paying for materials and labourers to build on the present site. I'm afraid it's nothing more than an exercise in hope over experience at the east side. It's not impossible to build there, but the buttressing and foundations needed to make it a success would need a lot of careful planning and far more finance. It's not just a wise man who builds his house upon the rock;" he grinned, "he would also be thrifty."

They began the journey back to the Cathedral. Pudsey was deep in thought the whole time. He left them on the opposite bank, still mulling it over.

"Let me discuss it and come back to me tomorrow morning. If it goes ahead, I would like your ideas for the interior work as well. If there is anything you need, just knock on that door there." He pointed across the green to one of the doors in the low building. "Whatever you need can be provided."

The two men shook hands and Pudsey left them to their own devices for the evening. Bran looked at Anna then at his hands. "If you allow me a little time to wash, we could have a walk; explore the town."

She nodded, smiling at his manners. "I'll wait here."

She seated herself at a bench, wondering what had happened to Marc and the boys. The atmosphere was different from Drysdale and Redgate. There was more of a holiday spirit: perhaps because so many of those standing in little clusters were pilgrims - away from home. There was constant movement in various directions as goods were delivered or young men ran errands for their masters. She looked to her left to the castle on its mound. She wondered about the people who were to-ing and fro-ing and the lives they led. Where were their families? Did they live with them here in the town, or were they away for long absences? Men like Joss or Bran, who had a lot of business to attend to. She felt very sheltered by comparison. She had not expected it to be quite so noisy, what with the sound of masonry being erected, or perhaps now, dismantled, and the voices of the travellers being amplified by the surrounding stonework. She did not normally eavesdrop, but the small group of females she had noticed earlier were still there and she was sure she heard one of them mention the Northern. It always surprised her. She knew they had a reputation, but she always felt a little surprised when strangers spoke about them with such a knowledgeable air. She decided to listen to see if they got it right.

She sat in the perfect place for eavesdropping: an alcove created by the stonework kept her from view. Still, it wasn't that easy a task. They spoke in their own local dialect, a dialect with which Anna had thought she was familiar, but she was not used to hearing it spoken so quickly, nor interspersed with so much giggling. One girl spoke more than the rest and it was obvious that one of the others was hanging onto her every word, albeit uncomfortably, while the third seemed to be more cynical.

"I don't care whether you believe me or not - it's true. Every one knows it."

"Why haven't I heard about it then?"

"You don't know everything. Besides, who would tell you? It's not exactly polite conversation is it?" Anna, who had been listening so carefully to decipher their conversation, felt herself blush as the topic became clear to her.

"Shush," said the shyest. "It's not the right place to be talking about things like that."

The first lowered her voice a little, but continued. "Well, it is true. They study it and everything." She laughed. "They are good at everything else, so why not that?"

"Shush!" said the third, again, her conscience pricking her. "You sound like the worst sort of troubadour."

"Oh, be quiet," scolded the first, obviously taking this as a compliment. "They are married so there's nothing wrong with talking about it? It's not a sin like promiscuity. That's different. It's more like - oh I don't know - chivalry. True love and all that."

Anna looked at her hands feeling embarrassed. Especially as her father was one of the three men who founded the Order.

The second girl was still dubious. "How do you know all this then?"

Without hesitation, the first retorted, "Because, Clever Clogs, my cousin Hilda's friend used to be resident at Braunspeth brew house and the Northern stayed over there one time to have talks about the troubles with Scotland."

The second girl scoffed derisively. "Knights aren't going to talk about such things in front of your cousin Hilda's friend."

"No," said the first loudly, to cut short her friends' protests, "exactly. They didn't talk about it - apparently they never do. It's all part of the attraction."

"So how do you know then? Are you a seer?"

"Because," sighed her friend, rather snootily, "none of the household got any sleep while the Northern was there because they were making love all night. And I mean," she added with the air of one who would know, "making love. It was the women you could hear, not the men."

"Shush. Look. He's coming back," said the shy one nervously.

Anna tried to make herself smaller, realising they would see she had been listening once Bran met with her. Oblivious to her presence, the loud one said, "Did you see who he arrived with? What a limping mess. He must pity her."

"I suppose you think you are far more perfect a match," scoffed her friend. "Anyway, I don't think you should be so mean. I felt sorry for her."

Anna stood up, face burning and moved further along the building in order that they might think she had been out of earshot all along. Suddenly, the beautiful cloak she wore did not seem so suitable and simply added further weight to her embarrassment.

As she moved away, she heard the cynical one say compliantly, "I suppose he is a lot fitter and better looking than any other man here. Tall as well."

"Umm," the loud one added with uncharacteristic wistfulness, "Imagine the climb."

Bran smiled as he approached her and took her arm. "Sorry I kept you waiting, Anna. Which way shall we go?"

She chose the riverbanks via the route they had taken that morning so that she would not have to walk past the gossipers, but she imagined their eyes burning into her back. She could not bring herself to talk for some time.

"This is where your father first saw your mother," recalled Bran as they stepped up the winding incline to the market place.

She allowed curiosity to push away some of her humiliation. "Did father tell you about it?"

"He was with Will and Joss. Love at first sight - for both of them."

"For Will and Joss?" she asked, and they both laughed. "What time of year was it?"

"Winter - an exceptionally cold one."

"What was she like?" she asked, remembering that Bran had once told her that she reminded him of her.

"Beautiful: in every way. She looked after me as if I was her own. She could speak and write in three languages."

"What did she look like?"

He smiled. "It always amazed me that some men could walk past her without giving her a second look. Auburn hair, big brown eyes - like yours. In fact," he looked at her a little tentatively, "your mouth is the same shape as hers too."

She smiled awkwardly, the words of the gossips looming large, but still appreciating the feeling of continuity it gave her. "Were they in love for a long time?"

"Of course," said Bran. "All the time. I imagine Ben still loves the memory of her. They were meant to be together."

Anna stopped. They had walked downhill and begun to cross Elvet Bridge. She looked over the side and up to the Cathedral from this different angle. The failed building work was more evident from here. She pondered a little and Bran waited. After a little while, she took his arm and they continued down the slope of the bridge so they could rejoin the meandering riverside path.

He noticed there was something on her mind. "Does it make you sad to talk about your mother?" asked Bran. He took his cloak and spread it on the grass so that they could sit and eat while there was still some evening sun to warm them. She shook her head as she seated herself.

"How do you know they were happy?"

Bran looked at her, a little taken aback at her cynicism. He shook his head slightly as he spoke, as if he had never had to apply logic to this before. "It was obvious to anyone who saw them. The way they looked at each other. The things they did for each other."

"But how do you know that they were like that when they were alone? They may have argued or said harsh things to each other in private. I mean, you said they were meant to be together, but how do you really know? Are ideas like that really possible?"

Bran thought carefully before he answered. He did not blame her for being cynical. Indeed, there were kindlier men than Roger whose treatment of their wives fell far short of the ideals held in the Northern. He looked across the river, a slight crease forming between his brows as he concentrated.

"How do I know they were meant to be together?" he repeated, turning it over in his mind. It wasn't a difficult question to answer, unless you happened to be in love with the person you were talking to.

"I won't be able to sum it up in a neat little package. I imagine Ben loved Margery at first, because she was beautiful, because of the things she spoke of, because of the way she listened to him. But as he knew her more, again I imagine that his love deepened for other reasons. Just as I know that the sun will always rise in the East, I also know that your father was not capable of hurting your mother. It would not even cross his mind. From what I could see, if he had something to say he would say it to Margery first - not because he needed her opinion, but because he wanted it - and simply liked listening to her. If he was happy about something he would share it with her first. He was comfortable with her." He looked at her. She was sitting hugging her knees. She looked at him expectantly when he stopped speaking.

He turned to face her. "They had an easy way with each other. And they delighted in being together. Their marriage was a big part of....of.... Well, who they were." He thought harder, not entirely happy with his answer. "I don't think a man loves a woman because of the way she looks or the things she does. That just starts it all. Eventually, I think a man loves the things she does because it is she that does them; he loves the ideas she speaks of because it is she who speaks of them."

Anna gave a little smile which didn't quite reach her eyes. "So she has the capacity to make him miserable, I imagine."

"Yes," he concurred, quietly. "But if he has chosen well, she never would. The only way Margery ever made Ben miserable was by leaving him behind. He still misses her."

"So you do believe in true love? Without the poisonous parts?"

"It exists, Anna."

Even surprising herself, she blurted, "Or rather true pity. The two could be easily confused." Her hand moved to the burn at her throat. He gently took her hand away and lowered his head a little so that she would look into his eyes and know that he spoke from his heart. "You are beautiful, Anna. I think you are beautiful."

She wanted to believe him, but could not hold his gaze. She gave the slightest of shrugs. "You are the kindest of gentlemen."

He looked at her, concerned at the comment, but unable to deal with it immediately as Marc, Adam and Stephen arrived out of the blue and informed them that Pudsey had had his staff prepare a meal for them. Ross was preparing things, as a penance for an incident which was glossed over, but involved Adam being wet through to the knees.

By the time Anna went back to her room that night with a full stomach and a slight buzz in her head, it was pitch black. She was not used to drinking ale rather than water, but she welcomed the way it had finally numbed the self-pity which had poisoned her insides since she overheard the Cathedral gossips. She discarded some of her clothes as tidily as she could; lay on her bed expecting to look back on the day's events, and then fell into a deep slumber which carried her through until morning.

Bran, in his own lodgings, sat at his desk, candle burning, parchment before him, quill freshly trimmed. In his slightly tipsy state, he had decided it would be a good idea to write Anna a letter showing how he felt; not to be a substitute for telling her, but she was special and he was used to recording special events. Besides, he doubted that he would do his feelings justice when he eventually plucked up the courage to tell her plainly. The letter might help her to see.

But now, seated at his desk, he did not know how to begin. He knew what he wanted to say, but could not decide which language would make the words sound the most pleasing in her head when she read it. He thought and mulled it over, wondering which sounded the best when he translated it different ways. English? Latin? Aramaic? Eventually, having decided on French, he began.

When he finished, the candle had burnt to half its length and his shoulders ached a little. Still, he sat a while longer, waiting for the ink to dry. It reminded him of a poem that his father had memorised and then written down for his mother. Bran had found it after her death and kept it to remember them by. He recalled various lines as he sat looking blindly at the sheet in front of him. It was a Hebrew poem called "The Laundress." He tried to piece the whole poem together from the fragments in his memory.

My love washes her clothes in the water of my tears

And spreads them out in the sun of her beauty.

She has no need of spring water,

She has my two eyes; nor of the sun,

She has her own radiance.

After a short while, he surveyed what he had written earlier, acting as reader now to see what impact it would have. Happy with it, he blew out the candle and crossed to his bed in the half light.

Chapter Thirty Seven

Honour Bound

Muffled footsteps and hushed voices circled about the vast interior of the Cathedral. At the back, Anna stopped breathing, her eyes wide at this fantastical petrified forest towering so high over her head. How could mere men have created something of this stature? Her gaze was drawn down the length of the nave by enormous pillars delicately chiselled with perfect geometric patterns. The walls behind were colourful with frescoes of arch- browed apostles and angels, who favoured her with their benevolent glances. She looked up the length of the nave to glimpse seemingly miniaturised Bran as he was led to the left and up to Cuthbert's shrine. Pudsey wanted him to have one last look at his original ideas even though they had spent an hour to the West of the building discussing the merits of Bran's new plans.

Being the only woman in the building made her feel conspicuous and she drew back behind the furthermost pillar, trying to make herself invisible. She glanced warily at the line, reassuring herself that she could not be accused of crossing it. Now she was here, she wondered if there was any truth in the stories of females who had been struck dead for deigning to enter the monastery. She could not help but glance heavenwards as if waiting for the thunderbolt. She took her mind from it by wondering how Bran's ideas would look should they go ahead. The walls of the Cathedral at the back had to be at least eight feet thick. She looked up the height of the huge pillar closest to her. Bran had told her that their circumference was the same measurement as their height. She studied the patterned stonework. It did not seem possible. She wished she really was invisible. Then she would see how many lengths of her girdle were needed to meet around one of the pillars - that way she could judge the length better. She stepped back a little and strained to see where the top of the pillar met the arch of the vaulting, as wary of crossing the line as she would be of falling over the edge of a chasm. She was so lost in her scrutiny that she did not realise that Bran had already rejoined her. He grinned at her.

They left the building, squinting a little in the brighter light outside. Adam and Stephen were waiting for them by the block with their mounts. It was a still grey day, much chillier than the day before. Anna was glad of the cloak Bran had given her. While she mounted, Marc had a quiet word with him. "We'll follow closely while we are still in the town, but fall back a little once we reach the road home. It's probably best to cross the river at Framwellgate - the banks will be very muddy. It rained heavily last night."

Bran nodded. He recognised the wisdom of having a friendly observer in a busy place. Drunkenness and squabbles were increasing as people became more prosperous and moved away from the watchful eyes of their fellow villagers.

The ground along Saddlergate was soft and he was watchful of Anna in case the mare slipped, especially in the bloody mess left by the butchers as they went by Fleshergate. He wondered if her back was paining her. As they passed through the hubbub of the market, he noticed that a few individuals amongst the general crowds stopped and eyed her. He urged Seer on a little so that they were in no doubt that she travelled with a companion. As they wound their way down to the buildings which lined Framwellgate Bridge, they heard two sharp raps from behind. Marc had struck the door of a building near him with the hilt of his sword. Bran and Anna turned quickly. Bran waved her to one side in case there was a scuffle, then turned quickly to join Marc and the Squires. She strained to see past them. It must be serious for them to use the two raps.

To either side of the steep street, she had noticed that there were narrower alleyways, providing short cuts for those on foot who wished to move quickly from one street to another. One of those on the left seemed particularly dark and dropped away suddenly, its endpoint quickly hidden from view by a sharp right turning bend. At the head of the entrance to this dark pathway, a roughly dressed man with dirty skin and unkempt looking hair and beard, was holding onto the arm of a girl, who was trying to pull away from him.

At first, Marc and Bran did nothing, wanting to ascertain that their suspicions were correct. No one else had bothered to intervene, but now that the Northern were involved, a small band of on-lookers began to gather. It seemed that the girl had simply been in the middle of an errand. She carried bundles of bread in her arms, presumably for sale at the market. As she tried to pull away from the man who held her, some of her goods dropped into the mud. It was obvious that she was finding it harder to protect herself because the load was precious to her and she did not want to lose all in the struggle. Marc edged his mount forward: the man so far oblivious to the attention he drew.

"Release her," he said.

The man looked up. When he noticed the two knights, he lost some of the furrows in his brow and began to smile up at them in a way he thought was disarming. He still held on tightly to his quarry; his fingernails had already left semi-circular indentations on her forearms.

"Just helping her on her way home, Sirs. She's my daughter."

Anna strained to see. There was something familiar in her looks: something around the eyes. Perhaps she had seen her the previous day as they walked through the town. She certainly was not one of the three gossips who had left her shame-faced and now doubtful of the nature of her friendship with Bran. The girl began to cry and shake her head. Marc drew his sword. Bran reiterated calmly and clearly, "The order was quite plain. Let her go. You are marking her arm."

The man's false smile switched from Marc to Bran, then vanished. He let go with a sharp upward movement of the hand, implying it was a pleasure to be rid of the baggage. He continued to glower at Bran.

Bran ignored him and spoke to the girl, who could only have been three or four years older than Janey. Twelve at most. She had bent to retrieve her soiled goods. Her hands were shaking so that she had trouble balancing the bread in the basket.

He dismounted. Anna saw the man give a sly look down the alleyway, as if considering taking his leave of them, but Stephen had also climbed down and blocked the way.

"Is this man your father?" Bran asked, helping the girl with her goods.

She shook her head.

"Do you live close by?"

She gave a nod. She felt all eyes on her and wished to be away." For the time being. I lodge with my Grandmother, but she is very ill."

"Do you know what is wrong with her?"

The girl shrugged and shook her head. "She's just dying, Sir."

"Has she an illness that could spread?"

The girl shrugged. "I have nursed her for weeks, Sir, and I am not ill."

"And your parents?"

The girl looked down at her feet. "Never known them, Sir."

Bran considered and then asked, "Are you clever? Are you good at learning?"

The girl was somewhat flummoxed at the question. She thought. "I'm told I have a good memory, Sir."

"What's your name?"

"Margaret Gill, Sir. My Grandmother is Mary."

Bran pointed out Ross and Adam to her. "These two Squires will escort you home, Margaret. They'll buy your bread and take it to the almshouses before the end of the day. Is your Grandmother well enough to travel?"

"She cannot ride, Sir."

Bran looked pointedly at the two young men. "Do you think your Grandmother would agree to come to Drysdale? We can keep an eye on the two of you."

Margaret looked up at him for the first time. "Drysdale?"

"Do you know of it?"

"Of course, Sir. Everyone knows. I would very much like to see it, Sir. They say all sorts of miracles happen there."

Bran beckoned to Ross and Adam who joined them. "Escort Margaret's grandmother to the Cathedral and ask that she is nursed until she is well enough to be transported to Drysdale. Pudsey will be quite willing to help after the money we have just saved him so he will probably offer you the use of a cart. Also ensure that this man," here he indicated the offender strung out between Marc and Stephen, "has his offence reported. Let it be known that we expect him to be punished for his actions. I will send an account of what we witnessed here and transport if it is needed."

Bran smiled his thanks, realising the young men would be disappointed at the lengthy delay to their plans. They were aware that a welcome home party for Ben was intended, and this might prevent them attending. The bemused girl was escorted back to her home.

"What's wrong for some is right for others is it?" called the prisoner.

Bran ignored him and remounted. This seemed to encourage him as he saw the advantage in ranting at someone with better manners than he, even if it was over his shoulder as Adam and Ross escorted him to Pudsey's Palace with Margaret in tow.

"Aye! Get off with yer. That's right. Ar knarr what goes on along that Dale. It'll be the last we see of that little lass once yuv got yer Divil's claws in her."

Anna felt infuriated at this sudden emergence of moral stature when he had been clearly up to no good. She shuddered at the thought of what might have happened to Margaret had they not intervened. Completely ignoring his ravings, Bran rejoined her and they continued across the bridge. As Marc and Stephen turned to follow, the man called out again.

"You've already got a whore of your arn. Ar knarr about knighthood. Ave got eyes y' knarr."

Knights and page stopped in their tracks. Anna stiffened, simply wanting to leave the place. Would people think she was another injured waif, simply staying at Drysdale as she had nowhere else to go? Marc glared at the man who still sneered at Bran. He knew what this was really about. Double standards always irked him. He said nothing, but indicated that Adam and Ross should step to one side, then gave a slight squeeze with his thigh, only perceptible to his mount. With the slightest creak of leather, the horse gave a swift, harsh, backward kick, catching the prisoner on his backside so that he landed face downward in the deeply pocked mud, the wind finally taken out of his sails. The small party continued over the bridge to rapturous applause from the onlookers. Bran gave Marc a look which almost managed to show disapproval.

Marc continued riding, and keeping his eyes ahead, said only. "She cannot be much older than Janey. I hope someone would come to her aid if she ever needed it."

Anna gave a shiver, pleased to be leaving the place at last. Bran leant in close to speak to her as they rode. "Try not to let it spoil your memory of the trip."

She put on a brave face. "I'm not as naive as I used to be."

By the time they left the busier streets for the country lanes, the sky seemed to have grown darker. The weather was kind to them, but the ground was not. As they approached Braunspeth, the mare began to snort and limp. She had thrown a shoe. Bran jumped down and helped Anna to dismount. He frowned down at the problem as he inspected the hoof, embarrassed at the shoddy workmanship. Marc and Stephen cantered up, realising something was wrong.

"You go on," Marc said to Bran. "The sky looks full. We'll take Anna's mount and have it sorted at Braunspeth. Try to get back to Redgate before the sky falls down." Anna looked up. The clouds were a leaden grey tinged with a mucky yellow. Secretly she was glad not to have the responsibility of solving the problem.

As the others left, Bran mounted Seer and looked down at her. "Trust me?"

She nodded and smiled up at him, her arms held upwards. He positioned his leg so that she would have a safe ledge to position herself and lifted her easily. Aware that she had been shifting her position to ease her back earlier in the journey, he moved in his saddle so that she could use his chest and arm as a backrest.

"Comfortable?"

"Perfect," she smiled. She was glad of it. Bracing herself against the chilly air, not to mention the tension caused by that man in the town, had pained her back more than she liked to admit. She felt the tension ease from her muscles as her nearness to Bran warmed her through.

He wanted to speak to her, but this delicious closeness seemed to have tied his tongue. Their destination grew closer, threatening to steal the moment from him. Conscious of the chill in the air, he leaned forward a little so he could enclose her more in his arms. She relaxed against him.

"How do you feel?"

She smiled, enjoying the feel of his voice close to her ear, and said simply, "Safe."

As they travelled, the daylight diminished in spite of the early hour. They stopped. Bran studied the sky. Anna waited for a decision.

"I think we should risk the mud and go through the edge of the forest where it's sheltered. If there is a storm, there are places where we can stay for a while on that route - just until it blows over."

He quickened their pace. By the time they reached the covering of the trees, drops of wetness began to fall. Not rain as expected, but snow. In Spring. They looked about them.

Anna held out a hand to catch a flake as if to check that her eyes were not deceiving her. Seer stepped into the covering of the trees where the air was still. Day had turned to night. The darkness that suddenly enveloped them was at first impenetrable. All creatures, human or otherwise, had been taken by surprise and grown still. There being no breath of air to disturb its course, the great white flakes fell in straight lines. Seer's coat and ears twitched alternately at the nearness of the soft white stuff. Anna's eyes were large and dark. She aimed to discern the origin of the flakes' descent, but they were too many and too various. It seemed they just appeared from nowhere. Looking up into the trace work of branches reminded her of the Cathedral again. Bran lowered his head to hers and whispered, "Look ahead."

In front of them, insentient, as if frozen within a diorama, stood a fallow deer. Travellers and beast gazed at one another. The creature raised its nose to sniff the air, then walked away from them into the inky security of the forest.

The motion of the snow was smooth and constant. It seemed like every living thing was transfixed by the teeming veil; except something else held Bran's eye. He gazed at Anna's pale uplifted face: hypnotised by her complexion, no more remarkable than pale, except for its luminescence; by the upward tilt of her chin, nothing out of the usual, except for the dreamy fascination it leant to her expression; by her bare throat, exposed and vulnerable, marked with the scars that simply made him consider her his gentle warrior; and by her brown eyes, no more beautiful than those of a great many women, except for the sentiment behind them as she turned to look at him now. He pulled the warmer, drier inner folds of his cloak about her, taking care to cover her hair and neck, then took a pale hand in his and gently rubbed the cold away. She smiled up at him.

Sometimes, eyes meet and a strange thing happens. Something injects the heart.

Bran put his misgivings aside and did the most obvious thing a man in a snowfall could do to show he was in love; he gently brushed his hand across her cheek to wipe away a crystal of snow. Ever so slightly, her head inclined towards his open hand. He traced the outline of her face and bent to kiss her then pulled her closer against him and they sat, warm and still, while the snow fell silently over them. Presently, he spoke.

"Come back with me to Drysdale, Anna. Marry me."

She stirred a little so she could see his face. The hush of the near-night made her whisper. "Please do not feel that you have to ask me this. I do not presume it of you just because you asked me before the troubles. I realise you may pity me, but …."

He shook his head. "Pity you? Pity me, Anna. Circumstance and cowardice may have worked against us, but my feelings for you have not changed; nor will they. I've always loved you, but I know I have been in love since that day I came back from Europe almost a year ago. Remember? The day before the hunt. You were climbing the hill to sit above the house." He smiled, remembering. "It wasn't pity that took my breath away. I knew I wanted to marry you then. Pity how I felt when you shared your problem of a proposal from an unknown suitor."

She remembered how he had spoken to her when the rest of the household had gone to their beds. She did not pull away from him, but the seconds passing felt like hours to Bran. He felt his heart begin to sink. Perhaps she was angry with him for not telling her before Roger's arrival. Perhaps she blamed him for losing her child.

"If you cannot love me I'll understand, Anna. I shall not speak of it again."

She shook her head and put her fingers almost to his lips. "A man like you should marry a lady of renown, a great lady, a princess, or even a...."

He shifted in the saddle so they could look at each other. "Anna. I love you. If I had the means and magic to conjure up my perfect woman, here she would be."

She smiled, but there was an awkwardness that worried him.

"Please tell me, Anna. Tell me why you think we would not be perfect as man and wife."

Apart from having had her confidence shaken from eavesdropping the day before, there was another issue and she felt it unfair not to speak of it. And she would not allow the tears pricking her eyes to hold sway in the matter. Even though she wanted desperately to give a simple yes there would be no emotional blackmail from this lady. But he had guessed her fears already. He held her closer to him. She paused until she was able to trust her voice, then said with as practical air as she could muster, "You should at least marry a lady who can give you a child. A man like you should have as many heirs as possible. There aren't enough good people in the world as it is."

"Is that what you think?" He rested his chin above her head and folded his arms more tightly about her. "Let's work this out, shall we?"

She waited for him to begin. Seer shifted a little.

"A man never knows before he marries whether a lady is able to have his child, or at least if he does, he probably hasn't chosen the most gentlemanly route to wedlock."

She answered, "But if he marries a lady, knowing full well that she has had problems in the past, would he not have been wiser to look for a wife elsewhere?"

"Wouldn't he be cruel to marry one lady knowing that his heart belonged to another, and always would?"

She didn't answer. He took her hands again and stayed close. "There is no certainty that you cannot have children in the future, and while finding out, I would rather it was me by your side to keep you safe. Besides which, a man can grow to love children who aren't his own: children of good parents who have been wrenched from us. Who still deserve the chance of a good life. Just as your father became a good father to me."

Against his chest, he felt her head move a little, as if she wanted to make sure that she heard him clearly. He continued. "But the same logic doesn't apply when it comes to the way a man loves a woman. True love, I mean. He can truly love and protect substitute children and give them as happy a life as possible, but he cannot love a substitute wife as much as the woman he truly loves. I love you, Anna. I marry you or I marry no one. And what of children then?"

She sat up so she could look at him. He asked again. "Will you marry me?"

She reached up to touch his face, finally allowing herself to see him: the shape of his mouth, the smoothness of his brow, the soft intensity of his eyes, the breadth of his chest. Not a Godfather; not a foster brother; not a mentor; but a man. She smiled and whispered, "Yes."

He gave her a lingering kiss that warmed and quickened her blood.

As if to dilute some of the intensity of the moment, she put her head to one side, frowning slightly. "Are we allowed? Will the Church be unhappy? Or the King?"

He laughed, nothing able to stop his euphoria at her answer. "I'm a diplomat. I'll solve it."

Their voices rang through the boughs. She gave a wicked smirk. "Even if they say no, I'll run away with you. We'll live on berries and melted snow."

He smiled, urging Seer forward. "We'll build another Drysdale. Only the Northern will know of its whereabouts."

"I almost hope they do turn us down," she mused. "A secret world peopled by Drysdale's brightest and finest." She sighed and then added as a modest afterthought, "And me."

The evening must have warmed a little as the snow had turned much wetter. As Seer moved forward, Bran held out a hand to catch a few drops, then felt the dark blue cloak that covered them both. "We need to find shelter before our clothes are soaked."

The pine offered little protection from the wet; indeed, the drops from the branches were even larger and wetter than those that fell directly from the sky.

"There is an empty croft not far from here. It won't take long if we ride harder for a short time."

She shifted position a little and held tight as he steered them quickly between the trees. Eventually, the track broadened and they joined a road with ruts worn deep by wagons over the winter. A few hundred yards further and they dropped abruptly to the left, where a building perfect for bedraggled travellers was nestled a little way below them. Bran dismounted first, tethering Seer at the most sheltered side of the building. He lifted Anna down and helped her find her way down the dark, overgrown path and through the doorway. The only window on this side of the building was next to the door, which needed a generous shove to open it. He retrieved the saddle to keep the leather dry, then set to work, lighting a fire before it became more difficult to see. Anna sat on the one bench while he struck the flints, his face periodically appearing like a golden mask, then disappearing again, until, finally, the fire caught and grew in strength, lending a lambent glow to the otherwise comfortless room. It was enough to see by and, presently, it was enough to keep them warm. This done, he brought the parcel of food given to him by Pudsey's staff. They sat facing the fire.

"Now for the feast." He waggled the water container at her, making her smile. The smoke meandered around the room, finding its way to the roof and its staggered exit which howled in the wind, but at least kept the rain outside. Anna became aware of a coldness spreading over her shoulder as wetness from her hair seeped through her dress. She decided to untie it to give it a better chance of drying. She spoke as she untwined the leather that held the braid. "Have you needed to stay here before?"

"Once or twice. With Marc. The weather can be foul up here."

A gust of wind gave a howling shove at the door as if to prove him right. She smiled across at him and then turned back to her task. There was something comforting about being sheltered from such a storm in spite of its nearness. Bran placed a chunk of wood on the fire from a ready made pile in the far corner of the room, then sat back on the bench next to her. The fire spat and sparked a little. "May I do that for you?"

She nodded. He straddled the bench so he could reach her hair more easily, putting his hands around her waist and pulling her a little towards him so that she could rest her back against him while he reached in front of her to unwind the thong woven into the braid. A smell of violets was freed as his fingers worked.

"Tell me if I hurt you." His voice tickled her ear and sent ripples down her side.

"You're very gentle." He separated the wet rope of hair and arranged it so it fell over his arm towards the firelight, allowing it to dry more quickly. He kept his arms about her, making a protective barrier between the dampness of her hair and her clothes.

Anna thought of the gossips outside the Cathedral. She found that today she could dismiss their remarks far more easily. She smiled, thinking how lucky she was to be right here, right now, and not caring what anyone else thought. He leaned forward a little. "That's a satisfied smile."

"I overheard something yesterday, while I waited for you by the Palace walls." She stopped, realising she could be talking herself into an embarrassing corner.

"I'm intrigued. Will you share what you heard?"

She paused and considered his hands as she leaned against him, her head to one side. "Some young women were discussing the men in the Northern. They had not seen me."

"God or bad?" he asked.

"Oh good; definitely good. They were rather overawed by you."

He gave a soundless laugh. "I suppose other men, like the one in town earlier, make it easy for us."

"Maybe," she said, doubtfully, then said no more, in spite of each other's smiles.

He loved her closeness, her warmth, the movement of her body as she breathed and spoke.

"Will and Leona are organising celebrations at Drysdale for your father's return. We can escort him from Redgate. And, of course, I have other reasons for being so eager to meet with him before anyone else – I would like his blessing on our marriage. Do you think he will be happy for us?"

She looked at him almost upside down. "Of course. He loves you dearly. He thinks I am in safe hands when I am with you."

"In that case, there is a gift I need to give you, which is also at Redgate."

"You have already given me a beautiful cloak and a fine mare."

"They were gifts to celebrate your recovery. This will be a wedding present."

She sat up a little so she could turn to look at him. "You must be careful not to spoil me."

"When you receive this gift, it should show you how long I have loved you. Besides, we can share it."

She could not help smiling as she pondered on what it might be and turned to lean her back against him once more, lest he think her last words were insincere.

"Would Queen Eleanor have been allowed to cross the line in the Cathedral?"

He laughed at her butterfly mind. "No, not even Eleanor."

"Not even if she could wax lyrical about groins and squinches?"

"You've been paying attention."

"Well, eavesdropping. It's not quite the same. I love the sound of squinches but I have no idea what they are."

"Remember the towers?"

"Um," she nodded. "Are they squinches?"

He shook his head and drew shapes in the air in front of her. "Across the angles of the towers' walls are squinches – platforms – Puiset may wish to extend upwards some day – or a future Prince Bishop. Perhaps add a roof or a differently shaped tower. Changing the shape of the cathedral changes Durham's skyline, so it makes quite a statement. If it happens, it will be the squinches that the new work will rest upon."

"Oh," she sounded disappointed. "I thought they had something to do with towers, but I was imagining squinches as winged, furry animals that make their home up there." She grinned. "And I could not possibly tell you what I imagined when I heard you discussing barrel and groin vaulting."

Bran smiled. "Now do you see the danger of allowing women into monastic buildings?"

"Will the Galilee Chapel resemble the rest of the cathedral?"

He thought awhile. "It will be lower and smaller, so the pillars will not need to be so thick and strong because they will not need to support so much weight. It should seem spacious and light, in spite of its size, because of the number of windows."

"Will they allow women in there as you suggested?"

"Perhaps. It will be a Lady Chapel in that it's dedicated to Mary, so it would be rather fitting if they finally allowed female worshippers to have access. I could suggest it again next time I meet one of Pudsey's hangers on."

"Is that one of the skills of diplomacy? To get others to suggest things?"

"It can help lay down a route through the political mire." She felt his breath warming her neck, and having considered what he had said more carefully, she turned to face him again. Her face was more serious. She hesitated, leaned forward and kissed his brow, then sat back and looked at him. "Everything has to be thought through so carefully. There is no easy way for you, is there?"

He stroked her cheek and rested his forehead against hers. "There are no easy ways for most of us."

"I'll do my best to make you happy, Bran," she whispered.

He let his fingers become entangled in her hair and kissed her mouth. They looked at each other a good long while. His head told him that the gentlemanly thing to do was to withdraw so that she could have the bench to herself and he would stop wanting her so much: but not yet. The rest of his body dictated that he should stay. They were intimate again and he did not want to dismiss the new mood so quickly. Besides, she had leaned against him again and it would also be gentlemanly to provide a backrest to ease the pain in her spine. He threaded his arms beneath hers and clasped his hands at her stomach once more, allowing himself the luxury of a kiss on the nape of her neck.

Both were aware of the other's heart beating faster and stronger. Absently, Anna felt her hair, her fingertips brushing his ear. He took her hand, holding it up gently in the firelight. "Such slender wrists." He traced a line along the back of her hand to the paler, smoother underside of her arm. She closed her eyes. His fingertips sent a line of pleasure through her as they moved towards her shoulder and breast.

Her voice was a whisper, "You feel so warm. Do I feel cold to you?"

"Beautifully cool." He kissed her cheek and slowly moved to get up, knowing there was a risk of things going too far before he had spoken to Ben. He imagined her father looking in at the window to spur him into action, but it did not prevent him feeling cold and neglectful of her feelings. He knelt on the floor in front of her and smiled, an air of reticence overcoming him.

"You know, just because a man will not dishonour his Lady, it does not mean that he…" he paused, "that he wouldn't like to." He grinned down at her self-consciously.

She smiled, understanding rather than judging his need to let her know. He leaned forward and kissed her brow. "Let me make you comfortable for the night, Anna."

He supported her back and helped her to ease herself down full length on the bench. A roar from outside and a whistle at the door frame signalled that heavier rain was on its way. As Bran arranged the blanket to cushion her better, a cold draught slid its way under the door.

"You must not sleep on the floor. It's turning colder."

He smiled down on her. "I won't be asleep."

The rain began its assault on the croft, allied with the wind which dashed clattering waves of pebble like drops against the door and window. Bran stood to discern whether Seer was at the most sheltered place now that the wind had changed. Satisfied, he pulled the saddle in front of the door, draped their wet clothes a little closer to the fire and returned to his place at her makeshift bedside.

"Is your bedding soft enough?"

She nodded, but he could tell her head was not resting comfortably. He pulled his robe over his shoulders and folded it to make a cushion. For the moment, he was doctor again.

"There. Try that. How is it?"

"Um. Soft." She almost purred. "And warm." She turned her head to look at him. "But what about you? Won't you be cold?"

"I'll be fine." He kissed her brow. "I'll keep a fire going. Besides, it's best if I stay awake. I talk in my sleep."

She grinned up at the ceiling. "I know." She noticed his confusion and laughed, turning to lie on her side so she could face him as she spoke. "You said a great many things," she raised an eyebrow.

He stroked away the hair that had fallen over her face. Even through his chemise, she could not help being aware of his body. He leaned closer to her, allowing his arm to fall across the bench above her head and his hand to rest at her shoulder. Outside, the rain had become so heavy that it was impossible to discern the separate drops. The droning of the downpour became suddenly louder, almost as if someone had opened the door. Both looked towards it, then smiled at each other's shared thought.

Bran asked, "Will you tell me what I said, or torment me mercilessly?"

"I don't think I could possibly tell you."

"Really? It was that bad?" He wondered if his hidden rage had shown itself.

She bent her arm so that she could clasp her hands under her ear to pillow her cheek. "Oh, not so much bad, as indecipherable."

He gave a relieved smile. He knew his vivid dreams had returned over the past few weeks and they were unlikely to go until Edwin was apprehended and his sentence carried out.

"You have been a good doctor to me."

He bent his head and kissed her ear. "Just returning the favour."

She raised her head to free a hand and gently pulled the thin stuff of his chemise to one side, revealing the area of his worst wound from the attack in the forest. She did it as tenderly as the day it had been inflicted. Her touch sent gooseflesh over the surface of his skin. He watched her face as she touched him.

"So hard to see now," she whispered. "But it was so close to your heart, I was afraid." She traced the scar that ran parallel with his rib and looked at him.

He whispered, "You healed me well." And bent again to kiss her mouth.

She looked back. There were other, newer scars that he must have accrued over the past few months. A particularly long, pale weal ran in an almost vertical line down his stomach. "This is a bad one." She lifted the hem of his shirt to follow the scar to its end. He obliged her and pulled it over his head, laying it over her so his body heat warmed her hip. She studied him the way an awestruck explorer studies a new map, taking in the shape of his body and the marks he had suffered.

"Who did this?"

"Someone fighting for the Scottish King."

She imagined the chaos and the hurt. His skin felt warm and smooth beneath her hand, making her more aware of his vulnerability. He watched her face and she looked up at him. "I can't bear to think of you being hurt."

He stroked her hair and kissed her throat where Roger had burnt her. "Nor I you."

She did not flinch away as he touched the old wound as she would have done in the past. She turned onto her back and he moved closer, kissing her mouth again, enjoying the fullness of her lips. She stroked his bare shoulder and they looked at each other for a long while, ignoring the drumming rain.

"I should let you sleep." They held each other's gaze.

She traced the outline of the muscle that ran from his shoulder down to his chest. The last thing he wanted was sleep. Unconsciously, her free hand travelled to her own scars. "You could rid me of him once and for all. Make it feel like it never happened."

Her eyes were large and dark in the shadows. He kissed her brow, her cheek, her mouth, her throat. He felt his heart quicken and forced himself to move onto his knees to put some distance between them. This wouldn't do for her. The last place he ought to be making love to Anna was in a deserted croft on a makeshift bed; but the longer he stayed close to her, the more their surroundings became insignificant. He found he could not draw his eyes away from her face. He was drunk on her.

"I'm sorry I couldn't keep him from hurting you, Anna. I should have let you know how I felt earlier."

"Any hurts I have felt have never been down to you."

He shook his head. "He was a fool. Not to see what he had." He kissed her gently, stroking her hair. She slipped her arms around his neck and he held her closer, kneeling upright as he sought her mouth with his. As they kissed, he lifted her and lowered her closer to the circle of warmth from the fire. He knelt over her, unable to look away. "Know how much I love you, Anna."

She reached up, stroked his bare shoulders and gently pulled him towards her so she could kiss his mouth once more. He ran his fingers under the collar of her gown and chemise, baring her shoulders, and trailed his lips along her throat. On raising his head, he gazed at her face, stroking her hair, able only to whisper. "I have to know that you are sure."

Her eyes darkened and she nodded. He allowed his forehead to rest against hers, a pounding euphoria in his heart. Shifting a little, she stroked her cheek against his, causing them both to close their eyes at the pleasure of simply being so close. He lay beside her and she watched him, doe-eyed and silent, as he undressed. As the rain continued its relentless battery, she allowed her eyes to explore his body: his fire-lit skin shone golden; old wounds only managing to highlight the smoothness of what remained undamaged. He watched her as her eyes moved down to his waist and hips, feeling almost abashed at how she seemed to want him when she looked back into his eyes. He loosened the ribbon at her side to allow her clothing to be pulled further from her shoulders and beyond then lightly trailed his fingers over the soft, pale skin of her stomach. He hardly touched her, but she felt every nerve arching towards him, wanting to feel him close against her. Leaning forward, he kissed her brow and whispered, "If I do anything that hurts you, let me know. I only want to make you happy."

She stroked his cheek and he kissed the palm of her hand, her brow, her mouth, her throat; moved over her and ran his lips over her stomach, her hips, her thighs; his warm hands pulling her gown over her feet, then stroking her skin, easing away her tension. She sighed and relaxed, enjoying her nakedness, feeling herself opening to him, and a fluttering over her abdomen. His touch, so slight, created ripples of warming pleasure. The tip of his tongue, quick and light as a candle flame, only just barely flickered against her. She closed her eyes. He was so gentle that she had no inkling of whether he was touching her with his tongue, his fingertips, or both – she felt nothing but the pleasure he created as it grew from a series of perfect ripples to a constant intense wave, which coiled and grew and threatened to break as her heart quickened and her blood pounded. As if he felt it too, he moved forward to lean over her so he could kiss her face, then gazed and gazed, enjoying the feel of her cool stomach against his warm skin. He stroked her hair from her brow and she closed her eyes at his touch. "Are you sure, Anna?"

She nodded. He kissed her brow, then looked into her eyes and, as he gently pushed into her, a mutual smile of pleasure passed between them and their eyes shone. Everything else was forgotten; they were lost in each other's healing, each brush of lips and meeting of eyes a powerful drug sending their hearts racing. The firelight made a shadow play of their lovemaking, surrounding them with inseparable, shifting figures. She was beautiful, making his head spin; her look an aphrodisiac.

How could such a powerful man have such a subtle touch? She stroked his back, feeling his tender movements drawing out the pleasures her body could reap, given the right look, the right touch, the right man. His warmth and the intermittent cool draughts of air from the door frame played across her in turn, making her heart quicken once more. She gave an almost languorous stretch and he bent to kiss her, then gazed down at her, smiling, feeling her coming closer. She met his gaze, whispering his name: his name; not Bran but Saul. She took him by sweet surprise and, as she saw this in his face, she whispered "Saul" again. The appetite in his abdomen grew and would be, had to be, satisfied, and he came and came and came. He slid his hands under her shoulders, holding her close, his face buried in her hair. He had done what he promised himself he would not do and a sharp pang of guilt stabbed at his chest. He cradled her head, kissed her cheek and looked at her. She guessed from his look what was on his mind and lifted her head to kiss his mouth, then placed her fingers gently against his lips. "Do not say sorry."

He kissed her fingertips, all guilt dispelled. Of course he wasn't sorry. No one would spoil this for them – especially himself. He reached for his now crumpled chemise, lay by her side and pulled it over them, lying so he could cradle her better and she could nestle her head under his chin. He put his arm about her shoulders and kissed her hair. Somehow, he felt stronger.

He felt her head shift on his arm and her whisper tickle his ear, "I love you."

The words made him smile. "God, I love you, Anna." And he buried his cheek more deeply into her hair and they lay quietly, enjoying the contrast of the stillness inside the room with the tumult outside. She took his hand and put it to her lips, wanting him to know how close she felt to him. He sighed again, "There cannot be a man in the entire world who loves a woman as much as I love you."

She tilted her face and they looked at one another.

"I won't let anyone spoil this for us, Anna." He stroked his thumb across her temple and lifted her gently. They both sensed a different type of want this time and paused, their breathing deep and matched. He knelt and helped her onto his lap, as they touched, teased, stroked, kissed, whispered gently, longingly, fiercely; he stroked his hands across her back as she raised herself to take him and held her closer as they moved. So overwhelmed by her that it almost felt like sadness, he stroked a hand through her hair and rested his chin on her shoulder, kissed her ear and whispered that he loved her – in English, French, Latin, Hebrew – and with each change in language she felt a new wave of pleasure wash over her. How did he know it would do that to her? And he whispered her name, again and again. She loved the sound on his lips. And the way his fingertips trailed down her stomach and found where they met, and played against her, magnifying the pleasure she already felt. He kissed her brow and told her how beautiful she looked; how beautiful she felt; how much he loved her; how many times he had dreamed of them making love; how she was always on his mind, no matter where he was; how good her body felt against his; how, when they were married, he would take her in every room in the house, at every time of day; how he would undress her slowly after finding an excuse to send everyone away; how he would kiss every inch of her body, while jealous knights would hide and watch because she was so beautiful. As he described how he would lie naked with her on the trace room floor where anyone might walk past and see them, she gave a beautiful, moaning sigh and he pulled her close against him, keeping her close, kissing her and telling her how much he loved her so that she might not feel guilty at their want. She nestled against him while her heart quietened. He put the blanket about her shoulders, and held her closely, hoping she did not think he had gone too far, too soon. Presently, she shifted against him and raised her head. He looked at her to judge her mood, careful not to break one of Joss's rules – never ask how it was. She smiled up at him. "I'm going to enjoy being married to you, aren't I?"

He relaxed, smiled and held her close.

Although the night was ugly and the light from the window inviting, Marc knew better than to join his friends in the croft. Much to a bedraggled Stephen's disappointment, they pressed on through the darkness, leading the mare through the two further miles of pitted mud that would spit them out at Redgate.

Chapter Thirty Eight

Fragments

A calm and shadow-dappled morning immersed the croft, with nothing to show for the previous wild night but damp-darkened thatch and light scatterings of twigs. Seer had moved himself from the makeshift shelter by the stonework and clambered out of the shade and up the bank to where the grass was a greener shade of lush. The morning sun managed to squeeze its way through the mud spattered window on the eastern side of the door to touch Anna's pale, bare shoulder. Bran lay on his side, gazing down at where she lay in her cloak, the silk lining against her skin. Finally content in the knowledge that she felt the same as he did, he took a deep, euphoric breath. He wasn't simply a puppet to Want. He cared for her, just as he always had, but now she was his. And it felt amazing.

He had no idea how long he stared down on her, but the sun finally moved across her face, causing her to stir a little and turn her head towards his chest. When she woke, he kissed her brow and continued to gaze. Eyes shining, she reached up and gently stroked his cheek. He took her hand and kissed her palm. "Still want to marry me?"

She wove her fingers into his hair and gently pulled him closer. Her whispered "Yes" sounded deliciously in his ear.

He rested his brow gently against hers. She gave a catlike stretch, allowing the cloak to fall open a little, revealing the patterned lining and her pale torso. Sleepily, she said, "The silk feels beautiful."

He smiled and lowered his head to kiss her stomach then rested his cheek against her ribs, listening to her heart beating. "Silk on silk."

Lying as they were, his manner showing a loving deference towards her, strengthened her somehow and as his voice sounded through her, she folded her arms about his shoulders, so he would know how much he meant to her. Without raising his head, he spoke again. "I wrote a letter to you."

"To me?"

"Yes. The night before last. After we supped with Pudsey."

"At such a late hour?"

"Um. In case I was too much of a coward to tell you how much I loved you before we reached home."

She ran a hand through his hair, enjoying the warm nearness of his cheek on her stomach. "There was no need. I have always loved you."

He raised his head and leaned on his elbow once more, liking her answer.

She smiled up at him coyly. "I used to daydream about you."

As he stroked her hair away from her brow, his fingers brushed against something behind her head. He picked it up and they exchanged a look of recognition. It was the now empty bottle of oil Marc had given him. He stretched over her to place it on the bench and she could not resist trailing her fingers over his skin, enjoying the novelty of intimacy with this man she had known since she was born. Bran lay by her side again, holding her closer. He cradled her head, kissed her hair and asked, "Would you share your daydreams with me?"

She blushed. "Perhaps one day."

She rested her cheek against his chest, and laid her forearm across him. It seemed impossible to touch him too much. "May I read the letter you wrote?"

He moved under her, giving a quiet laugh. "If you promise not to be cruel to a poor man when his heart and soul are laid bare."

She tilted her chin and kissed just below his ear. He said nothing more on the matter but stretched his bare foot towards the doorway and the saddle he had placed there the night before. She watched as he unhooked a leather bag by its strap with his toe and then bent his leg and took the bag with his free hand.

"You're very …..flexible," remarked Anna, raising her hand to take the proffered letter. "Are you sure you want me to read it?"

He nodded. "Even more so now than when I wrote it."

She turned onto her back in order that she might use both hands to unroll it and angle it towards what little light there was. Bran turned on his side to watch her as she read, uncomfortable, not so much at the prospect of Anna knowing how he felt, but at the thought that the letter was not good enough: that his expression might not have done his feelings justice. His heart as well as his language skills were open to scrutiny and he could not prevent himself from making her aware of parts of the letter he felt worthy of criticism – as if his criticism would prevent her own need to find fault. "I left it unsigned," he apologised, then tried to explain why. "Bringing it to an end never seemed appropriate. It would be like saying, all of the above is as much as I can find to praise in you. A signature seemed to cut short the way I felt….the way I shall always feel."

She looked at him and smiled. "That's a lovely thing to say."

Self-consciously, he lifted his arms and placed his hands over his eyes, remembering something from their love-making and wondering whether he should bring it up. He took a deep breath. "Perhaps it was the right decision after all. Last night, you called me Saul."

"Do you mind?"

He shook his head and when he looked at her his eyes shone. "It felt amazing." Then he lay on his back and looked into the rafters, deciding any further interruptions would simply delay rather than remove his torment. He tried to be patient: counting the beams, studying the existing smoke hole to see how it could be made more efficient, but all the while he was aware of Anna's raised hands. She seemed so very still. Finally, when far more time than she needed to read it had passed and she had rested her arms, but still said nothing, he could no longer bear it. Quite stupidly, he asked, "Have you read it?"

She lay still, her eyes closed. She nodded a little in response to his question, swallowed then whispered, "Three times." Her lashes were wet. He turned back onto his side, put his arm around her and pulled her closer. "I didn't want to make you sad, Anna."

She put her arms around his neck, holding him near. "You echo what I think and feel. It's as if there was a reason for what went before. No one could deserve this sort of happiness without paying through suffering first. And you wrote the same."

They lay quietly for a long while. Presently, she spoke again, "It is a beautiful letter. No one else should ever read it. It's too precious to risk being seen by prying eyes."

"Do you have an idea?"

She considered, then, rather self-consciously, said, "Perhaps we could memorise the whole, then each take a part of it. Each of us would know that the other always carried the other half – making it whole. But if it fell into the wrong hands, no one could share its full meaning."

"I like that," he said. "Especially if it was to be torn from top to bottom rather than side to side – so we shared everything from first to last."

"Yes." She sat up, leaning on her palm, and smiled down at him, "Thank you."

"For what?"

"Knowing me well enough to see that I hoped you would propose again."

He smiled and took her hand. "Your father should be back at Redgate by now. Shall we speak to him as soon as possible?"

She nodded. "I think he'll be pleased."

"I hope so."

"You think he has reason to be disappointed?"

Bran shook his head.

"He loves you very much," she reassured him, "and so do I." She reached to her side and picked up the letter again, smiling.

"That's a nice smile."

She held the letter carefully once more. "There are so many things to make me smile in here." She indicated the parchment, then looked down at him and stroked his cheek, "And here."

He sat up, edging himself behind her, and looked over her shoulder, putting his arms around her that they might read the letter together. She relaxed against him and watched as his hands straightened the parchment. He rested his chin on her shoulder. "I worried that you might think some of my words presumptuous."

She could already guess which parts, but said, "Show me."

Although his face was not visible to her, she could hear the smile in his voice. "Well, for instance, where I speak of two becoming one."

She put her head on one side, pretending to give the matter some serious thought. "I had imagined you meant that we thought as one."

He held her a little closer and whispered in her ear, "I already felt quite safe presuming we think the same way." He put the letter down and bared then kissed her neck. "I'm afraid I have to be honest with you, Anna. I was speaking of our minds, souls and bodies."

She bent her head, allowing him to brush her hair back from her shoulders and then lower her gently on her side. Lying behind her, he stroked her hip. He moved his hand over her stomach, shaping himself against her and stroking her skin as she arched her back in another catlike stretch. "What sort of wife would I be," she sighed, "if I was critical of my husband's honesty?"

Chapter Thirty Nine

Avowal

The day was chilly but the air calm with a brightness that made the snow on the hills west of Redgate dazzle. Ben, cloakless, stopped midway between the house and the start of the tree-covered slope, unfolded his arms and held his chilled fingers to his brow in order that he might survey Bran's architecture without squinting. His contented sigh momentarily left a swirl of mist in the air in front of him. He had known Bran would do Anna proud. Thank God that business with Harun's sister was over. He hoped Azra and Ralph's proposed visit to Drysdale before leaving for Spain would not give rise to any awkwardness.

Just as he had the night before, he stepped up to the entrance of the library, hoping to see the interior in daylight this time, but before he could enter, a piercing whistle sounded from behind him. He shook his head at Marc's newfound way of catching people's attention because he had discovered it worked so well with his children.

"They're back," called Marc. Ben followed his gaze through the near naked trees, thanking God under his breath that they were safe, even though their arrival made imminent some rather uncomfortable business.

Since the dawn sky had lightened to a red mottled pale blue, he had kept a wary eye on the road from Durham: in spite of Edwin being under lock and key; in spite of the rebellion being in its final death throes; in spite of the King's popularity being on the rise again since he had made it known that he would walk barefoot to Canterbury and do penance for his involvement in Beckett's slaying. Ben surveyed his land satisfied with his lot. Yes. He had made the right decision. This was all he had ever wanted. Contentment was not far off, but, as was usual in life, there were just a few more hurdles to jump before they were out of the woods completely. William the Lyon had still to be apprehended, and there would be those in England who would be poised and waiting to see whether France and the Princes still had an attack left in them. They had Edwin now, but he wondered, with so many of them having a score to settle with him, whether it would delay the sentence actually being carried out. There was a time when he would have put his own case for being the one to preside over the hearing, but he had grown a little weary with it all lately. He had other things on his mind. He sighed and rubbed some of the numbness from his hands. These problems seemed as nothing when compared to the issue he had yet to broach with Anna and Bran. Was broach the right word? It had been on his mind for so long it felt more like a conclusion. The two people...the two living people most precious to him would need to learn something he would rather they did not.

On seeing Ralph and Azra in Yorkshire, he could tell, more from things that were said than the fall of

Azra's dress, that she was with child. Ralph's or Bran's? He hoped he had done the right thing by agreeing to their stay. And of course, the other problem: there was Adela. He hoped Joss would not be angry. And if he was…well; there were some things the Northern's strength and the King's favour could not solve.

Behind him, Marc went into the stables to check that the mare would pass inspection should Bran and Anna want to check on her. He hoped Ben's uncharacteristically distracted manner was not a sign that he disapproved of Bran being alone with his daughter for so long. Passing a hand over the mare's polished shoulder, he wondered how the night had gone for them. "I hope you were right, Susan," he whispered.

Ben imagined that Bran would take his time on this final part of the journey and made a retreat into the house where he could wait in the warmth. Besides, if he greeted them from the doorway as they arrived, Anna's attention would not be drawn too quickly to the newly unveiled building.

With the household sadly depleted, Ben was able to sit on his own by the fire in the Hall. A shaft of honey coloured sunlight fell through the window to the south, freshening the colours in the wall hangings: the same tapestries Margery had brought with her from Beau Repaire. Reflecting, Ben rested his gaze blindly on the patterns and figures before him.

"I hope you don't mind, love. It never really was for me. You were the only part of Beau Repaire that I ever wanted." Ben knew the King did not really understand his refusal; such a vast area of fertile land, with good hunting too: but he did like the reasoning behind the land being used for a monastery. It would thrive under the monks and should prevent those with appetites to match Edwin's growing too ambitious.

Ben stirred himself on hearing hooves outside, realising it was nearly time. Marc had not exactly told him that Bran and Anna had grown close, but his inability to hide his smile on telling him that they would be arriving separately, as well as Will's exuberance on describing the gifts he had given her before the journey, said it all. At least Will was busy this morning, he and Leona having ridden over to Drysdale with Leonard, presumably to draw out how he felt about Tilly, although ostensibly, Will said the purpose for the trip was to look out for Adam and Ross and their escorts. And of course, Ben was pleased for his children. They were a perfect match. But that had not eased the queasiness that had irked him ever since he had seen how Bran had looked at her on the day of the hunt, nor prevented the sudden panic when Harun suggested Anna might need blood. To think, he had thought Walter would have allowed him to ignore the issue. He wondered whether Marc and Will would need to know. Probably not. And over time it would become insignificant.

He hoped Joss would be here soon, even if that meant knowing Edwin was in their midst once more. He needed Joss to be here for this. He could not do it without him – or should not. He tapped his fingertips across the torn page he had been holding as if he had finally made a decision, before easing it back inside Marge's diary. The little book, decorated with an M now so faded that Ben did not know whether he simply imagined it was still there, was pocketed deep inside his cloak. He sighed, stood up and passed through the shaft of light to the doorway. He hesitated to speak briefly with his dead wife. "Help me to tell it as it truly was, Marge."

Taking a deep breath, he crossed the threshold. Bran was already helping Anna down. Lingering looks and an almost tangible magnetism between the two told him they had recently made love. He could hardly criticize him for lack of respect. She would be dead if it was not for him.

"Your journey went well?" asked Bran.

Ben smiled, "Very. And yours?"

Bran nodded a little self-consciously.

They followed Ben into the house, through the Hall and into the private chamber. It was beautifully warm. Having discarded their cloaks, Ben indicated they should take a seat.

"I need to show you the land rights the king has granted various members of the Northern," he said and then waved a hand in the direction of the table top where what appeared to be a scattering of dust and rags lay.

Bran leaned forward to inspect it although his mind was really on other things.

Ben folded his arms and joined in the scrutiny. "This is what we took from Beau Repaire the night that Marion was killed. The evidence has been safely locked away for almost ten years."

Bran now saw the collection with fresh eyes: the bloodstained chemise, the monkshood leaves, quite dry now, and the cup that had held the juice from the yew berries. To one side of these were tatters of faded green, bloodstained cloth.

"Of course, it would be hard to convict Edwin with this evidence alone. The juice and leaves are unrecognisable now, but that will make little difference to the overall outcome. He has murdered and schemed throughout this rebellion, fanning the flames when the troubles might have ended otherwise. However," he said, picking up a crisp grey shred, "I simply could not feel a sense of completion if we did not show him that we knew of his crimes against Marion and Catherine."

"His trial is imminent then?" asked Bran.

Ben nodded, "Joss is bringing him here today."

Bran glanced at Anna, wondering how she felt about her father speaking of Catherine. Should he ask Ben about their marriage now or wait until this business with Edwin was over. As if reading his mind, Anna nodded.

Ben looked at them and waited while Bran tried to phrase what he wanted to say. "We have news..that is…with your blessing…we have news." Ben smiled at Bran's unusual floundering.

"You have something you wish to ask me?"

The couple smiled. Bran took Anna's hand then sighed and turned his head towards the window, hearing more arrivals outside.

"Please excuse me," Ben said apologetically, and left the room in order to meet his guests.

"Do you think he is displeased?" asked Bran.

Anna shook her head.

"I had hoped to speak with him before he was distracted by Edwin."

Anna stood up, leaned over him and kissed his brow. "We have all our lives to look back at this and smile."

"If Joss comes back with him, do you want me to wait until we have Ben alone, or to carry on?"

Anna considered, her head to one side, "Let's do it. Joss would be the first to know anyway."

He pulled her closer, resting his cheek against her waist. The transience of what he had had with Catherine made him relish the reality of Anna. "Did you notice anything different when you arrived?" he asked her.

She stroked his hair, looking down at him while she pondered. "About father?"

He looked up at her and smiled. "Not even warm."

On hearing footsteps, Anna took her seat once more. The latch lifted and Ben and Joss entered the room.

"Is Edwin here?" asked Bran.

Joss nodded. "Safely stowed in the oubliette." He took a seat at the window.

Ben smiled at the company, realising how awkward the couple must be feeling after all the interruptions. "I believe Bran and Anna have some news for us."

Joss gave Bran a steady look. Bran reached across to Anna, took her hand, then looked at Ben. He kept it simple. "Anna and I wish to marry. We hope to have your blessing."

The two older men looked at each other. "Of course you have," said Ben, then opened his arms to embrace Anna who had been far more nervous than she had cared to admit and was already on her feet with her arms about her father's neck.

Joss smiled at Bran. "A perfect match, I would say." He turned to his old friend. "And courteously dealt with by Ben. A lot of fathers like to torment their future sons first – just to keep them in line."

"I'm not the only one showing courtesy," added Ben. "Joss also has some good news, but has delayed telling us so as not to rob you of the joy following your own announcement."

Both Anna and Bran looked to him. Unusually for him, he gave an almost self-conscious laugh. "Adela is to have a child. Around Martinmas, God willing."

"That is good news." He had lost four children in one fell swoop. Until Adela it had seemed there would be no one to carry on his line.

As congratulations were passed back and forth, Bran noticed something in Ben's manner. He seemed to be preparing himself for something. His stillness was gradually noticed by all and they looked to him. It was not like Ben to sour the atmosphere. He asked them to be seated, but remained standing himself, his hands behind his back, wondering where to begin. "Forgive me my strange humour."

Anna, concerned, asked, "Are you unwell?"

"No." He shook his head, unclasped his hands and rubbed his brow. He gave an embarrassed laugh. "I am simply in a quandary as to where to begin what I have to say. I want you all to know that I hold you in the highest regard. And Anna," he gazed at her, smiling fondly, almost tearfully, "I love you very dearly." He turned to Joss. "And Joss, forgive me if this is not what you would have chosen to do. I find I need to…to do it this way."

An inability to understand had etched lines on Joss's brow.

"Two such welcome announcements make it necessary to … to provide you with some details."

Anna and Bran looked at each other for answers. They looked to Joss, but he seemed equally nonplussed. Ben stood with his hands on the back of the chair by the fire. He opened his mouth several times as if to speak but seemed to be unable to find the words he needed. It was so quiet in the room; they could hear the pages laughing as they carried out their errands in the kitchen and the fluttering of the flames about the logs in the hearth. Finally, Ben looked at Joss. "I think there is something we need to share with them, don't you?"

Although the sun behind Joss almost made a silhouette of his face, they saw the lines on his brow gradually smoothed away as Ben's meaning dawned on him. He seemed to turn to stone once more, clasping his hands on his sword in front of him with his head bowed.

"For the future," Ben pressed on gently.

Joss took a slow, deep breath, as if preparing himself for a deadly blow that he had previously promised he would take. As he inhaled, his back straightened, and he looked ahead as if his future was mapped out on the stonework opposite. Almost imperceptibly, he nodded.

Something in Ben seemed to relax and he said quietly, "Thank you, Joss." He turned to the other two. "Before I tell you this, I want you to open your minds." He looked at Anna. "And Anna, I want you to realise that this does not change anything – not fundamentally." He hesitated. Bran felt, once again, that the rug was about to be pulled out from under him. Nevertheless, he gave Anna's cool hand a reassuring squeeze. Anna's and Ben's faces reflected the same expression: they both seemed to be willing the other to be kind.

Joss spoke from the window. "Tell them, Ben. There is no easy way."

Ben pondered several seconds, then said, "Happily, as Adela and Joss are to have a child, and, also happily, as you are to marry, there is something that needs to be said, in order to safeguard future decisions." He paused and looked at Anna, then pressed on while his speech had momentum. "There is a fair chance that Joss is your father."

Anna looked at Ben, not truly comprehending what he had just said but feeling as if she had stopped breathing for some reason. Her expression remained the same, prompting him to ask, "Did you catch what I said, Sweetheart?"

She nodded dumbly. Bran was sure he felt her hand pull away a little from his. Joss looked to Ben, as if relying on him to speak out for him. Bran tried to distance himself and treat the case as he would if in the presence of strangers, knowing he would be better placed to help Anna this way.

"You said to keep an open mind, Ben. Could you help Anna to see how?"

Ben nodded and clasped his hands together tightly, searching for the words. Joss intervened, albeit briefly. "It wasn't..." He grasped for the right word, "It wasn't an infidelity."

Now that Joss had broken the ice, Ben found it easier to explain. "No, no. Nothing like that."

Anna remained silent, but looked from one to the other as if finding it hard to fathom who they were anymore.

Ben paused, then slowly sat down. "I have always found if I need to say something of import, I do it better in the guise of storyteller. So, I implore you to imagine." He looked from the couple to Joss. There were things he needed to know too. "Imagine three characters: first of all, Ben and Margery – man and wife. A couple very deeply in love. Always were and that never changed."

He noticed something behind Anna's eyes. Was it disbelief? He said pointedly, "Ever." He would not have Margery slighted by anyone.

"For thirteen years, they tried for a child. Eight times Ben thought Margery would die in the trying. At times she would reach a point much further than the last and their hopes would rise, only to be dashed once more. He could not bear to see her suffering and came to blame himself and would truly have been happy to worship her from afar; to have done without children of his own; but she would not hear of it. Ben tried to explain that his own mother had had problems- she had died bringing his only sister into the world, and she in turn had remained childless – perhaps it was something in his blood. In one rather self-pitying outcry he had said she would have been better off marrying someone else: someone who could have guaranteed her children. Of course, they both knew Ben did not mean this –it was the voice of despair, needing to hear reassurances to the contrary – but that childish comment sowed the seeds of an idea, which remained dormant for a year." He glanced to Joss, who was listening intently, obviously hearing this for the first time. "During this year, at the age of thirty one, Margery miscarried her ninth child; this time in the sixth month of the pregnancy, as on three previous occasions, she had to suffer long and arduous days filled with pain; had to suffer the desperation of being so close to holding a perfectly formed living child instead of a perfectly formed little corpse. Ben had never seen such suffering on the worst battlefield. The priest lingered thinking he would only be called back as Margery was so close to death." Ben looked to the doorway, "The little graves are amongst the trees, in a patch of grass that overlooks the Church."

He looked back at Joss. "They were not the only people suffering. Joss, our third character, had had his family swept away in the ridiculous quarrels between those who thought Stephen supported them and those who thought Matilda their champion. Such grievous and needless loss left us all reeling. The first anniversary of their deaths coincided with the weeks following Margery's latest stillbirth. It was May.

Margery had not been recovered long. The weather was improving and she had been making ready for guests as visits between households were increasing. One day she stood, thinking she was alone, in the corner of the room that had been prepared for the child. Always had been." Ben stopped and swallowed, obviously finding it difficult to carry on. "Ben watched her quietly from the doorway, watched her kneel at the side of the empty crib, watched her tenderly stroke her fingers over the swaddling cloth neatly folded and placed within, and watched her mouth suddenly twist and her hands come to her face as she sobbed." His brow creased as he remembered, shaking his head. "She was quite folded in two by grief and longing. I remember she held her arms across her belly, where the child had left her empty." He breathed deeply and continued. "Ben would have fought off any enemy who made her suffer so, but here the method of defence was much more difficult to fathom."

Ben paused and Bran glanced at Anna, hoping her grief for her own child would not be too harshly resurrected.

"It was such a private moment, but her suffering prompted her husband to go to her. And while he knelt and held her, thinking that this had to end, he heard Joss arrive. Joss who had never been himself since his own family was killed: Joss, the strongest and most discreet man they knew. Surely, a child of his would survive a premature birth, no matter how long the labour."

He stopped once more. It was obvious there were certain parts of his planning with Margery that he would rather not share. He seemed to shake himself out of the past and continued with a more matter of fact air, as if to have the confession over and done. "Of course, Joss was a man of honour and under any other circumstances would not have entered into such a contrived …coupling…without questioning the morality of it. But, it is a sad fact that we are most vulnerable when we are amongst those we feel we can trust absolutely. And, of course, Redgate ale has a lot to answer for. I am afraid, friend, that the…liaison… was…. opportunistic, if not planned. And I am heartily sorry to have abused your trust and your grief in such a manner. Although, not so sorry that I wish it had never happened. Our daughter has justified the means. I realise you must have been carrying a heavy burden of guilt for the past sixteen years and it is this that pains me." Ben seated himself as if awaiting punishment. "A man with no regard for your children's souls may have carried the secret with him to his grave, but, of late, I have felt the issue was reaching the point of no return." He smiled at the company. "It is a sorry fact that Destiny likes to play tricks on us all. Now I have said something, it may be that your offspring never wish to wed, but I could not help but feel that keeping silent on the matter would only tempt fate. I hope you can find it in your hearts to forgive me. Judge me as you find fit. And, Anna, I hope you can keep a place in your heart for me."

Joss stood, laying the sword on the sill, and rubbed his hand over his chin. "A lesser man would have been completely eaten with jealousy by now. You said nothing."

Ben gave a quiet laugh. "Oh believe me, there were times I wanted to, but something stopped me. In the hours leading up to Margery's death, she told me to read her diary. "I know you," she said, "and I want you to read it all." I knew what she meant and I knew she must have previously thought that this time she might not come through. The night she died, I locked myself away and read the diary from cover to cover, all apart from one page towards the end: the one page she probably thought the most important to me. When I read the first few words, I knew it referred to what had happened and I stopped reading." He shrugged a little at his own cowardice. "I was afraid to read what she had set down." He paused and then decided to be more honest. "I was afraid that she might have fallen in love with you." Joss shook his head as he spoke. "But then, the night before we left for the Borders, just incase it was my last chance, I read that page." He smiled. "Fifteen years of worry for nothing. She set my heart and mind at rest."

Joss folded his arms and scanned the company. "You know, there is no firm guarantee that Anna is my daughter. In fact, the probability is that she is not."

Ben nodded. "I have told myself as much a great many times over the past months, but while there is the slimmest of chances to the contrary, the next generation's souls should not be put at risk." He looked at Anna and held out his hand. "You were wanted so badly, Anna. I have never been disappointed and I know your mother would have felt the same."

She stood, took a few steps, stooped and kissed Ben's brow, looked a little awkwardly at Joss, bobbed him an acknowledgement which was half smile and half curtsey, then turned and left the room. Bran watched her go. She did not look back.

Joss and Ben looked at him. He rose to his feet and with an embarrassed "Excuse me," left the room.

Ahead of him, Anna stopped momentarily, then turned left to the mews. Not knowing what he would say once he had caught up with her, Bran followed. The light was dim in the building and apart from the slight movements of the birds, there was no sound. Anna had stopped before her own hawk, her back towards Bran. Although she was nothing more than a shadow within the grey, he saw her shoulders rise as she gave a deep sigh. Fearing that what she had just learned had made her cynical about their future marriage and that this might be magnified by memories of her lost child, he went to her, rather than allowing time to work its destruction on their hopes of happiness. From behind her, he put his arms around her waist and simply asked, "Anna?"

She leaned against him and reached up and back to stroke his cheek.

"I hate to see you cry."

She turned to face him. "I'm not crying." She took his hands so that she might guide him closer to the small window. "See?" she smiled. "I had to leave quickly so they wouldn't see how relieved I was."

"Relieved?"

She nodded. "I am so sorry. I know it's not appropriate when Joss and my father are so obviously distressed, and you had such respect for my mother, but…" She stopped and covered her hand with her mouth as she thought. She shook her head as if incredulous. "Forgive me. I am sure the enormity of what was just said will visit me soon. But, I truly thought, even though it is not logical given that news of our wedding had just been well received..." She took a deep breath. "Please do not think me an idiot, but I honestly thought he was going to say that you and I are brother and sister. I was convinced. His announcement came as wonderful news by comparison."

Bran gave a sigh of relief. "I'm not to worry that you're reeling under the weight of disillusion then?"

She tilted her face up to his, "God no," she smiled. "I am more concerned for Joss and what Adela might say or do?"

They left the building and looked for a private place which caught the sun. Not so easy since Joss and fifteen men had arrived with Edwin. Bran scanned the trees then smiled. "The sun seems to be shining on our favourite place if you are willing to put up with the climb."

She linked her arm through his and they meandered through the knights erecting tents, up the slope to gain the relatively level glade where Bran had first come across Anna over a year ago. He held out a corner of his cloak and wrapped it about her as they sat. She hugged her knees. "I imagine you are more disturbed than I about the revelation."

Bran shook his head and looked at her.

"What is it?"

"I thought exactly the same. About us being brother and sister." He shrugged and grinned. "I was thinking, all those years worrying about which God to choose, only to learn I had damned us both during the course of the night."

She smiled, leaning her head on his shoulder, "And the morning."

He put his arm round her and pulled her closer. He cast a watchful eye over the entry hole to the oubliette to satisfy himself that Edwin was out of earshot. "I can see why Ben thought he would have to tell us. It must have affected him much more deeply than he has said. He hasn't a selfish bone in his body. Still, no matter what we think, there is no way of changing it now. The important thing is how we manage what we know. How we prevent it from becoming a potential threat to the Northern or our children." He stroked his cheek against her hair and said, "That sounded well, didn't it?"

She tilted her face to his and kissed his cheek. He stood and helped her to her feet. He looked back through the tree tops to the house, wondering whether he should report the incident in Durham to Joss now or wait until later. Thinking that Marc would have already mentioned it to Ben and Ben would relay this to Joss at a time he deemed more appropriate, he turned to Anna. "I think it is time to show you your gift." Standing behind her, he rested his chin gently on her shoulder and asked, "Notice anything different?"

She followed his line of vision, gradually noticing the glass and stonework of the new building. From this angle it appeared to be much closer to the main house. "Oh, it has been unveiled. Is my gift in there?"

"Let's see." He took her hand and led her down and past the main building.

Inside, Ben watched the couple walk past the window where Joss had seated himself once more. "Are you disappointed that I spoke out?" he asked.

Joss shook his head and gazed into the fire. "I always thought that if you ever found out, the main thing I would want you to understand is that I never meant to slight you. At that time, my mind was brimming with what I had lost."

"And your unprepared belly with the household ale."

Joss's mouth momentarily became a thin line of self deprecation. He stood up and walked to the fireplace. "I feel I killed her. I felt that if you knew what had happened you would hate me – break away from the Northern – perhaps try to take supporters with you."

Ben gave a deep sigh. "Oh, Joss. What a legacy we left you with. I am truly sorry."

Joss shook his head at the apology. "You knew all along and yet have been a constant friend." He gave a soundless laugh. "You spoke of strength: you are the strongest man I know."

Ben simply shrugged. "Will you speak with Adela?"

Joss stretched with discomfort at the thought. "I cannot keep a secret from her. Logically, I have not been unfaithful to her, yet that is how it feels. Perhaps that's what secrets do to a man when he buries them. I suppose I could justify keeping it from her in the way I would keep a military secret to protect the Order: it does not sit well with our reputation for monogamy." He turned from the fire. "I really don't know yet. If I do not tell her now and it becomes necessary later, my reticence will seem less forgivable."

The friends fell quiet. Joss looked at his hands and, presently, spoke. "Margery talked to you through her diary. I feel I need to give you my viewpoint as well. It's just hard to put it into the right words."

"Tell me as you think it."

Joss seated himself at the window once more, leaned his elbows on his thighs and clasped his hands, looking at the floor. "I felt I owed the world another child. It was my neglect that led to Peter's death."

"You were not to blame for your children's deaths, Joss. You had to do your service. Their killing was not down to you."

Joss looked at his friend. "Maybe that is true of Judith and the three eldest, but Peter." He shook his head. "Peter's death I could have prevented."

Ben waited.

"When I was told of the smoke, I returned as quickly as I could, but too late. I allowed grief and anger to cloud my judgement. I had laid their bodies together and I kept thinking 'I wonder where poor Peter is'. As it was getting dark, I finally recalled something Judith had said. If the need ever arose, she would hide her children in the only place they would be safe from fire and from thieves: in the cold store cut into the rock behind the kitchen block. Even hungry thieves would not think to look there. I began to panic, the answer so obvious to me now, and although it seemed logical that if he lived I would have heard him crying for attention, I made the mistake of allowing myself to feel hopeful.

It was gloomy and the way to the place covered in bracken so I had to feel my way. At first, I thought he was not there. My fingers met something stone cold. But I also felt cloth and wool: quite a large bundle: well wrapped. I lifted it out and carried it into what was left of the bailey where the light was relatively stronger. I undid the layers and there he was: cold, still, his unhappy mouth tinged blue. She had left him just as she told me she would if the need arose and I had failed them both. Whether he had died from the cold or simply smothered as he turned in the swaddling, there was no need for his death."

"You were not to blame, Joss. If they were still here, they would tell you as much."

Joss looked at Ben. "When Margery came to me that night, describing quite humbly and plainly the idea that had crossed your minds, it was neither love nor lust that was on my mind, but absolution. It is a sign of how strong your love was that there was no flirtation or suspicion of deceit one way or the other. You mentioned the ale, and it is true that I had supped far more than usual, but I still recall how low I felt before I had put the first cup to my lips and before Margery spoke with me. There were many nights when I would lie awake going over and over how I could have done things differently to save Peter. It would churn my stomach so badly that I would throw up. Yes, I was drunk, but I have to be honest; I don't think things would have turned out any differently if I was sober."

Ben held his gaze for a while, then said, "Good." He said no more on the matter, but allowed his eyes to be drawn to the window by Bran and Anna now making their way up the steps to the library. "They make a good couple," he judged. "They will be happy together. Although their love has yet another tricky test to withstand," he said recalling Azra. Before telling what he knew of this, he remembered Marc's message. "Apparently there was some unpleasantness on their departure from Durham. Bran will keep you fully informed of what happened. I gather they prevented a crime and the two would-be victims are to reside at Drysdale."

"Do we know the names?"

Ben shook his head.

Joss watched the library door close. "I'll allow them some private time before speaking with Bran, although I'd like to be extra vigilant until we are completely rid of Edwin."

Ben nodded. "It's hard to believe the time has finally come," he said, looking to the library door once more, eager to have another tour of the building himself.

****

Bran watched Anna's face as she looked around her. She took in the empty shelves, imagining them brimming with rolls and bindings; walked to the table where several documents and books, some of them her own and some not, had been laid ready; ran her hand over the smooth wooden surfaces, a score of colours revealed in the grain by the sunlight that fell in broad patterned sheets through the trace work of the large windows. When she thought she had looked all around her, her eyes were drawn yet again, upwards this time, by a broad stairway of shallow steps to the gallery. She turned on the spot to follow its course, as it bridged the fireplace beneath; ran under the windows, each housing a different design; then encompassed an enormous wheel which reached from floor to ceiling in order that books might be lowered or raised between storeys. She turned to find Bran had been replaced by a bookcase which she was sure had not been there before. As she watched, the casing slowly revolved and Bran was revealed once more. Following his lead, she gave a tentative push on another set of shelves. He indicated the wedge holding it in place at its base and pushed down on it for her to free the motion.

"They will always move in this direction so the thick end of the wedge is lowered when the shelving moves over it, but it will not budge when turned the opposite way."

"How clever. Do they all move so?"

Bran nodded. "That is why each shelf has a lip, to hold everything in place when the case is in motion. Do you like the window?" he asked, pointing directly above their heads.

She smiled, placing her palms on the table top in order to balance with her head tilted back. "It's beautiful. I'm impressed."

"And I. The masons only began work on it the day before we left for Durham. They must have used their entire team to have it finished for our return."

"Stunning." She looked about her. "It's all so beautiful. I envy the monks who will spend so many hours in here." She drew a deep breath. "Um. It even smells beautiful. Newly worked wood."

"So you like your gift?"

She glanced over table top and shelves, looking for the gift. "I'm not sure what it is," she admitted at last.

Bran smiled and held out his arms whilst slowly turning about. When he had turned full circle he put his head on one side, awaiting her reaction, but could tell by her expression that she was going to need a little more help. "This is yours. The library. I built it for you, although I have to confess, it began as Ben's idea."

If Anna had not grown so accustomed to balancing on her own two feet she would have fallen. "Mine?"

He nodded and looked up at the window above them once more. "Look again."

She began to smile the sort of smile that animates the whole body just before it turns to laughter. Amidst the branch-like pattern of the trace work was lodged an elaborate A. It was the design he had been working on in the trace room a few days earlier. "And I was wondering how long I should wait before asking permission to use one of the tables to work at."

He wandered about, moving shelves and revealing further tables and differing views as he went. His voice echoed about the place, "No need to choose a favourite. Reconfigure to your heart's, or your eyes', content." He stopped momentarily at the centre of the room and waved a hand where the light fell on the floor casting a shadow A.

She laughed as he moved from view then reappeared in the most unexpected places, until eventually he was standing before her once again. "Would you invite me to sit by the fire with you?"

She smiled and took his arm, leading him to the fireplace, which had been set and lit for them. The rest of the building seemed large, capacious, almost cathedral-like, but the area round the fire was built to ensconce and comfort. They immediately felt intimate on seating themselves. They heard the door's latch being lifted and moved away from each other, a little self-consciously. Joss and Ben were tactfully loud in their praise and slow in their progress through the library in case the couple needed time to compose themselves.

They got to their feet and stood dutifully. Ben noticed that Anna had overcome her shock at his earlier revelation. When he spoke, he made no reference to it. "Marc tells me a celebratory feast is being prepared at Drysdale, to be held tomorrow night."

Bran nodded.

"Would it be a little presumptuous of me to suggest we also make it the beginning of the wedding celebrations? It seems completely unnecessary to make you wait any longer." He smiled at Anna. "And I am sure you would both like to marry sooner rather than later." Personally, he thought it best to set the marriage celebrations in motion before Ralph and Azra arrived.

Bran squeezed Anna's hand. "I think that is a wonderful idea."

Joss stood, arms folded, looking about him. Taking in the empty shelves he remarked, "There's a life's work here."

She grinned and said as if it was something to be looked forward to, "Yes, isn't there." She hugged Bran. "Thank you. And thank you too." , remembering it had originally been his idea.

As they made their way to the main house, Bran asked, "Do we deal with Edwin before or after the wedding?"

"I thought before would be best," said Joss. "It would be better not to have him looming over the celebrations."

"We wondered whether you would like to preside. Have the trial at Drysdale. Pudsey has already given permission if you are agreeable," added Ben.

Bran nodded. "Yes. Besides, it will give us something extra to celebrate." He pondered. "Are the accusations drawn up?"

Joss nodded. "And character witnesses have been told to make ready should he call for them, but it is unlikely given that he holds no sway over them any longer. Even those who would speak for him out of greed have no incentive now that he is landless."

They seated themselves by the fire, Anna noticing with some satisfaction that her favourite stool by the hearth gave her a good view of her library. She glanced at Bran who was watching her already, smiling at her obvious liking for her wedding gift.

"Ben tells me there was some trouble as you came out of Durham," said Joss.

Bran reluctantly turned his mind to matters less pleasant. "Yes. An attempted abduction. Adam and Ross are accompanying the victim and her grandmother, who is ill, to Drysdale. They may even be there by now, depending on the level of bureaucracy they face. I usually find it depends on who is dealing with the matter."

"I'll make a record of all names involved, just to be on the safe side while the rebels are still irking us by making their presence felt. I suppose there is no point hearing the culprit's name as yet – he would probably try giving a false identity first."

"Pudsey's men will check out his name for us. The young woman was Margaret Gill and her grandmother was Mary..." A sudden shock of recognition made Bran's heart miss a beat. The others looked to him. Bran unconsciously raised his hands to his head, and then with a "damn him" he jumped to his feet and ran out to the oubliette. Peering down into the darkness, with the guards above looking slightly bewildered, he yelled, "Edwin! Show yourself."

There was no movement below. His three companions came out to join him. "What is it?" asked Joss.

"Edwin is definitely down there isn't he?"

Joss nodded. "I put him there myself." He wandered to the edge of the entry hole. "You heard Sir Drysdale, Edwin. Show yourself or I shall join you."

A pale face gradually moved into the light and glowered up. Joss looked at Bran, who, having satisfied himself that their prisoner actually was Edwin, composed himself and said, "I need to speak with you inside."

Ben and Joss looked at each other then followed him back to the house. Bran found it hard to control his agitation. "I am afraid I have been a fool. The name of the grandmother, I have finally come to realise, is Mary Gill."

Joss's brow creased and he looked to Ben as if he had missed something, but his friend seemed equally unenlightened.

Bran continued. "The day my mother was hanged, I was there. I was hiding in a corner of the room they took her to. Just before she was executed, the King's men came to the door and demanded that the woman named Mary Gill ought to be released. Obviously, there was no one there of that name and the execution continued."

Anna still could not follow his train of thought, but Joss seemed to be remembering now. "Edwin sent orders for the execution to be stopped, but he deliberately gave the wrong name, Mary Gill: the name of one of his mistresses. He had no intention of ensuring Joanna survived."

Bran nodded. "It is too much of a coincidence." He shook his head at his own stupidity. "I knew it was unusual for the mare to have been shod so poorly, but I thought no more of it. Adam and Ross could be in danger."

Joss rubbed his chin, glad that he had a vigilant man like Will there already. "We have quite a force of men here and more on the way, thanks to Edwin. The two women themselves will pose no threat, so we must assume there are plans afoot. I say we take a small group and Edwin now and get to Drysdale. We leave a guard here and carry on with the trial as planned. It is best we feign ignorance but have a watch ready to catch the culprits, rather than simply scare them into hiding."

Ben agreed. "Say nothing of this to Edwin. If we do not question him on the matter, he may assume we are still in the dark. I will make the new orders known to the men." He turned to Bran and held out a protective arm towards Anna. "Bran, would you please explain to Anna the clever idea you incorporated into the library in case trouble ever darkened our doors again."

Bran nodded and took Anna's arm.

"Remember," added Ben, "we need to be seen behaving as usual."

Anna felt a sudden chill realising Ben meant that it was likely they were being watched.

Once back in the library, Bran, having sensed Anna's fear, held her close. "It will all be well, Anna. Forgive me. We are so close to being rid of him after all these years that I magnify every little detail which might delay the problem of Edwin being solved."

She savoured his closeness while she could, leaning her cheek against his chest. "Promise me you will be careful."

"Now of all times, I have great reason to be careful. This present danger will be over and done with soon. Tomorrow night we will feast at Drysdale, and by the end of the week, we will be man and wife."

She smiled and he took her hand. "Remember this," he said, leading her to the centre of the room, midway between the entrance and the fireplace.

He held out his arms. "At present these shelves are rather like the spokes of a wheel, with the hub being the table in the centre."

She nodded. One at a time, he began to slide the six sets of shelving through ninety degrees. On the sixth, he beckoned to Anna and she joined him. Moving the final case into position meant that they were both now fully surrounded by a high wall of shelving. "You cannot be seen even from the balcony once these shelves are all configured so." He knelt down under the table and lifted three boards from the floor by what at first had appeared to be knotholes in the wood. A stairway was revealed. He looked up at her. "It's dark down there, but don't be afraid should you need to use it. It is well built. The floor has been beaten smooth. The roof is well supported. You will need to feel your way but eventually you will find the path has an uphill gradient and you will be brought out well beyond the manor walls on the other side of Redgate Bank." He held his hand out to her and together they descended the steps. His voice echoed as he continued to explain. "It is unlikely that anyone pursuing you will realise that the bookcases swivel, so even if they guess where you are, they will waste a lot of time breaking their way through. Even then, there are five doors to pass through; all of them a hand's span in thickness; none of them locked to you."

Anna stepped gingerly behind Bran who was already invisible in the darkness. He took her hand so she could feel the door ahead of them. "The door's surface is smooth. It will push open quite easily in spite of its weight. Once through there is a bolt that can be slid in place preventing you from being followed." He took her hand and demonstrated for her so that she could feel the freedom of the bolt's motion. "Even during the panic of an attack, you should be able to do this quite easily."

They climbed back to the surface. Before sliding the shelving back to its original, spoke-like position, they held each other, knowing Bran would have to leave at once. "I imagine Ben will stay here with you and act as commander if need be. I'm sure it won't be necessary."

He gently placed his brow against hers. "It will be over soon." He reached inside his clothing and took out the letter they had read together in the croft. "I know this by heart now. Learning it may take your mind off things in the short time we are away from each other."

She tilted her face and kissed his mouth. "Promise me you will come back safely," she whispered.

"I promise," he said.

Chapter Forty

Azra

At Drysdale, Ralph stared out at the westward view. It seemed to encompass all types of landscape in one: forest framed fields gave way to moorland then snowcapped hills. He would miss it when they returned to Spain. He turned back to the room and watched as Azra combed her long black hair. She was worth it. She noticed him looking and gave a nervous smile. He stood behind her and stooped to kiss her shoulder. "Still worrying?"

She put down the comb and nodded. "Now that we are here, I feel an even bigger fool. I don't know what it was that made me behave that way."

Ralph found it hard to know what to say. Shrugging, he offered, "I suppose the men from the Northern are like characters who stepped straight from the pages of an epic tale. They fuel the imagination of men and women." He wished they were on their way now. For the most part, he simply wanted to forget about it all, but he understood her shame and her need to make amends, especially with her brother. If that meant coming back here to face Bran in the hope he would pass on her feelings to Harun, then so be it. He had things to see to in Spain, but if it made her happy to do this, then he was happy.

He sat on the bed and watched her. She came to him and knelt before him. "How can you bear to be with me?" she asked.

He looked at her smiling. "It's very easy."

She rested her head on his lap. "Shall we go?"

He stroked her hair. "If you wish."

She looked up at him. "If I do not make my peace with them, it will constantly haunt me."

He nodded and helped her to her feet.

"Thank you," she said. "For understanding."

Chapter Forty One

Absolution

The kitchen window gave Mary Gill, seated at a table with her granddaughter, a good view of the main building. Tilly ran from the Hall, then stopped in the courtyard, wiping her eyes hastily with the cuff of her sleeve. Leona had been in the throes of explaining how new residents usually had accommodation built for them before their arrival, when Mary, greedily lapping up the view, interrupted her. "Well, well. Looks like someone has been chased from her warren. Someone must be less of a gentleman than he looks."

The only sign of annoyance on Leona's part was a deep breath as she turned to the window. At that moment, Leonard came to the doorway and watched as Tilly hurried across the courtyard.

"I can assure you," said Leona, as demurely as possible, "that man is a gentleman. We tend not to judge too quickly here at Drysdale – or any Northern household for that matter." She looked pointedly at Margaret's black eye.

"Oh, I am aware of that," replied Mary, in such a way that Leona felt obliged to study her face to read the intent behind her statement.

A step at the door took some of the awkwardness from the moment. Will entered. He smiled broadly; which was not unusual for him on entering kitchens. Mary sat with her hands folded on her lap and her face set, obviously feeling put out by Leona's reproof. Although both women were of roughly the same years, Mary's sagging frown aged her considerably.

"Welcome, ladies," beamed Will. "I trust you are starting to feel settled in already. You are to have the luxury of a room of your own until we can deduce whether your illness is infectious."

Mary gave a short sharp sniff, which caused Leona to raise a querying eyebrow at her husband. She wondered from what infirmity this ill natured woman was supposed to be suffering. Margaret, by contrast, sat visibly squirming under the tension her Grandmother was causing, her knuckles whitening as she clenched her fists in embarrassment. Will, realising that social niceties were going to be non-existent never mind over and done, decided he would cut to the chase. Keeping the same cheerful resonance in his voice, he said, "Ross and Adam tell me that Mary's eye was blacked after the event in Durham, not during." He looked at the girl. "How did it happen, Sweetheart?"

The girl blushed and opened her mouth to speak, but was interrupted by her Grandmother. "Clumsy thing fell down the step to the street. Covered in clarts she was. As if there's not enough to do."

Will looked at the girl, and raised his eyebrows as if asking her to verify the story. She cleared her throat, but only managed to say "Step," and give a nod.

It was obvious to Leona and Will that this was a lie, but they said nothing. Robert was on his way back from Durham, not wanting to entrust anyone else with the extra provisions for the feast, so Leona hid her annoyance by busying herself with their meal and placed two bowls of broth on the table before the guests.

Margaret gave a whispered "Thank you" but Mary gave another snort.

"I am not accustomed to eating in the kitchen," she complained.

Leona could have pointed out that she was unused to serving in the kitchen, but again she chose to remain silent. She could see no earthly use this woman might provide at Drysdale.

"Ross described the room where you have been living with your grand daughter," said Will, his tone brimming with concern. "Perhaps you were not used to that either."

The older woman's mouth twisted as she repeated stubbornly, "Not used to being fed in the kitchen." She turned her head at the sound of another step in the doorway and Bran entered. "Used to it or not, I would not have you dining with the swine just to make you feel at home, Mary."

In spite of his instant dislike for the woman's manners, Will looked rather taken aback at Bran's tone.

Bran looked at Margaret, assessing the severity of the bruising the pages had just told him about. "Eat your meal, Margaret, while I take your Grandmother to the Hall. There are a few questions I need to ask her before we see if there is any point in allowing you to settle in."

Mary glared at him. "I am in no fit state to be shifted from pillar to post. The road we travelled was so ill kept that we are battered and bruised senseless."

"So that's her excuse," Will whispered to Leona.

"Let me help you, Mary," said Bran. He walked behind her and placed his hands under her arms and lifted her from her seat.

"Get off me. What are you doing?"

Margaret's eyes widened as Bran lifted her grandmother bodily from her stool.

"No time for quibbling, Mary. Or perhaps you were planning to wait for Edwin to lead you into the Hall in a far more leisurely manner." He marched her through the kitchen door. "I can inform you that those who wait for him are invariably let down."

As he guided the kicking and struggling Mary across the courtyard, she finally managed to free herself from his grasp and rounded on him. "I am aware of that," she hissed between heaving breaths. "My son was one who waited."

Bran put his head to one side. Joss came from the Hall and joined them. She looked from one to the other. "Roger was my son: father to the girl in there."

Considering her, then raising his eyebrows at the undercurrent of pride revealed in her tone, Bran queried, "You mean that same Roger who pretended to be Walter Espec that he might take Drysdale from me?"

She glowered at him.

"That same Roger who brought about the death of his own child and almost killed my God daughter in the process?"

Sensing an uncharacteristic anger building in Bran, Joss narrowed his eyes, quickly calculating the likelihood that what she had said was true. His dispassionate voice neutralised the vehemence of the enquiry, only leaving room for cold, hard fact. "He must have started young to have a daughter Margaret's age."

She gave a sneer. "Oh, he did that. Just like his father." She looked from one face to the other, a strange pleasure in her eyes, now that she had their attention. Suddenly, her demeanour changed and she spoke far more softly, "I need a seat. I need to take my medicine." She closed her eyes and rubbed her forehead. "Forgive me my ill temper. The pain makes me most impatient."

Bran gave a sarcastic bow and indicated the entrance to the Hall, where he had wanted her to go in the first place. Every breath she took and movement she made oozed self pity as she ambled to the doorway, remembering midway to walk with a limp. Joss and Bran looked at each other, taking a deep breath.

Will joined them. "Ross seems to have a lot of sympathy for the girl. That is, he has been trying to put her at ease by playing the clown even more than usual. He thinks she was beaten at some point before collecting them this morning. She would not say why it happened. He says she would only blush, as if humiliated by the bruising."

Bran gave it some thought. "I would risk a bet that it is because she gave away the name of Gill. Have a discreet word with Leona. Perhaps she can get to the bottom of it while they are alone in the kitchen."

Joss gave a quiet sigh. "Let's get this over and done, Bran. Delaying the treatment only allows time for the canker to spread."

Mary walked into the Hall alone and took the opportunity to cast her eyes about. It seemed quite gloomy but she could make out the trestle on which were placed several empty bowls. At the fireplace a steaming pot was hanging. Knowing she would have to be quick, she scuttled across the room as if to take a sniff. She glanced back to the doorway, then quickly pulled out a phial from her cloak. As she unstopped it and held it to what little remaining light there was, she smiled and muttered, "Medicine." Then poured the liquid into the pot. She stirred it and stepped away as Joss and Bran entered the room.

"It smells quite delicious," she said, a smile now sitting, rather uncomfortably, on her face.

Steps from the stairs drew their attention as Azra and Ralph descended.

Although Ben had spoken of them, Bran had not expected them to arrive so soon. He greeted them, hiding his annoyance at being sidetracked just at the point where he felt he needed to stay focused.

"Is your room to your liking?" he asked Ralph, still too uncomfortable with Azra's past accusation to look her in the face.

"Perfect, thank you. It is most kind of you. I promise our visit will be a short one. Our ship sails in three days."

Bran found this raised his spirits considerably.

"Congratulations on your marriage. Speaking of which, I hope you will be able to join us for part of our celebrations. Anna and I are to wed soon." He turned and looked at Mary who had seated herself on the most comfortable chair by the fire and was dabbing at her eyes with a handkerchief. "Just one or two problems to solve first."

Ralph sensed the tension and asked, "Would you like us to leave you?"

Bran considered Mary, then slowly shook his head. "No, I think you might as well stay. I do not intend to spend too much time on this." He looked to Joss. "Shall we bring Edwin in?"

Joss walked to the doorway and nodded at Edwin's guard.

Bran called to Mary. "Come and take a seat at the table please."

She looked rather put out at being made to move, but did so slowly. Bran stood across the table from her. If she was ignorant of etiquette, he would ignore it too. Ralph and Azra sat by the fire and observed the seemingly informal proceedings with interest.

Bran spoke. "While plotting against the Crown and helping others to do likewise, your son came to Drysdale under a false persona and killed fifteen of Drysdale's friends and family members, including his own unborn child. The mother would have died too if not for the miracle-working of this lady's brother." He indicated Azra. "He cut the throats of a defenceless ten month old girl and her mother. These are just the crimes of which we are aware. You seemed upset that Edwin let him down. What was the plan?"

Mary shuffled and frowned. "There was no plan," she grimaced.

"Then why imply Roger's death was down to Edwin?"

"You have no right to question me like this; I have done nothing wrong."

"In a time of rebellion we have every right," growled Joss. "Are you saying you do not recognise the jurisdiction of men appointed by the King?"

She shook her head and reached inside her cloak. "I cannot think straight. I need to take my medicine." She pulled a second phial from her pocket. Bran reached forward and took it from her hand.

A voice from the shadows by the fireplace spoke, causing Mary to give a start. "Sir Drysdale is quite learned in medical matters. It is unwise to take some medicines on an empty stomach." Marc stepped forward from where he had been quietly observing her since she entered the building alone.

Mary straightened her back haughtily. "I am not hungry."

Joss entered with two guards either side of a dishevelled, mud smeared Edwin. He did not look at Mary.

"Not greeting your old friend?" Bran asked.

Edwin remained silent but stared coldly down his long nose at Bran.

Marc fetched an empty bowl from the table then went to the pot by the fire and spooned a generous helping of pottage into it. He brought it back and set it before Mary. "I really think you should eat. Once you have tasted my Uncle's cooking, nothing else will do."

She pushed it from her, shaking her head. "No. I am not hungry. Besides, my medicine makes me feel quite sickly."

Bran, sensing what Marc was up to, sat on the stool facing her. He gave her a level look. "Margaret said you were finding it hard to make ends meet. I had thought you would be grateful for a wholesome meal."

Mary made no answer. Marc picked up the bowl and the spoon next to it and carried it to Edwin. "Now I know you must be starving, Edwin, having been in hiding for so long, with no household willing to give you shelter."

Edwin said nothing.

Marc placed the bowl back on the table. "For two people who say they are estranged you seem to have a lot in common. A poor appetite for one."

The company watched with interest as he bent low to Mary, pretending to whisper conspiratorially. "Is the medicine you poured into the pot when you first came in too foul tasting?"

Mary said nothing but sat with her head bowed looking at her hands.

"A reluctance to talk would seem to be another shared trait," observed Bran. "Let me make it simple for you. All that is required is a yes or no answer. Mary, tell me. Have you poisoned the pot?"

"Don't be ridiculous!"

Azra looked at the pot, then back to Mary.

Bran turned to Edwin. "Edwin, did you know of Mary's plan to poison the pot?"

Edwin looked ahead, his dirt-coloured eyes blank. Maintaining his stubborn silence and his assumed air of indifference, only made his contempt more apparent.

Marc sighed impatiently. "They have poor manners in common as well."

Bran stood, "Well, children, we are going to be here a long time until someone starts to explain what is going on."

Joss pulled up a stool and sat with his arms crossed. "I could always beat it out of him."

Azra stood and all but Mary and Edwin looked to her. She crossed to the pot. Perhaps she could offer information based on the aroma, they thought. She stirred the spoon about and before her surprised observers could stop her, she raised the spoon to her lips and took a taste.

Ralph jumped to her side and dashed the spoon from her lips, but too late.

Bran went to her. "Azra! If she has poisoned it, we have no idea which antidote to use."

Azra shrugged and smiled. "All seems well. It is the least I could do after causing so much trouble for you."

Ralph placed a concerned arm about her. He was the first to notice beads of sweat appearing on her brow.

She became a little unsteady on her feet, and gave a brief laugh as if scolding herself for clumsiness.

"Azra. The child," said Ralph, as if there was still time to prevent her from doing the damage. Feeling a trembling begin, he quickly pulled a chair closer that she might take the weight from her legs.

Mary snorted from the table. Her confidence had grown since Edwin's arrival. "One less of your sort isn't going to be missed."

Ralph seethed but stayed at his wife's side as she gave a cry and held her stomach. He yelled across the room. "What have you put in there?"

Mary watched with interest and said, "Just wolf bane."

Joss looked at Edwin and noticed a flicker of a smile behind his eyes. "She's lying," he said and gave Edwin a swipe which knocked him to the floor.

Bran thought quickly. "She must have the antidote in the phial. That is why she was so eager to take it before the food was served. Quickly!" Marc struggled with Mary who had the audacity to cling to the bottle, hoping to delay the treatment. He unclasped her stubborn fingers from the phial and threw it to Bran who uncorked it and, in spite of her swollen throat which was already making it difficult to breathe, helped Azra to swallow. Ralph knelt before her willing the spasms to pass. At length, her breathing became more even and gradually her colour returned, but the pains in her abdomen did not stop.

Azra straightened herself and looked directly at Mary. "There," she said, her voice still hoarse. "Now we can move on."

Marc, Joss and Bran looked at each other. Marc spoke first, his voice a snarl. "I am all for executing them here and now. I'll do it myself if you wish. Just as I kicked Roger into Hell."

Joss stroked his chin. "We have procrastinated too long. People like these need a different type of law."

Edwin sneered from the floor. "Won't that be going against your King's wishes? I demand to be tried by Pudsey."

"Is that right?" asked Joss. "Bad luck, Edwin. Pudsey demands that we take care of this. Since turning a blind eye to rebel activity up here, he has had quite a few of his toys confiscated. They are of far more value to him than you are Edwin." He feigned another swipe aimed at Edwin's face.

Edwin flinched. "I know when William the Lyon plans his next attack and who his supporters are."

Joss smiled. "That is most kind of you, Edwin. I think June was the earliest they could gather more troops together, wasn't it. We have men in the Borders all ready and waiting, some of whom were present at these oh so secretive meetings. To catch a rebel, think and act like a rebel."

Edwin scrabbled about for an answer that might delay things further. "I was at those meetings for the same reason: to bring the rebels down."

Bran gave an impatient growl of a sigh. With one hand he lifted Edwin to his feet by the scruff of his neck, then kicked back at the table and overturned it. Mary started up from her stool as Bran came for her. With his free arm, he lifted her bodily from her seat and dragged them both across the floor to the doorway.

"I have had more than enough of this pandering to vermin. How many victims did you think it would take before we finally reached the end of our tether?"

Joss and Marc followed them quickly outside while the two guards watched from the window. Azra gave a stifled moan and held her arms across her belly. The guards turned back to the couple.

"Shall we fetch Sir Drysdale? He could be of some help."

Ralph nodded, "Please do."

"No!" Azra interrupted.

"Azra, please."

She shook her head and sat straighter as the latest spasm began to dwindle. "Please, do not interrupt them. I shall be well again if I lay down for a while."

Ralph looked to the door and back again. She did seem a little better now. "As you wish, but I will carry you up the stairs and as soon as Bran is finished outside, perhaps these gentleman could inform him that we wish to see him."

The guards nodded and Azra put on a brave face, even laughing as Ralph struggled to lift her from the stool.

When they turned to look back through the window, Will had joined them. Marc and Joss held the prisoners close while Bran brought a rod and levered up a large wooden disc set into the ground, uncovering what seemed to be a large water tank beneath. Without pause, he then grasped one at a time and threw them in. Edwin and Mary splashed frantically, trying to keep themselves afloat in spite of the sudden shock of cold. Edwin's voice echoed up at them. "This is unlawful! You know it, Joss. The King will finish you rather than tolerate you ignoring his system."

Joss approached the edge and smiled at the couple's slowly frantic movements. "Can't hear you, Edwin."

"Allowing a Jew to kill a Christian would ruin your reputation!" he spluttered.

Joss considered him, head to one side, one corner of his mouth puckered with an almost comical concern. "Surely you are not likening yourself to Christ, Edwin."

Mary seemed to be having more difficulties than Edwin and thrashed the water violently in an effort to keep her head above water. "I can tell you of other things he has done. The people he has killed." She began to cough and splutter at the effort of shouting above the splashing while fighting for breath. "And plans to kill."

Joss simply brushed away some drops of water from the front of his tunic then stood up and stepped backwards out of their sight.

Indifferently, Marc watched the progress of those who had created the man that murdered his wife and child. If they died of pneumonia before giving a confession he would not care. The world needed to redress its balance. It would take a hell of a lot more Edwins and Marys to make up for Susan and Maud alone.

Bran walked purposefully to what seemed to be a raised, flat-topped, circular stone mound, with a thick T shaped beam at the top. He beckoned to Joss to help him and each took one end of the T and began to turn the beam anti-clockwise. As they did so, a new movement of the water began to roar as more of it now it poured into the small reservoir containing Edwin and Mary. Bran then strode to the edge of the foaming chasm, the couple floundering now, buffeted against the further wall, with the churning foam gushing in at them. His face remained inscrutable as he stooped to heave the wooden cover back into place.

Joss looked at him. "I hate him too, but he had a point about the King. This method is good for giving us more information but I do not think we should let them die in there."

Bran stood defiantly in front of the cover, barring Joss's way. "Trust me," he said.

Beneath the cover, their cries were absorbed in the melee. After several minutes, the rushing calmed, leaving an awkward silence. Bran did not bother to explain himself, until it was quiet enough to be heard without him having to raise his voice. "There are a great many people wanting to be the one to personally end Edwin's life when it comes to the execution. This solves a problem I have mulled over for some time. If they stayed calm and helped each other, they will have discovered that the water is deep enough to prevent them from climbing out, but not so deep that they will no longer be able to breathe. The water in this container can never rise higher than the water level in the reservoir it is fed from: a simple law of physics. I designed the container so it would be safe." He stooped over the wooden covering and looked back at Joss. "A few minutes of panic is nothing compared to what they have put others through."

Will asked, "And if they did not help each other?"

Bran began to move the cover back. "That is what we are about to find out."

"So, not so much a trial by water as a trial by character," surmised Will.

The handful of men stood over the opening and looked down. There was no sign of either of them.

"Is there a way out?" asked Marc.

Bran shook his head and began to remove his clothes. "Even if they could swim against the force of the water, which is highly unlikely, I covered the end of the feeder with a strong lattice to prevent debris from entering from the reservoir." Once naked, he jumped into the water. The onlookers were immediately wary of Bran's apparent disregard for his own safety and stood with swords at the ready in case he was held under. After Bran's initial dive, he came quickly back to the surface. They could just about make out the outline of his blanched legs, as he trod water and wiped the wet black hair away from his face, looking up at his friends. "It's very, very cold," he informed them in a voice that juddered, then upturned duck like and disappeared from view.

Under the surface, Bran was forced to feel rather than see his way. He circled gradually deeper and deeper, until at last his sweeping fingers brushed against something more resistant. He moved his hands over the shapes below him. He could feel one face, an arm, hair, then another face. They seemed to be very close to each other and anchored somehow. He began to haul at them and very slowly, they began to move to the surface. He had just enough breath left to reach the air where the others took the bulky burden from him.

Bran climbed out, picked up his clothes and walked to the fire in the Hall where he might dry off and dress out of the cold. He noticed as soon as he entered that Ralph and Azra were no longer there. As he dressed, he asked the guards, "Where are our guests?"

The two men seemed to wake themselves up, the spectacle outside having made them forgetful. "The lady did not feel well, Sir. Her husband carried her to their room and asked if you could spare the time to look in on her."

Without even as much as a glance outside, he ascended the stairs, hair still dripping.

On entering the room, he saw Azra's pained face and Ralph kneeling over her, stroking her hair. He looked to Bran. "Thank God. Can you help her, Bran?"

"I shall try," he answered and went to them.

He felt her brow, asked questions, gently felt her abdomen, asked more questions. "You mentioned a child," he said to Ralph.

Ralph nodded. "Yes."

Bran realised that either he or Ralph might be the father. Gently he asked, "Do you mind me looking to see if you are bleeding?"

Azra shook her head. "I feel I am," she whispered.

Bran lifted her slightly and saw there was no need to look further for the bedcovers themselves were already stained with fresh wet blood. Ralph threw Bran a look of panic.

Once more, Azra's pains began to subside. Bran gave them both a sympathetic look. "I can save you Azra, but you must take the medicine I give you."

They said nothing but it was obvious to Bran that they were waiting to hear about the unborn baby. "The antidote has taken away the threat of the poison for Azra, but I am afraid your baby cannot have survived the ordeal."

"Are you sure?" she asked, surprised at the strength of the sadness that suddenly swept over her. He nodded and squeezed her hand.

"Just like that?" asked Ralph.

"I am afraid so, Ralph." He turned to Azra once more. "To ensure your health, you must take the medicine I give you. We need to make sure we prevent any infection. I can give you something for the pains too, but you will have some discomfort for roughly a week. I want you to stay here. Tilly will tend to you. She will bring fresh bedding and dressings."

He walked to the door with the couple looking after him, dazed. Even from the other side of the room he could see the tears in her eyes. He felt it would be too callous to leave without saying something further. "It is no consolation, Azra, and I would not have wished any harm on you or your child, but your actions have helped to finally bring to a conclusion years and years of strife. The people responsible for this and much more have already been executed."

Her mouth momentarily became a thin line. Then she said, "Do you think Harun might find it in his heart to forgive me one day?"

He smiled, not really sure of the answer, but said kindly, "I have."

Chapter Forty Two

Burying the Past

Bran paused and absorbed the tableau under a just-beginning-to-darken sky before stepping outside again. Will was crossing the bailey to speak with Joss, while Marc was kneeling over the still-dripping mass Bran had dragged up out of the water. Will waited until he had joined them.

"Leona has managed to put Margaret at ease," he began. "Just as you surmised, Bran, she was beaten by the old woman. She was obviously using Margaret and her own feigned illness as the means to enter Drysdale. It would seem the fellow you arrested yesterday was in it for the money. He was quite prepared to serve a short sentence under false pretences then spend his earnings afterwards. Apparently, Edwin had promised him land as well."

"My land, I suppose," said Bran.

Will nodded, "Such a lowborn fellow could not believe his luck. Just as well really: he should not be too disappointed when we inform Pudsey of his real crime and he is charged with something far weightier."

"Was she beaten for giving away the name of Gill?" asked Bran.

Will placed his hand before him, palm down, and tilted his wrist one way then the other as he weighed it up. "Partly," he said. "She began crying when Leona spoke with her, but not just because she was recalling her beating. She is only eleven years old and had her first bleed last night. When she asked her grandmother what was happening to her, she received another thrashing for her ill timing. Poor girl thought she was dying because she had done something wrong. No one had bothered to explain things to her, and her grandmother did nothing for her last night. She has been on a knife's edge all day; half of her hoping no one would notice and the other half thinking she had not long to live before she bled to death."

"How much more of their plans did she know?" asked Joss, ignoring the sentiment. "Are there any others involved?"

"She knew of the poison and said Edwin had been to their home, but not for a long time. As the old woman said, Roger was her father, but apart from a visit with Edwin last Spring, she had never seen him before. She seems unaware of anyone else being involved, but I guess it is best to be wary all the same."

Bran pondered. "Who was her mother?"

Will shook his head. "I asked her that, but she simply said she had never known her. She was brought up solely by her grandmother."

"If the mother was dead, she would have said so. It seems strange that, with only the old woman's influence, she has such a gentle temperament."

Marc spoke from where he knelt. "Perhaps she has received too many beatings to dare to show another side."

"Or the sudden change in her body has made her timid," said Will.

"Does she know what has happened to her grandmother and Edwin?" asked Joss.

Will shook his head. "Not as yet. Leona will break the news gently. Although it would seem she was expecting them to receive some sort of punishment for plotting against us."

Joss considered. "I'll have her taken to Asterby in the Midlands. We have more females in that household. That way she can start life afresh without what has happened here hanging over her – and us."

Bran was relieved. That was one less problem for him to solve. He turned to Marc. "Apart from the obvious, can you tell how they died?"

"Arguing," was the blunt reply. Marc pointed to Mary's turkey-skinned neck. "You see this? To me that looks like the sort of bruising that would occur if someone had tried to choke her. And here," Marc pulled the clinging, saturated cloth of Edwin's sleeve so more of his forearm was revealed, "you can see that Mary's girdle has been removed: one end wound tightly about Edwin's wrist and the other tied round her own. So tightly the skin is bruised."

"You were right," Joss said to Bran. "Instead of helping each other, one has tried to out-survive the other."

Bran knelt down and studied the waxy faces still contorted by desperate fury. He imagined how, amongst the churning foam, Edwin would have tried to silence Mary, his hands at her throat after her threats to reveal all; then how Mary, knowing she was going to die, had out done him in the end by binding her to him, keeping him with her beneath the water.

Bran looked to Joss. "We need to let Pudsey know exactly what has happened as soon as possible, incase someone tries to twist the truth."

Joss nodded. "I shall see to it, then after the wedding, I shall persuade Adela to go to her father's house. It is safer for her there until we know all rebel activity has been curtailed. William the Lyon has still to be suppressed. There are plenty of men who would think nothing of killing her if they knew she was with child."

Bran sighed and considered the wide-eyed anger of Edwin's face. "I thought that seeing him like this would bring a sense of relief, but there always seems to be something left lingering in the air."

"Like a fart after griping stomach pains?" asked Will so politely that they all laughed.

Joss gave a rare, reassuring smile. "That is all the rumination they deserve. You have done well today, Bran. The end of Edwin will not mean the end of all of our troubles, but it will certainly cut them down to size." He grasped Bran's arm and pulled him to his feet. "Your parents would be proud, just as I am." He looked to the sky then back at Bran. "You should make it at a canter. I imagine you want to get back to Redgate as soon as possible to check that your future bride is safe and sound."

"And that your future father-in-law is not trying to talk her out of it," grinned Will.

"Go with him, Marc. It's not much of a detour on the way back to pass by Bradley Hall to speak with the watch there. That way, we can lie easy when the wedding celebrations begin. "

Bran looked back to the Hall, thinking of his guests. "Azra and Ralph may need me. It seems callous to leave when she is in the throes of losing her child."

All three looked at him, not having realised the extent of the sacrifice Azra had made. Joss spoke. "We shall see she is looked after. Tilly knows what she is doing. We will reassure them that you will be back tomorrow."

Bran wanted nothing more than to get straight back to Anna, but his duty of care pricked at his conscience. "Do not let them go home. Azra needs time for her body to heal itself."

Marc got to his feet and held out his arm as if to guide Bran to the stables. "Come on, friend. Let this go. Edwin deserves no more of our time."

Bran shook his head. "I know. It is hard to believe we are finally free of him."

"Marc is right," said Joss. "And just because the cure does not taste good, it does not mean it has not worked. You need to go now, or it will be too dark."

Bran's mouth became a thin line as he pondered. "Give me time to do one more thing. I will be back as soon as Seer is ready to ride."

He quickly re-entered the Hall and ran up the three flights of twisting steps to his private chamber. He crossed to the window which looked onto the hill top that divided him from Redgate. He read the horizon from left to right, taking account of every detail, just as he had since he was a boy whenever he felt insecure, whether staying at Drysdale or Redgate. He began to recite the familiar lumps and lines: three crooked trees, all bent eastwards; an even rectangular block then a gap where the wall was down; one tree; one pole where people were hanged in Stephen's time (push image of mother from head); nineteen trees, all obligingly separate and distinct, up to the westward point where the hill was creased. All was as it should be. He held his gaze for a while longer, making sure there were no extra shapes or unexpected movements. And still, all was as it should be. On hearing hooves in the bailey, he forced himself from the window and made his way down.

Knowing full well where he had been and what he had been doing, the others looked at him expectantly as he mounted.

"Just setting my mind at rest," he smiled, knowing he would be watched every step of the way regardless, and he and Marc set off at a gallop.

Back at Redgate, Anna wandered into every nook and corner of the library, stopping now and then to peer round shelving or feel the smoothness of the stone trace work. At intervals, she paused in her wanderings to look back at the letter she held, checking the accuracy of her memory when recalling a particular sentiment or phrase against Bran's writing. Finally, she looked up to the window in the ceiling and reluctantly surrendered to the idea that it was now far too dark indoors to carry on reading his words. As she made her reluctant way to the door, it opened and there was Bran, as if she had conjured him by thinking of him so much. She went to him, smiling; not asking him how things had gone, just in case the answer spoilt the moment.

He took her hands, pulled her to him and kissed her. "Let's go to our favourite place to make the most of the fading light."

He wrapped his cloak around her to ward off the increasingly chilly breeze. They made their way through the dusky canopy: linking arms, shaking heads, talking, smiling.

By the time they had completed their climb, they were speaking of Tilly and Leonard.

"Is there any news of them?"

"No," Bran shook his head. "I think it will take time. Leonard likes the idea of quests: perhaps he feels he should prove himself to her."

As they sat down, Anna waggled the rolled letter at him. "I believe I have this by heart now."

"Very seemly to involve the heart," smiled Bran.

"Would you like to test me?" she grinned offering the letter.

He shook his head. "I trust you." He took it from her, unravelled it and held it, fingers poised and ready to tear. "Like this, from top to bottom?" he asked.

Anna bit her lip. "It's such a beautiful text," she said, but then nodded resolutely. "Yes, just so."

Bran tore it slowly and handed her one half, then rolled the other and placed it inside his cloak. "Next to my heart," he said, smiling at her.

The breeze was picking up, and eventually they had to concede that sitting outdoors in wintry conditions may not have been such a romantic idea after all. As Bran helped Anna to her feet, he stole another kiss and she momentarily lost her grip on the parchment. The wind snatched at it, dangling it teasingly just out of reach before sending it flying above the tree tops.

Anna's dismayed eyes hopelessly followed its spiralling journey. "Oh. Shall we ever find it again? What an idiot I am."

Bran interrupted her with a kiss. "The parchment is not important, remember. We have it by heart."

"Can you forgive me?" she asked.

He put his head to one side as if it was a strange question, then grinned at her, reached inside his cloak, took his half of the parchment, held it aloft, and let it go. They both watched as the fragment simply rolled back on itself and landed at their feet.

He gave her a wry look. "That wasn't quite what I had in mind."

"Let's pretend we did not see," whispered Anna, and they made their way back down to the warmth and light of the Hall, where Marc, their father and a pitcher of Redgate ale were already settled by the fire, waiting for them.

And perhaps another evening, there would be time to sit in the moonlight and talk of happier times.

Epilogue

The view from one of Redgate's many perches still shows the route from a hidden Drysdale. The narrow road tumbles down to the bridge, which crosses the river, which flows past ancient Bradley Hall, which stands across the road from where the archers practised, just in case.

Streets like Meadhope and Angate still follow their narrow medieval pattern, causing vehicles that have just descended Redgate's swollen slopes to pause courteously, allowing on comers to pass by. Those descending find it hard to stop, while those ascending find it hard to start and, still, those wagons hauling heavy loads climb at a similar rate as when they were horse-drawn and only very gradually overtake those on foot.

Sheep still speckle the hillside and half-hidden, ankle-twisting pathways still branch away from the main route to snake past lime, chestnut, pine and cloth-tearing gorse. One passes Godric's well; another skirts round a bastle that has long since crumbled; another rises short and sharp to the memorial where the priest, John Ducket, was arrested, and whose body was broken and buried at Tyburn four hundred and seventy years after Anna and Bran were wed. Tenacious ramblers may stop, gaze and take a deep breath. And perhaps the group of pine will remind them of ladies holding the hems of their gowns away from muddy ground. And it may be that, in the grass at their feet, they might see, not stumble-making rubble, but mementoes of lives past: a lintel from a manor house where royal decisions were taken; a shard of iron where a kitchen once stood and mouth-watering feasts were prepared; and the ruined fragment of a once wind-tossed letter, whose words may have eventually faded to nothing, but the love that prompted them never did.

Lightning Source UK Ltd.
Milton Keynes UK
09 April 2010

152542UK00001B/2/P